James Madison, Public Servant: A Biography

Gary L. Rose

James Madison, Public Servant: A Biography

Gary L. Rose

Academica Press
Washington~London

Library of Congress Cataloging-in-Publication Data
Names: Rose, Gary L. (author)
Title: James Madison, public servant : a biography | Rose, Gary L.
Description: Washington : Academica Press, 2025. | Includes references.
Identifiers: LCCN 2024944060 | ISBN 9781680534252 (hardcover) | 9781680534269 (e-book)

Also By Gary L. Rose

Connecticut Republicans: Past, Present and Future (2023)

New England Local Government: The Case of Connecticut (2021)

Haywire: A Chronology of the 2016 Presidential Contest (2017)

No Holds Barred: The 2012 Connecticut Senate Race (2013)

Connecticut's Fourth Congressional District: History, Politics and the Maverick Tradition (2011)

Shaping a Nation: Twenty Five Supreme Court Cases That Changed the United States (2010)

The Emerging Catholic Electorate: Political Perspectives of College Students at a Catholic University in the Northeast (2008)

Connecticut Government and Politics: An Introduction (2007)

Public Policy in Connecticut: Challenges and Perspectives, editor (2005)

Connecticut Government at the Millennium (2001)

The American Presidency Under Siege (1997)

Controversial Issues in Presidential Selection, editor 2nd edition (1994)

Connecticut Politics at the Crossroads (1992)

Controversial Issues in Presidential Selection, editor (1991)

Contents

Preface

While on one of my many trips to the nation's capital, my son and I decided to pay a visit to the Library of Congress. I had been to the ornate and majestic Jefferson Building several times where I looked in awe at the thousands of books that comprise the Library's holdings. I often marveled at the remnants of Thomas Jefferson's personal collection, which served as the original body of books for this extraordinary institution. Oddly, however, I had never set foot in either the Madison Building or the Adams Building; both buildings, like the Jefferson Building, named after two of our nation's foremost Founders. The Jefferson Building officially opened to the public in 1897. This building clearly attracts the most visitors. The Adams Building opened in 1939, while the Madison Building, the last of the three, opened in 1980. Compared to the Jefferson Building, traffic tends to be light in the Adams and Madison buildings.

What I could not help but notice during our tour of the Madison Building is how the statue of Madison seated on a chair in Memorial Hall seemed more subdued and less captivating compared to the magnificent outdoor monuments of Washington, Jefferson, Lincoln and Martin Luther King, Jr. Although Madison's statue is located inside a building, which imposed structural limitations, I still could not help but wonder why a statue of the "Father of the Constitution" was not located outdoors and in a more visible location for the public. The location and size of Madison's statue located within the Madison Building seemed to suggest that Madison is perceived as an important figure in American history, but perhaps not to the same extent as that of the nation's more iconic figures. Because the Constitution of the United States is the most successful and oldest written Constitution in the world, and because the Constitution has weathered the storms of a civil war, world wars and civil strife, and because the freedom of the American people can be attributed to the Bill of Rights, I decided during my visit to the Madison building that someday, when time permitted, that I would devote a book to the public service of James Madison.

I find it troubling that as our nation is poised to celebrate the 250th anniversary of our nation's founding, a large majority of the American people, college students in particular, know so little about James Madison. This is apparent whenever I post the portraits of the Founding Fathers on PowerPoint slides and ask students to identify their names. Students can identify George Washington, Benjamin Franklin, Thomas Jefferson, and sometimes Alexander Hamilton, but never Madison. Moreover, students seem perplexed when I ask whether contemporary American government still reflects "Madisonian" ideals of government; "Madisonian" is an alien word for most students. Thus, the purpose behind my writing this biography is to introduce James Madison to students. My treatment is a straight-forward account of Madison's life and all that he did for the American republic. I distilled what students and general readers should know about this extraordinary and overlooked Founding Father. My biography unfolds as follows.

Chapter One examines James Madison as a boy and young man. His education at a boarding school and by a private tutor on his father's plantation, along with his education at the College of New Jersey (which became Princeton University) where he was introduced to thinkers of the Scottish Enlightenment by the President of the College, the Reverend John Witherspoon, will show how Madison's education heavily impacted his views towards government and his conception of human liberty. Madison's participation as a delegate in 1776 to Virginia's Constitutional Convention where, at the age of twenty-five, he helped write a portion of the Virginia Declaration of Rights provide insight into the Madison's firm belief in religious freedom and his sharp intellect.

Chapter Two covers Madison's first attempt to win a seat in the Virginia House of Delegates. His attempt was unsuccessful due to the politics of personal favors, in this case free shots of whiskey. Nevertheless, Madison's stellar reputation earned as a delegate to his state's constitutional convention resulted in a prestigious appointment to the Councils of two Virginia governors: Patrick Henry and Thomas Jefferson. Although only serving on Jefferson's Council for less than a year, Jefferson would become a lifelong mentor to Madison. This would have profound implications for the future of Madison's political career. One will also learn from this chapter about Madison's time as a member of the Continental and Confederation Congresses, where he quickly impressed his fellow lawmakers as a detailed and thorough lawmaker. Upon leaving the Congress due to term limits, Madison returned to Virginia where he served in the Virginia House of Delegates. Madison's historic *Memorial and Remonstrance* in which he argued for the separation of church and state in Virginia, along with his support for *The Virginia Statute for Religious Freedom* proposed by Jefferson are covered in this chapter. Chapter Two also covers Madison's efforts to increase the powers of the Confederation Congress, which her knew as a former member were insufficient. This resulted in the Annapolis Convention in 1786 where Madison along with Alexander Hamilton strategized to create a stronger federal government. Due to Madison's determination and prompted by a farmers' uprising in western Massachusetts, a convention was convened in the summer of 1787. It is at the convention held in Philadelphia where Madison, who authored the Virginia Plan, contributed in a direct way to the formation of the Constitution of the United States.

Chapter Three is devoted to Madison's important contributions related to the ratification of the U.S. Constitution. In this chapter, one will learn about the historic fight between proponents and opponents of the Constitution. Proponents were known as *Federalists*, while opponents were identified as *Antifederalists*. The writings of Antifederalists and Madison's participation as one of the three authors of the historic *Federalist Papers* are examined in this chapter. Writing under the pseudonym of *Publius*, the *Federalist Papers* helped to persuade delegates to the New York ratifying convention to vote for the Constitution. Madison's key role at the Virginia ratifying convention is also covered in this chapter. Readers will gain great respect for Madison after learning how Madison in a magnificent debate with Patrick Henry, a leading Antifederalist, methodically defeated Henry's attempt to block ratification. Had it not been for the writings and debating of James Madison, New York and Virginia may not have ratified the Constitution.

Chapter Four covers Madison's time as a member of the Congress of the United States. His opponent, who he narrowly defeated in his first campaign for Congress, was none other than James Monroe. This was the first and only time in the history of the United States, that two future presidents faced one another in a congressional election. Madison's election was quite remarkable in light of Patrick Henry's attempt to prevent his election by gerrymandering his congressional district. What is particularly important in this chapter is Madison's impressive work as a federal legislator and how he was directly responsible for authoring and securing ratification of the Bill of Rights. Included in this chapter is Madison's vehement opposition to the controversial Jay Treaty supported by Alexander Hamilton and the Federalist Party. The Jay Treaty, one of the most divisive and controversial treaties in the history of the United States, was among the chief contributors to the so-called "Quasi-War" that erupted between France and the United States. Madison's strong opposition to Hamilton's successful proposal to establish the Bank of the United States is discussed in this chapter. Chapter Five also includes the fascinating debate that occurred between Madison and Hamilton regarding the proper scope of presidential and congressional authority in the area of foreign affairs. The *Pacificus* v. *Helvidius* debate, which erupted over President Washington's Proclamation of Neutrality announced in

1793, is an important component of this chapter. The debate brings into focus important questions regarding the separation of powers doctrine.

Chapter Five explores Madison's efforts devoted to building an opposition party to challenge Hamilton's Federalist Party. Madison's party, originally known as the Republican Party, not only eclipsed the Federalist Party as the dominant party in electoral politics, but also transformed the entire character of American politics. Although Jefferson was the leader of this party, which supported states' rights and an agricultural economy, it was Madison's grassroots party-building efforts that were responsible for the development and viability of the Republican Party. In this chapter, the reader will also learn about the Federalist Party's attempt to crush the Republican Party by passing the Alien and Sedition Acts in 1798. Jefferson and Madison anonymously responded with the controversial Kentucky and Virginia Resolutions, which potentially could have landed both of them, particularly Jefferson, in prison for sedition. Readers will learn that the first two-party system that pitted Federalists against Republicans emerged due to opposing political positions over the Jay Treaty, the Bank of the United States and the French Revolution. Partisan divisions were intense between Federalists and Republicans.

Madison's role as President Jefferson's Secretary of State is the focus of **Chapter Six.** The many challenges that confronted Madison during his eight years as secretary of state are examined in this chapter. A Supreme Court ruling which resulted in judicial review, the Barbary Wars, the Louisiana Purchase which doubled the size of the United States, the infamous Yazoo Scandal in Georgia, Jefferson's disastrous embargo on British trade, which Madison championed, along with Madison's desire to acquire "the Floridas" all arose during his time as secretary of state. Although Madison is not rated as one of our country's top secretaries of state, he nevertheless was involved in a very direct way to every foreign policy decision issued by Jefferson. Madison is among the longest serving secretaries of state in U.S. history.

Chapter Seven provides readers with an opportunity to learn about Madison's two-term presidency. In this chapter readers will learn that despite identified as the heir apparent to Jefferson's presidency, Madison not only faced opposition from Federalists but also from a faction of Republicans within his own party. Yet despite attempts to derail his ascent to the presidency, Madison, with the help of his politically astute wife, Dolley, was able to win two presidential elections by comfortable margins. In this chapter The War of 1812, referred to as "Mr. Madison's War" is the subject of extended discussion. A difficult war to comprehend, the War of 1812, was strongly supported by not only Madison but also a very pro-war, anti-British faction of newly elected congressional

Republicans known as the War Hawks. The war from the very start was characterized by partisan and sectional divisions. The Treaty of Ghent, which ended the war, but solved virtually none of the underlying conditions that led to the war, is also covered in this chapter. Additional decisions made by Madison when he was president, one of which involved a controversial cabinet appointment, are also discussed. Readers should find it interesting that towards the end of his presidency, Madison supported the rechartering of the Bank of the United States, an arm of the federal government that he opposed when he served in Congress.

Chapter Eight is devoted to Madison's twenty years in retirement. Readers in this chapter will learn that Madison hardly led the quiet life of a retired president. His meticulous editing of his convention notes that were released after his death, the assistance he provided to Jefferson related to the creation of the University of Virginia, his participation once again as a delegate to Virginia's constitutional convention, and his effort related to creating a colony in Liberia for emancipated slaves are discussed in this chapter. Because Madison was a slave owner, a portion of this chapter is devoted to an interview he had with a writer during which his views towards slavery and the colonization effort were discussed. The chapter ends with a brief treatment of what several Founders, Madison included, had decided to do with their slaves as instructed within their wills.

Madison's legacy is the focus of the **Conclusion.** Several questions regarding what Madison might have to say about contemporary developments in American government are also presented in this chapter. More specifically, the extraordinary growth in presidential power at the expense of congressional power is the subject of discussion. Such developments quite frankly threaten the separation of powers doctrine, a core doctrine of Madison's political science.

My treatment of Madison depends on a number of major biographies pertaining to James Madison, several of which are classics. A number of scholarly articles are also referenced along with helpful websites devoted to the Founders.

My goal in writing this biography was not to produce a masterpiece, such as those that are referenced, but rather to write a smaller and more succinct volume regarding Madison's life and public contributions. My volume is intended for a variety of academic courses. Those can include Introduction to American Government, Introduction to U.S. History, Constitutional Law, and the American Presidency. Professors who teach these subjects should find my biography of Madison helpful.

I have enjoyed Mr. Madison's company during the writing of this book, and trust that my readers will find my treatment of James Madison fair, interesting and educational.

Gary L. Rose

Acknowledgments

First and foremost, I must acknowledge the several classic and exceptionally informative books and academic articles which guided my writing on James Madison. When I decided to write this biography, I immersed myself in many scholarly works related to Madison. These books and articles served to educate me on his life and career as a public servant. Although every book and article listed in my bibliography was in one way or another helpful when researching and writing this biography, there were several that I must give particular recognition to. They include the extraordinary and multi-volume biography of James Madison by Irving Brant (1941-1956), along with the exceptional single volume works of Francis F. Bierne (1949), Richard Brookhiser (2011), Lynne Cheney, (2014, 2020), Jay Cost (2021), Noble E. Cunningham, Jr. (1957), Noah Feldman (2017), Kevin R. Gutzman (1990), Donald B. Hickey (2012), Ralph Ketcham (1971, paperback edition 1990), Jack N. Rakove (1990) and Robert Allen Rutman (1987). The writings of J.C.A. Stagg must also be identified.

Professor Burton Spivak, a faculty member in the history department at Sacred Heart University, deserves very special recognition. Burton devoted many hours to reading and thoroughly critiquing a draft of my manuscript. An exceptional historian and author of the acclaimed *Jefferson's English Crisis: Commerce, Embargo and the Republican Revolution,* Burton's assistance contributed in numerous ways to a more substantive and precise treatment of James Madison's public life.

My wife, Laurie, read a draft of the manuscript and provided insightful recommendations regarding style and substance. My son, Garrison, a history and government teacher with impressive knowledge of U.S. history, also offered helpful observations that further strengthened the final draft. I am appreciative of their support regarding this project.

Because I write books for classroom use with the goal of educating students, I often ask students to read draft chapters of my manuscripts and to provide constructive edits and criticism. I was fortunate in the spring of 2024 to have five dedicated students assigned to me as research assistants. The five students were tasked with a larger project related to presidential elections yet found time to review chapters associated with my Madison project. Special thanks to Abby

Conrad, Liam Conway, Ava Hufford, Will Kurnik and Ciara Mooney for their helpful comments. My former student and long-time research assistant, Bridget Hughes, also provided helpful assistance with this project. My colleague, Professor Sidney Gottlieb, also deserves recognition for his expertise related to formatting the final manuscript. Tracey Mauro, my former administrative assistant, provided valuable assistance when I was responsible for managing an academic department.

Last, but not least, Professor Paul du Quenoy, proprietor of Academica Press, must also be acknowledged. I am thankful to Paul for recognizing the value of a biography regarding one of our nation's preeminent Founders. I am grateful to him and his staff at Academica Press for accepting my manuscript and for bringing this biography to light.

Gary L. Rose

Dedication

To Laurie, my soulmate

Chapter One

Madison's Early Life, Education, and the Virginia Convention

The Madison Family Tree in Brief

The Madison family had deep roots in Virginia dating back to 1653 when James Madison's great-great-grandfather was given six hundred acres of land under what was known as the "headright" system.[1] As described by Ralph Ketcham, under this system of land acquisition, individuals were allotted land for sponsoring and paying for the travel of immigrants from England to Virginia. For each qualified immigrant the sponsor was given 50 acres.[2] Madison's great- great-grandfather whose name was John Maddison (spelled with two ds) was given a large tract of land for funding the travel of 12 English immigrants. Although the "headright" program allowed for funding the travel of relatives, such as cousins, aunts and uncles, in most instances those who arrived in Virginia under the "headright" program were designated as indentured servants of the individual who paid for their travel.[3] Before his passing, John Maddison paid for the passage of more "headrights" and expanded his land ownership by an additional 1300 acres. John Maddison's son, John Maddison Jr. i.e. James Madison's great-grandfather, continued to expand the family's estate, thus establishing the Maddisons as a family with substantial land holdings.[4] Land acquisition would continue with the three sons of John Maddison, Jr. The sons' names were John, Henry and Ambrose. Modifying the family name to Madison, the sons would acquire large tracts of land amounting to approximately 5,000 acres.[5] Although 5,000 acres might seem like an extraordinary amount of land, the Madisons were not considered among

---

[1] Ralph Ketcham, *James Madison: A Biography* (Charlottesville: University of Virginia Press, paperback edition, 1990), p. 3.
[2] Ibid.
[3] Ibid.
[4] Ibid.
[5] Jay Cost, *James Madison: America's First Politician* (New York: Basic Books, 2021), p. 15.

the largest landholders or planters in Virginia. As Jay Cost writes, "This placed them in the middle tier of Tidewater land owners – well above the class of small freeholders, but hardly at the level of the elites who dominated the top of Virginia society."[6]

John Jr.'s son, Ambrose, i.e. James Madison's grandfather, married Frances Taylor who had four sisters and four brothers. One of her brothers was named Zachary. Zachary's grandson, also named Zachary, would become the 12th president of the United States.[7] Ambrose and Frances had three children, two girls and one boy. James was the name they chose for the boy. James would eventually become the father of James Madison, Jr., the subject of this biography.

After acquiring more land and clearing forests, Ambrose in 1729 established a new plantation for himself and family, which they named Mount Pleasant.[8] Ambrose's plantation "was about halfway between Fredricksburg and the eastern side of the Blue Ridge and thirty miles northeast of the future site of Thomas Jefferson's Monticello."[9] Tragedy would strike the family when Ambrose was apparently murdered in 1732. "Three slaves . . . were tried and convicted of poisoning the master."[10] The slave directly responsible for Ambrose's murder was put to death, while his accomplices were whipped for their involvement.[11]

Upon turning 18, James assumed management of the family's estate. He was now able to relieve his mother of the day-to-day responsibilities associated with overseeing the plantation. At the time, the family owned twenty-nine slaves, although only ten of the slaves were old enough to toil in the plantation's tobacco fields.[12] It was in Orange County, Virginia at the base of the Blue Ridge Mountains, a geographical area referred to as the Piedmont, where the Madison plantation was located and where it would continue to expand. Montpelier would eventually be the name chosen for the plantation.

In addition to managing the family's plantation, James immersed himself in various activities associated with county government. Although he was not a member of the House of Burgesses in Williamsburg, which was quite far from his home, he was nevertheless very involved in public affairs. He served in a variety

---

[6] Ibid.
[7] Ketcham, *James Madison*, p. 4.
[8] Cost, James Madison, p. 15.
[9] Ibid.
[10] Noah Feldman, *The Three Lives of James Madison: Genius, Partisan, President* (New York: Random House, 2017), p. 24.
[11] Ibid.
[12] Ketcham, *James Madison*, p. 5.

of offices including "overseer of local roads, justice of the peace, county lieutenant of the militia, and coroner."[13]

James' two sisters married into wealthy and respected families, which further elevated the reputation and political connections of the Madison family. In 1749, James married Nelly Conway whose family lived on a plantation in Port Conway, Virginia. This plantation was located in King George County, not far from James' plantation. After being married for eighteen months, Nelly gave birth to a boy who they decided to name after his father.[14] The official birthdate of James Madison Jr. is listed as March 15, 1751. The birthplace was at the Conway plantation located near the Rappahannock River. The original house no longer exists.[15]

James Madison Jr. was the first of twelve children born to James and Nelly Madison. Three of Madison's siblings died while they were infants, while two siblings died when very young from intestinal complications.[16] Madison survived, despite being born with health issues that would affect him throughout his adult life. Little did James Madison's father and mother know that their first child would eventually be known as the "Father of the U.S. Constitution" that he would author the Bill of Rights, be appointed secretary of state, form a major political party, and win election as the fourth President of the United States.

James Madison – the Young Boy

The seminal biographies regarding James Madison unfortunately contain scant details regarding what sort of young boy he was, or what his childhood interests were. He was raised along with his many siblings on his father's plantation in Orange County, which had expanded in both land and slaves. Due to the availability of slave labor, Madison as a young boy did little work on the plantation. Irving Brandt suggests that the absence of work and physical exercise allowed Madison to focus more on reading and studying which although sharpening his mind did little to improve his "physical weakness from which he suffered so greatly."[17] His siblings were his confidants and playmates. Among Madison's siblings, he had the closest association with his two brothers nearest to

---

[13] Cost, *James Madison*, p. 16.
[14] Ibid., p. 17.
[15] The birthplace of James Madison is now a bed and breakfast known as Belle Grove Plantation; online at virginiaplantation.wordpress.com.
[16] Jeff Broadwater, *James Madison*, (Chapel Hill: University of North Carolina Press, 2012), p.1.
[17] Irving Brant, James Madison: The Virginia Revolutionist 1751-1780, (New York: The Bobbs Merrill Co., 1941), p. 45.

his own age.[18] Cousins also lived nearby, and seven boys were born on the Taylor plantation, some of whom were close to Madison in age.[19] He had a network of friends, suggesting he was not a lonely boy. In addition to his white playmates, Madison also played with the children of slaves. This was typical among most slave owning families.[20] Bonds were formed among white and black children.

As the plantation grew in size and the number of slaves owned by the Madison family increased, there was an abundance of children for Madison to play with.[21] Unfortunately there is no record of what he and his playmates did for fun. One thing seems certain however -- as a young boy growing up in the Piedmont region of Virginia and viewing on a daily basis the beauty of the Blue Ridge Mountains, and having many children to play with, young James Madison likely had a fulfilled childhood.[22] His was not a hardscrabble or aimless childhood.

Yet despite a childhood filled with friends and cousins, Madison as a very young boy, like all children his age who lived in the Piedmont, lived in constant fear of Indian attacks, particularly during the time period known as the French and Indian War (1754-1763). The possibility of an Indian attack was a constant concern, not only on the minds of children in the Piedmont who heard horror stories of Indian atrocities, but also on the minds of their parents. Throughout his entire life, James Madison, as Brant notes, would reflect on "the terror that gripped the people of the Piedmont as they saw their land, stripped of its frontier defenses, exposed to the creeping approach of the French and Indians."[23]

James Madison's Education

Like the children of plantation owners throughout much of the South, Madison received a rigorous education. Along with other boys from surrounding plantations, he began his studies at a boarding school in King and Queen County.[24] The boarding school was run by a Scotsman named Donald Robertson who firmly believed that young boys needed to be educated in not only the classics but also in foreign languages. Boys who attended Robertson's boarding school

---

[18] Ketcham, *James Madison*, p. 12.
[19] Ibid.
[20] Ibid.
[21] Ibid.
[22] Ibid., p. 10.
[23] Brant, *James Madison: The Virginia Revolutionist 1751-1780,* p. 45.
[24] Kevin R. Gutzman, *James Madison and the Making of America* (New York: St. Martin's Press, 2012), p. 1.

were taught "Greek, Latin and French, albeit with a Scottish brogue."[25] It was in Robertson's classes where Madison, known as "Jemmy," was introduced to the writings of Greek and Roman philosophers, several of whom would influence his understanding and perspectives towards government. In Robertson's courses, as Carl J. Richard notes, young James Madison was introduced to the writings of "Virgil, Horace, Justinian, Cornelius, Nepos, Julius Caesar, Tacitus, Lucretius, Eutropius, Phaedus, Herodutus, Thucydides and Plato."[26] Later in life, Madison, would attribute much of his knowledge to what he had learned from Robertson.[27]

After attending Robertson's school for six years, Madison's father decided that his son, who was now 16, would be better served and more prepared for college if he was instructed at home by a private tutor. The tutor, a Scotch-Irish Episcopal Priest named Thomas Martin who James' father hired to educate his children, would also live on the Madison plantation and teach the Madison children.[28] Arriving from New Jersey, The Rev. Martin, who was twenty-five at the time, had also been hired as the rector of the church that the Madison family attended. It was not at all unusual in colonial times for instructors at boarding schools, such as Robertson, or those who served as private tutors on plantations, such as Martin, to be ordained ministers.[29] Instruction by Martin included foreign languages, history, mathematics and literature. Education was a serious affair on the Madison plantation. Madison's education with his private tutor continued until he was 18 and ready to attend college. By the time he applied to college, Madison was proficient in several subjects including Greek and Latin.[30] James Madison was thus a very educated young man and exceptionally prepared to handle a rigorous college curriculum.

Madison's College Choice

Madison chose the College of New Jersey to pursue higher education. The College would officially become known as Princeton University in 1896. Madison decided on the College of New Jersey due to the college's reputation for academic

---

[25] Carl J. Richard, *The Founders and the Classics: Greece, Rome, and the American Enlightenment* (Cambridge: Harvard University Press, 1995), p. 18.
[26] Ibid.
[27] Ibid.
[28] Gutzman, *James Madison*, p.1
[29] Mary-Elaine Swanson, "The Education of James Madison: A Model For Today," *The Foundation for American Christian Education*, 2010. - Excerpts from a book by the same title published by the Hoffman Center, Selma, Alabama, 1991; online at https://face-net-wp-content-upload-2018/11/ (Accessed February 1, 2024.)
[30] Gutzman, James Madison p. 2.

rigor. He considered attending the College of William and Mary where the sons of many plantation families often went, but this college did not appeal to him. The College of William and Mary, which Thomas Jefferson had attended, was not known at the time for having the most demanding academic standards.[31] Standards were important to Madison. Nor did Madison decide to attend one of the prestigious colleges in England or Scotland, where boys from elite plantation families often attended.[32]

In addition to the College of New Jersey's rigorous academic reputation, Madison, in his short autobiography, also attributed his college choice to the influence of his private Episcopal tutor, Thomas Martin. Martin was a graduate of the College of New Jersey and had urged James to attend his alma mater.[33] Martin's older brother, Alexander, who visited his brother at the Madison plantation, was also a graduate of the College. Alexander further encouraged James to attend the same college that he and his brother had attended.[34] Yet another reason cited by Madison for his selection of the College of New Jersey over the College of William and Mary was that the Virginia college was located in what was known as the Tidewater region of Virginia. The heat, humidity and mosquitos were present among the coastal communities of Virginia. This would have been problematic for James, particularly since he was not a healthy young man. His life had been spent in the Piedmont, where the mountain air was cooler and the humidity less punishing.[35] Attending the College of William and Mary would have caused health complications. As Noah Feldman put it, "Throughout his life, Madison felt he had a propensity for getting sick. As a result, he protected himself as much as possible from places and activities thought to produce disease."[36]

Arriving at the College of New Jersey, it was likely apparent to Madison that his background was substantially different from many of his classmates. He was from Virginia, a southern slave-owning colony, while a majority of his classmates were from mid-Atlantic and Northeastern colonies, particularly New Jersey, Pennsylvania and New York.[37] Additionally, Madison was a member of the Anglican Church of England. This too placed him in the minority, as the College of New Jersey was a Presbyterian institution that attracted students aligned with

---

[31] Ibid.
[32] Ibid.
[33] Feldman, *The Three Lives of James Madison*, p. 6.
[34] Brant, *James Madison: The Virginia Revolutionist 1751-1780,* p. 71.
[35] Feldman, *The Three Lives of James Madison,* p. 7.
[36] Ibid.
[37] Ibid., p. 4.

Protestant denominations at odds with the Anglican Church.[38] And to further separate James from his classmates, he not only was from a slave owning plantation, which must have seemed barbarous to many northern students, but he had also arrived at the college with the services of a slave who had been willed to him by his maternal grandmother. Sawney was the name of the slave who traveled with James to college and who tended to his personal needs.[39] One can only wonder what his fellow students from colonies where the institution of slavery was less ingrained and where some of the students may never have been from a slave owning family must have thought when they first met James with a slave in tow.

Although there were several reasons why James selected the College of New Jersey to pursue his college education, there can be little doubt that another reason had much to do with the towering reputation of the college's revered and renowned president. Here the name of the Reverend John Witherspoon looms large in the education of James Madison.

The Reverend John Witherspoon

John Witherspoon was a Presbyterian minister who had emigrated to Virginia from Scotland. Well before his appointment as the College of New Jersey's president, and before he left Scotland, he had acquired the reputation as a distinguished and renowned scholar. He was born on February 5, 1723 in East Lothian, Scotland. The son of a Presbyterian minister, Witherspoon first attended a preparatory school followed by his enrollment at the University of St. Andrews. It was at St. Andrews where he earned a bachelor's degree in divinity.[40] He then enrolled at the University of Edinburgh where he extended his education by earning a master's degree. It was then onto divinity school at St. Andrews where by the age of twenty, he earned a doctorate and became ordained.[41] As an ordained Presbyterian minister, Witherspoon's first church was in Beith, Scotland. It was there that he met and married Elizabeth Montgomery, whose ancestral tree could be traced to John Knox, the minister and theologian known as the founder of

[38] Ibid.

[39] Ibid.

[40] "John Witherspoon: Pastor, College President and Signer of the Declaration;" online at https://nassauchurch.org/about/princetoncemetary-bios/cemetary-bio10/ (Accessed March 1, 2023.)

[41] "John Witherspoon (1723-1794);" online at https://www.ed.ac.uk/alumni/services/notable-alumni/alumni-in-nistory/john-witherspoon/ (Accessed March 1, 2023.)

Presbyterianism.[42] The Witherspoons then moved to Paisley, Scotland where he continued to serve as the pastor for another church.

During his years as a Presbyterian minister in Scotland, Witherspoon's scholarly reputation soared as a result of the books he authored, as well as the reputation of his sermons. A prolific scholar, Witherspoon's writings and reputation became well known not only among Scottish and English theologians, but also among prominent and highly educated colonists. James H. Smylie describes Witherspoon in this manner, "Witherspoon was a Calvinist. He stood in this tradition as it manifested itself in eighteenth-century Scotland. He was a Presbyterian evangelical under the sway of the common-sense philosophy of the University of Edinburgh and with a record of dissatisfaction with ecclesiastical autocracy in the Church of Scotland."[43]

When the College of New Jersey's president, the Reverend Samuel Finley, died, a concerted effort was launched to recruit Witherspoon as the college's next president. Finley was the college's fourth president in nine years who had unexpectedly passed away. The board of trustees was concerned about the future of the institution.[44] The board decided to make a concerted effort to stabilize the College by recruiting a renowned scholar. Prominent New Jersey lawyer, Richard Stockton, who was in England on a business trip, was asked by the board of trustees to personally visit and persuade Witherspoon to accept the vacant presidency. Stockton's visit was unsuccessful due in large part to resistance from Witherspoon's wife, Elizabeth. She had a fear of traveling over deep water, a condition known as "hydrophobia."[45] The thought of traveling on a ship across the Atlantic Ocean was truly terrifying to Elizabeth.

Repeated attempts to recruit Witherspoon continued for several months until the stalemate was finally broken. Benjamin Rush, a physician and graduate of the College of New Jersey, who was in Edinburgh, decided to use his persuasive skills to recruit Witherspoon.[46] After Rush had corresponded with Witherspoon and insisted that he alone could stabilize the college and elevate its reputation, Witherspoon invited the young doctor to visit him at his home so they could

---

[42] Mark Grossman, *Encyclopedia of the Continental Congresses*, First Edition, Volume 2., L-Z (New York: Grey House Publishing, Inc., 2015), p. 1513.

[43] James H. Smylie, "Madison and Witherspoon: Theological Roots of American Political Thought," *The Princeton University Library Chronicle,* Vol. 22., No. 3 (Spring 1961), p.120. online at http://www.jstor.com/stable/2640297 (Accessed April 1, 2024.)

[44] Stephen Fried, *Rush* (New York: Crown Publishers, 2018), p. 53.

[45] Ibid.

[46] Ibid., pp. 53-54.

further discuss the prospect of him becoming the college's next president.[47] Rush accepted the invitation and traveled to Witherspoon's home where he stayed as a houseguest for several days. Rush's discussions not only with Witherspoon, but also with Elizabeth, proved to be effective. After several intimate conversations and apparently impressed with Rush's persuasive talking points, Elizabeth finally consented to the move.[48]

Several months later, the couple and their five children arrived at the College of New Jersey where the Reverend John Witherspoon began what would be a legendary twenty-five year college presidency.[49] As a result of Witherspoon's leadership, enrollment at the college increased, the college's finances greatly improved, and more faculty were hired. Witherspoon by every account was a transformative and successful college president.[50]

Madison's Academic Mentor

College student James Madison would be introduced to the great philosophical thinkers in Witherspoon' seminars. Witherspoon, like other Scottish professors during the mid-eighteenth century, was an exceptionally skilled instructor. His pedagogical approach was honed at Scottish universities, which at the time were known for embracing the most rigorous academic standards in English speaking countries.[51] In his seminars, Witherspoon introduced Madison and his classmates to an array of Scottish philosophers which included a "powerful Presbyterian critique of religious oppression."[52] Madison's respect for religious liberty was likely formulated in Witherspoon's seminars. From Witherspoon, Madison would learn that Protestantism, not Catholicism with its popes, cardinals and autocratic edicts, was the brand of religious thought most conducive to religious liberty and personal independence. Yet he would also learn from Witherspoon that the Church of England had a blemished history of persecuting dissenting religions.[53] Most importantly, and at the heart of Witherspoon's lectures, Madison became intimately familiar with the powerful thinkers associated with the "Scottish Enlightenment." The Enlightenment, which overlapped the 17th and 18th centuries brought forth a number of important

---

47 Ibid., p. 54.
48 Ibid., p. 55.
49 Ibid., p. 55.
50 Grossman, *Encyclopedia of the Continental Congresses,* p. 1513.
51 Richard Brookhiser, *James Madison* (New York: Basic Books, 2011), p. 18.
52 Andrew Burstein and Nancy Isenberg, *Madison and Jefferson* (New York: Random House, 2013), p. 12.
53 Ibid., p. 13.

political philosophers whose controversial works served to stimulate debates regarding human rights and the divine right of kings. This time period, which does not have a specific start and end date, was one of the most intellectually stimulating periods in the history of the western world.[54] According to Jack N. Rakove, "Witherspoon remade the college into a major outpost of the Scottish Enlightenment, introducing his students to the moral philosophy of Frances Hutchenson, Thomas Reid, and Lord Kames, and the social science of Adam Ferguson, Adam Smith and David Hume."[55]

As a student, Madison was very serious and dedicated to his studies. His pre-college tutorial sessions with the Rev. Thomas Martin and his several years at the boarding school studying under Rev. Donald Robertson had prepared him so well that he earned his bachelor's of arts degree in two years. But rather than head back to the family plantation, he chose to stay an additional year beyond graduation to take more courses in theology and ethics with Witherspoon.[56]

Beyond his intense commitment to academics, Madison also participated in the Whig Society, a debating club that challenged the views of the college's more prominent Cliosophic Society.[57] A reserved young man and on the shy side, it was through the pressure and demands associated with face-to-face collegiate debating that Madison was able to refine and further develop his critical thinking and oratory skills; skills that would greatly serve him throughout his career as a public servant.[58] Yet despite overcoming his shyness, he was the only student among his twelve member graduating class who chose not to speak at his graduation. A health related issue was the reason.[59]

Witherspoon's students were well-educated and well-versed in the classics by the time of graduation. His gripping and challenging seminars likely included, among others, the writings of John Locke. Locke's *Second Treatise on Civil Government* which appeared in 1689 during England's Glorious Revolution must have been on Witherspoon's required reading list. Locke's emphasis on God-given inalienable rights, which included life, liberty and property, as well as the God-given right to revolt against abusive government, most surely resonated with

---

[54] Feldman, *The Three Lives of James Madison,* p. 6.
[55] Jack N. Rakove, *James Madison and the Creation of the American Republic,* (New York: Harper Collins Publishers, 1990), p. 3.
[56] Smylie "Madison and Witherspoon," p. 120.
[57] Feldman, *The Three Lives of James Madison*, p. 5.
[58] The two debating societies merged in 1928 to create the Whig Cliosophic Society, aka "Whig-Clio;" See "The American Whig-Cliosophic Society;" online at whigclio.princeton.edu/history/ (Accessed June 25, 2024.)
[59] Broadwater, *James Madison*, p. 3.

Madison. The writings of French nobleman and political theorist Baron de Montesquieu, particularly Montesquieu's *The Spirit of Law* (1748), would also have been on Witherspoon's syllabi. Montesquieu's endorsement of the separation of powers and how this governing doctrine was essential for preserving human liberty must have influenced Madison's appreciation for balanced and limited government. The classic writings of Athenian, Greek and Roman philosophers would also have served to shape Madison's thinking regarding the principles of government and leadership.[60] Cost writes, "Thucydides would instruct him in warfare. Aristotle in philosophy, Cicero in ethics, Polybius in politics, Justinian in law."[61] Witherspoon also introduced James to the writings of the Scottish Enlightenment philosopher David Hume whose writings on moral philosophy Witherspoon criticized with regularity. The "infidel writer" was how Witherspoon referred to Hume.[62] Richard Beeman notes that Hume's "observations about governance in an 'extended republic' would have a profound influence on Madison in later years."[63]

American independence from Great Britain was also a topic of much discussion during Madison's days in college. Revolution was hotly debated, with Witherspoon's lectures by no means neutral on this subject. Indeed, after Madison had graduated, Witherspoon, while still serving as president of the college, was elected in 1776 to the Continental Congress where he served three consecutive terms. It was the Second Continental Congress, of which Witherspoon was a member, which spearheaded the war for independence against Great Britain. Moreover, due to his fluency in French, Witherspoon while a member of the Congress, wrote a letter to his contact in France urging French support for the American Revolution.[64] Witherspoon was the only clergyman among the fifty-six patriots who signed the Declaration of Independence. During the American Revolution, Witherspoon participated as one of the coauthors of the Articles of Confederation.[65] Many of Witherspoon's students, including James Madison, would join the revolution when independence from Britain was formally declared.[66]

---

[60] Carl J. Richard, *Greeks and Romans Bearing Gifts: How the Ancients Inspired the Founding Fathers* (Lanham: Rowman and Littlefield, 2008), passim.
[61] Cost, *James Madison*, p. 25.
[62] Ketcham, *James Madison*, p. 42.
[63] Richard Beeman, *Plain, Honest Men: The Making of the American Constitution* (New York: Random House, 2009), pp. 25-26.
[64] Grossman, *Encyclopedia of the Continental Congresses*, p. 1514.
[65] Ibid.
[66] Burstein and Isenberg, *Madison and Jefferson*, p. 12.

The impact of Witherspoon's seminars, his vast knowledge of religion, politics and philosophy, along with his academic mentoring of students, was evident in the number of his former students who chose to pursue public service careers. The list is impressive: "a president and vice president of the United States, nine cabinet officers, twenty-one senators, thirty-nine congressman, three justices of the Supreme Court, and twelve state governors."[67] To date, it is unlikely to discover a college professor or college president who has had such a profound influence on so many students.

In 1772, with college completed, Madison returned to his father's plantation. His seminars with Witherspoon had molded his philosophy of government and strengthened his support for religious liberty. Feldman writes, "What Madison learned in college, much of it from Witherspoon himself, would influence the course of his thinking for the rest of his life."[68]

Home From College

When Madison returned to Montpelier, he was not in the best of health. Health problems became more acute during his last year of college and had become even more severe after he had returned home. Writing to his close college friend, William Bradford, Madison expressed a morose outlook towards his future. He described himself as "too dull and infirm now to look out for any extraordinary things in this world," nor did he anticipate "a long or healthy life."[69] Attempting to cheer up his friend, Bradford in a return letter reminded Madison, "Persons of the weakest constitutions, by taking a proper care of themselves often outlive those of the strongest."[70] Bradford's encouraging words were prophetic, as Madison would live to be eighty-five.[71] Exactly what was wrong with Madison's health was never medically diagnosed. His health problems which began when he was a boy and became more serious while in college persisted throughout his entire life. He would have what he described as "sudden attacks somewhat resembling epilepsy" which impeded for a particular period of time his "intellectual functions."[72] It was after college and when Madison was back home that very contentious political developments between the colonists and the British

[67] Grossman, *Encyclopedia of the Continental Congresses,* p. 1512.

[68] Feldman, *The Three Lives of James Madison*, p. 5.

[69] Madison writing to Bradford, November 9, 1772, *Papers of James Madison*; quoted in Cost, *James Madison,* p. 27.

[70] Bradford writing to Madison, March 1, 1773, *Papers of James Madison*; quoted in Cost, *James Madison*, p. 27.

[71] Cost, *James Madison*, p. 27.

[72] Madison quoted in Cost, *James Madison*, p. 26.

government were now surfacing. Such events would be a turning point in the life of James Madison and the start of his long career in public service.

The Revolution Was Beginning

When Madison was a young boy living on his father's plantation, tension between the thirteen colonies and Great Britain had been festering since the end of the French and Indian War. This was a war fought from 1754-1763 between Britain and France to determine which of the two powerful European countries would have control over North America.[73] The war was taking place during a much larger conflict occurring in Europe between France and Britain, along with allies of both countries. In Europe the war, once it ended, was known as the "Seven Years War." During the North American conflict, several Native-American tribes had aligned themselves for different reasons with the French. Colonial regiments loyal to Britain fought against the French in the interest of defending the British Empire's colonies and territorial possessions. In the end, Britain defeated France and maintained control over her thirteen colonies and much of Canada.[74]

Even though Britain had defeated France, the war had plunged the treasury of Great Britain into serious debt. As a response, taxes and other harsh economic measures were imposed on the colonists by the British Parliament. The clear intent was to replenish the depleted British Treasury. Such taxing measures included the Sugar Act 1764, the Stamp Act 1765 and the Townshend Acts passed in 1767 and 1768. The taxing measures passed by the British Parliament and without the consent of the colonists, served to fuel resentment and tension between colonists and British soldiers. One incident that clearly reflected the growing animus occurred on March 5, 1770 in the city of Boston when a contingent of frightened British soldiers fired on a jeering mob of more than three hundred angry colonists, some of whom were throwing snowballs and rocks at the soldiers. When the skirmish ended, five colonists lay dead.[75] Colonial propagandists, such as Paul Revere, depicted the killings as the "Boston Massacre."[76]

Exhibiting little respect for the colonists and describing them as disloyal British subjects, the British Parliament in 1773 passed the infamous Tea Act. The act, which served to further inflame the colonists, placed the British owned East

[73] Fred Anderson, *The War That Made America: A Short History of the French and Indian War* (New York: Penguin Books, 2006).
[74] Ibid.
[75] David McCullough, *John Adams* (New York: Simon and Schuster, 2001), p. 65.
[76] Ibid., p. 66.

India Company in a privileged trading position, while simultaneously suppressing the economic interests of colonial tea companies. As Stacy Schiff notes, "It allowed the East India Company to export tea directly, without additional duty, and to appoint agents to sell that tea to retailers, eliminating the merchants in the middle."[77] Members of the British Parliament anticipated the colonists' resentment, but found their level of anger surprising. "Few in Great Britain thought to use the words "tea" and "liberty" in the same sentence, when by 1773 the words were inextricable in America."[78]

The Boston Tea Party followed. On the night of December 16, 1773, rebellious colonists disguised as Native Americans boarded British ships anchored in Boston's harbor. Over the course of two hours and with exceptional precision, the "Sons of Liberty" pried open and dumped more than three hundred chests of tea into the freezing waters of the harbor.[79]

Rather than recognize the intense hostility caused by the Tea Act and deciding to negotiate a compromise with the colonists, the British Parliament with the support of King George III responded by passing a body of four acts in 1774 collectively titled the "Coercive Acts." Colonists chose to label the laws as the "Intolerable Acts." The acts were specifically intended to punish the colonists and the city of Boston for the rebellious incident. One of the acts was the "Boston Port Act," which officially closed Boston's harbor. The specific intent of this act was to isolate and ruin the economic life of Boston.[80] The harbor was to be officially closed until Boston reimbursed the East Indian Company for the damaged tea. One of the acts required the arrest and trial of those responsible for the damaged tea.[81]

James Madison was no longer a boy, nor for that matter a college student, when the Tea Act was imposed on the colonists and when the Boston Tea Party occurred. He was home from college and living comfortably on his father's plantation. Yet at this point in his life he had already become a strong supporter of American independence, His opposition to the harsh taxing measures imposed by Britain, the teachings of Witherspoon, the bold actions of the Sons of Liberty in Boston, and the Coercive Acts had convinced Madison that revolution and independence from Britain was the one and only option for the thirteen colonies.

---

[77] Stacy Schiff, *The Revolutionary: Sam Adams* (New York: Little and Brown, 2022), p. 230.
[78] Ibid.
[79] Ibid., p. 242.
[80] Ibid., p. 258.
[81] Ibid., p. 259.

In April 1775, colonists clashed with British soldiers in the Massachusetts towns of Lexington and Concord, With the revolution against Britain now starting, Madison in October 1775 was appointed by Virginia's Committee of Safety as a colonel in the Orange County militia. This appointment, despite his impressive rank, required little official or strenuous activity on Madison's part. His health was poor and he knew that serving as an officer in the militia would not be a part of his future.[82] Madison recognized that his commitment to the revolution would not be in the form of military service, but instead would be in a different but equally important way.

The Virginia Constitutional Convention

In April of 1776, James Madison entered the world of public service as a delegate to an important convention held in Williamsburg, the current seat of government in colonial Virginia.[83] The purpose of this convention was to write a constitution for the colony of Virginia. Conventions at the time were formed in several of the colonies for the purpose of providing colonists with more autonomy over matters related to independence.[84] The conventions, which consisted of delegates elected from local communities, circumvented the colonial legislatures that many colonists had concluded were unresponsive to the movement for independence. Richard Brookhiser describes the colonial conventions as "protorevolutionary institutions, outside the law, but in Virginia they were run by the local gentry, who felt as threatened by London's behavior as radical Bostonians."[85] Constitutions were written in several colonies where these conventions were held. In Virginia, Britain's Royal governor had decided by 1776 to abdicate his appointed office. His abdication permitted colonists supporting the revolution to engage in uncontested control over political matters.[86]

It was at the Virginia Convention in 1776 where Madison met George Mason. At the age of twenty-five, Madison's interactions with Mason would prove to be a transformative and highly educational experience. Perhaps to his surprise, Madison was invited to serve on a committee headed by Mason to draft the Virginia Declaration of Rights and a new constitution for Virginia. Regarded as one of the most learned and well-versed individuals with respect to the history of England and law, Mason, who owned a large plantation alongside the Potomac known as Gunston Hall, would guide the committee's deliberations while

---

[82] Gutzman, *James Madison and the Making of America*, p. 8.
[83] Brookhiser, *James Madison,* p. 22.
[84] Ibid.
[85] Ibid.
[86] Cost, *James Madison*, p. 29.

educating Madison on the nuances of rights and religious liberties.[87] Mason, a rather gruff and no-nonsense sort of man, who Ketcham describes as "aloof from colonial politics,"[88] was an admirer of England's Glorious Revolution of 1688 and the writings of John Locke. The revolution in England culminated in limits placed on the powers of the King, while simultaneously transferring more powers to the British Parliament. Mason based many of his own governing principles on those principles associated with the anti-monarchial Whigs of England.[89] Mason was regarded as the colony's foremost expert regarding the core principles of republican government. On complex questions related to law, delegates often looked to Mason for guidance.[90]

The committee to which Madison was appointed worked diligently on a Declaration of Rights and a constitution. It was a large committee consisting of more than two dozen members. In his capacity as committee chair, Mason directed the business of the committee.[91] A number of learned Virginians were also selected to serve on Mason's committee, one of whom was Patrick Henry, a strident supporter of American independence.[92] Henry would be elected Virginia's first governor in 1776.

A number of proposals to help the delegates with their work were delivered from several individuals, one of whom was Thomas Jefferson. Jefferson at the time was serving in the Continental Congress located in Philadelphia. Jefferson forwarded three different versions of a proposed constitution to Mason's committee. The committee accepted some of Jefferson's proposals, but in the end the committee's final draft more closely reflected the ideas of the individual committee members. [93] The writings of political philosophers were consulted, like those studied in Witherspoon's seminars. The committee also drew from the recent work of John Adams' *Thoughts on Government* (1776) for guidance.[94]

Although Madison as a committee member made contributions to the Virginia Declaration of Rights and the colony's new constitution, his contributions according to most accounts were limited. As the youngest member of the committee, Madison out of respect deferred to the wisdom of Mason and

---

[87] Ketcham, *James Madison*, p. 71.
[88] Ibid.
[89] Gutzman, *James Madison* and the Making of America, pp. 9-10.
[90] Ketcham, *James Madison*, p. 71.
[91] John Boles, *Jefferson: Architect of American Liberty* (New York: Basic Books, 2017), p. 63.
[92] Ketcham, *James Madison*, p. 71.
[93] Boles, *Jefferson*, pp. 64-65.
[94] Ketcham, *James Madison,* p. 71.

felt obligated to defer to the views of the more senior members of the committee.[95] Yet there was one provision of the Declaration of Rights that reflected Madison's direct influence. This was the sixteenth provision regarding religious freedom. Madison, after some diplomatic negotiation with Mason, was able to modify "that all men should enjoy the fullest toleration in the exercise of religion" to "All men are equally entitled to the free exercise of religion."[96] The difference between "toleration" and "free exercise" was significant to Madison. The term "toleration" suggested that while different religions would be tolerated, the Anglican Church in Virginia would still be deemed superior to other religions and would remain the established church. "Free exercise," however, was a much stronger term and indicated that all religions would be viewed as equal to one another. Madison further believed that church and state should be separated. Yet despite Madison's support for a separation of church from state, he was unsuccessful in his attempt to convince the more senior committee members that the Virginia constitution should separate the two institutions

Although Madison had been baptized as an Anglican, which was the denomination of the Madison family, he had never undergone formal confirmation within the Anglican Church.[97] His strong opinions against an established church in Virginia apparently stemmed from watching how Baptists were systematically persecuted by the Anglican controlled colonial government.[98] Ketcham describes the persecution, "The decade of the 1760s was one of violent persecution of the dissenters, specifically the Baptists who were very active in the Piedmont. They were stoned out of Culpepper County in 1765 and jailed in Spotsylvania County in 1768."[99] Despite Madison's objections, Mason, the respected committee chair, along with the more experienced Edmund Pendleton, rejected Madison's recommendation to disestablish the Anglican Church.[100]

The merger of church and state was not unusual among the American colonies, nor for that matter when colonies became states following independence. Indeed, several state constitutions required tax supported churches. Establishment varied from one state to the next. In Virginia it was the Anglican Church. In Connecticut, taxes were paid to support the Congregational Church.

---

[95] Ibid.
[96] Cost, *James Madison,* p. 33.
[97] Broadwater, *James Madison*, p. 5.
[98] Cost, *James Madison,* p. 31.
[99] Ralph L. Ketcham, "James Madison and Religion – A New Hypothesis," *Journal of the Presbyterian Historical Society*, Vol. 38., No 2 (June 1960), p. 67; online at https:??www.jstor.org/stable/23325326. (Accessed March 26, 2024.)
[100] Cost, *James Madison*, pp. 32-33.

The Virginia Declaration of Rights reflected the writings and views of Enlightenment philosophers, such as John Locke. In his treatment of the Virginia Declaration of Rights, Chester James Antieu states, "This was the first deliberate adoption of the natural rights philosophy as the basis for political organization anywhere in the world."[101] Although Madison was certainly a contributor to the Virginia Declaration of Rights, credit for this profound document belongs almost exclusively to George Mason. Leonard C. Helderman describes Mason in this manner, "Never covetous of public office, deeply read in the classics and political literature of the 17th and 18th centuries, he lacked the magnetism of Jefferson and the fire of Henry. Yet he was one of the greatest of the Virginians of the golden age. As his essentially scholarly mind pondered the problems of his day, he envisioned a Virginia Commonwealth, free, tolerant, somewhat aristocratic."[102]

Madison was surely in awe of the committee with whom he had been selected to serve. He must have found this experience to be an extraordinary opportunity to learn about history, liberties, and republican government from not only Mason, but also from several other learned convention delegates. It is important to note that the convention Madison attended not only devoted its attention to composing a Declaration of Rights and a new constitution for Virginia, but also went a step farther by unanimously supporting a resolution that called upon the Continental Congress to declare America's independence from Britain.[103]

Whether it was due to the unanimous vote of Virginia's constitutional convention, or growing support among the colonies for independence, the Continental Congress in the summer of 1776 had finally come to the conclusion that revolution was the only possible road to achieving independence from Britain. A five-member committee was subsequently selected to write a Declaration of Independence. Due to his eloquent writing style and masterful grasp of political philosophy, the committee deferred to Thomas Jefferson to author the document. Although the revolution had already started in 1775 with the deadly confrontations between colonists and British soldiers in Massachusetts, the American quest for independence became official on July 4, 1776, the day in which the Continental Congress formally approved Jefferson's final draft.

---

[101] Chester James Antieau, "Natural Rights and the Founding Fathers – The Virginians," *Washington and Lee Law Review* Vol. 17, No. 1 (Spring, 1960) p. 44; online at https://scholarlycommons.law.wlu.edu/wlulr/vol17/Iss1/4. (Accessed March 26, 2024.)

[102] Leonard C. Helderman, "The Virginia Bill of Rights," *Washington and Lee Law Review* Volume 3, No. 2 (1942), p. 234; online at https://scholarlycommons.law.wlu.edu/wluir/vol3/Iss2/3. (Accessed March 1, 2024.)

[103] Brookhiser, *James Madison*, p. 22.

Chapter Two

Madison's Entry into Public Service and the Constitutional Convention

An Unsuccessful Bid for Public Office

Madison served one term in the Virginia House of Delegates immediately following approval of the state's constitution. A clause in the new constitution allowed those who served as delegates to the convention to continue as members of the assembly during the first legislative session.[1] Thus, it was in 1776 as a member of the Virginia House of Delegates that Madison began his long career as a public servant.

Intrigued by the give and take of legislative politics, Madison, when his term expired decided to seek a second term in the House of Delegates. His confidence as a member of the assembly had grown and his intellect had impressed fellow delegates. However, despite Madison's desire to continue as an elected legislator, he quickly learned that politics is not always about impressing voters with one's intelligence and ideas, but rather by cultivating personal loyalties in the form of small favors for people. One such favor within the district where he was seeking election involved serving shots of whiskey to voters. Although winning votes by serving whiskey might seem totally incongruent with how a candidate should win public office, the fact of the matter is that whiskey and votes had long been happy companions in colonial times. Unfortunately for Madison, his opponent, Charles Porter, was a likeable tavern keeper who understood the relationship between votes and free shots of whiskey.[2] Madison, not surprisingly, viewed the use of whiskey to gain votes beneath his personal values. Feldman writes, "The ordinary person did not want to have a pint of ale with James Madison, and the feeling, Madison demonstrated, was mutual."[3] Madison thus lost his first bid for public

---

[1] Brant, *James Madison: The Virginia Revolutionist 1751-1780,* p. 272.
[2] Feldman, *The Three Lives of James Madison,* p. 30.
[3] Ibid.

office due to the favors his opponent provided to voters, in this case free shots of whiskey. This was hardly the style of politics that Madison respected, nor did he intend to ever engage. "One public argument used against him at this time, according to the Reverend Dr. Balmaine, was that he was better fitted for the pulpit than the legislature."[4] Reflecting on his loss to Porter many years after, Madison noted that the use of liquor by candidates for public office had its roots in England and was brought to Virginia by English settlers.[5]

The Governor's Council

Despite his defeat, the word had circulated among the political class in Virginia that the young James Madison should be given a meaningful role in Virginia's new government. His sharp intelligence and his penchant for precision were attributes deemed beneficial to Virginia's interests. Accordingly, Madison was appointed by Virginia's House of Delegates to serve on the Governor's Council of Virginia's first governor, Patrick Henry. The Governor's Council was modeled after the privy councils of England where a small group of learned individuals served as advisors to the monarch. The privy councils functioned as the "executive arm of the British government from as early as the 13th century."[6]

From 1777 to 1779, Madison first served on the Council of Governor Patrick Henry. This was an important position, as Virginia's new constitution required the Governor's Council to participate in every decision made by the governor. Reflecting on his time as one of the eight councilors to Governor Henry, Madison, rather than recalling the situation as one of eight councilors and a governor, felt the more accurate description was one of "eight governors and a councilor."[7] Madison truly loved serving on the Council for Henry. Indeed, so devoted to his work as a councilor that in 1778 when he was elected by Orange County voters to serve in Virginia's House of Delegates, a position he had previously sought but lost due to the politics of whiskey, he declined to serve out of his devotion to the Council.[8]

In June of 1779, Thomas Jefferson was elected governor of Virginia.[9] Madison, due to his diligence and insight, was once again appointed as a

---

[4] Brant, *James Madison: The Virginia Revolutionist 1751-1789,* p. 307.
[5] Brant, *James Madison: The Virginia Revolutionist 1751-1789,* p. 306.
[6] The House of Commons, "The Privy Council: history, functions and membership," November 15, 2023; online at commonslibrary.parliament.uk/research-briefings/chp-7160/ (Accessed March 8, 2024.)
[7] Madison quoted in Burstein and Isenberg, *Madison and Jefferson*, p. 59.
[8] Feldman, *The Three Lives of James Madison*, p. 33.
[9] Brookhiser, *James Madison*, p. 29.

councilor. For six months, Madison would serve as a personal advisor to Jefferson. Like George Mason, Jefferson would provide an invaluable mentorship to the young man from Orange County.[10] Although Madison had briefly met the older Virginian when Jefferson stepped down from the Continental Congress in 1776 to occupy a seat in the Virginia legislature, the two at the time were not close to one another.[11] That changed very quickly when Madison served on Jefferson's Council. The two bonded and a mentoring relationship developed. As Brookhiser put it, "The man who had never had an older brother, found one in Jefferson, along with unfailing stimulus and inspiration."[12] Ketcham notes that their social and intellectual bonding was due not only by their "zeal for the revolution" but also due to their mutual love for "words and ideas of books."[13] Lynne Cheney captures their relationship in these terms, "Each was probably the brightest person the other ever knew, and both were well schooled, giving them a vast fund of common learning on which to draw as they talked and planned."[14]

During his time as a councilor, Madison boarded at the home of his cousin, the Reverend James Madison. In 1776, the Reverend Madison had been selected as the president of the College of William and Mary. Living at the stately home of his cousin, an Episcopal Minister, was a convenient and comfortable form of lodging for Madison.[15] He had a comfortable and rewarding existence while serving on the Councils of Henry and Jefferson.

Madison as a Member of the Continental Congress

In 1779, Madison was chosen by the Virginia legislature to serve in the Continental Congress. He enthusiastically accepted the opportunity to serve as a congressional representative in light of the Congress' central role related to the revolution. The revolution was now in its fourth year with the outcome far from certain. As a representative in Congress, Madison felt certain he could be an important contributor to the war for independence. At the age of 29, Madison was the youngest member of the Continental Congress.[16] Yet despite his age and lack of legislative experience, his

---

[10] Ibid.

[11] Lynne Cheney, *James Madison: A Life Reconsidered* (New York: Viking Press, 2014), p. 64.

[12] Ibid., p. 30.

[13] Ketcham, *James Madison*, p. 84.

[14] Cheney, *James Madison,* p. 71.

[15] Cost, *James Madison*, p. 34.

[16] Donald Dewey and Barbara Bennett Peterson, *James Madison: Defender of the American Republic* (New York: Nova Science Publishers, 2009), p. 20.

commitment to law making far surpassed the other Virginians who had been selected to serve in the Congress. As Dewey and Peterson note, "The quality and especially the attendance record of Virginians in (and mostly out of) Congress was embarrassing to the state and distressing and depressing to General Washington."[17]

Formed as a reaction to the abuses of King George III and resistance to the harsh measures imposed on the colonies by the British Parliament, leaders of the thirteen colonies had formed a Congress to protect and advance colonial interests. Members of the Continental Congress had selected Philadelphia as its meeting place. Historians describe the Continental Congress as consisting of two distinct periods. The First Continental Congress lasted only a short while, from 1774 to 1775, while the Second Continental Congress existed from 1775 to 1781. Although members of the First Continental Congress favored independence from Great Britain, it was the Second Continental Congress that appointed a committee to draft the Declaration of Independence and which served as the assembly that spearheaded the American Revolution. The Second Continental Congress has gone down in history as a bold and fearless Congress consisting of strident revolutionaries and patriots. It would be as a member of the Second Continental Congress where Madison would earn his reputation as an outstanding and highly dedicated lawmaker. It was also during his time in the Continental Congress that he would recognize the need for a stronger national government and a stronger union among the states.

Madison's contributions as a member of Congress were significant. Like his performance at the Virginia Convention and during his time as a member of the councils that advised of Henry and Jefferson, Madison's reputation as a learned public servant with a keen eye towards detail impressed his fellow lawmakers. As Irving Brant notes, when Madison took to the floor to speak, "the effect was startling upon those who did not know him well."[18]

One of the policy areas in which Madison made an important contribution while serving as a member of the Continental Congress pertained to resolving land claims which speculators had acquired in regions west of the thirteen colonies. Speculators prior to the war for independence included such notable individuals as John Hancock, George Washington, Benjamin Franklin and George

---

[17] Ibid.

[18] Irving Brant, *James Madison: The Nationalist 1780-1781* (New York: Bobbs Merrill Co., 1948), p. 13.

Mason.[19] The rights to western land purchased by wealthy colonists had become complicated due to the Proclamation Line of 1763 established by King George III following the French and Indian War. The Line established by the King prohibited colonists from buying land beyond the Appalachian Mountains. Unfortunately for the speculators, the King's proclamation drastically devalued the land they had purchased.[20] With the war for independence underway and a firm rejection of the policies established by the British government, land claims of not only speculators but also individual states surfaced as a major issue in Congress. It was not unusual for states in those days to lay claim to land well beyond their western borders. To further complicate matters, there were border and land disputes between the states.[21] Recognizing the complexity associated with land claims and the urgency to resolve these difficult issues, Madison focused his efforts on establishing solutions for resolving land disputes. One important development which can partially be credited to Madison involved the final agreement of several states to cede their land claims. Congress, Kevin R. Gutzman writes, "adopted the provisions regarding eventual statehood for the ceded lands and congressional reimbursement of the military expenses borne by the ceding states, but it rejected the provision regarding Indian purchases."[22] Madison also supported the right of the states that were ceding their land to "affix whatever conditions they chose to their cessions . . . "[23] The ceded land in Madison's view would be helpful for the creation of new states beyond the original thirteen.[24] The disposition of land claims and the ceding of lands was a complex and key issue that faced the Continental Congress. It was an issue that James Madison helped resolve.

Madison's intellectual and political reputation resulted in his appointment to every key legislative committee in the Continental Congress. On virtually every major issue that came before the Congress, Madison was a contributor to final resolutions. "As he learned that his insights, his pen, and his political skills were extraordinary useful in Congress, he knew he had found his place."[25] Madison's love and respect for the legislative process was reflected in the fact that he had near perfect attendance during his time in Congress and never missed

---

[19] Kevin R. Gutzman, *James Madison and the Making of America* (New York: St. Martin's Press, 2012), p. 18.
[20] Ibid.
[21] Ibid., p. 19.
[22] Ibid. p. 20.
[23] Ibid.
[24] Ibid.
[25] Ketcham, *James Madison,* p. 101.

deliberations or key votes.[26] Dewey and Peterson summarize Madison's performance as a lawmaker, "By spring of 1783 James Madison had become an unquestioned legislative leader, a spectacular advancement from the shy and quiet member who had arrived three years earlier. He chaired most of the committees on which he served and wrote many major reports, especially on foreign affairs and finance. Most important were his efforts to move the United States toward fiscal responsibility."[27]

Although during his time as a member of the Second Continental Congress, Madison expressed support for state sovereignty, studies of his legislative behavior suggest that at this point in his life he had become a proponent of national solutions and often gravitated to the "nationalist faction" of lawmakers.[28] Adam Tate observes, "During spring 1781, the nationalists proposed two measures: the impost and the coercive powers amendment. Madison supported both measures. Historians have long viewed Madison's support as evidence of his growing nationalism and have tended to plot his position in 1781 as the first indication of Madison's push for constitutional reform, while usually ignoring his previous discussions of sovereignty."[29] Commenting on Madison's nationalist orientation, Jeff Broadwater offers this perspective, "A Virginia republican, he was also a Virginia nationalist, a term that, in Madison's case, was not an oxymoron." Madison firmly believed that the country "should be governed by Virginia values."[30]

While Madison was serving in the Second Continental Congress, the Congress with the approval of the thirteen states adopted a national constitution titled the Articles of Confederation. This constitution would last for only seven years, 1781 to 1788. With the exception of the Northwest Ordinance passed by the Confederation Congress in 1787, which outlined procedures for admitting new states into the Union,[31] the Articles of Confederation were a noble, but unsuccessful, experiment in self-government. The national government consisted of only a unicameral Congress, very similar to that of the Continental Congress.

---

[26] Ibid.

[27] Dewey and Peterson, *James Madison*, p. 27.

[28] Adam Tate, "James Madison and State Sovereignty, 1780-1781, *American Political Thought* Vol. 2, No. 2 (Fall 2013), p 187; online at https://www.jstor.org/stable/10.1086/673130. (Accessed March 26, 2024.)

[29] Ibid.

[30] Jeff Broadwater, *James Madison: A Son of Virginia & a Founder of the Nation* (Chapel Hill: University of North Carolina Press, 2012), p. xiii.

[31] "Northwest Ordinance 1787" online at archives.gov/milestone-documents/northwest-ordinance. (Accessed July 11, 2024.)

Due to legitimate fear of executive power, there was no chief executive in a separate branch of government. There was a president of the Congress, but this was a legislative rather than an executive role. There was no judicial branch of government or a Supreme Court. The powers of the Congress were limited in scope with the majority of power contained within the individual state legislatures. But despite the fact that the thirteen separate states retained many of their powers, the Congress, as Jack N. Rakove writes, "began to function much like a national government."[32] Although Madison supported the Articles of Confederation, it was only a matter of time for him to notice the new constitution's inherent deficiencies. Madison knew a better governing document could and must be created. But it would not be as a member of the Congress that Madison would work to reform the Articles, as his time as a congressman expired in 1783 due to term limits. Madison was thus required to vacate his seat.

With public service his calling, Madison returned home to Orange County where after only three months he decided to serve as a member of the Virginia House of Delegates. As Sidney Howard Gay notes, "Mr. Madison's reputation was already made by his three years in Congress, and he now easily took a place among the political leaders of his own State."[33] To protect the assembly from the British, the Virginia House of Delegates in 1780 had been relocated from Williamsburg to Richmond.[34]

Madison as a Member of the Virginia House of Delegates

Madison's "Memorial and Remonstrance"

While a member of the Virginia House of Delegates, Madison, a firm believer in religious freedom, which was evident when he helped draft The Virginia Declaration Rights, led a challenge to Virginia's tradition of supporting public policies intended to sustain the Anglican Church. Church and state in Virginia were closely intertwined with one another, as they were in several other states.

In 1785, Governor Patrick Henry had introduced a bill to the legislature titled "Establishing a Provision for Teachers of the Christian Religion." The bill required the use of property tax dollars to pay for educational programs run by

[32] Jack N. Rakove, *The Beginnings of National Politics: An Interpretive History of the Continental Congress* (Baltimore: The Johns Hopkins University Press, 1979), p. 194.
[33] Sidney Howard Gay, *James Madison* (New York: Chelsea House Publishers, 1983), p. 45.
[34] Cost, *James Madison*, p. 56.

Christian ministers in Virginia.[35] The bill did not specify Anglican ministers, but rather Christian ministers in general. Henry's bill allowed taxpayers to designate which Christian religion their tax dollars should be directed. In the view of Vincent Munoz, "Henry's bill may have erased distinctions among Protestants, but it was not nonsectarian."[36] Nevertheless, despite the generic support for all Christian ministers, it was apparent that the true intent of Henry's bill was to support Episcopal clergy.[37] Moreover, even though the bill identified the educational function of Christian ministers, it was also evident that the bill "granted a direct subsidy to Christian clergymen."[38]

Madison knew what Henry's motivations were and decided to oppose the bill in writing. His written objections presented to the Virginia legislature were titled *Memorial and Remonstrance*. In this impressive body of objections, Madison presented fifteen separate articles in which he not only challenged Henry's bill, but also argued in forceful terms for the God-given right to religious liberty.[39] Reflecting on Madison's written objections and support for religious freedom, Munoz states, "The 'Memorial and Remonstrance' offers Madison's most comprehensive and philosophical statement on the fundamental political principles excluding religion as such from civil jurisdiction. It stands as the pinnacle of his theoretical reflections on the subject of church and state."[40] Madison's opposition to policies which blended church and state would be on full display when he authored the First Amendment to the U.S. Constitution which prohibits government support for religion, while at the same time protecting the free exercise of religion.

Jefferson's Virginia Statute for Religious Freedom

While a member of the House of Delegates, Madison also shepherded a bill that Jefferson had proposed protecting religious freedom. Fortunately for Jefferson, who at the time was serving as Minister to France, Madison was able to use his political leverage to navigate Jefferson's bill. The bill passed on January

---

[35] Vincent Phillip Munoz, "James Madison's Principle of Religious Liberty," *The American Political Science Review,* Vol. 97, No. 1 (February 2003), p. 21; online at https://www.jstor.org/3118218 (Accessed March 26, 2024.)
[36] Ibid.
[37] Ibid.
[38] Ibid.
[39] Ibid., pp. 21-22.
[40] Ibid., p. 34.

16, 1786.[41] The bill, titled the "Virginia Statute for Religious Freedom," represented Jefferson's views, as well as Madison's, regarding the rights of religious minorities. Both Jefferson and Madison were well aware of how Baptists had been persecuted in Virginia. For years, both had felt that legal protection for Baptists and other religious minorities should be a paramount concern. Madison, as noted in the previous chapter, was adamant about protecting religious freedom when he helped draft the Virginia Declaration of Rights. When Jefferson was governor, he received letters from Baptists insisting on religious freedom in Virginia.[42] Jefferson scholar John B. Boles notes that Jefferson's papers from 1776 suggest that his thoughts regarding the rights of religious minorities was influenced by John Locke's "A Letter Concerning Toleration" (1689).[43] The state of Virginia was thus the first state to ever pass a bill protecting religious freedom.[44] The historic statute, according to Boles, "was one of the most important intellectual and political victories of the entire revolutionary era and one of three accomplishments Jefferson wanted memorialized on his tombstone."[45] The bill was Jefferson's, but it was Madison who helped turn the bill into a law.

While serving in the House of Delegates, Madison remained in close contact with several Virginians he had served with when he was a member of Congress. Deeply concerned about the viability of the Articles of Confederation, in 1785 Madison traveled to Philadelphia to meet with his former colleagues for the purpose of discussing what reforms were needed to strengthen the Congress.[46] His conversations were not only informative but also convinced him to encourage the Virginia assembly to draft a resolution providing Congress with the authority to regulate interstate commerce. Expanding Congress' authority to regulate interstate commerce, in Madison's view, would at least be a step towards strengthening the national government and a step towards creating unity among the states. Moreover, free trade among the states would be enhanced, along with the establishment of a more prosperous national economy.[47] Rakove notes,

"Positive instructions from the largest southern state might help to break the impasse within Congress, defuse the sectional tensions that had already alarmed

---

[41] John B. Boles, *Jefferson: Architect of American Liberty* (New York: Basic Books, 2017), p. 84.
[42] Ibid., p. 80.
[43] Ibid., p. 81.
[44] Ibid., p. 85.
[45] Ibid. p. 84.
[46] Rakove, *The Beginnings of National Politics,* p. 368.
[47] Ibid.

Madison and facilitate later ratification by the states."[48] Much to Madison's disappointment, however, his proposed resolution was not supported by the Virginia legislature. This was predictable, as the commerce power under the Articles of Confederation was the exclusive domain of the individual states. State lawmakers in Virginia were unwilling to cede such an important power to Congress.

Yet to Madison's satisfaction, the Virginia assembly under the leadership of Speaker of the House John Tyler, the father of the future president by the same name, approved an alternative resolution calling for the thirteen states to meet in a convention for the purpose of reviewing trade and commercial relations among the states. The Virginia resolution called upon the thirteen states "*to take into consideration the trade of the United States, to examine the relative situations and trade of the said States; to consider how far an uniform system in their commercial regulations may be necessary to their common interest and permanent harmony; and to report to the several states such an act relative to this great object , as, when ratified by them, will enable the United States in Congress effectually to provide for the same.*"[49] Thus, it was the state of Virginia, due to Madison's concerns, that took the lead in calling for a convention for the purpose of reviewing the current problems related to interstate commerce. Support for a convention devoted to interstate commerce would at least in Madison's view begin the process of reviewing and rectifying one of the most glaring deficiencies of government under the Articles of Confederation.[50] The convention was scheduled for September 1786. The chosen location was the city of Annapolis, Maryland. Madison intended to use this convention to strengthen Congress' power over interstate commerce and to begin serious discussion regarding the creation of a stronger and more centralized form of government.

The Annapolis Convention

Despite an invitation to the thirteen state legislatures to send delegates to the Annapolis Convention, delegates from only five states attended: Delaware, New Jersey, New York, Pennsylvania and Virginia.[51] Collectively, there was a total of twelve delegates who attended the convention, all of whom, as Louis Ottenberg

---

[48] Ibid.

[49] The Virginia Resolution quoted in Louis Ottenberg, "A Fortunate Fiasco: The Annapolis Convention of 1786," *American Bar Association Journal*, Vol. 45, No. 8., p. 836., (August 1959); online at https://www.jstor.org/stable/25720900 (Accessed March 27, 2024.)

[50] Rakove, *The Beginnings of National Politics,* p. 369.

[51] Cost, *James Madison*, p. 68.

notes, "were in favor of the same thing – strengthening the Federal government."[52] Massachusetts, New Hampshire, North Carolina and Rhode Island had selected delegates to attend the convention, but for a variety of reasons their delegations never made the trip. Maryland, with reservations regarding the purpose of the convention, chose not to attend, despite the convention's convenient location.[53] With less than a majority of states participating, the convention did not have a quorum and thus was unable to conduct official business. Nevertheless, Madison and other delegates who favored reform of the Articles of Confederation used the convention to make the case for a stronger and more nation-centered form of government.

One of Madison's allies at the Annapolis Convention who had arrived as a delegate from New York was Alexander Hamilton. Madison had become acquainted with Hamilton when both served together in Congress. Hamilton, like Madison, favored a much stronger national government with a broad set of powers. He was one of the most strident critics of the Articles of Confederation. At the Annapolis Convention, Hamilton authored a report titled "Address of the Annapolis Convention." In this report, Hamilton called upon the thirteen states to participate in a "general meeting" for the purpose of addressing a wide range of contemporary governing problems beyond the problem of commerce.[54] The delegates at the convention unanimously supported Hamilton's address.[55] It was evident that momentum was growing for a convention to either reform the Articles of Confederation, or perhaps to write a new constitution.

Despite poor attendance and the absence of a quorum to conduct official business, the Annapolis Convention held from September 11 to 14, 1786 merits historic importance, as it served to create momentum for the Constitutional Convention that was convened the following year. In addition to Hamilton, Madison loomed very large behind this development. Commenting on what transpired at the Annapolis Convention, Brookhiser suggests that Madison and Hamilton not only benefitted from poor attendance, but were likely pleased that only a handful of state delegates participated. Their goal of advancing support for a stronger federal union faced little resistance from the convention's participants.[56] "No one had asked the Annapolis Convention to call for full-scale political reform. In stretching their mandate and then getting out of town, Madison

---

[52] Ottenberg, "A Fortunate Fiasco," p. 837.
[53] Cost, *James Madison,* p. 68.
[54] Ibid., p. 68- 69.
[55] Brookhiser, *James Madison,* p. 46.
[56] Ibid., p. 47.

and Hamilton had pulled a fast one – a clever and opportunistic maneuver."[57] Burstein and Isenberg further observe that Madison used the Annapolis Convention to not only cultivate support for reform among the delegates who attended this convention, but also to generate support for reform among members of the Virginia House of Delegates whose support for reform he deemed essential for proceeding with the Constitutional Convention.[58] It was the Annapolis Convention, as Ottenberg put it, where "the seeds" were planted and which soon "germinated" in the Constitution of the United States.[59]

Shays' Rebellion

By the end of 1786, Madison, Hamilton and other advocates for a stronger federal government had successfully convinced a number of key individuals, which included several members of Congress, that the Articles of Confederation were deficient and that a convention was necessary to save the fledgling republic. To help buttress their call for reform, in the summer of 1786 and extending into 1787, a farmers revolt led by former revolutionary war captain, Daniel Shays, occurred in western Massachusetts. Due to extremely poor economic conditions and heavy taxes imposed on farms, farm foreclosures began occurring with regularity. Farm families were plunged into poverty and destitution. The result was a farmers' uprising against the state government. In the words of Catherine Drinker Bowen, "Desperate farmers, ruinously taxed – by 'Boston' they said – and seeing their cattle and their land distrained by the baliffs, had risen in revolt. With staves and pitchforks they had marched on county courthouses after the best Revolutionary technique, frightening sound-money men out of their wits and rousing General Washington to express disgust and anger that a country that had won a difficult war was not able to keep order in peacetime."[60] The rebellion convinced a number of political and military leaders that change in government was now needed. One prominent patriot who recognized the need for reform was General Henry Knox of Massachusetts. Knox, who Alpheus Mason and Richard Leach identify as the "sower of the seeds of fear,"[61] sent numerous letters to Washington in which he described the farmers' rebellion in catastrophic terms, "The Theoretic government of Massachusetts has given way, and its laws are trampled under foot. . . . Our government must be braced, changed or altered to

---

[57] Ibid.

[58] Burstein and Isenberg, *Madison and Jefferson,* p. 138.

[59] Ottenberg, "A Fortunate Fiasco," p. 882.

[60] Bowen, "*Miracle in Philadelphia*, p. 10.

[61] Alpheus Thomas Mason and Richard H. Leach, *In Quest of Freedom*, 2nd ed. (Englewood Cliffs: Prentice Hall, 1973), p. 68.

secure our lives and property."[62] Madison received word of the rebellion in a letter from fellow Virginian Henry Lee that approximately forty-thousand members of the Massachusetts militia were supporting the rebels.[63] Recognizing that the rebellion could generate support for a stronger federal government, Broadwater notes that Madison also exploited the rebellion by circulating "unfounded reports of violence and foreign intrigue, suggesting the turmoil showed the need to add 'vigor' to the national government."[64]

Although the rebellion was eventually suppressed by the Massachusetts militia, "Shays' Rebellion," as it became known, caused much consternation among members of the Confederation Congress. The rebellion, although confined to one region and in only one state, further bolstered the argument of those calling for a stronger centralized government that could provide order and stability to the country. Madison had called on the Congress to take forceful measures against the rebels, although he realized that the limited powers of Congress prevented meaningful action on the government's part against the uprising.[65]

Shays' Rebellion is often described in textbooks as the "catalyst" that led to the Constitutional Convention in 1787. The revolt certainly elevated the urgency for a convention to carefully review the inherent flaws of the Articles of Confederation, and perhaps overhaul or even jettison that decentralized and distrustful scheme of government. Although support for a convention had been growing prior to the rebellion, the uprising, which some felt might spread to other states, provided Madison, Hamilton and others with more leverage for initiating reform.

In 1787, Madison was once again elected to Congress, a position beneficial for building support for a convention. The Congress in 1787 was now meeting in New York City. Since 1774, the Congress had met in seven different locations due to the mobility and constant presence of British troops.[66] Madison's efforts to orchestrate a convention along with the efforts of Hamilton and other pro-convention members of the Congress would soon be successful.

The Congress, apparently swayed by Hamilton's Annapolis report, Madison's persuasive support for another convention, and the disturbing farmers' rebellion in western Massachusetts, finally voted for a convention to review the

---

[62] Knox quote in Mason, *Free Government, p. 185;* quoted in Mason and Leach, *In Quest of Freedom*, p. 68.
[63] Broadwater, *James Madison*, p. 40.
[64] Ibid.
[65] Gutzman, *James Madison*, p. 65.
[66] Catherine Drinker Bowen, *Miracle at Philadelphia: The Story of the Constitutional Convention May to September 1787* (Boston: Little Brown and Co., 1966), p. 12.

problem of national governance. Congress' call for a convention did not suggest that the convention's purpose would be to write a new constitution, but rather for "the sole and express purpose of revising the Articles of Confederation."[67] Although a majority of congressional delegates agreed that reforms were necessary, many still felt that the Articles of Confederation, despite problematic with respect to promoting commerce and providing for national security, was still a governing document worth preserving. Thus, it was a revision of the Articles of Confederation, not the drafting of a new constitution that was the original purpose of the historic Constitutional Convention in 1787.

James Madison at the Constitutional Convention

May 14, 1787 was selected by Congress as the start date of the convention. The city of Philadelphia was selected as the convention's site. The convention would be held in the Pennsylvania State House, which since 1776 had been renamed "Independence Hall." It was an appropriate city for the convention and an appropriate building in which to conduct such a convention. The room in which the convention would be held was the same room where the Continental Congress had originally met and where Thomas Jefferson's eloquent draft of the Declaration of Independence had been signed by fifty-six patriots committed to American independence from Britain.[68] To conduct the business of the convention, the delegates from the individual states would be required to caucus and cast one block vote per state. The block vote would represent the position of their respective state. To conduct formal business, a quorum of seven states was required.[69] Of the thirteen states invited to the convention, Rhode Island was the only state that chose not to send delegates. Although fifty-five delegates from twelve states participated in the convention's proceedings, several delegates arrived in Philadelphia on different days and even different months throughout the summer. Some delegates departed before the convention adjourned. Rarely were all fifty-five delegates present on a given day, and rarely was business conducted with all twelve state delegations on the convention floor.[70]

Many of the delegates who attended the convention were learned individuals with experience in government and public affairs. Political novices were not among the delegates. Yet among the fifty-five delegates who attended the convention, there was one delegate who stood apart from the others with respect

[67] Quoted in Bowen, Miracle in Philadelphia, p. 11.
[68] Bowen, Miracle in Philadelphia, p. 23.
[69] Ibid., p. 17.
[70] Ibid., p. 24.

to his grasp of large and small republics, his familiarity with the writings of Greeks and Romans, and his knowledge of philosophers associated with the Scottish Enlightenment. That delegate was James Madison, who in no uncertain terms had arrived at the convention with a major goal in mind. In the words of Rakove, "James Madison went to the Constitutional Convention of 1787 intent on seizing the initiative from the opening moments. But the proposals he carried with him represented far more than a list of his own priorities. They amounted to a comprehensive theory of government that consciously challenged many axioms of eighteenth-century political science."[71]

Although Madison's knowledge regarding the complexities of government can certainly be traced to the teachings of Witherspoon, along with his own independent reading, his intellectual preparation for the convention can also be attributed to the assistance provided to him by his mentor, Thomas Jefferson. Several months before the convention, Jefferson, while serving as Minister to France, sent chests of books to Madison to help prepare him for debate on the convention floor. Catherine Drinker Bowen describes the massive number of books Jefferson sent to Madison.

> The books arrived not by ones and two, but by the hundreds; thirty seven volumes of the new *Encyclopedie Methodique,* books on political theory, and the law of nations, histories, works by Burlamaqui, Voltaire, Diderot, Mably, Necker, d'Albon. There were biographies and memoirs, histories in sets of eleven volumes and such timely productions as Mirabeau on The order of the Cincincinnati.[72]

Forever the serious student, Madison's note taking was extensive while reading the books Jefferson had supplied. He focused in particular on the success and failure of the more recent and ancient confederacies, studying each one thoroughly and separately. These included, "the Lycian Confederacy, the Amphicytonic, the Achaean, the Helvetic, the Belgic, the Germanic."[73] Based on his extensive reading and note taking, Madison authored a paper that he intended for use at the forthcoming convention. His paper was titled *Vices of the Political System of the United States.*[74] This was a clear and very direct critique of government under the Articles of Confederation. "Finished in April, on the very eve of the meeting to revise the structure of American government, this brief

---

[71] Jack N. Rakove, *James Madison and the Creation of the American Republic* (New York: Harper Collins, 1990), p. 44.
[72] Bowen, *Miracle at Philadelphia*, p. 14.
[73] Brant, *James Madison: The Nationalist 1780-1787*, pp. 410-411.
[74] Ibid., p. 411.

article not only probed the weaknesses of the state and federal structures, but put into words the thoughts on government which its author had distilled out of the world's past and his own mind."[75] Madison's support for a stronger national government was quite direct and perhaps astounding, "Let the national government be armed with a positive and complete authority in all cases where uniform measures are necessary. Let it have a negative, in all cases whatsoever, on the legislative acts of the states, as the King of Great Britain heretofore had. Let this national supremacy be extended also to the judiciary department."[76]

The Virginia Delegation

Madison was part of a seven-member delegation selected for the convention by the Virginia state legislature. The Virginians were a most distinguished group. They included the retired and revered General George Washington who had been coaxed out of retirement by Madison to not only attend the convention but to also serve as the convention's presiding officer. As Robert Allen Rutland notes, "That settled the matter of whether good men or second-raters would attend."[77] Virginia's current governor Edmund Randolph led the delegation, while George Mason, known for his vast political expertise, was also a member. Because the Virginia delegation arrived in Philadelphia well before the arrival of the other state delegations, they had much time to meet among themselves to strategize and to refine the plan they intended to present to the convention. "The Virginians met each day after a leisurely breakfast and listened as Madison dissected the political corpse of the Confederation, delving into causes and effects."[78] Among the seven delegates from Virginia, Madison was not only familiar with the history of republican governments and the writings of political philosophers, but he was already an experienced lawmaker. As noted by Harold S. Schultz, "Madison was well-prepared by practical experience for the role he played in 1787 in drafting the U.S. Constitution. Although only thirty-six years old, he had already served for two years on the council of the Virginia governor, five years in the Virginia legislatures, and four years in the Confederation Congress. In every office that he held, he had been known for his serious attention to business." [79]

---

[75] Ibid.

[76] Madison's paper quoted in Bowen, *Miracle at Philadelphia*, p. 14.

[77] Robert Allen Rutland, *James Madison: The Founding Father* (Columbia: University of Missouri Press, 1987), p. 14.

[78] Ibid., p. 15.

[79] Harold S. Schultz, "James Madison: Father of the Constitution?" *The Quarterly Journal of the Library of Congress*, Vol. 37, No. 2 (Spring, 1980) p. 216; online at https://www.jstor.org/stable/29781852 (Accessed March 13, 2024.)

The Virginia Plan

It was on May 29, 1787, that Randolph presented the "Virginia Plan" to the convention. This was a comprehensive reform plan consisting of fifteen separate resolutions. Although it was Randolph who presented the Virginia Plan, the Plan in reality represented the handiwork of Madison. Despite the fact that some of the Plan's resolutions were voted down by the delegates, it was nevertheless the Virginia Plan that ultimately persuaded a majority of delegates to forego a revision of the Articles of Confederation and to write an entirely new constitution. Scholars who have studied the convention suggest that it was the Virginia Plan, more than any other plan presented at the convention, that provided the "framework" for the U.S. Constitution.[80]

The original fifteen resolutions of the Virginia Plan that Madison drafted and which Randolph presented have unfortunately never been found.[81] Yet what does provide evidence regarding the content of the fifteen resolutions can be discerned from the notes of the convention that were recorded by Madison. Madison, not surprisingly, meticulously recorded the day-by-day proceedings that have provided a treasure trove of material for historians and constitutional scholars to draw upon. Although some scholars have questioned whether Madison's transcriptions of the resolutions are in fact a word-for-word description of each resolution presented by Randolph, his notes nevertheless are still considered the most reliable source of information regarding not only the content of the Virginia Plan, but also what transpired inside Independence Hall during the sweltering summer of 1787. The convention was conducted in total secrecy with journalists prohibited from covering the proceedings.

Despite the fact that some of Madison's resolutions were not supported by the delegates and some subject to modification, a review of the Virginia Plan will still reveal clear connections to the governing system established by the Constitution. These include a bicameral national legislature with the lower chamber directly elected by the people with population determining the number of representatives allotted to the individual states. There is also an upper chamber, although Madison proposed that this chamber should also be based on population with members chosen by the lower chamber.[82] Power would be equally shared between the two chambers. There is also a strong statement endorsing Congress' ability to legislate for the nation, which represented a major shift from the state-

---

[80] Rutland, *James Madison.*, p. 15.

[81] Editorial Note, "The Virginia Plan, 29 May 1787; Founders Online; at https:?? founders.archives.gov/documents/Madison/01-10-02-0005. (Accessed May 31, 2023)

[82] Founders Online, "The Virginia Plan"

centered system of government established by the Articles of Confederation. A resolution authorizing Congress to exercise a veto over any state law that Congress deemed harmful to the republic was also included in the Virginia Plan. One of Madison's resolutions also recommended a separate executive, but one that would be chosen not be the people, but by Congress. One of Madison's resolutions also called for a Council of Revision consisting of members of the executive and judiciary who together who would review and possibly veto bills before, not after, they were legislated.[83] One of his resolutions also called for an independent judiciary.[84] Thus, it was the Virginia Plan that moved delegates towards supporting a new constitution that embraced a more powerful and federal style of government along with a system of separated powers with checks and balances. Although Madison through his own independent readings and the books provided by Jefferson was by the time of the convention intimately familiar with the success and failure of different sized republics, including the difficulties faced by large republics, he nevertheless pressed ahead in making the case that an enlarged federal republic with constitutional safeguards would be best for the United States. The Virginia Plan, which to this day is attributable to Madison, is what guided the delegates as they forged a new constitution, albeit with an abundance of compromises.

State Constitutions Were Also Consulted

Somewhat overlooked in treatments of the Constitutional Convention and the decisions that were reached was the important role that state constitutions played in helping to guide the thoughts of the delegates. While it is true that the philosophical works of Locke and Montesquieu as well the historical experiences of European republics influenced the views of Madison and other delegates, so too were the practical experiences that some of the delegates had with their own state constitutions. Between the start of the American Revolution in 1775 and the Constitutional Convention in 1787, eleven states, due to their desire for self-governance, had already adopted their own state constitution.[85] It is within these early state constitutions that one will find some of the core principles contained within the federal constitution.[86] As Benjamin F. Wright writes, "The men who drafted the national Constitution dealt with the materials familiar to them in their

---

[83] Founders Online, "The Virginia Plan"
[84] Founders Online, "The Virginia Plan"
[85] Benjamin F. Wright, Jr. "The Origins of the Separation of Powers in America," *Economica,* No. 40 (May 1933), p. 176; online at https://www.jstor.org/stable/2548765 (Accessed March 30, 2024.)
[86] Ibid.

States. Agreement without serious opposition was reached in the Convention upon those problems where colonial and State experience was clear and relatively undivided. Where experience was unclear or conflicting, dispute, and ordinarily compromise resulted."[87]

Madison's Two Major Defeats at the Constitutional Convention

Representation in the Upper Chamber

Although Madison favored a system of representative democracy, the Virginia Plan was nevertheless viewed by delegates from the small and less populated states as deficient with respect to providing fair representation for states in Congress. According to the Virginia Plan, representatives in both the lower and upper houses of Congress would be based on the population of each state. Clearly, states like Virginia, New York and Pennsylvania would dominate states like New Jersey, Connecticut and Delaware.

In response to Madison's proposed model of representation, New Jersey's governor, William Patterson, presented what became known as the "New Jersey Plan." Patterson's Plan deviated from Madison's Virginia Plan by supporting a unicameral legislature with equal representation for every state regardless of a state's population or status.[88] Every state would therefore have equal power related to the legislative process. To make his point, Patterson delivered a forceful speech before the delegates that was highly critical of Madison's Plan. Patterson argued that if the Virginia Plan's formula for representation was accepted, this would result in small states dominated by the larger and more populated states. Small states would be subject to despotic rule.[89] Madison countered Patterson by suggesting that if the New Jersey Plan were supported by the delegates, then the states would have far too much power to control the future of the country and that the national government would be unable to respond to internal crises when they arose, such as Shays' Rebellion.[90] Support for equal representation among the states was also expressed, although in a more pointed and dramatic manner, by a delegate from Delaware named Gunning Bedford. On June 30, another hot and steamy day, Bedford directed his ire at the delegates from the large states by aggressively proclaiming, "I do not, Gentlemen, trust you. . . . there are foreign powers who will take us by the hand." Compelled to respond to Bedford's

---

[87] Ibid., p. 184.
[88] Bowen, Miracle at Philadelphia, p. 106.
[89] Ketcham, *James Madison*, p. 202.
[90] Cheney, *James Madison*, p. 135.

comments, Massachusetts delegate Rufus King rose and spoke to the convention, "I am concerned for what fell from the gentleman from Delaware. . . . Whatever may be my distress, I never will court a foreign power to assist in relieving myself from it."[91]

A "Grand Committee" was formed to resolve the large state versus small state controversy. The work of the committee resulted in the "Great Compromise," or "Connecticut Compromise," which reflected the astute recommendations of Roger Sherman, one of the three delegates representing Connecticut. The Grand Committee recommended that representatives in the lower house of Congress would be apportioned based on the population of individual states, which is what Madison proposed, while in the upper house each state would have equal representation regardless of population, which accommodated Patterson and supporters of the small states. On July 16, the Grand Committee's presentation of the Great Compromise was supported by a state vote of 5 to 4.[92] Although support for the Great Compromise was clearly a defeat for Madison, he was nevertheless determined to keep the convention moving towards the final goal of establishing a new constitution for the American republic. The man from Montpelier was too much of a statesman to sulk and undermine those who did not support his proposal for representation. Following his victory over the issue of state representation, Patterson, also a statesman, supported every subsequent proposal recommending a stronger and more nation-centered federal republic.[93]

Included within the "Great Compromise" was the provision for counting the slave populations within the individual states for the purpose of representation and taxation. A number of delegates from the northern states felt that slaves, because they were property, should be counted for the purpose of taxation, but should not be counted for allocating congressional representatives to states. Many southern delegates felt differently. They argued that slaves should be counted when allocating representatives to the states, but not for the purpose of taxation. Although there was a north/south split among the delegates on this issue, delegates from their respective regions were not uniformly in agreement with one another regarding how best to count slaves.

The result was the notorious three-fifths compromise. The compromise involved the counting of three-fifths of a state's slave population for the purpose

---

[91] Statements of Gunning Bedford and Rufus King, in Pierce, "Sketches" and Yates's notes, debates, June 30, Records, III, 92, I, 490-93; 500-502; quoted in Ketcham, *James Madison*, p. 210.
[92] Ketcham, *James Madison*, p. 213.
[93] Ibid., p. 215.

of taxation and representation. The compromise provided southern states with additional representatives in Congress, a strategic decision for bolstering southern support for the Constitution. Although critics of the compromise have suggested that the Founders viewed a slave as three-fifths of a person, an understandable criticism, the three-fifths fraction, according to Richard Beeman, reflected instead "a rough approximation of the measure of wealth that an individual slave contributed to the economy of his or her state."[94] Beeman notes that although there was no empirical evidence to document the value of wealth a slave generated, there was nevertheless a general understanding that "the wealth-producing capacity of a slave was roughly three-fifth of that of a free person."[95] Despite the lack of evidence, "the idea of a three-fifths ratio, however arbitrary, it may have been, obviously stuck in the minds of many Convention delegates."[96]

Congressional Veto Power Over State laws

The second defeat for Madison involved his resolution that would give Congress a veto power over the actions of state legislatures. Madison had argued that Congress should be authorized under the Constitution to veto any state law that federal lawmakers deemed harmful to the national interest. Madison's support for this congressional power, which he believed was necessary for preserving the Union, was perplexing given his subsequent and strong support for federalism during the fight to ratify the Constitution. A majority of the delegates found Madison's recommendation a threat to state sovereignty and rejected his resolution.[97] Garry Wills suggests that perhaps one reason why Madison did not want the convention proceedings to be made public was that he did not want the public to know that he had vigorously advocated a congressional veto over state laws, "That position would always have been embarrassing to him."[98]

The Constitutional Convention continued throughout the summer with the delegates completing their work in September. On September 17, thirty-nine delegates signed their name to the proposed Constitution of the United States. Although Madison is the principal figure associated with the U.S. Constitution,

---

[94] Richard Beeman, *Plain, Honest Men: The Making of The American Constitution* (New York: Random House, 2009), p. 154.
[95] Ibid.
[96] Ibid.
[97] Frank Garver, "Propositions Rejected by the Constitutional Convention of 1787," *The Historian*, Vol. 6., No. 2 (Spring, 1944), p. 115; online at https:www.jstor.org/stable/24435972 (Accessed March 13, 2024.)
[98] Garry Wills, *James Madison* (New York: Time Books, Henry Holt and Co., LLC, 2002), p. 43.

one would be remiss not to call one's attention to the fact that a number of individuals from the twelve state delegations each in their own way contributed to the structure and content of the final document. According to Brant, "From the written record, perhaps half of the fifty-five who attended the convention can be put down as active builders of the Constitution. The silent ones knew how they were voting. Of deliberate obstructors or self-promoters there were few indeed, of marplots not one."[99]

In his comprehensive treatment of the Constitutional Convention, Akhil Reed Amar posits that in addition to Madison, much credit should also belong to James Wilson from Pennsylvania and certainly George Washington who presided over the convention.[100] Wilson, in Amar's view, could conceivably be called the "father of the Constitution." "When it became clear that the Articles were failing, Wilson theorized a brilliant new approach – popular sovereignty – that underpinned and unified the Constitution crafted at Philadelphia. At that drafting Convention, Wilson participated vigorously, contributing from start to finish and present every day or nearly so."[101] Amar further notes that following the Constitutional Convention, Wilson's printed statements were highly instrumental in securing ratification of the Constitution, not only in his home state of Pennsylvania but also in several other states.[102] Brant also comments on the impressive role of Wilson at the Constitutional Convention, "Ranking among the foremost in legal and political knowledge, he knew all the political institutions of the world in detail, and drew attention not by the charm of eloquence but the force of reasoning."[103]

Regarding Washington's role, Amar points to the creation of the American presidency located within Article II of the Constitution. It was because of Washington that the Constitution established, "a presidency far more muscular than any state counterpart, with an independent electoral base, a substantial (four year) term of office, unlimited reeligibility, a powerful pair of veto and pardon pens, broad appointment and removal powers, military and diplomatic heft, personal control over executive department heads, and more."[104] Amar writes that although Washington's "voice almost never appears" in Madison's recorded

---

[99] Irving Brant, *James Madison: Father of the Constitution 1787-1800* (New York: The Bobbs Merill Company Inc., 1950), p. 154.
[100] Akhil Reed Amar, *The Words That Made Us: America's Constitutional Conversation, 1700-1840* (New York: Basic Books, 2021).
[101] Ibid., p. 210.
[102] Ibid.
[103] Irving Brant, *James Madison: Father of the Constitution 1787-1800,* p. 57.
[104]Amar, The Words That Made Us, p. 212.

notes, Washington, knowing that he would be the first president under the Constitution "got everything he wanted" with the result a "breathtakingly strong chief executive."[105] Madison apparently had little to do with the creation of the presidential office.[106]

The Ratification Process

Printed copies of the proposed Constitution were sent off to the states for ratification once it had been approved by the Convention. Article VII of the Constitution stated that the affirmative votes of nine states would be required to ratify the Constitution. Sending the Constitution to state conventions was strategic, as state conventions, unlike state legislatures, would consist of a cross section of people within each state, as opposed to a body of elected state lawmakers. Elected state lawmakers, more than state convention delegates, would likely be suspicious of the national powers embedded in the proposed Congress and presidency. National powers in their view could pose a threat to states' rights as well as their own political power. By allowing state convention delegates, rather than state legislators, to vote for the Constitution, the Framers could legitimately claim that the United States Constitution, once ratified, was based on the will of the American people. The state convention votes would therefore correspond to the first three words of the Constitution's Preamble, "We the People…."

The Framers knew that despite sending the proposed Constitution to state ratifying conventions that a major fight still loomed ahead. Not surprisingly, the little man from Montpelier would be instrumental in securing the Constitution's ratification. Writing to Jefferson on October 24, 1787, a little more than a month after the Convention adjourned, Madison described how remarkable it was that the Constitution, in light of the deep political divisions that existed among delegates, was able to produce a document for ratification. He described the Convention as "a task more difficult than can be well conceived by those who were not concerned in the execution of it. Adding to these considerations the natural diversity of human opinions on all new and complicated subjects, it is impossible to consider the degree of concord which ultimately prevailed as less than a miracle."[107] Madison knew that the fight to ratify the Constitution would

---

105 Ibid., pp. 212-213.

106 Regarding Wilson and Washington, Amar presents a very balanced treatment regarding the role of both individuals at the Convention. He presents the "case for" and the "case against." Only the "case for" is presented here.

107 Madison to Jefferson, October 24, 1787, *Papers of James Madison*; quoted in Lynne Cheney, *The Virginia Dynasty* (New York: Viking, 2020), p. 94.

be as divisive and political as the summer convention, but he was confident that in the end the Constitution would be supported.

James Madison --- "Father of the Constitution"

Although James Madison is identified as the "Father of the Constitution" due to his efforts at the Constitutional Convention, there are scholars, such as Amar, who believe the title gives Madison too much credit for the governing document that finally emerged from the Constitutional Convention. Harold Schultz also objects to the title. As Schultz put it, "The exalted title 'Father of the Constitution' exaggerates Madison's influence at Philadelphia. The Constitution that was finally approved in September 1787 was more at variance with his thinking than with that of a majority of delegates."[108]

Yet despite legitimate questions regarding Madison's influence at the Constitutional Convention, there can be no denying that the "framework" of the Constitution belongs to Madison, more than any other delegate. Moreover, Madison was highly instrumental in spearheading the call for a convention, and as the next chapter will show, he was a key figure in helping to win ratification of the Constitution in two key states - New York and Virginia. Also on the list is the Bill of Rights that Madison authored. Granted, some of Madison's resolutions that were part of the Virginia Plan were defeated at the Constitutional Convention; that fact cannot be denied. Yet when one considers his collective efforts before, during, and after the Constitutional Convention, it should be apparent that James Madison was the principal figure responsible for the existence and ultimate success of the United States Constitution. He deserves the title, "Father of the Constitution."

---

[108] Schultz, "James Madison: Father of the Constitution?" p. 222.

Chapter Three

Madison Fights to Ratify the Constitution

There was little doubt in the mind of James Madison following the Constitutional Convention that a major political fight would commence once the proposed Constitution was presented to delegates at the state ratifying conventions. Securing the support of at least nine states would be a major challenge. If ratified, the Constitution would transform the nation's governing system from that of a confederal form of government in which states were supreme, to that of a federal government in which states, although still empowered, would be subordinate to the federal constitution and federal laws. Cost describes the enormity of the task that awaited those who would be selected as delegates to state ratifying conventions.

> The coming fight over ratification would be the greatest democratic event in the history of the world up to that point in time. White male freeholders across the thirteen states would be tasked with electing delegates to special ratifying conventions that would determine whether the Constitution would be adopted.[1]

Those who opposed the proposed Constitution and who preferred a continuation of the Articles of Confederation, were identified as "'anti-federal men' with an 'anti-federal disposition.'"[2] At some point, the opponents of the Constitution became known as Antifederalists. The title of the opponents was understandable, as it was a broadly empowered *federal* government that was being proposed for ratification. Those who supported the Constitution and a new *federal* form of government were identified quite simply as Federalists. Although the dividing line between the two factions was evident, there was nevertheless a spectrum of support and opposition within both groups. For some Federalists and Antifederalists only minor disagreements separated their views on government,

---

[1] Cost, *James Madison*, p. 114.

[2] W.B. Allen, Gordon Lloyd and Margaret Lloyd, eds. *The Essential Antifederalist* (Lanham: University Press of America, 1985), p. viii.

while on some contentious issues there was consensus and overlap. Pauline Maier clarifies the division that existed between the two factions, "The terms 'Federalist' and 'Antifederalist,' which were used mainly by 'Federalists' oversimplify the debate over the Constitution by suggesting there were only two sides."[3] Yet with regard to the fundamental issue regarding the dividing line between federal and state power, there was serious disagreement.[4]

Federalists and Antifederalists were located in towns and cities among the thirteen states. In some states, such as Hamilton's home state of New York and Madison's home state of Virginia, there was a clear division between Federalists and Antifederalists, while in other states, such as Delaware and Connecticut, the divisions were mild. Although Madison recognized that it was possible to win the support of nine states without the support of Virginia and New York, he knew that to bring the Constitution into existence without the support of both states would inherently undermine the legitimacy of the new Constitution. Virginia and New York were both large states with large populations and inhabited by many prominent people. Madison deemed it essential to win ratification in both of those states.

High Profile Antifederalists

New York's Governor George Clinton

In the state of New York, Governor George Clinton, the most powerful figure in New York politics, was a leading Antifederalist. Clinton was in his sixth term as governor and had an exceptionally strong base of political supporters known as the "Clintonians." To complicate matters for the Federalists, Clinton was scheduled to be the presiding officer at the New York ratifying convention. The convention with Clinton presiding was scheduled to take place in Poughkeepsie, New York.[5]

Virginia's Former Governor Patrick Henry

Patrick Henry, who served as Virginia's first governor from 1776- 1779 and again as governor from 1784-1786, was also a strident opponent of the proposed Constitution. Like Clinton in New York, Henry had a loyal base of supporters. It was Henry who proclaimed that he "smelt a rat" when the Constitutional Convention was initially called for. It was therefore understandable that he was

---

[3] Pauline Maier, *Ratification: The People Debate the Constitution, 1787-1788* (New York: Simon and Schuster, 2010), p. 94.
[4] Ibid.
[5] Bowen, Miracle at Philadelphia, pp. 109-110.

not a member of the seven member Virginia delegation that attended the Convention. Although Henry was a great patriot and strident supporter for the American Revolution, Madison was nevertheless convinced that Henry was "committed to the destruction of the republic."[6]

Governor Edmund Randolph

Randolph, who served as Virginia's governor from 1786-1788, was also a problem for Madison. Ironically, it was Randolph who had led the Virginia delegation in Philadelphia, and it was Randolph who presented the Virginia Plan. However, as the convention progressed, Randolph withdrew his support for the Constitution. He expressed concern about a potential aristocracy in the Senate and a presidency tantamount to that of "a little monarch."[7] Madison however still felt that Randolph, who had succeeded Henry as governor and who was a major voice in Virginia politics, could still become an ally when it came time to vote for the Constitution. Randolph's contradictory positions on key components of the proposed Constitution suggested that he might in the end support ratification.[8]

The Learned George Mason

Madison had also lost the support of George Mason at the Convention. Mason's primary reason for not supporting the Constitution was that it did not contain a bill of rights. In Mason's view, a bill of rights was essential for protecting the American people from the newly created federal government. As the principal author of the Virginia Declaration of Rights, which protected and expanded civil liberties to the people of Virginia, Mason's objection was understandable. At the Convention, Mason's support for a federal bill of rights was countered by Roger Sherman from Connecticut who convinced most of the delegates, but not Mason, that the bills of rights contained within state constitutions were more than sufficient for protecting the American people from government encroachment.[9] Yet despite Sherman's argument, Mason warned that a government unrestrained by a bill of rights could evolve into a system of government in which civil liberties were abused and disrespected.[10]

---

[6] Feldman, *The Three Lives of James Madison*, p. 198.
[7] Randolph, August 13, 1787, Madison's *Debates*, 448; quoted in Feldman, *The Three Lives of James Madison*, p. 164.
[8] Feldman, *The Three Lives of James Madison, p. 165.*
[9] Ibid., pp. 165-166.
[10] Ibid., p. 167.

Encouraging Words about Randolph

After the Convention, Madison had received a letter from Randolph suggesting that the shortcomings of the proposed Constitution could perhaps be remedied in a second constitutional convention.[11] Madison however saw no need to call for a second convention, particularly after how contentious the Philadelphia Convention had been. He also suspected political mischief in calls for a second convention. He thought that the ratification battle could be won without further changes to the proposed Constitution. Moreover, much to Madison's delight, he received word from some friends that despite Randolph's original opposition at the Convention, he was now reevaluating his position and that he might after all vote for the Constitution.[12]

Despite the strong opposition of key political figures in both New York and Virginia, Madison was confident that a majority of delegates in the ratifying conventions of both states could eventually be persuaded to vote for ratification. Yet he knew it would require a grand political strategy to win the support of both state conventions, particularly after eloquent essays penned by Antifederalists began appearing in newspapers.

Antifederalist Essays

Shortly after copies of the Constitution were circulated to the states, a number of essays in opposition to the Constitution began appearing in newspapers throughout the Northeastern and Mid-Atlantic states.[13] The articles were penned by authors writing under pseudonyms associated with Roman patriots. There were essays authored by "Brutus," "Agrippa," "Cato," "Centinel," and the "Federal Farmer." The essays expressed strong opposition to the proposed Constitution and underscored what the authors viewed as potential dangers lurking within this proposed federal government.

The Antifederalist essays raised valid arguments, which Madison and supporters of the Constitution could not ignore. In addition to the Antifederalist articles penned under pseudonyms, Patrick Henry without concealing his identity was speaking forcefully against the Constitution, as was the governor of Massachusetts, Elbridge Gerry. Gerry, despite serving as a member of the Massachusetts delegation to the Convention, had decided that the Constitution should not be supported. Both Henry and Gerry, along with the anonymous essays published in leading newspapers, posed serious obstacles to Madison and his

[11] Gutzman, *James Madison*, p. 135.
[12] Ibid.
[13] Cost, *James Madison*, p. 121.

allies supporting the Constitution. Excerpts that capture the views of Antifederalists follow.

The Brutus Essays

Appearing in the *New York Journal* from October 1787 to April 1788, readers were exposed to several essays against the Constitution authored by an Antifederalist under the name of "Brutus." Of all the Antifederalist articles published in newspapers calling for the defeat of the Constitution, the Brutus essays are considered by historians to be the most persuasive and cogent.[14] Brutus warned those who would be voting to ratify the proposed Constitution of the inherent dangers associated with Congress' authority to regulate interstate commerce, and how the Supreme Court could potentially infringe on the rights of the American people. Brutus also focused on the taxing and borrowing powers of Congress and how such powers, along with Congress' authority to raise an army, would likely be used to diminish states' rights and civil liberties.[15] Expressing his concern over a large republic, which Madison strongly favored, Brutus argued that the people under the Constitution would lose control over their state governments and that federal office holders would not only use their authority to serve their personal interests but would also use their powers to oppress the citizenry. As Brutus stated in his article published on October 18, 1787, "If then this new constitution is calculated to consolidate the thirteen states into one, as it evidently is, it ought not to be adopted."[16] In his essay published on November 15, 1787, Brutus warned his readers that the proposed Constitution, although appearing on its face to be virtuous, contained several hidden dangers, "On a careful examination, you will find, that many of its parts, of little moment, are well formed: in these it has a specious resemblance of a free government – but this is not sufficient to justify the adoption of it – the gilded pill, is often found to contain the most deadly poison."[17]

The Agrippa Essays

Essays from "Agrippa" appeared in the *Massachusetts Gazette* from November 1787 to January 1788. The central concerns of Agrippa pertained to the Constitution's potential harm to local governments, personal freedom and commerce. Agrippa's essays were directed to the forthcoming Massachusetts

---

[14] Herbert J. Storing, *The Anti-Federalist: Writings by the Opponents of the Constitution* (Chicago: University of Chicago Press, 1981), p. 103.
[15] Storing, pp. 103-107.
[16] Brutus quoted in Storing, p. 116.
[17] Brutus quoted in Storing, p. 122.

ratifying convention, as well as the people of Massachusetts.[18] Agrippa was especially concerned that personal freedom would be compromised by the Constitution and how a reduction in freedom would compromise economic productivity and the work ethic of the people. In his essay published on November 23, 1787, Agrippa posited the following, "It is a fact justified by the experience of mankind from the earliest antiquity down to the present time, that freedom is necessary to industry. We accordingly find that in absolute governments, the people, be the climate what it may, are in general lazy, cowardly, turbulent, and vicious to an extreme. On the other hand, in free countries are found in general, activity, industry, arts, courage, generosity, and all the manly virtues."[19] On December 3, another essay authored by Agrippa appeared in which he directly challenged the benefits of an expanded republic. Creating a larger republic was among the principal goals of Madison. Agrippa expressed his negative view towards large republics in this manner, "It is the opinion of the ablest writers on the subject, that no extensive empire can be governed upon republican principles, and that such a government will degenerate to a despotism, unless it be made up of a confederacy of smaller states, each having the full powers of internal regulation. . . . Large and consolidated empires may indeed dazzle the eyes of a distant spectator with their splendour, but if examined more nearly are always found to be full of misery."[20]

The Federal Farmer Essays

Essays from the "Federal Farmer" were printed in the *County Journal* in Poughkeepsie, New York from October 8, 1787 to January 1788. In his first essay, The Federal Farmer expressed reservations about the structure of federalism contained within the proposed Constitution and what he viewed as a potential loss of states' rights. As the Federal Farmer put it, "It appears to be a plan retaining some federal features, but to be the first important step, and to aim strongly, to one consolidated government of the United States. It leaves the powers of government and the representation of the people so unnaturally divided between the general and state governments, that the operation of our system must be very uncertain."[21] The Federal Farmer also felt it was important to alert his readers to the fact that the delegates who attended the Constitutional Convention in the summer of 1787 were misled into believing that a revision of the Articles of

---

[18] Storing, p. 227.
[19] Agrippa quoted in Storing, p. 230.
[20] Agrippa quoted in Storing, p. 235.
[21] Federal Farmer quoted in W.B. Allen, Gordon Lloyd, and Argie Lloyd, *The Essential Antifederalist* (Lanham: University Press of America, Inc.,1985), p. 75.

Confederation was the principal purpose of the Convention when in fact the Convention organizers intended to write an entirely new Constitution from the very start. "The states still unsuspecting and not aware that they were passing the Rubicon, appointed members to the new convention for the sole and express purpose of revising and amending the confederation and probably not one man in ten thousand in the United States, till within these ten or twelve days, had an idea that the old ship was to be destroyed, and he put to the alternative of embarking in the new ship presented, or of being left in danger of sinking."[22] Centralization of government was also among Agrippa's concerns. "The plan proposed appears to be partly federal, but principally however, calculated ultimately to make the states one consolidated government."[23] The Federal Farmer had expressed similar concerns about the powers that were delegated to the federal government, including the power to declare war and to raise taxes. In the view of the Federal Farmer, there were not enough limits structurally or legally placed on the proposed central government.[24]

The Centinel Essays

In addition to Brutus, Agrippa and the Federal Farmer, an opponent of the Constitution was writing persuasive essays against the proposed Constitution under the pseudonym of "Centinel." Centinel's essays appeared in the *Independent Journal* distributed in the city of Philadelphia, the same city where the Declaration of Independence was read and where the proposed Constitution was drafted. In his essay published on October 5, 1787, Centinel expressed great concern over the potential loss of liberty under the proposed Constitution. "All the blessings of liberty and the dearest privileges of freemen are now at stake and dependent on your present conduct."[25] Centinel's examination of the Constitution found the potential powers of the Senate to be particularly troubling. He considered the allocation of two Senators per state, regardless of a state's population, as unfair to the larger and more populated states. Centinel also expressed concern over the Senate's power to confirm executive branch appointments, along with the six- year term provided to Senators with no limit on reelection. Because Senators, in Centinel's view, would be of the "better sort" and "well born," there would be a strong chance that many of them would serve for life. Because of the Senate's extraordinary influence, Centinel suggested that presidents would likely be a pawn of the Senate, or what he described as the

---

[22] Federal Farmer quoted in Allen, p. 80.
[23] Federal farmer qoted in Allen, p. 81.
[24] Allen, pp. 87-91.
[25] Centinel quoted in Allen, p. 94.

Senate's "minion."[26] The Constitution in Centinel's view was laying the groundwork for "a permanent Aristocracy." Centinel also identified the absence of a bill of rights in the proposed Constitution as problematic. He was especially troubled over the fact that the Constitution did not contain a provision for press freedom, nor a provision guaranteeing jury trials in civil disputes. Centinel concluded his essay by suggesting that if the state conventions chose not to ratify the Constitution, then a second convention should be conducted for the purpose of creating a more "suitable government."[27]

The Cato Essays

Essays authored by "Cato" appeared in the *New York Journal* from November 22, 1787 to January 3, 1788. In essays 5-7, Cato addressed the problems he perceived in the office of the presidency. Cato noted that the language contained in Article II of the Constitution establishing the presidential office was "vague and inexplicit." Cato compared the vague and broad powers assigned to the presidency as similar to that of a monarch. He noted, the "president possessed of the power given him by this frame of government differs but very immaterially from the establishment of monarchy in Great Britain . . ."[28] Cato also suggested that the possibility existed of electing a president with "the unbridled ambition of a bad man."[29] Examining the Senate, Cato suggested that the six-year term for senators would remove the Senate from the will of the people, and that the Senate in conjunction with the president would likely undermine the bills passed by the House of Representatives. Cato challenged his readers to contemplate this question, "But the liberties of this country, if this system is adopted, will be strangled in their birth; for whenever the executive and Senate can destroy the independence of the majority of the House of Representatives, then where is your security?"[30] Cato dismissed the argument of Federalists that the amendment provision in the Constitution would provide a safeguard for rectifying unforeseen constitutional problems. "But you are told to adopt this government first, and you will always be able to alter it afterwards. This would be first submitting to be slaves and then taking care of your liberty; when your chains are on, then act like freemen."[31]

---

[26] Centinel quoted in Allen, p. 100.
[27] Centinel quoted in Allen, p. 101.
[28] Cato quoted in Allen, p. 159.
[29] Cato quoted in Allen, p. 160.
[30] Cato quoted in Allen, p. 165.
[31] Cato quoted in Allen, p. 165.

The most ambitious opposition to the Constitution was evident in the essays penned by Brutus, Agrippa, the Federal Farmer, Centinel and Cato. Yet there were other Antifederalists who authored informative and well-crafted essays that have received less attention compared to their more famous counterparts. These essays were also sophisticated and convincingly argued. For example, on November 28, 1787 an essay opposed to the Constitution was submitted to the *Independent Gazette* in Philadelphia from "An Old Whig."[32] In 1788 in New York, an essay appeared in a newspaper authored by "A Plebian."[33] The same year in Poughkeepsie's *County Journal* Antifederalist essays were authored by "Sidney."[34] Also in 1788, essays appeared in Baltimore's Maryland Gazette authored by a "Maryland Farmer."[35] while insightful essays against the Constitution appeared in 1787 in the *Gazette of the State of Georgia* penned by "A Georgian."[36] A reading of the lower profile Antifederalist essays, of which there were many, will disclose similar themes regarding the dangers to liberty posed by the Constitution. In one essay by "A Georgian," the author pleaded with his readers to vote against the Constitution, "I beg you to call to mind our glorious Declaration of Independence; read it, and compare it with the federal constitution; what a degree of apostasy will you not then discover."[37] The Georgian also warned against excessive taxation on the part of the federal government, a potentially oppressive standing army, a legislature inadequate to represent the citizenry, and the unfortunate failure on the part of the Constitution to protect trial by jury and freedom of the press.[38]

Madison, although expecting opposition to the proposed Constitution, may have been startled by the volume and sophistication of the Antifederalist essays appearing in newspapers throughout several of the states. Such essays, much to his chagrin, noted few if any positive features of the Constitution. In addition to the plethora of essays in opposition to the Constitution, Madison was also aware of the many speeches and letters against the Constitution delivered by esteemed political leaders such as Henry and Gerry. Gerry's letter must have especially concerned him.

---

[32] Allen, pp. 27-30.
[33] Allen, pp. 31-40.
[34] Allen, pp. 50-53.
[35] Allen, pp. 117-121.
[36] Allen, pp. 226-228.
[37] A Georgian quoted in Allen, p. 228.
[38] Allen, p. 228.

Governor Gerry's Letter

Governor Elbridge Gerry's letter to the Massachusetts legislature on October 18, 1787 identified several serious flaws with the Constitution's three-branch model of the federal government. Gerry noted, "there is no adequate provision for a representation of the people – that they have no security for the right of election -- that some of the powers of the Legislature are ambiguous and others indefinite and dangerous – that the Executive is blended with and will have an undue influence over the Legislature – that the judicial department will be oppressive … and that the system is without the security of a bill of rights."[39]

Madison's Correspondence with Jefferson

Shortly after the Convention had concluded, and while opposition to the Constitution among Antifederalists was rising, Madison had sent the proposed Constitution to Jefferson in Paris with the hope that his mentor and the governor he once served would find the Constitution a more desirable governing document than the Articles of Confederation. Jefferson's response, while not totally opposed to the Constitution, must have troubled Madison. In Jefferson's view, without a bill of rights, the proposed Constitution would fail to protect the people from the forthcoming federal government. Jefferson also expressed serious concern over the absence of term limits imposed on those elected to the presidency. Jefferson suggested that a president might become similar to that of a monarch.[40] He also suggested that as long as America was weak with respect to military might, that presidents might be inclined to solicit arms and money from European powers, thus becoming beholden to foreign interests.[41] Jefferson even went so far as to question why a Constitutional Convention was necessary in the first place. In his view, the threat from Shays' Rebellion was terribly exaggerated and hardly presented the threat to stability that proponents of the Constitution had suggested. France, in Jefferson's view, was where insurrections that threatened stability were occurring, not a short-lived farmers' uprising in western Massachusetts.[42] Jefferson placed Shays' Rebellion in context by noting, "one rebellion in 13 states in the course of 11 years, is but one for each state in a century

---

[39] "Elbridge Gerry's Objections Letter to Massachusetts Legislature;" online at teaching americanhistory.org/document, (Accessed June 16, 2023.)
[40] Burstein and Isenberg, *Madison and Jefferson*, p. 171.
[41] Ibid.
[42] Ibid.

and a half."[43] Jefferson, much to Madison's dissatisfaction, expressed support for a second constitutional convention to amend the deficiencies in the Constitution.

Jefferson's opposition to the Constitution was further evident in a letter he sent to William Carmichael, a prominent political figure in Maryland. The intent of his letter to Carmichael was to dissuade delegates to Maryland's ratifying convention from voting for the Constitution. In his letter, Jefferson predicted that the Constitution would likely be defeated in Virginia, which in his view would justify a second convention.[44] In addition to Carmichael, Jefferson also sent excerpts of a letter he had sent to Madison to another influential Marylander named Uriah Forrest. Jefferson encouraged Forrest to distribute his letter among the delegates to the Maryland ratifying convention with the request that his identify be kept a secret.[45] It was apparent that Jefferson found the Constitution deficient in several respects. This is not to suggest that Jefferson, like many of the Antifederalists, favored a continuation of the Articles of Confederation. Instead, Jefferson seemed to believe that the Constitution, despite having a number of flaws, could still be transformed into a better governing document at a second convention. Given Madison's reverence for Jefferson, it is likely that he was dismayed by his mentor's critique of the Constitution.

The Federalist Papers

Alexander Hamilton who was instrumental in promoting the Constitutional Convention and who strongly supported the proposed Constitution, recognized that a public relations campaign would be required to win the support of state ratifying conventions, particularly in those states where Antifederalist sentiment was strong. Hamilton recognized that the most effective way to influence the views of delegates selected to attend the contentious ratifying conventions would be to publish a series of persuasive essays in defense of the proposed Constitution. This, in Hamilton's view, would be the best way to counter the Antifederalist essays that potentially could influence opinions about the Constitution.

Hamilton resided in New York where he was a high profile and prominent lawyer. The political class in New York also knew that Hamilton had served as an aide-de-camp to George Washington during the war for independence, and that as one of the thirty-nine delegates who signed the Constitution he was a strong supporter of a new and broadly empowered federal government. To assist him

---

[43] Jefferson to Madison, December 20, 1787, *The Republic of Letters;* quoted in Burstein and Isenberg, *Madison and Jefferson, p. 171.*
[44] Cheney, *The Virginia Dynasty*, p. 97.
[45] Ibid.

with his public relations project, Hamilton sought the services of several learned individuals capable of articulating a strong case for the Constitution. His first choice was John Jay, a respected lawyer and distinguished public servant from New York. Jay was the principal author of the New York State Constitution. In 1783, Jay had participated side-by side with Benjamin Franklin and John Adams in negotiating the Treaty of Paris, which secured American independence from Britain. The Congress under the Articles of Confederation had also appointed Jay as the nation's foreign affairs secretary.[46] Hamilton knew that Jay's expertise in the area of foreign policy would effectively bolster the argument that the Constitution would strengthen the country's role in foreign affairs.[47] Chernow recognizes why Hamilton sought Jay's involvement, "With his first-rate mind and unquestioned integrity, he was a superb choice to collaborate on the project."[48]

Hamilton also approached Gouverneur Morris who had served in the Continental Congress from New York. Morris, a signer of the Constitution, had relocated to Pennsylvania. Morris declined the invitation due to previous obligations.[49] Hamilton also sought the services of William Duer, another well-known New Yorker and former member of the Continental Congress. Like Morris, Duer was a strong proponent of an empowered federal government. Although Duer was unable to commit to Hamilton's project, he did submit two essays for Hamilton's consideration, neither of which were published as part of the final project.[50]

Hamilton also asked James Madison to participate in his project, a most logical choice. Madison was serving as a member in the Confederation Congress that was located in New York. His proximity to Hamilton was convenient. Moreover, Hamilton and Madison already knew one another from their days together as delegates to the Constitutional Convention and their combined efforts at the Annapolis Convention. Chernow comments that by the time both Hamilton and Madison worked with one another at the Annapolis Convention they "were kindred spirits in their common distaste for the parochial tendencies of the states."[51] Hamilton was impressed with Madison's grasp of philosophy, the history of republics, and his precise intellect. Although Hamilton and Madison

---

[46] Ron Chernow, *Alexander Hamilton* (New York: The Penguin Press, 2004), p. 247.

[47] Benjamin Fletcher Wright, ed., Introduction: *The Federalist* (Original copyright 1961 by the President and Fellows of Harvard University, reprinted - New York: Barnes & Noble, 2004), p. 7.

[48] Chernow, *Alexander Hamilton*, p. 247.

[49] Ibid.

[50] Ibid.

[51] Ibid. p. 223.

were not simpatico with respect to every provision within the Constitution, the two were nevertheless committed to securing the Constitution's ratification and finally ending the Articles of Confederation. Madison recognized that Hamilton's project presented itself with a tremendous opportunity to promote the Constitution, the document that reflected his views towards effective government.

Once the writing team was in place, Hamilton, Madison and Jay embarked on an elaborate writing campaign intended to win support for the Constitution. Their main target was the New York ratifying convention where they anticipated strong opposition to the Constitution. Accordingly, each of their published essays in New York newspapers, which included the New York Packet, were addressed "To the People of the State of New York."

Although the target was the New York ratifying convention, the *Federalist* essays also appeared in newspapers in several states outside of New York, although not in large numbers. Pauline Maier's research discovered that some of the early *Federalist* essays were sent by Hamilton and Madison to George Washington at Mount Vernon with a request to forward them to newspapers in Virginia. A small number of these essays submitted by Washington were reprinted in the *Virginia Independent Chronicle* located in Richmond.[52] At the same time, eighteen of the *Federalist* essays were reprinted in Philadelphia's *Pennsylvania Gazette*, seven essays were reprinted in the *American Herald* located in Boston, while a small handful of essays appeared in newspapers in other states.[53] The *Federalist* essays although not widely distributed among the thirteen states, were read, albeit on a limited basis, in states outside of New York.

A total of 85 essays were published beginning in October 1787 and extending into May of 1788.[54] Each essay was titled *Federalist* and given a number 1 to 85. The authors wanted their readers to understand that the proposed federal government established in the Constitution was superior to that of the Articles of Confederation and contained governing principles that would further strengthen the country. At the same time, Hamilton, Madison and Jay chose to write under the pseudonym of "Publius." According to Chernow, the pseudonym they chose to write under was based on the name of the Roman patriot, Publius Valerius, who "had toppled the last Roman king and set up the republican foundations of government."[55] Following the publication of the 85 essays, they were published in 1788 as a two volume compilation by the New York printing company of John

---

[52] Maier, *Ratification,* p. 84.
[53] Ibid.
[54] Ibid.
[55] Chernow, *Alexander Hamilton*, p. 248.

and Archibald McLean. The publication was titled, *The Federalist.*[56] Although to this day there is still some debate regarding who authored each *Federalist* essay, there is a consensus among scholars to whom each essay should be credited. Benjamin F. Wright's thorough treatment of the *Federalist* essays identifies a computer analysis and "scholarly detective work"[57] that has allowed researchers to identify which essay was authored by which collaborator. Fifty-two of the *Federalist* essays were authored by Hamilton: *Federalist Nos. 1, 6-9, 11-13, 15-17, 21-36, 59-62*, and *Nos.65-85*. Madison is credited with writing twenty-eight of the essays: *Federalist Nos. 10, 14, 18-20, 37-58*, and *No. 63.* Jay, who was the first person Hamilton recruited for the project, had to withdraw from the project due to health problems. He is credited with five essays: *Federalist Nos. 2-5* and *No. 64.*[58]

The *Federalist* essays were not however the first time that Hamilton resorted to essays under a pseudonym for the purpose of generating support for the Constitution. Prior to launching the *Federalist* project, Hamilton had penned four essays critical of the Confederation that appeared in *The New York Packet.* His four essays were published under the pen name, *The Continentalist.*[59] Hamilton's essays warned of impending anarchy in the absence of a stronger federal government and that state secession was a distinct possibility. Chernow identifies Hamilton's *Continentalist* essays as the "spirited precursors to the *Federalist Papers.*"[60]

Although Hamilton was clearly the initiator and main contributor to the *Federalist* project, it is Madison's essays, particularly *No. 10* and *No. 51*, that scholars often regard as the most persuasive and profound essays among the eighty-five. Indeed, *Federalist No. 10* and *No. 51* often appear in the Appendices of introductory American Government textbooks.

Important to note, however, is that although the 85 *Federalist* essays *are* routinely lauded by scholars as the definitive defense and interpretation of the Constitution, caution needs to be exercised for those who seek from the 85 articles an understanding of how government under the Constitution was supposed to function. As Wright notes, "*The Federalist* is a masterpiece of political argument intended more to persuade its readers to adopt the Constitution than to explain how it would operate. Though this truth does not prevent those who would

---

[56] Wright, ed., Foreword, *The Federalist*, p. ix.
[57] Wright, ed., Foreword *The Federalist*, p. x.
[58] Wright, ed., *The Federalist*, passim.
[59] Chernow, *Alexander Hamilton,* p. 158.
[60] Ibid.

interpret the Constitution from citing Publius as persuasive authority, it should restrain them from invoking Publius as conclusive authority."[61] Moreover, although the 85 essays were instrumental in persuading a majority of the delegates to the New York ratifying convention to vote for the Constitution, one should be careful about assigning too much credit to the *Federalist* essays for persuading the convention delegates. In a volume published in 1941, historian Edward Mead Earle noted that although the *Federalist* essays were certainly relevant to what transpired in the New York ratifying convention, other factors were also at work that helped win the support of the convention. As Earle observes, "the decisive factors were Hamilton's amazing performance of argumentation and strategy at the New York Convention and, perhaps even more important, the fact that ten states already had ratified before the vote was taken in New York (thus assuring the inauguration of the new government regardless of the outcome there)."[62]

Nevertheless, despite Earl's words of caution regarding the significance of the *Federalist* project, there can be little doubt that the arguments presented in the 85 essays revealed not only the many strengths of the Constitution compared to the feeble and dysfunctional Articles of Confederation, but also the extraordinary brilliance and foresight of Hamilton, Madison and Jay. The essays, despite containing elements of political propaganda, should be viewed, as they often are, as among the core documents that contributed to the oldest and most successful written Constitution in the history of humankind.

Federalist No. 10

Madison's first contribution as Publius was *Federalist No.* 10. Hamilton and Jay in previous *Federalist* essays had made compelling arguments for a stronger federal government and how under the Constitution the hand of the federal government would be significantly strengthened, particularly in the area of foreign affairs. Madison's intention in *No. 10* was to convey to his readers how an expanded federal republic, such as that which the Constitution would create, was a more stable and effective form of government compared to the state-centered Confederation. In Madison's view, an expanded republic would be far more effective at balancing and mitigating the corrosive influence of political factions, thus preserving the liberties of the people. An enlarged republic with political interests distributed within an empowered federal government, as opposed to small republics dominated by majority factions would inherently allow

---

[61] Wright, Foreword, *The Federalist*, p. xii.

[62] Edward Mead Earle, Introduction, *The Federalist* (New York: Random House, 1941), p. x., footnote 2.

for more competition and reduce factional power. An expanded federal republic with competing interests was thus the solution in Madison's view for "curing the mischiefs of faction." Many scholars have examined Madison's thinking in *Federalist* 10 along with his other contributions to the project. In one treatment of *No. 10,* Mark M. Arkin contends that Madison's line of thinking reflected his familiarity with the writings of the Scottish theologian David Hume regarding the deleterious impact of religious factions. Arkin states, "that it is likely that Hume's treatment of religion as an ordinary faction within the polity --- indeed, the primary and most dangerous form of faction --- provided the critical connection in Madison's thinking between his Virginia experience and his argument in the *Tenth Federalist* that the multiplicity of political and economic factions would lead to a stable governmental order."[63] Madison, as mentioned in the previous chapter, had been exposed to the writings of Hume when he was a student of Witherspoon's.

> The smaller the society, the fewer probably will be the distinct parties and interests composing it; the fewer the distinct parties and interests, the more frequently will a majority be found of the same party; and the smaller the number of individuals composing a majority; and the smaller the compass with which they are placed, the more easily will they concert and execute their plans of oppression. Extend the sphere, and you take in a greater variety of parties and interests; you make it less probable that a majority of the whole will have a common motive to invade the rights of other citizens.[64]

Madison's view that an enlarged republic as a check on factional power had also been expressed by Hamilton in *Federalist 9*. The lead author of the *Federalist* project stated very clearly in his first sentence that a strong Union was the best antidote to factional politics and anarchy. Madison in *No. 10* felt it was necessary to expand upon Hamilton's essay to demonstrate the virtues of a stronger and expanded Union. As Hamilton stated in *Federalist* 9:

> A Firm Union will be of the utmost moment to the peace and liberty of the States, as a barrier against domestic faction and insurrection. It is impossible to read the history of the petty republics of Greece and Italy

---

[63] Marc M. Arkin, "'The Intractable Principle:' David Hume, James Madison, Religion, and the Tenth Federalist," The *American Journal of Legal History*, Vol. 39., No. 2 (April, 1995), p. 174; online at https://www.jstore.orgstable/845897. (Accessed March 10, 2024.)

[64] *Federalist No. 10.*

> without feeling sensations of horror and disgust at the distractions with which they were continually agitated, and at the rapid succession of revolutions by which they were kept in a state of perpetual vibration between the extremes of tyranny and anarchy.[65]

Reflecting on *Federalist No. 10*, historian Burton Spivak notes that "Madison flipped the traditional view that only small republics could maintain the republic form over time. Madison believed that small republics, like the several states, were prone to class conflict over property, but extended republics held the answer to public tranquility."[66] Expanding on the thrust of *No. 10,* Spivak notes that "Madison believed that in an extended national republic, the multitude of different religions, occupations, cultures, histories, viewpoints, and work arrangements (slave labor versus free labor) would camouflage and complicate the issue of class and make it much harder for people and parties to organize on the fundamental issue of the few versus the many."[67]

Federalist No. 51

Among Madison's many contributions to Hamilton's project, it is in *Federalist No. 51* where one finds Madison's eloquent defense of the separation of powers doctrine, along with his support for a system of checks and balances. It is *Federalist 51* that scholars point to when discussing the "Madisonian" model of government. The Virginia Plan is where one finds, as Rutland noted, the basic "framework" for this form of government. As discussed by John Fairlie, Madison, "accepted the doctrine as an established political truth, holding that the accumulation of all powers, legislative, executive and judicial in the same hands would be tyranny. But he argued that the doctrine does not mean that various departments should be completely and absolutely independent of each other."[68] Madison clearly recognized that overlap in lawmaking was a necessity.

In *No. 51*, Madison states that human beings are naturally inclined to seek power and control over others. Because of this natural lust for power, a government must be constructed in a way to ensure that power can be checked. As Madison put it, "Ambition must be made to counteract ambition." In

---

[65] *Federalist No. 9.*

[66] Comments regarding Madison's perspective in *Federalist No. 10* provided to author by Sacred Heart University history professor, Burton Spivak, June 20, 2024.

[67] Ibid.

[68] John A. Fairlie, "The Separation of Powers," *Michigan Law Review*, Vol. 21., No. 4 (February 1923), p. 399; Online at https://doi.org/10.2307/127683. (Accessed March 10, 2024.)

Madison's view, three branches of government, each with its own sphere of power and with each branch constitutionally empowered to constrain the other two, is the most effective way of keeping the powers of government limited. Limited government, in Madison's view, is how the liberties of the American people will be preserved. The following passage from *Federalist* No. 51 captures Madison's pragmatic understanding of human nature.

> If men were angels, no government would be necessary. If angels were to govern men, neither external nor internal controls on government would be necessary. In framing a government, which is to be administered by men over men, the great difficulty lies in this: you must first enable the government to control the governed; and in the next place oblige it to control itself. A dependence on the people is, no doubt, the primary control on the government; but experience has taught mankind the necessity of auxiliary precautions.[69]

Despite the brilliance of *Federalist* 51, it is important to note that what Madison articulated in his classic essay was not the first time that the doctrine of separated powers was introduced. As discussed in Chapter 1, while studying under Witherspoon, Madison was most certainly required to read John Locke's s *Second Treatise on Civil Government* published in 1689 and Baron de Montesquieu's *The Spirit of Law* published in 1748. Both Locke and Montesquieu supported a form of government with powers separated into departments.

Additional *Federalist* essays authored by Madison that have never received the same recognition as *Nos. 10 and 51,* yet are exceptionally insightful include *Federalist Nos. 39, 45* and *No. 46*. In *No. 39*, Madison described how the Constitution once ratified would inherently sustain a republican form of government by virtue of the fact that the people would directly elect the members of the House of Representatives. Moreover, senators and the president, although not directly elected, would reflect the will of the people. Madison also spent considerable space in *No. 39* articulating the difference between a *federal* government, which the Constitution established, and that of a *national* government. The Constitution, Madison demonstrated, is a federal system that includes states' rights, while a national government does not include state sovereignty. In the following passage from *No. 39,* Madison underscores the key role of states in securing ratification of the Constitution.

---

[69] *Federalist No. 51.*

> Each State in ratifying the Constitution, is considered as a sovereign body, independent of all others, and only to be bound by its own voluntary act. In this relation, then the new Constitution will, if established, be a *federal* and not a *national* constitution.[70]

To further allay the fears of Antifederalists that the states would lose all their powers under the Constitution, Madison in *Federalist No. 45* explicitly discussed how the states would continue to have a broad range of powers under the Constitution and would continue as vibrant components of the new federal system.

> The powers delegated by the proposed Constitution to the federal government are few and defined. Those which are to remain in the State governments are numerous and indefinite. The former will be exercised principally on external objects, as war, peace, negotiation, and foreign commerce. . . . The powers reserved to the several states will extend to all objects which, in the ordinary course of affairs, concern the lives, liberties, and properties of the people; and the internal order, improvement and prosperity of the State. [71]

Madison expanded his argument regarding the preservation of states' rights in *Federalist No. 46.* Here he demonstrated that even those elected to serve in the federal government would remain wedded to the interests of their respective states.

> It has already been proved that the members of the federal will be more dependent on the members of the State governments, than the latter will be on the former. . . . The prepossessions, which the members themselves will carry into the federal government, will generally be favorable to the States; . . . A local spirit will infallibly prevail much more in the members of Congress, than a national spirit will prevail in the legislatures of the particular States.[72]

Madison Heads to Virginia for a Showdown

The New York ratifying convention was expected to be a very close vote, as well as the vote in the Virginia ratifying convention. Washington, concerned about the distinct prospect of the Virginia convention voting against the

---

[70] *Federalist No. 39.*
[71] *Federalist No. 45.*
[72] *Federalist No. 46.*

Constitution, wrote to Madison requesting that he return to Virginia to participate as a delegate at the state's ratifying convention.[73] Although Madison had reservations about those who drafted the Constitution also participating as delegates in ratifying conventions, he agreed to travel from New York to Richmond to participate in what he knew would be a confrontational and divisive convention.[74] There he would face strong opponents to the Constitution, including the charismatic former governor Patrick Henry, along with the learned and revered George Mason. Madison had hoped that by the time he arrived in Virginia and was selected as a convention delegate from Orange County that at least nine states would have ratified the Constitution. This would give him more leverage against Henry, Mason and the other Antifederalist delegates when the convention was convened.

Bad weather delayed Madison's trip to Virginia. After traveling several difficult days in early March, his first stop in Virginia was to visit Washington at Mount Vernon to discuss the forthcoming convention. "After the cold winter in New York, Madison enjoyed the early signs of spring along the Potomac as he and his host visited in the pleasant parlors of Mount Vernon."[75] Madison encouraged Washington to openly communicate to the people of Virginia his support for the Constitution, while delicately letting him know that the people would expect him to serve as president once the Constitution was ratified.[76] Following his visit to Mount Vernon, Madison then traveled to Orange County, arriving only one day before the delegates to the state convention were elected.[77] Delegate selection was a spirited affair in Virginia with delegate candidates campaigning and delivering speeches to sway the voters. Maier notes that because the speeches so clearly identified where delegate candidates stood on the Constitution that once the elections were over, it was somewhat predictable based on who was chosen what the convention ratification vote would be.[78] Yet despite the speeches and election, there was still uncertainty regarding what would transpire at the ratifying convention. Some predicted a slight majority in favor of the Constitution, while others expected a close vote against ratification. "The results were reassuring to nobody."[79]

---

[73] Maier, *Ratification*, p. 216.
[74] Ibid.
[75] Ketcham, *James Madison*, p. 250.
[76] Ibid.
[77] Maier, *Ratification* p. 225.
[78] Ibid., p. 237.
[79] Ibid.

Madison was elected as a convention delegate from Orange County by an overwhelming vote of 202 to 56.[80] An important component of his support can be attributed to the support he received from Baptist voters who viewed Madison as a strong supporter of religious liberty and the rights of dissenting religions. In particular, support from the influential Baptist preacher John Leland, although perhaps not a sole determinant of the outcome, appears to have contributed in a significant way to Madison's landslide election.[81]

Madison had meticulously prepared for the ratifying convention scheduled for June. With so much of his time and energy already having been devoted to advancing the Constitutional Convention, formulating the contents of the Constitution, and demonstrating the virtues of the Constitution in his *Federalist* essays, Madison felt confident that he could convince a majority of the delegates that the Constitution was a governing document worth supporting.

By late spring 1788, eight states had ratified the Constitution, with the conventions of New Hampshire, New York and Virginia scheduled for conventions in June.[82] Yet Madison understood that even if New Hampshire or New York provided the ninth ratification vote to bring the Constitution into existence, it would still be harmful to the future of the United States if Virginia remained outside of the Union. The Constitution, in Cost's view, would for all intents and purposes be "stillborn" without Virginia's support.[83] It was essential therefore for Madison to win the support of the Virginia convention, even if the vote for ratification was by a slender majority.

To make sure the delegates were fully aware of the Constitution's contents and why this governing document was superior to the Articles of Confederation, Madison distributed printed copies of *The Federalist* to the convention delegates.[84] He suspected that some of the delegates had not read in any careful way the proposed Constitution, nor for that matter were they intimately familiar with the *Federalist* essays. Madison was pleased to learn that the pro-Federalist Edmund Pendleton was selected to preside over the ratifying convention. Pendleton's control over convention proceedings would be helpful. Reviewing the list of delegates scheduled to attend the convention, Madison did his arithmetic

[80] Ketcham, *James Madison*, p. 251.

[81] Mark S. Scarberry, "John Leland and James Madison: Religious Influence on the Ratification of the Constitution and on the Proposal of the Bill of Rights," *Dickenson Law Review*, Vol. 113., Issue 3 (2009), p. 763. online at https: //ideas.dickinsonlawpsu.edu/dira/vol113/iss3/3. (Accessed April 1, 2024.)

[82] Maier, *Ratification*, pp. 252-253.

[83] Cost, *James Madison*, p.148.

[84] Ketcham, *James Madison*, p. 253.

and estimated that a very slight majority of delegates would support the Constitution when the roll call was conducted. He anticipated victory.[85]

The Virginia Ratifying Convention

Patrick Henry

The Virginia ratifying convention was conducted from June 2 to June 27, 1788. The delegates met from 10:00 am to 4:00 pm for the first several days of the convention and then from 9:00 am to 5:00 pm from the middle of June to the convention's adjournment.[86] Multiple and passionate speeches were delivered by the delegates, with some speaking several times to drive their key points home. Patrick Henry, as Madison anticipated, vehemently opposed the Constitution and delivered powerful and commanding speeches against ratification. Gutzman writes, "By all accounts, Henry was a hypnotic speaker. His oratory was at once sermonic and fiery. One could not help but be swept up in the mighty river of persuasion that Henry could unleash."[87]

The Constitution in Henry's view, failed in every respect to protect the liberties of the people and to ensure adequate representation of the people in Congress. The great orator, who "smelt a rat" regarding the purpose of the Constitutional Convention in Philadelphia, identified the Constitution as a threat to private property and targeted the monarchial character of the presidency.[88] In Henry's view, the powers afforded to the presidency in the proposed Constitution were clearly "an awful squinting . . . toward monarchy."[89] Henry reminded the delegates that he was always an American patriot and reminded them of his strong opposition to the despotic Stamp Act of 1765, which fueled colonial resistance to British rule.[90] Yet he saw no reason to be pressured into voting for the Constitution to save the Union and claimed that it made little difference if the state of Virginia was, or was not, a part of the United States, "What is to be the consequence, if we are disunited?" Henry encouraged delegates to wait and see how the new government functioned under the Constitution before supporting it.[91] Henry also questioned the legitimacy of the Constitutional Convention held in

---

[85] Cost, *James Madison*, p. 151.

[86] Gutzman, *James Madison and the Making of America*, p. 200.

[87] Ibid., p. 203.

[88] Ibid., p. 207.

[89] Speech of Patrick Henry quoted in Maier, *Ratification*, p. 266.

[90] Gutzman, *James Madison and the Making of America,* p. 207.

[91] Speech of Patrick Henry, June 5, 1788, *Documentary History of the Ratification of the Constitution,* 9:951-68; quoted in Gutzman, *James Madison and the Making of America,* p. 208.

Philadelphia, suggesting that it violated procedural requirements for conducting a convention. He questioned who gave the drafters of the Constitution the authority to write "We the People" in the Preamble. "Who authorized them to speak the language of We, the people, instead of, We, the states?"[92] Reviewing Henry's speech, Feldman observes that Henry was not only suggesting that the Constitutional Convention was conducted without proper authority, but that the proposed Constitution had the appearance of a conspiracy.[93]

Edmund Randolph

Madison knew that Henry could never be convinced to support the Constitution, while Randolph, despite his original opposition to the Constitution, was now moving towards ratification. Randolph admitted that although he initially refused to support the Constitution when he was a delegate to the Constitutional Convention, he now felt that preservation of the Union was paramount. He announced that he had finally come down on the side of the Constitution. The fact that eight states had already ratified the Constitution was in his view a very important development, "I refused my signature, and if the same reasons operated on my mind, I would still refuse; but as I think that those eight states which have adopted the Constitution will not recede, I am a friend to the Union."[94]

Responding to Henry's claim that it made little difference if Virginia was a member of the Union, Randolph reminded the delegates that under the Confederation there were frequent conflicts between states and that national security along with interstate commerce had been problematic.[95] It was foolish in Randolph's view for the state of Virginia to remain outside of the Union. Feeling the need to employ drama to win his audience, Randolph standing before the delegates raised his arm and boldly proclaimed, "I will assent to the lopping of this limb before I assent to the dissolution of the Union."[96] Feldman notes that Randolph's switch to the side in favor of the Constitution after having refused to sign his name to the Constitution was not atypical of his political behavior, as he normally wanted to be on the "winning side of any question." With eight states having ratified the Constitution, Randolph, who had previously "hedged his bets,"

---

[92] Speech of Henry, quoted in Gutzman, p. 204.
[93] Feldman, *The Three Lives of James Madison*, p. 221.
[94] Randolph speech, June 4, 1788, *The Documentary History of the Ratification of the Constitution*, 9:931-36; quoted in Gutzman, p. 206.
[95] Gutzman, *James Madison and the Making of America*, p. 209.
[96] Randolph Speech, June 4, 1788; quoted in Gutzman, p. 206.

now concluded the time had arrived to join the Federalists.[97] Ecstatic over Randolph's support for the Constitution, Madison penned a letter to Washington and fellow Federalist Rufus King, in which he expressed great satisfaction that Randolph had finally come onto the side of the Constitution.[98]

James Monroe

James Monroe, who would serve as the Secretary of State under President Madison, and would be elected as the country's fifth president, was also a delegate to the ratifying convention. At the time, Monroe was serving in Virginia's House of Delegates.[99] Monroe apparently was not pleased that he had been passed over as one of Virginia's seven delegates to the Constitutional Convention. He also felt somewhat snubbed by both Madison and Randolph when the ratifying convention began. He wrote to Jefferson that neither Randolph or Madison were exhibiting much respect to him as a convention delegate.[100]

Monroe, well before the Virginia convention had started, also had issues with George Washington, who he felt was calculating every move so that he would be remembered as a magnificent and heroic leader. "The Statesman" is how Monroe pejoratively referred to Washington.[101] As a delegate, Monroe shared Jefferson's critical views towards the Constitution and suggested that the proposed presidency, which Washington would inevitably occupy, would be similar to that of a monarch.[102] Like Henry, Monroe spoke forcefully against the Constitution. It is ironic that a future president of the United States viewed so many flaws within the Constitution and chose not to support the Constitution primarily due to the powers afforded to the presidential office.

George Mason

George Mason, as expected, also spoke against the Constitution. Among his several objections was the taxing power that was delegated to Congress in Article I, Section 8 of the Constitution. Mason proposed that the Constitution should be amended to give state legislatures the authority to determine how much in the way of taxes a state should provide to the federal government. In his view, Congress' taxing power was too discretionary without any limitations.[103] He asked if it was

---

[97] Feldman, *The Three Lives of James Madison*, p. 222.
[98] Gutzman, *James Madison* p. 207.
[99] Cheney, *the Virginia Dynasty*, p. 101.
[100] Ibid., p. 102.
[101] Ibid., p. 102.
[102] Ibid., p. 103.
[103] Maier, *Ratification*, p. 262.

appropriate for the people to be taxed by both states and the federal government?[104]

Mason's argument to allow state legislatures to control the amount of taxes paid to the federal government was not acceptable to Madison. Although "no taxation without representation" was a battle cry of the American Revolution, the taxing power of the federal government was, as Maier notes, "a sine qua non of an effective national government."[105] Yet Mason's objections, although deemed unacceptable to supporters of the Constitution, were nevertheless serious and thoughtful. Mason drew from the writings of Montesquieu and argued that republican government was only possible in small republics, with such republics federated to further limit the power of government.[106] In Mason's view, the taxing power afforded to Congress in the Constitution was contrary to Montesquieu's conception of republican government. Feldman writes, "If Henry presented himself as the people's tribune unmasking conspiracy, Mason posed as the last classical republican revealing the historical impossibility of Madison's bold, theory-driven design."[107]

James Madison

Madison was not in the best of health when the convention began. Yet despite having health issues, which he had experienced since childhood, he rose to the occasion and delivered extremely detailed and persuasive speeches in defense of the Constitution. Madison knew that he was unable to match Henry with respect to oratory, so his strategy would be to carefully dissect the Constitution line-by-line and in methodical fashion win the support of the delegates based on the merits of the Constitution.[108] As Madison put it, "We ought not to address our arguments to the feelings and passions ... but of those understandings and judgments which were selected by the people of this country to decide this great question, by a calm and rational investigation."[109] Drawing on his debating skills learned in college, his grasp of ancient confederacies, along with the practical knowledge he had gained as a member of the Continental and Confederation Congresses, Madison brilliantly and without histrionics systematically disassembled every argument raised by opponents of the Constitution, including the mesmerizing deliveries of

---

[104] Ibid.
[105] Ibid., p. 273.
[106] Feldman, *The Three Lives of James Madison,* p. 223.
[107] Ibid.
[108] Gutzman, *James Madison,* p. 209.
[109] Madison speech, June 6, 1788, *The Documentary History of the Ratification of the Constitution,* 9;989-98; quoted in Gutzman, *James Madison*, p. 209.

Patrick Henry. Madison's low keyed and analytical style moved delegates towards his position.

In a scholarly article lauding Madison's performance at the Virginia ratifying convention, the Hon. Charles Evans Hughes, who served as the Chief Justice of the U.S Supreme Court from 1930-1941, described Madison's persuasive oratory in this manner, "Cool, cautious, deliberative, he was capable of prolonged concentration in intellectual work, which resulted in convictions securely based in profound study and adequate reflection. His mental equilibrium was not upset by gusts of passion and he had no aptitude for attempts to sway others by tempestuous eloquence. He sought to convince and he became formidable in debate because he was thorough in preparation and precise in statement."[110] Archibald Stuart, a delegate to the convention, was so impressed with Madison's performance that he forwarded a letter to a friend in which he praised Madison's impressive speeches before the convention delegates. "Madison came boldly forward and supported the Constitution with the soundest reason and most manly eloquence I ever heard. He understands his subject and his whole soul is engaged in its success and it appeared to me he would have flashed conviction into every mind."[111] In one of his typically low-keyed and substantive speeches, Madison, reflected on Henry's statement that the people of Virginia were satisfied with life under the Articles of Confederation. In response to Henry's assertion, Madison presented a set of very simple and straightforward questions:

> If this be their happy situation, why has every State acknowledged the contrary? Why were deputies from all the States sent to the General Convention? Why have complaints of national and individual distresses been echoed and re-echoed throughout the Continent? Why has our General Government been so shamefully disgraced, and our Constitution violated? [112]

Foreign Policy Was Also Debated

Although the highly spirited debate that occurred between Madison and Henry was mostly over where the locus of governing power should be and which model of government best served the interests of liberty, it would be remiss to

---

[110] Charles Evans Hughes, "James Madison" *American Bar Association Journal*, Vol. 18., No. 1 (January 1932), p. 854; online at https://www.jstor.org/stable/25708450. (Accessed May 1, 2024.)

[111] Stuart to Breckinridge, June 19, 1788; *Documentary History of the Ratification of the Constitution;* quoted in Cheney, *The Virginia Dynasty*, p. 101.

[112] Madison speech, June 6, 1788; quoted in Gutzman, *James Madison,* p. 210.

overlook the fact that foreign policy also surfaced during their lengthy and historic debate. According to Robert W. Smith, because shipping firms in Virginia participated in trade with Britain and depended heavily on the Mississippi River for commercial purposes, foreign policy also became an important point of contention. "On 12 and 13 June, the convention spent the entire day discussing the Mississippi River. No other convention saw this much time devoted to foreign policy."[113] How the proposed federal government would impact Virginia's use of the Mississippi River was of great concern to Henry and his fellow Antifederalists. "Like its southern neighbors, Virginia bordered the Mississippi and depended on its use for the sale of its western land and the export of its produce."[114] In some respects, the Antifederalist delegates at the convention felt that foreign affairs was a policy area best left to the states, not the federal government.[115] However, as he did on practically every contentious issue, Madison in his low keyed, steady and persuasive style, convinced a majority of delegates that Virginia's use of the Mississippi River, and more generally the state's foreign trade, would not be constrained under the new Constitution.

Thomas Jefferson

Jefferson was in Paris when the Constitutional Convention was conducted during the summer of 1787. He was still in Paris when delegates selected to state ratifying conventions were voting on the Constitution. Jefferson, as previously discussed, had expressed to Madison a number of his concerns regarding the Constitution, most notably the absence of a bill of rights. Yet despite serving his country in France, Jefferson still chose to insert himself into the ratification process by submitting a proposal which Madison must have found objectionable. In his proposal circulated in June and slightly before the New Hampshire convention, Jefferson recommended that after the ninth ratifying vote, which the New Hampshire vote would be, that the four remaining states should hold off on ratifying the Constitution unless a majority of the delegates to those four conventions agreed to include a bill of rights.[116]

Madison was alarmed over Jefferson's position. If what Jefferson was recommending resonated with delegates to Virginia's convention, then it was possible that those who were leaning towards ratification, but who favored a bill

---

[113] Robert W. Smith, "Foreign Affairs and the Ratification of the Constitution in Virginia," *Virginia Magazine of History & Biography* Vol. 122, Issue 1 (2014), p. 40; online at https://www.jstor/stable/24392923. (Accessed March 1, 2024.)
[114] Ibid., p. 41.
[115] Ibid., p. 47.
[116] Cheney, *The Virginia Dynasty*, p. 100.

of rights, might hold off on voting for the Constitution until a bill of rights was agreed to.[117] Jefferson's proposal was obviously intended to force the Federalists, Madison in particular, into accepting a bill of rights. Jefferson's circulated proposal was hardly welcomed by Madison who was determined to bring the Constitution into existence based on the vote of thirteen, not nine, states. A favorable vote of all thirteen states, in Madison's view, had to be the first order of business. A bill of rights, which he originally did not see as necessary, was something the Congress could address after, but not before, the Constitution was ratified.

Virginia's Ratification Vote

With the debating and floor speeches over, the delegates on June 25 voted on the Constitution. Two separate votes were taken, with each vote favorable to Madison and his fellow Federalists. The first vote, which Henry was sponsoring, was a vote to amend the Constitution with a declaration of rights, and if supported by the convention, to forward this amendment to the other state conventions for their consideration. Henry's proposal was defeated, 88-80.[118] The second vote was to ratify or not ratify the proposed Constitution. The vote to ratify passed 89-79, an almost identical vote as the first vote regarding Henry's amendment.[119] It was evident that the Federalist and Antifederalist factions were united with one another on both votes.

Madison had thus won the battle. He had beaten Henry through his calm, analytical and clear treatment of the many virtues of the Constitution. Describing Madison's stellar performance, Garry Wills notes, "Good as Henry was as an orator and debater, he was not a reflective or studious person, and he was up against a man who had thought and debated and persuaded on this subject through two years that sharpened all of Madison's analytical power and parliamentary deftness. The tiny David slew the mighty Goliath."[120] Brant notes that Madison was able to defeat Henry "by placing every disputed issue before the convention in terms so clear and logical offered with such sincerity and fairness, that they held their ground against the passionate oratory, the distortions and exaggerated alarms of Henry, Mason and Grayson."[121] Although Virginia's convention vote

---

[117] Ibid.

[118] Maier, *Ratification*, p. 305.

[119] Ibid.

[120] Garry Wills, *James Madison*, (New York: Times Books, Henry Holt and Co., 2002), p. 36.

[121] Irving Brant, *James Madison: Father of the Constitution 1787-1800* (New York: The Bobbs-Merrill Co. Inc., 1950), pp. 227-228.

was essential for the purpose of establishing the legitimacy of the Constitution, little did the delegates know that only four days prior to their ratifying vote that the New Hampshire convention had formally ratified the Constitution. New Hampshire, after having held two conventions, the first in February and the second in June 1788, was thus the ninth state to ratify the Constitution, 57-47. New Hampshire's vote allowed the Constitution of the United States to become the law of the land.[122]

Approximately one month later, due to the influence of the Federalist essays and Alexander Hamilton's persuasive performance at the New York ratifying convention,[123] delegates to New York's convention, despite stiff opposition from the Antifederalist governor George Clinton and the Clintonians, voted on July 26 to ratify the Constitution. Like Virginia, the New York vote was close, 30-27.[124] Although he was not a delegate to the New York Convention, Madison's influence was nevertheless present in the form of his *Federalist* essays.

The entire ratification process was a fascinating and highly politicized affair. In several states, the ratifying convention was largely a formality with minimal opposition. Yet in other conventions, such as in Massachusetts, New Hampshire, Virginia, New York, North Carolina and Rhode Island, Antifederalist opposition was fierce. Where there was strident opposition to the Constitution, debates revolved around serious and philosophical disagreements regarding where the locus of governing power should be. Should the power be in the federal government, or should power remain in the states? That was the central point of contention in several conventions. The dates of ratification and the votes of the original thirteen states are presented below. Vermont, which achieved statehood after having been a part of New York, chose to have a convention in 1791 to show its support for the Constitution. The ratification votes of the original thirteen states and Vermont presented below in no small part can be attributed to the brilliance of James Madison.

Ratification of the Constitution

State	Date of Vote	Vote to Ratify
Delaware	December 7, 1787	30-0
Pennsylvania	December 12, 1787	46-23
New Jersey	December 18, 1787	38-0

[122] Maier, *Ratification,* pp. 314-316.
[123] Ibid., pp. 352-353.
[124] Ibid., p. 396.

State	Date of Vote	Vote to Ratify
Georgia	December 31, 1787	26-0
Connecticut	January 9, 1788	128-40
Massachusetts	February 6, 1788	187-168
Maryland	April 26, 1788	63-11
South Carolina	May 23, 1788	149-73
New Hampshire	June 21, 1788	57-47
Virginia	June 25, 1788	89-79
New York	July 26, 1788	30-27
North Carolina	August 2, 1788	75-193
	November 21, 1789	194-77
Rhode Island	May 29, 1790	34-32
Vermont	January 10, 1791	105-4

Source: Center for the Study of the American Constitution, Department of History, University of Wisconsin; online at csac.history.wisc.edu. (Accessed July 3, 2023.)

In addition to philosophical differences, the variation in votes were also a reflection of how the convention delegates viewed the benefits of the Constitution with regard to the interests of their own state. There were reasons why in Virginia and in New York the votes were close, while in Delaware, New Jersey and Georgia the votes were unanimous. Ketcham offers this view of the variation, "In short, antifederalism flourished where states, or groups, within states, saw no need in terms of the matters then facing them, for a stronger central government. Federalism, on the other hand, was strong in the states least able to deal individually with their problems."[125]

North Carolina and Rhode Island, two of the original thirteen states, had to be convinced that a bill of rights would be added to the Constitution before they would vote to ratify. This was a pre-condition for both states to support the Constitution. When the First Congress of the United States was convened in 1789, both North Carolina and Rhode Island, along with the states that had ratified the Constitution, were sent copies of a proposed bill of rights. Finally persuaded that a bill of rights would be added to the Constitution, both states decided to vote for the Constitution.[126]

---

[125] Ketcham, *James Madison*, p. 237.
[126] Amar, *The Words That Made Us*, p. 314.

Chapter Four

Madison in the United States Congress

The United States Constitution was established for the purpose of strengthening the arm of the federal government and to create a larger federal republic capable of promoting interstate commerce, enhancing national security and establishing a stronger union among the states. At the same time, the Constitution established limits on the newly created federal government in the form of separated powers with checks and balances, a system of federalism that respected states' rights, and a republican form of government with elected representatives. Missing however was a bill of rights that would preserve the liberties of the American people from potential abuses on the part of the federal government.

As previously discussed, the absence of a bill of rights was the main reason why George Mason who served as a delegate to the Constitutional Convention refused to sign his name to the Constitution. Moreover, the absence of a bill of rights was among the chief reasons why a number of Antifederalists opposed the Constitution and why Thomas Jefferson expressed reservations about the proposed document. Jefferson, a strong proponent of a bill of rights, had not only shared his concerns to Madison, but had also shared his concern to a number of public servants. Writing to William Carmichael, who at the time was serving the Confederation as the charge d'affairs in Madrid, Jefferson noted that the Constitution had "fenced the people by no declaration of rights."[1]

After the Constitution was ratified by nine states, Jefferson congratulated Madison on his extraordinary efforts to create a new Constitution and to secure its ratification. Yet he continuously reminded Madison, sometimes in a subtle way, that a bill of rights was still a necessity. "I sincerely rejoice at the acceptance

---

[1] Jefferson to William Carmichael, December 15, 1787, *Papers of Thomas Jefferson,* 425; quoted in Boles, *Jefferson*, p. 194.

of our new constitution by nine states. It is a good canvas, on which some strokes only want retouching."[2]

It is difficult to think of the U.S. Constitution as existing without the Bill of Rights. Yet that was the Constitution signed by 39 delegates in Philadelphia, and that was the Constitution that was ratified by the states. Madison during the Constitutional Convention and during the ratification process did not see the need for a bill of rights. One of his principal objections was that an enumeration of rights in the Constitution could potentially empower the federal government to abuse those not listed. Madison, as Jack N. Rakove writes "was genuinely worried than an incomplete enumeration of some rights might render other rights equally valuable more precarious precisely because they lacked an explicit constitutional sanction."[3] Yet despite his objections and concerns, Madison eventually acquiesced to those insisting that a bill of rights should be added to the Constitution. Indeed, not only did Madison acquiesce, but he soon became the principal advocate for a body of rights to be included as a set of amendments to the Constitution. The question this raises is why did Madison, who was at first firmly opposed to a bill of rights, soon become its supporter? Although it may detract from his historical reputation, particularly since Madison has always been regarded as a man of high principles, the answer to this question can be traced to the realities of electoral politics.

Madison's First Campaign for Congress

Following ratification of the Constitution, elections were held in fourteen states to elect candidates to the First Congress of the United States. Madison was determined to represent Virginia. He was already an experienced legislator having served in the Virginia state legislature, as well as the Continental and Confederation Congresses. Madison also knew that for the Constitution to succeed, it would require members of Congress who strongly believed in the Constitution and who supported the powers provided to the newly established federal government.

Madison's preference was to serve in the U.S. House of Representatives, a legislative position he was most familiar. Despite his preference, his supporters nevertheless placed his name in nomination for the U.S. Senate. At the time, and

---

[2] Jefferson to Madison, July 31, 1788, *Papers of Thomas Jefferson,* 442; quoted in Boles, *Jefferson*, p. 195.

[3] Jack N. Rakove, "James Madison and the Bill of Rights: A Broader Context," *Presidential Studies Quarterly*, Vol. 22., No. 2 (Fall 1992), p. 668; online at https://www.jstor/stable/27551030. (Accessed April 26, 2024.)

for many years thereafter, the two senators from each state were not popularly elected, but rather selected by state legislatures. This method for choosing U.S. Senators remained a constitutional requirement until 1913 when the seventeenth amendment transferred U.S. Senate elections to the voters.

Unfortunately for Madison, the state legislature in Virginia was filled in Virginia was filled with Antifederalists loyal to the former governor, Patrick Henry. Henry was therefore positioned to exact his revenge on the man who through firm and reasoned debate had defeated his efforts to block ratification of the Constitution during the state ratifying convention. Henry could now return the favor and block Madison's election to the Senate. Madison was certain that Henry would do his absolute best to prevent him from becoming one of the two senators from Virginia in the First Congress. Madison's expectation was correct, as that is exactly what Henry did. True to form, Henry resorted to hyperbole by arguing that Madison, if chosen by the state legislature to represent Virginia in the Senate, would clearly pose a danger to the country's freedom.[4]

Through his behind the scenes maneuvers and exercise of political leverage, Henry successfully blocked Madison's selection as a U.S. Senator. Although the Virginia state legislature was firmly in the former governor's grip, Madison, quite surprisingly, placed a strong third behind Richard Henry Lee and William Grayson, the two Senators handpicked by Henry.[5] The recorded votes in the state legislature were 98 for Lee, 86 for Grayson and 77 for Madison.[6]

Having been blocked by the Virginia legislature to serve in the U.S. Senate, Madison then concentrated on winning a seat in the U.S. House of Representatives, his first choice to begin with. Virginia had been allocated ten congressional seats, several of which were located in large geographical districts that included several counties. The fifth congressional district, which included Orange County, was the district Madison was hoping to represent. Yet here again, Henry's political chicanery was evident. The governor had orchestrated a law requiring all congressional candidates to reside for at least one year in the congressional district they were intending to represent.[7] Knowing that Madison as a result of this law could not switch districts, Henry, with the assistance of his

---

[4] Editorial Note, "Madison's Election to the First Federal Congress October 1788-1789:" Founders Online, at https://founders.archives.gov/documents/Madison/01-11-02-0219. (Accessed February 10, 2024.)
[5] Ibid.
[6] Hilarie M. Hicks, "The Congressional Election of 1789," Montpelier's Digital Doorway; online at https://digitaldoorway.montpelier.org/2021/11/02/the-congress-election-of-1789. (Accessed February 10, 2024.)
[7] Editor's Note, "Madison's Election"

fellow Antifederalists in the legislature, drew the geographic shape of the fifth district in a manner which purposely included a large number of Antifederalists whom he was certain would doom Madison's bid for Congress. Henry's devious manipulation of the fifth district's shape and composition has been described as one of the very first "gerrymanders" in American political history, long before the term became popularized.[8] Madison learned of Henry's devious efforts while he was concluding his term of office in the Confederation Congress.[9] "In the districting scheme enacted by the Virginia General Assembly, the most controversial district by far was that which included James Madison's home county of Orange; the Federalists claimed that Henry designed this district specifically to ensure 'Little Jemmy's defeat.'"[10] There was ample reason to conclude that the Fifth District had been gerrymandered by Henry in light of the fact that every one of the delegates in five of the district's eight counties who had been elected to the ratification convention had voted against the Constitution. In one county, the delegates evenly split on the ratification vote. Collectively, among the sixteen delegates who attended the ratification convention from the Fifth District, eleven had voted against the Constitution.[11]

Dismayed over what he perceived as pending defeat of his bid for a congressional seat, Madison on December 8, 1788 wrote to Jefferson in Paris, stating that Henry "has taken equal pains in forming the Counties into districts for the election of Reps. to associate with Orange such as are most devoted to his politics, and most likely to be swayed by the prejudices excited agst me."[12]

With the district drawn in a manner that was less than receptive to Madison and the Federalist point of view, Madison recognized that to win the district he would have to express strong support for a bill of rights. Voters in the fifth district needed to be assured that the federal government would not compromise their personal liberties. With Henry packing Antifederalists into the fifth district, Madison recognized that to win the seat his support for a bill of rights had to be firm and robust.

---

[8] Hicks, "The Congressional Election of 1789"

[9] Editor's Note, "*Madison's Election*"

[10] Thomas Rogers Hunter, "The First Gerrymander? Patrick Henry, James Madison, James Monroe, and Virginia's 1788 Congressional Districting," *Early American Studies*, Vol. 9., No. 3 (Fall, 2011), p. 791; online at https://www.jstor.org/stable/23546676. (Accessed March 30, 2024.)

[11] Ibid.

[12] Madison to Jefferson, December 8, 1788, *Jefferson Papers*, 14: 342; quoted in Hunter, "The First Gerrymander?" p. 795.

Madison versus Monroe

Madison's opponent in the fifth congressional district was Col. James Monroe, one of the leading Antifederalists in the state of Virginia. Like Madison, Monroe was also a great admirer of Thomas Jefferson and considered him a mentor. Monroe had spoken forcefully against the Constitution at the Virginia ratifying convention. His candidacy was strongly supported by Henry. This would be the only time in American history that two individuals, both of whom were destined to become presidents, would face one another in a congressional contest.

To win this election, Madison knew that his support for a bill of rights had to be widely advertised among the freeholders who would be voting on Election Day.[13] To broadcast his position, he sent two letters to newspapers in which he promised voters that if elected to Congress he would sponsor a bill of rights.[14] To be viewed by voters as the principal advocate of a bill of rights, Madison reasoned that he could cut into Monroe's support among Antifederalists, while holding on to voters aligned with Federalists; an electoral coalition was a necessity.

But to win this election, Madison, who still had duties as a member of the Confederation Congress located in New York City, recognized that he would have to come home and vigorously campaign, a form of activity that he frowned on. Nevertheless, with Monroe already campaigning within the gerrymandered district and calling for another convention to consider amendments to the Constitution, which included a bill of rights, Madison knew that his presence in the district and his support for a bill of rights was essential. As a highly skilled debater, Madison was hoping to debate Monroe in front of large audiences. He also vividly remembered when in 1777 he campaigned for a seat in the Virginia House of Delegates and how his opponent by treating voters to shots of whiskey cost him the election. For some freeholders, Madison reluctantly concluded that he might have to resort to personal favors to win their support.[15] Eager to begin his campaign for the congressional seat he coveted, "in December he made the 330-mile trip back to Orange to begin his campaign for Congress."[16]

Although the issues Madison and Monroe debated during the campaign were a mix of issues facing the federal government, including how taxes should be levied and collected,[17] Madison made sure he was perceived as the most knowledgeable of the two candidates with respect to the importance of a bill of

---

[13] The term "Freeholders" refers to property owning males who had the right to vote.

[14] Amar, *The Words That Made Us*, p. 312.

[15] Hicks, "The Congressional Election of 1789"

[16] Hunter, "The First Gerrymander?" p. 796.

[17] Hicks, "The Congressional Election of 1789".

rights. With Baptist congregations increasing within his legislative district, Madison strategically stressed the importance of religious freedom.[18] He made it a point to pay "special attention to reminding these voters about his views on religious liberty."[19] Like Madison's election as a delegate to the Virginia ratifying convention during which he received strong support from Baptists and the Baptist preacher John Leland, Madison's election to the First United States Congress would also be dependent on the support he received from Baptist voters and Leland's commitment to his candidacy.[20]

Leading Antifederalists who were familiar with Madison's original opposition to a bill of rights labeled him a candidate without convictions. They attempted to brand him as a political opportunist who had latched onto the notion of a bill of rights as an expedient way of winning his election. George Mason had serious doubts about Madison's authenticity with respect to his support for a bill of rights. He suggested to his son that Madison, with respect to this particular issue, was a fraud.[21]

Whether Madison's position had truly evolved in favor of a bill of rights, or whether his position during the campaign was calculated to win votes, one may never know. Regardless, when freeholders went to the polls on February 2, 1789 and when the votes in the eight counties within the fifth district were finally tabulated, Madison was declared the winner. He had defeated Monroe 1,308 to 972, a margin or 336 votes.[22] The temperature on election day was well below zero with close to a foot of snow covering the district.[23] The brutal weather, which likely affected voter turnout, might have benefited Madison. Besides winning his own election, Madison must also have been overjoyed when he learned that among the ten congressional elections across the state of Virginia, six candidates aligned with the Federalists had won their contests.[24]

The congressional contest between Madison and Monroe has gone down in history as one of the most unusual but vitally important elections in the annals of congressional politics. Yet in addition to the unusual fact that two future presidents competed against one another, what is often forgotten is how civil this

---

[18] Editorial Note, "Madison's Election"
[19] Hunter, "The First Gerrymander?" pp. 797-798.
[20] Mark S. Scarberry, "John Leland and James Madison: Religious Influence on the Ratification of the Constitution and the Proposal of the Bill of Rights, *Dickenson Law Review*, Vol. 113., Issue 3 (2008-2009) pp. 789-792.
[21] Cost, *James Madison*, p. 165.
[22] Ibid.
[23] Hunter, "*The First Gerrymander?*" pp. 802-803.
[24] Editorial Note, "Madison's Election"

contest was. More to the point, although the contest was highly competitive, Madison and Monroe conducted themselves in a collegial and statesmanlike manner throughout the entire campaign. Never once did the contest become personal, nor were there character assassinations or mudslinging. The election was very unlike what voters are exposed to in contemporary congressional campaigns. Gracious in victory, Madison had this to say in a letter to Jefferson. "It was my misfortune to be thrown into a contest with our friend, Col. Monroe. The occasion produced considerable efforts among our respective friends. Between ourselves, I have no reason to doubt that the distinction was duly kept in mind between political and personal views, and that it has saved our friendship from the smallest diminution."[25] Reflecting on the election after he had retired from public service, Madison described one of the debates between himself and Monroe. "We used to meet in days of considerable excitement, and address the people on our respective sides, but there never was an atom of ill will between us."[26]

Most treatments of Madison's victory make note that he was able to overcome Henry's gerrymander that was intended to put Madison at a distinct disadvantage to Monroe. Although there is strong reason to believe that Virginia's Fifth Congressional District was drawn by Henry and his fellow Antifederalists in a manner to deny Madison his election, not every scholar who has studied this historic election has concluded that the district was in fact gerrymandered by Henry. Thomas Rogers Hunter has argued that the district was drawn largely due to geographical, rather than political, considerations. Reviewing the geographic dimensions of the Fifth District, Hunter notes the following, "Not only are the counties closely grouped within the same region, but the district is also bounded on the all four sides by natural geographic features: the southern boundary is the James River, the northern boundary to Rappahannock River, to the east is the Fall Line, and the westernmost counties end at the Blue Ridge. In short, in all of Virginia history it would be nearly impossible to find a rural congressional district significantly more compact or as defined by geography."[27] Although Hunter recognizes that Henry was a "dictator during the 1788 General Assembly," he nevertheless concludes that the repeated claims of Henry's gerrymander are

---

[25] Madison to Jefferson, March 29, 1789, Montpelier Research Data Base; quoted in Hicks, "The Congressional Election of 1789."
[26] Madison's observations, December 3, 1827, Montpelier Research Data Base; quoted in Hicks, "The Congressional Election of 1789."
[27] Hunter, "The First Gerrymander?"p. 807.

"entirely unwarranted."[28] Hunter's perspective is clearly an alternative view regarding the congressional contest between Madison and Monroe.

Congressman Madison

Having won his congressional election, Madison returned to New York City to begin his work as a member of the U.S. House of Representatives. The First Congress of the United States, no longer referred to as the Confederation Congress, met in Federal Hall in New York City for its first year of existence, March 4, 1789 to April 12, 1790. The Congress would then move to Philadelphia where it conducted legislative business from December 6, 1790 to May 14, 1800. The Congress would then make a final move to its current site in Washington, D.C. where it has remained since November 17, 1800.[29] The Congress in 1790 had authorized President Washington to select a permanent sight for the nation's capital. Washington selected a sight along the Potomac, not far from his own plantation at Mount Vernon. The location, which would be designated a federal district, would become known as Washington, D.C.

Madison served in the United States Congress for four consecutive terms, from March 4, 1789 to March 4, 1797. During his first year in Congress, he quickly earned the reputation as an exceptionally skilled legislator. As Rutland notes, "Every congressman who heard Madison talk was impressed. The breadth of his knowledge, his willingness to compromise, and his focus on the need for immediate action marked him as a leader during that First Congress."[30] He was, in essence, the "floor leader" on several key issues, among them the passage of legislation designed to generate revenue for the federal government.[31] During his first term in Congress, Madison delivered a floor speech at least 150 times, an extraordinary number of speeches for any member of Congress.[32] Reflecting on Madison's performance as a lawmaker, Massachusetts Congressman Fisher Ames described him as "our first man."[33]

---

[28] Ibid., p. 820.
[29] Congressional Research Service Reports; online at https://crsreports.congress.gov. (Accessed January 17, 2024.)
[30] Rutland, *James Madison*, p. 56.
[31] Ibid.
[32] Feldman, *The Three Lives of James Madison*, p. 259.
[33] Ames, April 9, 1789, *Papers of James Madison,* 12:71; quoted in Feldman, *The Three Lives of James Madison*, p. 259.

Madison Resolves a Separation of Powers Controversy

One of Madison's finest moments in the first Congress involved his leadership during a dispute regarding how a cabinet officer could be removed.[34] Madison, who was instrumental in introducing legislation that created the first set of cabinet departments,[35] skillfully addressed what was one of the many perplexing ambiguities contained within the Constitution. The Constitution was very clear that the president, and the president alone, had the constitutional authority to nominate a cabinet officer. It was also evident that the U.S. Senate under the Constitution was given the authority to confirm or reject a cabinet nominee. The Constitution was also unambiguous in describing how a public official, which included a cabinet officer, could be removed. The process involved impeachment by the House of Representatives followed by a vote in the Senate to remove. What was not clear in the Constitution, however, was whether the president had the sole authority to fire a cabinet officer.[36] Was the removal of a cabinet officer embedded within the president's authority as chief executive under Article II of the Constitution? If the president could nominate a cabinet officer, did not the president also have the authority to remove the officer? The ambiguity raised a separation of powers question. Feldman notes that Madison, after considerable discussion among House members, finally resolved the removal controversy by "arguing for a pragmatic reading of the Constitution, not a literal one."[37] Impeachment in the House and removal by the Senate in Madison's view was not always the most realistic solution, as the process was too cumbersome and time consuming. The Senate, Madison noted, would always have to be in session and ready to handle an impeachment trial, which could erupt with little prior notice. This, in Madison's view, was simply impractical.[38] The better solution, in his view, would be to interpret the Constitution in a pragmatic manner. This would allow the president in his role as chief executive to personally remove a cabinet officer. This in Madison's view was the more efficient and more practical solution. Madison also noted that because President Washington was a man of virtue, it seemed reasonable to trust the president's judgment with respect to removal. Feldman summarized Madison's perspective: "The president enjoyed

---

[34] Feldman, *The Three Lives of James Madison*, pp. 264-266.
[35] Ibid. 265.
[36] Ibid.
[37] Ibid.
[38] Ibid.

distinct and unique legitimacy under the Constitution. He was therefore worthy of more confidence than the Senate."[39]

After addressing the removal process from a pragmatic perspective, Madison drew upon his wisdom regarding the separation of powers doctrine to further settle the issue. The distribution of powers as established in the Constitution prevented the Congress from limiting the president's authority. Thus, to involve Congress in the removal of cabinet officers would invade the executive authority of the president. This would be a violation of the Constitution.[40] Madison's intimate knowledge of the Constitution and how he addressed the separation of powers settled the issue, at least for the time being. The constitutional ambiguity involving the president's authority to remove executive branch officials, along with other ambiguities contained within the Constitution, would be further addressed in future Supreme Court rulings.

The Bill of Rights

During Madison's first congressional term, there was one legislative contribution that stood out among his other contributions and the one he is most remembered for. This was Madison's leadership related to adding a bill of rights to the Constitution. As Gordon Wood put it, "There is no question that it was Madison's personal prestige, and his dogged persistence that saw the amendments through the Congress. There might have been a federal Constitution without Madison, but certainly no Bill of Rights." [41]

Once he was elected to Congress, Madison was determined to fulfill his campaign pledge promised to freeholders during his congressional campaign against Monroe. Thus, it was during his first term in Congress that Madison penned a bill of rights. Ketcham writes, "He advocated measures to satisfy the large number of people who objected to the Constitution only because it lacked a bill of rights. . . . He hoped as well that Federalist support of a bill of rights would convince North Carolina and Rhode Island to ratify the Constitution."[42]

Although American government textbooks credit Madison with authoring the Bill of Rights, it is important to note that the various rights contained within this bill were not rights that Madison conceived. For example, one will find rights contained within the Bill of Rights that are drawn from the Magna Carta adopted

---

[39] Ibid., p. 266.
[40] Ibid.
[41] Gordon S. Wood, *Empire of Liberty: A History of the Early Republic, 1789-1815* (New York: Oxford University Press, 2009), p. 69.
[42] Ketcham, *James Madison*, p. 290.

in 1215. Due process of law are among the rights contained within the Magna Carta. The Magna Carta was intended to limit the power of the English King, while simultaneously expanding liberties to the nobility. The English Bill of Rights of 1689, adopted during England's Glorious Revolution, which resulted in the establishment of a constitutional monarchy, also contains a listing of rights that Madison likely drew from. Closer to home, Madison also extracted portions of the Virginia Declaration of Rights that was adopted in 1776. One will recall that Madison at the age of twenty-five served as a delegate to Virginia's constitutional convention where, under the watchful eye of George Mason, he helped draft this impressive body of rights, particularly the section pertaining to religious freedom. A reading of the Virginia Declaration of Rights will find that Madison incorporated sections of the Virginia document almost verbatim into the Bill of Rights. The right to confront witnesses against oneself, the right to a speedy trial before an impartial jury, protection from self-incrimination, the prohibition of excessive bail and fines, protection from self-incrimination, protection from unreasonable search and seizure, the right to bear arms, and the free exercise of religion are rights that appear throughout the Virginia Declaration of Rights and obviously guided the pen of Madison when drafting the Bill of Rights.[43] Moreover, Madison was very familiar with the various bills of rights that were included in state constitutions, several of which were written and approved when independence from Britain was declared in 1776. At the Constitutional Convention in 1787, several state constitutions were reviewed and served as guides for the delegates.

Ratifying Madison's Bill if Rights

According to Article V of the U.S. Constitution, an amendment can be added to the Constitution in one of two ways. One procedure is to propose an amendment by a vote of two-thirds of each chamber of Congress, followed by a vote of three fourths of the state legislatures. The second procedure allows two-thirds of the state legislatures to call a convention for the purpose of proposing an amendment. Once the convention votes for an amendment, it is then sent to either the state legislatures or state conventions for ratification. The support of three-fourths of the state legislatures, or three fourths of the state conventions, is required for ratification. To date, the twenty-seven amendments to the Constitution, which

[43] Ms. Morgan O'Brien, a former history major at Sacred Heart University, wrote an outstanding senior thesis titled "George Mason: Father of the Bill of Rights." Morgan's thesis demonstrated the close relationship between Mason's Virginia Declaration of Rights and Madison's Bill of Rights.

include the Bill of Rights, have been added by way of the first constitutional procedure. The concept of federalism is evident whenever an amendment has been added to the Constitution.

Madison's first draft of the Bill of Rights included twenty amendments. He also felt it was important to include a preamble for the Bill of Rights.

> *The Conventions of a number of the States, having at the time of their adopting the Constitution, expressed a desire, in order to prevent misconstruction or abuse of its powers, that further declaratory and restrictive clauses should be added: And as extending the ground of public confidence in the Government, will best ensure the beneficent ends of its institution.*[44]

During the summer of 1789, The House of Representatives reviewed Madison's twenty proposed amendments and voted in favor of seventeen.[45] The seventeen amendments were then forwarded to the Senate for approval. After extensive review and debate regarding the seventeen amendments, the Senate approved twelve amendments. On September 25, 1789, a joint resolution was passed by both chambers approving the twelve amendments.[46] The twelve amendments were then sent to the state legislatures for ratification.

The original First Amendment, known as the "representation amendment," described the formula for allotting representatives to the states. This amendment was rejected by the states. The original Second Amendment described when Congress could adjust pay for its members. This amendment stated, "No law varying the compensation for the services of the Senators and Representatives, shall take effect until an election of Representatives shall have intervened." In short, this amendment required an election to first take place before a pay raise could be authorized for members of Congress. Voters were thus permitted to vote out of office representatives they deemed unworthy of a pay raise. It was also Madison's intention to give Congress, not the President, the authority to determine a congressional pay raise.[47] Only six state legislatures ratified this amendment when it was proposed. This was below the required number of states to ratify an

---

44 Mark Grossman, ed., Constitutional Amendments: Volume I (New York: Grey House Publishing, 2012), p.3.

45 National Archives, "The Bill of Rights," online at archives.gov. (Accessed January 18, 2024.)

46 Ibid.

47 Steven Calibresi and Zephyr Teachout, "The Twenty-Seventh Amendment," National Constitution Center; online at constitutioncenter.org/the-constitution/amendments/amendment-xxvii/interpretation/165/ (Accessed July 19, 2023.)

amendment, which in 1789 numbered eleven states.[48] However, there was no time limit placed on the ratification of this proposed amendment. This meant that because it had not been rejected, like the proposed first amendment, it would continue to languish as a proposed constitutional amendment. The status of this amendment was eventually discovered by a University of Texas student named Gregory Watson when writing a research paper on governmental procedures.[49] Watson argued in his paper that because there had not been a time limit placed on ratification of the original Second Amendment that it still had the status of a proposed amendment that the state legislatures could vote on. Watson's professor graded his paper a C, which Watson appealed but to no avail. Watson then went public to secure passage of the amendment and found an ally in U.S. Senator from Maine, William Cohen. Cohen championed Watson's crusade and convinced the Maine legislature in 1983 to ratify the amendment.[50] This led to a domino effect with more states ratifying the amendment. By 1992 thirty-eight, i.e., three-fourths, of the states had voted to ratify the amendment. Madison's amendment, originally identified as the Second Amendment, was thus included as the Twenty-Seventh Amendment to the U.S. Constitution. On May 20, 1992, the U.S. Senate unanimously voted to accept the validity of this amendment. The House voted 414-3 to also accept it. To date, forty-six of the fifty state legislatures have voted to ratify what was the original Second Amendment.[51]

Some legal scholars have questioned the legality of this amendment by suggesting that Article V of the Constitution requires a coherent time frame for an amendment to be ratified, although Article V does not specify this.[52] Thus, James Madison's original Second Amendment finally became the law of the land thanks to a student research paper that received a C. Watson's former professor, perhaps embarrassed by grading the paper a C, changed the grade to an A.

Although the original First Amendment was rejected, and the original Second Amendment never ratified or rejected (until it finally entered the Constitution in substance as the 27th Amendment}, states did however ratify what at the time were amendments three to twelve. As a result, amendments three to twelve thus became amendments one through ten, which together comprise the Bill of Rights.

It is important to note that the original intent of Madison's Bill of Rights was to impose limits on the federal government, not the states. This was

---

[48] Ibid.

[49] Ibid.

[50] Ibid.

[51] Ibid.

[52] Ibid.

understandable, as it was powers afforded to the federal government that worried many Americans. Madison and other Federalist however felt that the bills of rights in state constitutions were more than sufficient to protect the people from the actions of state lawmakers. He thus saw no compelling reason to apply the Bill of Rights to both levels of governing authority. Beginning in the twentieth century, however, and through a series of historic Supreme Court rulings, the Bill of Rights was deemed applicable to the states by way of the Due Process Clause of the Fourteenth Amendment. By "incorporating" the Bill of Rights into the Due Process Clause, the Bill of Rights now imposes limits on both the federal and state governments. Whether Madison would have agreed with the incorporation doctrine is difficult to tell. What follows is a brief summary of the Bill of the Rights. This collective body of amendments that protects the freedoms of the American people is very much attributable to the efforts of Madison when he was a member of the U.S. Congress.

The First Amendment

The very first right contained within the First Amendment pertains to freedom of religion. The government is prevented from establishing a religion, which is stated in the "establishment clause," while the people also have the right to freely practice religion, which is guaranteed in the "free exercise clause." Madison, having intimate knowledge of how Baptists were discriminated against in Virginia, and having been the principal author of the religious provision in the Virginia Declaration of Rights, was determined to make a strong statement in defense of religious freedom. As Ketcham states, "religious liberty stands out as the one subject upon which Madison took an extreme, absolute, undeviating position throughout his life."[53] Thomas Jefferson writing to the Danbury Baptist Association in 1802 described the religious provisions within the First Amendment as creating a "wall of separation" between church and state. This is precisely what Madison erected when he authored the First Amendment. Additional rights contained within the First Amendment include the freedoms of speech, press, assembly and petition. One can reasonably argue that the First Amendment is the bedrock of American democracy.

Second to the Tenth Amendment

The Second amendment provides the people with the right to bear arms, which is understandable based on the colonists need for firearms during the Revolutionary War, while the Third Amendment prevents soldiers from

---

[53] Ketcham, *James Madison*, p. 165.

quartering in private homes, a practice that occurred during the American Revolution when British soldiers without permission and at their discretion quartered in the private homes of colonists. The Fourth, Fifth and Sixths Amendments provide an accused person with due process of law. This is a central tenet of the American legal system.

The Seventh Amendment allows citizens the right to have a jury trial in common law cases, providing the amount of money being sought justifies a trial. The dollar amount has been adjusted over time. The Eighth Amendment's prohibition on excessive fines and bail, as well cruel and unusual punishment, is a reflection of colonial experiences with the British.

The Ninth Amendment reflects Madison's legitimate concern that enumerating rights would allow the government to deny rights not listed; hence a broadly worded amendment intended to protect rights beyond those identified in the previous eight amendments. What James Madison had in mind with respect to unenumerated rights is subject to speculation. The Tenth Amendment reflects Madison's legitimate concern with protecting the principle of federalism. This is the amendment which guarantees a body of "reserved powers" to the states. The rights of the people are also protected in the Tenth amendment.

Ten extraordinary amendments comprise the Bill of Rights. James Madison, more than any other Founding Father or member of the First U.S. Congress, is the individual who deserves the credit for bringing into existence an impressive body of rights that have in so many ways preserved the liberties of the American people. Deeply concerned with the prospect of tyrannical majorities, which he had expressed very clearly in *Federalist 10,* Madison considered a bill of rights as an absolute necessity. In the perspective of Stuart Leibiger, Madison had always favored a system of government that would ensure "the requisite balance and stability against sudden impulses from the masses."[54] Thus, in addition to constitutional safeguards contained within the original seven Articles of the Constitution, the federal bill of rights, in Madison's view, would further contribute to balance and stability.

The Bank of the United States

Although an impressive legislator with a reputation for detail and extensive preparation, not all of Madison's legislative efforts during his time in Congress

---

[54] Stuart Leibiger, "James Madison and Amendments to the Constitution:1787-1789: Parchment Barriers," *The Journal of Southern History*, Vol 59. No 33 (August 1993), p. 444; online at https://doi.org/10.2307/2210003.
(Accessed April 20, 2024.)

were successful. One issue that he fought vigorously against, but lost the battle, involved The Bank Bill of 1791 proposed by Alexander Hamilton. Hamilton, a strong believer in a national economy based on federal control over commerce, had been appointed by President Washington as Secretary of the Treasury. Hamilton, who had collaborated with Madison at the Annapolis Convention, served as a delegate to the Constitutional Convention, and had recruited Madison for the *Federalist* project, envisioned a national bank which could serve multiple functions essential to the nation's economic development. As Chernow writes, "Lacking a uniform currency acceptable to all states still suffering a hodgepodge of foreign coins, the country required an institution that could expand the money supply, extend credit to government and business, collect revenues, make debt payments, handle foreign exchange, and provide a depository for government funds."[55] Because Hamilton had serious concerns regarding the interplay between politicians and monetary policy, he proposed that the National Bank, although formally established by the federal government, should be placed under private, rather than federal control.[56] The National Bank was clearly a dramatic departure from the decentralized system of banking in the United States, "Its ten million dollars in capital would be several times larger than the combined capital of all existing banks."[57]

As a member of the first Congress, Madison strongly opposed the National Bank. He also had a trusted ally in Jefferson who after returning from Paris had been appointed by Washington as Secretary of State. Jefferson and Madison were among the most vocal and steadfast critics of Hamilton's Bank. "As members of the Virginia plantation world, Jefferson and Madison had a nearly visceral contempt for market values and tended to denigrate commerce as grubby, parasitic, and degrading."[58] Surprisingly, John Adams, not a southern plantation owner and not as committed as Madison and Jefferson to preserving an agricultural-based economy, also had serious reservations about Hamilton's Bank. In the words of Adams, "Every bank in America is an enormous tax upon the people for the profit of individuals." Bankers, in Adams' view, were "swindlers and thieves."[59] In defense of his National Bank proposal, Hamilton argued that the federal government had a broad range of implied constitutional powers contained within the "necessary and proper clause" and the "general

---

[55] Chernow, *Alexander Hamilton*, p. 347.
[56] Ibid., p. 349.
[57] Ibid.
[58] Ibid., p. 346.
[59] Adams in Ellis, *Passionate Sage,* p. 161; quoted in Chernow, *Alexander Hamilton*, p. 346.

welfare clause." Such clauses in his view supported the constitutionality of the Bank. Madison firmly disagreed with Hamilton and did not view these constitutional clauses as giving the federal government the authority to enact a national banking system.[60] In addition to different constitutional interpretations, what further separated Madison from Hamilton with respect to the Bank was the issue of public debt, which Hamilton, but not Madison, viewed as having important benefits. According to Spivak, "The word 'debt' to southern planters like Jefferson and Madison was a curse word, the bane of their agricultural holdings and enterprises, a scourge that hounded them in life and from which even in death, as their heirs could attest, offered no escape or relief."[61] The most serious disagreement between Hamilton and Madison regarding the debt issue pertained to repayment of the debt, in particular who the recipients should be. Hamilton supported repayment to the *present holders* of debt, while Madison felt that the *original holders* of the debt should be first in line for debt repayments.[62]

Hamilton, in Spivak's view, had a better understanding of the debt issue. "What Hamilton understood and what Madison may not have understood was that the Revolutionary War debt was useless as a tool of national economic growth if it were divvied up among thousands of original holders, but was a vital engine of growth if it was concentrated in the hands of the speculator class, mostly northern, commercial and urban, with their entrepreneurial energy and plans for the future. A national debt was a national blessing Hamilton understood, because it could serve as the capital fuel of national economic growth."[63]

Nevertheless, despite both Madison's and Jefferson's objections, in 1791 both chambers of Congress passed the Bank Bill which chartered the Bank of the United States for a period of twenty years. The votes in Congress reflected a regional divide, with strong support for the Bank Bill among northern members of Congress, while strong opposition was evident among the southern members of Congress.[64] The Bank of the United States was signed into law by President Washington on February 28, 1791, a most historic piece of legislation. Madison and Jefferson, despite raising legitimate objections to Hamilton's proposal were unable to prevent passage of the legislation.

---

[60] Cheney, *The Virginia Dynasty*, p. 115.

[61] Comments regarding the Bank and the national debt provided to the author by Sacred Heart University history professor, Burton Spivak, June 21, 2024.

[62] Ibid.

[63] Ibid.

[64] National Park Service, "Congress Establishes the First Bank of the United States"; online at nps.gov/articles/000/establishing-the-first-bank.html. (Accessed July 24, 2023.)

Madison and the French Revolution

During Madison's first term in Congress, the French Revolution erupted, resulting in the violent end of the French monarchy and the dawn of republican government in France. Both Jefferson and Madison, unlike Hamilton and his supporters, looked upon the Revolution with admiration. As Rutland put it, "Madison, looking through republican-tinted spectacles, saw the events of 1789 as part of the worldwide movement started in 1776. He welcomed French aid in spreading the doctrines and blessings of republicanism."[65] Jefferson, perhaps more than Madison, was a staunch admirer of the French Revolution. Having served as Minister to France from 1784 to 1789, Jefferson was able to see firsthand how the French King, Louis XVI, mistreated his subjects and how the French nobility lived in splendor compared to the squalor of so many Frenchmen. "On the whole, Jefferson calculated, kings were a rather worthless lot."[66]

Opposing views of the French Revolution were quite stark in the First Congress. Madison found it reprehensible that Hamilton and his supporters were disdainful of the French Revolution. Despite having fought a war to gain independence from Britain, Hamilton still supported economic relations with the mother country over France. In addition to the divisive issue involving the Bank of the United States, it was perceptions of the French Revolution that now served to separate Hamilton and his followers from those aligned with Madison and Jefferson. Hamilton and his supporters however had the political leverage and were driving the policies of the federal government. The party eventually formed by Hamilton, known as the Federalist Party, would be instrumental in providing a strong political base upon which government policies were established.

Madison and Jefferson Take a Mysterious Trip Together

When the first Congress adjourned, Madison, exhausted from his legislative work and his unsuccessful fight against the Bank, decided to take a trip with Jefferson. The trip, as historian Garry Wills observes, was "under cover of a botany expedition."[67] Their trip, despite claims of wanting to study plant life in the Hudson Valley, was in reality a carefully planned trip to secure allies and supporters for the political party they were planning to form.[68] The party they

---

[65] Rutland, *James Madison*, p. 101.
[66] Ibid.
[67] Wills, *James Madison,* p. 45.
[68] Ibid.

envisioned would serve as an opposition party to the emerging Federalist Party of Hamilton.

Madison and Jefferson made their first stop on their "botany expedition" in New York City to meet with Philip Freneau, one of Madison's former classmates from college.[69] The meeting was intended to persuade Freneau to start a newspaper in Philadelphia that would be favorable to the party Jefferson and Madison were starting to form.

"Republican" was the name Jefferson and Madison chose for the name of their new party.[70] At the time, pro-Federalist Party publications were proliferating, particularly in the city of Philadelphia, the current site of the U.S. Capital. Both Madison and Jefferson had decided that a newspaper to counter Hamilton's economic policies and Hamilton's call for an empowered federal government was overdue.[71] In their view, Freneau's newspaper "would provide republicans with a rallying point."[72]

After having some reservations about the proposal, Freneau eventually agreed to publish the newspaper. To entice Freneau, Jefferson, who was serving as the nation's first secretary of state, offered Freneau a clerkship in the State Department at an annual salary of $250.00. Freneau's job would be to interpret documents printed in foreign languages. Cost notes that the job created by Jefferson with partisan politics in mind may very well have been the first use of patronage for party building purposes in the history of American politics.[73] Describing Freneau's job, H. W. Brands put it this way, "Freneau's qualifications for the job were modest, but so were the demands. He understood that he would be judged on the quality not of his translations but of his defense of the positions Jefferson called Whig."[74]

The newspaper started by Freneau was named *The National Gazette.* The paper would serve to counter the views expressed in the pro-Federalist *Gazette of the United States.*[75] Between November 19, 1791 and December 20, 1792, Madison would use the *National Gazette* to express his opposition to Hamilton's

---

[69] Cheney, *the Virginia Dynasty*, p.116.

[70] Although the Republican Party eventually became known as the Democratic-Republican Party, the party will be referred to as the Republican Party throughout the remainder of this work, which is common in many Madison biographies.

[71] Rutland, *James Madison*, p. 105.

[72] Ibid.

[73] Cost, *James Madison*, p. 212.

[74] H.W. Brands, *Founding Partisans: Hamilton, Madison, Jefferson, Adams and the Brawling Birth of American Politics* (New York: Doubleday, 2023), p. 189.

[75] Rutland, *James Madison,* pp. 105-106.

policies in a series of eighteen essays, all of which were published anonymously.[76] Despite his warnings of the dangers of faction in *Federalist* No. 10, Madison's essays nevertheless had a partisan thrust, further revealing his intentions to form an opposition party to Hamilton's party. Gutzman states, "Each of these essays took a nakedly partisan position, opposed to Hamilton and, through Hamilton, to the Washington administration."[77] Madison's essays were not however of the same intellectual or scholarly caliber as his *Federalist essays*. This was intentional, as he was attempting to reach a broader and more popular audience for the purpose of building a grassroots party.[78]

The Proclamation of Neutrality

During Madison's second term in Congress, war broke out between France and Britain. The two powers were longtime foes which was further evident in the previous French and Indian War. France's Ambassador to the United States, Edmond Charles Genet, sought the support of the United States with the expectation that President George Washington, who undoubtedly was grateful to France for its vital support during America's war for independence, would be amenable to the French request. Moreover, in 1778 the United States had entered into a Treaty of Alliance with France, which, in Genet's view, had bound the United States into supporting France in its wars.[79]

Yet France's request for American support quickly evolved into a conflict between Jefferson and Hamilton. Jefferson, having served for several years as Minister to France, and as an avid admirer and supporter of all things French, felt that the treaty had bound the United States into supporting France in its war with Britain. Hamilton, who wanted nothing to do with France, suggested that the better approach with respect to this conflict would be for the United States to remain neutral. Hamilton, who was much closer to Washington than was Jefferson, presented two specific reasons for the United States to adopt a neutral posture. First, the United States was not prepared to participate in another war. Second, the original treaty with France was no longer binding on the United States because it had been agreed to during the reign of King Louis XVI. In Hamilton's view, the termination of the French monarchy by the French Revolution had

---

[76] Gutzman, *James Madison*, p. 262.
[77] Ibid.
[78] Ibid.
[79] Stuart Leibiger, "George Washington and the Proclamation of Neutrality," *The Bill of Rights Institute*; online at billofrightsinstitute.org/essays/George-washington-and-the-proclamation-of-neutrality. (Accessed August 15, 2023.)

invalidated the treaty.[80] Hamilton's urging of Washington to declare neutrality was however to the advantage of Britain, which at the time had the stronger military. In disagreement with Hamilton, Jefferson felt that the 1778 treaty with France should be honored. Treaties, in his view, were not with the government of a nation, but rather with the nation itself irrespective of who was in power.[81]

Unwilling to become involved in a foreign war despite the treaty with France, President Washington in 1793 issued, without congressional approval, a neutrality proclamation. The proclamation stated in clear terms that the United States would not take sides in the European conflict. The president's proclamation at the time was officially titled "A Proclamation" without the term "Neutrality" included. The Proclamation soon thereafter became known as President Washington's "Proclamation of Neutrality."[82]

The Proclamation was controversial from the moment it was issued because Congress had not been involved in such an important foreign policy decision. Constitutional questions were raised: did the President of the United States have the authority to unilaterally issue a proclamation regarding the foreign policy of the United States, or did the Constitution require congressional approval? More broadly, the question became which branch of government, the executive or legislative, should have the final word on foreign affairs. Due to the Constitution's ambiguity, a separation of powers issue became the subject of a fierce debate.

The Pacificus v. Helvidius Debate

To defend the President's unilateral proclamation, Hamilton, writing under the pseudonym of "*Pacificus,*" began submitting a series of essays, seven in total, to the pro-Federalist *Gazette of the United States* whose owner was John Fenno, an admirer of George Washington and staunch supporter of the new federal government. The paper's motto was "he that is not for us, is against us."[83] In his pro-neutrality essays, Hamilton articulated the view that the United States was no longer bound by the Treaty of Alliance, and that the Neutrality Proclamation issued by President Washington was clearly within the president's constitutional authority. In his first essay, published in the *Gazette of the United States* on June 29, 1793, Hamilton argued that the president's constitutional role in the field of foreign affairs was broad and inclusive.

---

[80] Ibid.

[81] Ibid.

[82] Ibid.

[83] "Gazette of the United States" (New York [N.Y.]) 1789-1793, *Library of Congress; online at loc.gov/item/sn-83030483.* (Accessed September 10, 2023.)

> A correct and well informed mind will discern at once that it [foreign affairs] can belong neither to the Legislative nor Judicial Department and of course must belong to the Executive. . . . The Legislative department is not the organ of intercourse between the UStates and foreign Nations. . . . It is equally obvious that the act in question [the Treaty of Alliance] is foreign to the Judiciary Department of the Government. . . . Hence, though treaties can only be made by the President and Senate, their activity may be continued or suspended by the President alone.[84]

Hamilton's strongly worded defense of the Proclamation and his support for broad presidential power in foreign affairs would continue to appear in his "*Pacificus*" essays. Jefferson, recognizing that Hamilton's persuasive writing was structuring public opinion towards the president's proclamation, while simultaneously laying the groundwork for an expansion of presidential powers, pleaded with Madison to start rebutting Hamilton's essays. Writing to Madison, Jefferson expressed his exasperation over Hamilton's essays, "Nobody answers him, and his doctrine therefore will be taken for confessed. For God's sake, my dear sir, take up your pen, select the most striking heresies, and cut him to pieces in the face of the public. There is nobody else who can and will enter the lists with him."[85] Despite having reservations about entering into a public debate with Hamilton, particularly in light of Hamilton's keen mind, grasp of the Constitution, and persuasive writing style, Madison reluctantly accepted Jefferson's challenge. Thus, applying pen to paper and selecting the pseudonym, "*Helvidius*," Madison began submitting a series of essays in which he rebutted Hamilton's position while simultaneously defending the role of Congress in foreign affairs.

The first of five essays authored by "Helvidius" appeared in the *Gazette of the United States* on August 24, 1793.[86] This was the same paper in which Hamilton's essays were published. Madison and Hamilton, who had previously collaborated as colleagues on the *Federalist* essays under the pseudonym "*Publius*" were now engaged in an intellectual duel with another regarding the separation of powers doctrine. The pseudonyms of "*Pacificus*" and "*Helvidius,*"

---

[84] Morton J. Frisch, ed., "The Pacificus-Helvidius Debates of 1793-1794: Toward the Completion of the American Founding," Indianapolis: Liberty Fund, 2007; online at oll.libertyfund.org/page/1793-pacificus-hamilton-no-1-pamphlet. (Accessed September 10, 2023.)

[85] Jefferson to Madison, July 7, 1793, *Papers of James Madison, 15;* quoted in Cost, *James Madison,* p. 229.

[86] Cost, *James Madison*, p. 230.

not surprisingly, were the names of Roman historical figures. The essays began in the summer of 1793 and extended into 1794.

Citing both Locke and Montesquieu, political theorists he undoubtedly studied while a student under Witherspoon, Madison in his first essay identified both the war making and treaty provisions of the Constitution which he identified as powers belonging to the President and the Congress. "If we consult for a moment, the nature and operation of the two powers to declare war and make treaties, it will be possible not to see that they can never fall within a proper definition of executive powers." To strengthen his argument, Madison suggested that the executive power advocated by "*Pacificus*" was little different from that of a tyrannical king. "To say then that the power of making treaties which are confessedly laws, belongs naturally to the department which is to execute laws, is to say, that the executive department includes a legislative power. In theory this is an absurdity – in practice a tyranny."[87]

The several essays authored by Hamilton and Madison are among the finest arguments ever presented regarding where power should reside in the conduct of American foreign policy. Each essay is a deep dive into the Constitution by two brilliant Founders. Although the debate has never received the same recognition or status as the debate that occurred between "*Publius*" and "*Brutus*" during the fight to ratify the Constitution, there can be little doubt the contentious essays stand to this day as a profound treatment of the separation of powers doctrine, one of the most distinguishing features of the U.S. Constitution.

The Jay Treaty

The year after Madison and Hamilton debated one another over President Washington's Neutrality Proclamation, another controversy arose that was not only related to the Neutrality Proclamation, but which also had consequences for the country's relationship with both Britain and France. This controversy would further divide Hamilton and his fellow Federalists against Madison and Jefferson. This was the treaty negotiated in 1794 between Britain's Foreign Minister, Lord William Grenville and America's appointed negotiator, John Jay. The treaty that Jay and Grenville finally agreed to in 1794 was formally titled "The Treaty of Amity, Commerce and Navigation, Between His Britannic Majesty and the United States of America." In the United States, the treaty became known as "Jay's Treaty" or "The Jay Treaty."[88] The treaty was intended to resolve lingering

---

[87] "Helvidius," No. 1, August 24, 1793, Founders Online at founders. archives.gov/documents/Madison/01-15—02-0056. (Accessed September 10, 2023.)
[88] Americanhistorycentral.com (Accessed August 18, 2023.)

problems between the United States and Britain which had been festering since the end of the Revolutionary War.

As discussed in a Chapter Three, John Jay was a prominent New York lawyer who had served in the Continental Congress. He had also collaborated for a short while with Hamilton and Madison on the *Federalist* project. He had served as Minister to Spain during which time he tried to secure Spain's support during the American Revolution. Moreover, Jay was on the team of Americans who negotiated the Treaty of Paris in 1783 which had ended the Revolutionary War and which acknowledged independence for the United States.[89] Jay had been appointed by President Washington as the first Chief Justice of the U.S. Supreme Court, a position he held when negotiating the treaty with Grenville. Given Jay's stature and diplomatic experience, he was the natural choice to negotiate a treaty intended to resolve grievances between the United States and Britain, of which there were many.[90] Among the unresolved issues that Jay was expected to negotiate and resolve included: the continued existence of British forts around the Great Lakes region; Britain's continued practice of providing arms to Native American tribes who were hostile to American settlers; payment of debts that were still owed to both countries that had accrued prior to the American Revolution;[91] friction regarding trade relations between the United States and Britain; Britain's policy of seizing American merchant ships that were headed to France; Britain's continued practice of impressing American sailors into the British navy; and how to compensate American slave owners whose slaves were freed by the British during the Revolutionary War and who had been relocated to Great Britain.[92]

Having won its independence from Britain, the United States however was still not equal to Britain in terms of military might or economic power. Despite the 1783 Treaty of Paris, there remained much tension between the two countries. As Joseph J. Ellis, notes, "Washington had sent Chief Justice John Jay to London to negotiate a realistic bargain that avoided a war with England."[93]

The economic and military disparity between the two countries did not give Jay much leverage during his negotiations with Grenville. Moreover, Jay's strength as a negotiator had already been compromised by Hamilton who, as Ketcham reveals, "had secretly assured the British Minister that the United States

[89] History in Charts, "The Significance of the 1794 Jay's Treaty," December 19, 2022); online at historyincharts.com. (Accessed August 18, 2023.)
[90] Ibid.
[91] Ibid.
[92] Ibid.
[93] Joseph J. Ellis, *Founding Brothers* (New York: Alfred A. Knopf, 2000), p. 136.

would not under any circumstances enter into agreements of armed neutrality hostile of Great Britain, and that learning this, the British negotiators of the treaty were emboldened to resist every American claim."[94] Hamilton was determined for the United States to maintain favorable relations with Britain, regardless if such relations would undermine the interests of France.

The Treaty with Britain was signed by Jay on November 19, 1794 and subsequently ratified on June 24, 1795 by the Senate, which at the time was under the control of the Federalist Party. The Senate vote was 20 to 10.[95] Signed by President Washington, the "Jay Treaty" went into effect in 1796. H.W. Brands notes that knowing that the treaty's provisions would cause a political firestorm, Washington tried his best to keep the treaty from public scrutiny. His efforts were compromised however when a Republican from Virginia named Stevens Mason "smuggled the gist of the treaty out of the Senate and had it published."[96]

When the terms of the Jay Treaty became public, it was glaringly evident that Hamilton and the Federalists had, as they intended, reestablished close economic ties with Britain and that Jay had been unsuccessful in extracting concession from the British government. Although the British agreed to abandon their forts around the Great Lakes, British merchants were still allowed unrestricted access to the Northwest Territory and the Mississippi River.[97] Pre-Revolutionary debts, British impressment of American sailors, and payment for freed slaves were left unresolved. Particularly disconcerting to American commercial interests was the Treaty's provision that prohibited American ships from participating in British controlled West Indian trade, while Britain, quite astonishingly, was allowed a "most favored nation" status in its trade relations with the United States.[98]

Madison's outrage against the Jay Treat was on full display. He described the Treaty as a "ruinous bargain" and depicted Jay's conduct as showing "the blindest partiality to the British Nation and Government and the most vindictive sensations toward the French Republic. Indeed, the Treaty from one end to the other . . . must be regarded as a demonstration that the Party to which the Envoy belongs . . . is a British party systematically aiming at an exclusive connection with the British Government and ready to sacrifice to that object as well the dearest interests in our commerce as the most sacred dictates of National honour."[99]

---

[94] Ketcham, *James Madison*, p. 358.
[95] History in Charts, "*The Significance of the 1794 Jay's Treaty*"
[96] H.W. Brands, *Founding Partisans,* p. 268.
[97] Ketcham, *James Madison*, p. 356.
[98] Ibid., p. 357.
[99] Madison to Robert R. Livingston, August 10, 1795, Hunt, VI, 234-6; quoted in Ketcham, *James Madison*, p. 357.

Both Madison and Jefferson knew that France would feel betrayed by the Treaty and would view the Washington administration as having little, if no, appreciation for France's crucial support during America's war for independence. France, Madison surmised, would now consider the United States as an ally of Great Britain, despite President Washington's Proclamation of Neutrality. Madison's perspective was perceptive, as France viewed the Jay Treaty "as a repudiation of American earlier treaties with France."[100] Moreover, in the view of the French government, "If American merchants were going to trade with France's enemies, France was going to treat them like enemies."[101] France, the arch-enemy of Britain, had now decided to turn its wrath on the United States.

The X, Y, and Z Affair

The last thing that President John Adams, who had succeeded President Washington, wanted was a war with France. The American military was hardly prepared to engage in such a conflict. Recognizing the military weakness of the United States, the devious French Foreign Minister, Charles Maurice de Talleyrand Perigord, decided to hatch a scheme to extract payments from the United States which in turn would secure a pledge from France not to wage war. Talleyrand dispatched three agents on his behalf to meet with American envoys in France to present what in no uncertain terms was a bribery plot. In dispatches sent to President Adams, the American envoys identified the three French agents as X, Y and Z. Their names were Jean Conrad Hottinger, Pierrer Belamy, and Lucian Hauteval.[102] Talleyrand's bribery plan presented by X, Y and Z called for the United States to provide a direct payment of $250,000 to Talleyrand, along with an American loan to France of $10,000,000.[103] The money, according to X, Y and Z, would be deemed sufficient for guaranteeing peace between the two countries. But despite being reminded of France's military power and the harm that would come to the United States should France decide to wage war, Talleyrand's bribery scheme was rejected by the American envoys. The United States would not under any circumstances secure peace by way of bribery.

The Quasi War

The Jay Treaty and France's disdain towards the pro-British Federalist Party of Alexander Hamilton and President John Adams led to the so-called "Quasi-

---

[100] "The Quasi-War with France (1798-1801);" online at ussconstitutionmuseium.org/major-events/the-quasi-war-with-france. (Accessed August 20, 2023.)
[101] Ibid.
[102] David McCullough, *John Adams* (New York: Simon and Schuster, 2001), p. 495.
[103] Ibid.

War" between the United States and France. President Adams referred to the war as the "Half War."[104] The war would last from 1798 to 1801. Over three hundred American ships involved in commercial trade were seized by French privateers in the waters of the Caribbean and along the Eastern seaboard of the United States.[105] France was clearly waging a war against the United States.

The seizure of so many merchant ships prompted the United States government to convert a number of merchant ships into armed naval vessels equipped to confront any French ship that attempted seizure.[106] In addition to converting merchant ships for battle, the United States government authorized the creation of a separate Naval Department, along with the construction of twelve new battle ships. The government also authorized the establishment of a "Provisional Army" in light of concerns that the growing conflict could lead to a French invasion of the United States.[107] An "Additional Army" was also authorized which further expanded the American military with "ten thousand infantry regiments and six cavalry companies."[108] "These numbers exceeded what Adams wanted, though they fell short of Hamilton's fantasies. Adams, who sometimes portrayed himself as a passive spectator of his presidency, blamed Hamilton for pushing through this larger army."[109] American naval ships were deployed to the Caribbean to protect with force American ships engaged in trade.[110]

The "Quasi War" between the United States and France was never a declared war. Although French ships seized a number of American ships and goods, American commercial activity due to protective measure by the U.S. Navy were eventually restored. Between the years 1799 and 1800, the U.S. Navy had captured more than eighty French ships owned by privateers. The British Royal Navy was also instrumental in suppressing the actions of French privateers in the Caribbean.[111] The "Quasi-War" officially ended in 1800 with the Treaty of Mortefontaine. This Treaty not only brought an end to the conflict, but also ended the Treaty of Alliance between the United States and France.[112] Although

---

[104] Ibid., p. 508.
[105] "The Quasi War with France"
[106] Ibid.
[107] Chernow, *Alexander Hamilton*, p. 553.
[108] Ibid., p. 553.
[109] Ibid.
[110] Ibid.
[111] "The Quasi-War with France"
[112] Ibid.

hostilities between the United States and France had finally ceased, it was evident that relations between the two countries had become severely strained.

Emergence of an Opposition Party

The Bank of the United States, the Jay Treaty, the Quasi War with France, and what appeared to be autocratic behavior on the part of Presidents Washington and Adams spurred Jefferson and Madison to accelerate their plans to establish a strong opposition party capable of challenging the policies of Hamilton and the Federalist Party, or what Madison viewed as "the British Party." The opposition party, which had started to emerge during the second term of the Washington administration and which had succeeded in electing Jefferson as the nation's vice president, was now a top priority for Madison. So significant was Madison's role in developing a party to counter the policies of the Federalist Party that a separate chapter must be devoted to his historic efforts.

Chapter Five

Madison Builds a Political Party

The record is quite clear that political parties were not regarded as favorable instruments of democracy in the minds of the Founding Fathers. Richard Hofstadter offers this view, "Political discussion in eighteenth-century England and America was pervaded by a kind of anti-party cant."[1] When authoring the *Federalist Papers*, both Hamilton and Madison treated factions and parties as similar terms, neither of which, in their view, were helpful for the implementation of the new government.[2] When leaving the presidency after two terms, President George Washington in his Farewell Address warned against the divisive impact of political parties, while his successor, President John Adams, described parties as political instruments detrimental to the American republic.[3] Jefferson, who would lead the opposition party against the Federalists, once proclaimed that if he "could not go to heaven but with a party," then he "would not go there at all."[4] Despite fundamental differences among the Founders concerning issues related to governance, the one issue where there seemed to be consensus was that political parties were not consistent with democratic government. In the words of historian Arthur Scheslinger, Jr., "The Founders were reared in an anti-party tradition. . . . Parties were particularly at war with the philosophy, strong in colonial America, of civic republicanism and its emphasis on public good beyond the sum of individual and group interests."[5]

Yet despite the strong misgivings the Founders may have had about parties, and despite such strong warnings about the deleterious effect of party politics, it

---

[1] Richard Hofstadter, *The Idea of a Party System* (Berkeley: University of California Press, 1969), p.2.
[2] Ibid.
[3] Ibid.
[4] Jefferson to Francis Hopkinson, March 13, 1789, *Papers of Thomas Jefferson;* quoted in Cheney, *The Virginia Dynasty,* p. 118.
[5] Arthur M. Schlesinger, Jr., *The Cycles of American History* (Boston: Houghton Mifflin Co., 1986), p. 257.

did not take long for a two-party system to develop during the early days of the American republic. The genesis of this development was noticeable in the voting behavior of congressmen during the first several Congresses. In one study of thirty five roll calls recorded during the Second U.S. Congress, which did not include private bills, it was discovered that seventeen members of the House of Representatives voted identically as Madison did on at least twenty-three or more bills. This accounted for two-thirds of the bills before the House. Conversely, thirteen to fifteen members normally voted against Madison and his supporters. With the Second Congress consisting of sixty-five members, the roll calls revealed that close to fifty-percent of members were routinely divided on important legislative measures.[6] Although these clusters were factions, not political parties, the foundation for a two-party system was present.

The timeline regarding when the first two-party system in the United States came into existence is difficult to pinpoint with absolute certainty, as accounts when the factions evolved into parties tend to vary. For the purpose of providing instructional clarity, the archives of the U.S. House and Senate regarding the composition of Congress following the first set of federal elections can offer guidance. As Table One demonstrates, the first three Congresses which include the years 1789 to 1795 were not populated by parties, but instead by "pro-administration" or "anti-administration" factions. That changed in 1794 with the election of the Fourth U.S. Congress. Starting with the Fourth Congress, which was seated from 1795-1797, members of Congress would no longer be identified with pro or anti-administration factions, but instead with one of the two political parties. Table One is instructive.

[6] Noble E. Cunningham, Jr., *The Jeffersonian Republicans: The Formation of Party Organization 1789-1801 (*Chapel; Hill: The University of North Carolina Press, 1957), p. 22. (Private bills, which this study did not include, are bills introduced by individual members of Congress to benefit a specific individual or a specific business enterprise.)

Table One: Emergence of Parties in the U.S. Congress

U.S. House	U.S. Senate
1st Congress 1789-1791	
Pro-Admin - 37 seats	Pro-Admin - 18 seats
Anti- Admin - 30 seats	Anti-Admin - 8 seats
2nd Congress 1791-1793	
Pro-Admin - 39 seats	Pro-Admin - 16 seats
Anti-Admin - 30 seats	Anti-Admin - 13 seats
3rd Congress 1793-1795	
Pro-Admin - 51 seats	Pro-Admin - 16 seats
Anti-Admin - 54 seats	Anti-Admin - 14 seats
4th Congress 1795-1797	
Federalist Party - 47 seats	Federalist Party - 21 seats
Republican Party - 59 seats	Republican Party - 11 seats
5th Congress 1797-1799	
Federalist Party - 57 seats	Party - 22 seats
Republican Party - 49 seats	Republican Party - 10 seats
6th Congress 1799-1801	
Federalist Party - 60 seats	Federalist Party - 22 seats
Republican Party - 46 seats	Republican Party - 10 seats
7th Congress 1801-1803	
Federalist Party - 38 seats	Federalist Party - 15 seats
Republican Party - 68 seats	Republican Party - 17 seats

Source: Party Divisions of the U.S. House of Representatives, 1789-Present; online at History.house.gov/institution/party-division/; U.S. Senate Party Division; online at Senate.gov/history/party-division.htm.

The Federalist Party

The pro-administration faction, which by 1794 had evolved into the Federalist Party, was led by Treasury Secretary, Alexander Hamilton. Presidents Washington and Adams were associated with this party. The Federalist Party, which won the first three presidential elections (1789, 1792 and 1796) and controlled a majority of seats in several of the early Congresses, was identified as the party of the U.S. Constitution, federal power, the National Bank, and the Jay Treaty.

The Jeffersonian Republicans

Although the Federalist Party was controlling the reigns of government during the early years of the republic, it did not take long for the political faction in Congress opposed to the Federalist administration to emerge as a viable opposition party. This party was closely associated with Thomas Jefferson and James Madison. Initially identified as the political faction in Congress that supported a "Republican interest," the Jeffersonian/Madison faction soon became known as the Republican Party. The name was consistent with the party's commitment to core republican principles.[7]

The party of Jefferson and Madison, determined to challenge the Federalist Party, won 59 seats in the House of Representatives, while the Federalists won 47 seats in the congressional election of 1794. The Republican Party was clearly emerging and cutting into the Federalist Party's strength. The Republican Party however was not yet strong enough to overtake the Federalists. In the 1796 presidential election, the Federalist Party's candidate, John Adams, who served as vice president under President Washington, was elected president. The Federalists also won a majority of seats in both the House and Senate in the 1796 and 1798 elections. Yet as evidence of the Republican Party's increasing viability, Jefferson placed second in the 1796 presidential contest and hence was elected vice president. The U.S. Constitution at the time required the presidential candidate who placed second in the election, regardless of party, to serve as vice president. Thus, from 1797 to 1801, the president was a Federalist, while the vice president was a Republican. The possibility of having a president and vice president from two different parties would end with passage of the 12th Amendment in 1804. This amendment required presidential electors to cast separate votes for president and vice president, a process that has continued to this day. Norman Graebner writes, "As early as 1796 some modification of the

---

[7] Cunningham, Jr., *the Jeffersonian Republicans*, p. viii.

election procedure was called for by the election of two men of different political faiths."[8]

With respect to the elections of 1796, it is important to note that Jefferson had been retired from his post as secretary of state for three years. He had not publicly pursued the presidency. It was largely due to Madison's efforts related to party building, more than Jefferson's desire to be president, that contributed to the election results. The 1796 presidential election was not only a contest between two of our nation's Founders, but also a contest between two political parties with very different views towards government and foreign affairs. Noble E. Cunningham, Jr. captures the partisan division:

> The election of 1796 was clearly a contest between Republicans and Federalists. And as each party sought to give victory to its candidate, party lines tightened, party spirit rose to new heights, and political parties became a more ineradicable part of American life than ever before. No politically conscious citizen could have been unaware that the contest lay between Thomas Jefferson and John Adams, and that both these men were party candidates.[9]

Madison's Efforts

In 1800, Jefferson was elected President of the United States and the Republican Party overtook the Federalist Party in Congress, Much of what happened in that historic election year was due to Madison's leadership and party-building efforts. According to Cunningham, it was Madison, more than any other individual, who "laid the groundwork for the party organization which Jefferson was to perfect and lead to victory in 1800."[10]

Thus, the opposition party conceived by both Madison and Jefferson in 1791 during their trip to "study plant life" in the Hudson Valley had not only grown into a full-fledged opposition party to the Federalists, but by 1800 had eclipsed the Federalist Party as the nation's dominate party. What makes this development particularly noteworthy was that Madison, like Washington and other Founders, initially shunned the existence of parties, regarding them as divisive and harmful to the cause of good government. Madison's views towards political parties had obviously evolved to the point where he now viewed parties as essential checks

---

[8] Norman Graebner, "Political Parties and the Presidency" *Current History* Vol. 25, No. 145 (September 1953), p. 143; online at https://www.jstory.org/stable/45308516. (Accessed April 27. 2024.)

[9] Cunningham, Jr., *The Jeffersonian Republicans*, p. 94.

[10] Ibid., p. 88.

on power. In fact, Madison's evolution regarding the value of political parties may have begun as early as 1792 when he authored several essays in Freneau's *National Gazette*. According to Hofstadter, in these essays Madison had expressed a favorable position towards political parties.[11] Brands identifies a statement made by Madison in one of his essays which reveals his acceptance of parties, "In every political society, parties are unavoidable."[12]

Although it was Jefferson's illustrious name that was synonymous with the Republican Party, the evidence is convincing that it was James Madison, not Thomas Jefferson, who took the lead in organizing and developing the Republican Party. Yet despite Jefferson's election as president in 1800 and the Republican Party's success in the congressional elections, Madison knew that a vast amount of grassroots organization still had to be done if the Republicans were to maintain their control over the government.

Were the Antifederalists a Natural Base for the Republicans?

Before expanding on Madison's efforts related to party building, it seems fitting to first examine the frequent claim that those who aligned themselves as Antifederalists during the constitutional ratification process served as the building blocks for the Republican Party. It certainly would seem that Antifederalists with their insistence on states' rights and support for an agricultural-based economy would provide the foundational base upon which the Republican Party could depend for electoral support. Yet despite what one might conclude regarding a connection between Antifederalists and the Republican Party, the historical evidence does not support this claim. According to Cunningham, Antifederalists had largely disbanded and fragmented into factions once the Constitution was ratified, with many Antifederalists, including the strident opponent of the Constitution, Patrick Henry, aligning themselves not with the party of Madison and Jefferson, but with the Federalist Party. At the same time, many who supported the new Constitution and the need for a more powerful federal government and a stronger Union gravitated instead not to the Federalist Party but to the Republicans [13] Cunningham concludes that the evidence simply does not support the long standing view that party allegiances during the early days of the American republic were rooted in the debate to ratify the Constitution.[14] In a footnote, Cunningham challenges historian Charles Beard's position that a

---

[11] Hofstadter *The Idea of a Party System*, pp. 80-81.

[12] Madison in *National Gazette, January 23*, 1792; quoted in Brands, *Founding Partisans*, p. 192.

[13] Cunningham, *The Jeffersonian Republicans*, p. 23.

[14] Ibid.

correlation existed between the two factions that opposed one another during the ratification process and the eventual formation of the two-party system. Cunningham challenges Beard by noting that his perspective was based on the party alignments of the fifty-five delegates who attended the Constitutional Convention in 1787, a sample too small to make such a generalization.[15]

Madison's Commitment to the Grassroots

There was little doubt that despite his previous collaborative efforts with Hamilton, which included the Annapolis Convention, the Constitutional Convention in Philadelphia, and the *Federalist Papers*, Madison had come to the realization that Hamilton and the Federalist Party weres taking the country in a direction inconsistent with not only the core values of the Constitution, but also the economic welfare of the American people. In Madison's view, the elite and wealthy would be the direct beneficiaries of Hamilton's policies, one of which was the Bank of the United States. In Madison's view, the majority of the American people, particularly those in agricultural states and who made their living by farming, would be less fortunate under Federalist Party rule. Rutland captures the impact of Hamilton's policies, "Fortunes were built on mounds of public securities, as banking interests thrived because Hamilton's program was enacted into law and a new set of millionaires blossomed while the farmers watched as their tobacco and wheat crops barely provided much more than subsistence."[16] Madison knew that the only way to counter the policies of Hamilton and the Federalist Party, would be to build a strong and structurally sound political party; not from the top down, but rather from the bottom up. As Cost put it, Madison's and Jefferson's vision of a political party that effectively could challenge Hamilton was that of a grassroots organization that would serve as "the avatar of a broad majority, anchored on the general principles of self-government in pursuit of the common interest."[17] The party they were determined to build would serve as the "antidote to the factionalism of Hamilton and his 'Federalist' allies, as they would become known."[18]

To build a lasting and viable party, Madison knew that help would be needed. He knew that a true opposition party would require the assistance of several key individuals with extensive political connections and who believed in the principles of Jeffersonian republicanism. As Brookhiser observes, Madison

---

[15] Ibid.
[16] Rutland, *James Madison*, p. 102.
[17] Cost, *James Madison*, p. 211.
[18] Ibid.

recognized that to build his party, it was essential to find "like-minded men, not peers, who could do the work, much of it tedious, some of it dirty."[19] With the help of Freneau and the *National Gazette,* Madison already had a pro-Republican newspaper, essential for articulating the values of his party. But for his party to compete as a permanent national force, he knew that it had to be organized in every state and in as many local communities as possible.

In 1793, Freneau's paper went out of business due to a yellow fever which claimed the lives of 5,000 people in the city of Philadelphia.[20] Two of the fever's victims were John Todd and William Todd, the husband and baby son of Dolley (Payne) Todd. Dolley and her oldest son, Payne, luckily survived.[21] Widowed by the pandemic, Dolley would soon be introduced to James Madison by Congressman Aaron Burr. On September 15, 1794, Dolley became the bride of James Madison.[22]

Yet despite the termination of Freneau's newspaper due to the deadly pandemic, newspapers favorable to the Republican Party were now starting to blossom in several cities and states. The newspapers, Brookhiser notes, expressed views that were more partisan than the *National Gazette.*[23] Such papers would prove beneficial to Madison in his efforts to build a powerful grassroots party.

One of Madison's principal concerns related to party building was to avoid creating a party that would be perceived as having a distinctive geographic identify. Based on his experience in the Continental Congress, Madison had witnessed first-hand how members of the Congress were prone to dividing into factions that reflected geographic interests, as opposed to working for the good of all thirteen colonies. Madison, as Rutland notes, was troubled by the predictable political divisions between northern and southern congressmen.[24]

While Madison deserves most of the credit for elevating the Republican Party into a formidable political organization, it is important to also recognize the contributions of several individuals who were instrumental in helping Madison achieve his party-building goals. One such individual who worked behind the scenes to organize the Republican Party was John Beckley. Cunningham

---

[19] Brookhiser, *James Madison*, p. 100.
[20] Ibid., p. 116.
[21] Bruce Chadwick, *James and Dolley Madison: America's First Power Couple* (New York: Prometheus Books, 2014), p. 35.
[22] Ibid., pp. 37, 38. Chadwick notes the contrasts between Dolley Todd and James Madison. Dolley was 5'8, James was 5'4;. Dolley was a Quaker, James was an Episcopalian; Dolley opposed slavery, James owned slaves.
[23] Brookhiser, *James Madison,* p. 116.
[24] Rutland, *James Madison*, p. 100.

describes Beckley as, "a man who displayed much skill in the realm of practical politics, a man who knew how to win elections and to advance a party cause. As a party organizer, a campaign manager, and ever-faithful party worker, Beckley had few equals."[25] To advance the cause of the Republican Party, Beckley wrote and distributed numerous pamphlets extolling the virtues of Jeffersonian republicanism. His pamphlets were distributed in New York, Massachusetts, New Hampshire, Vermont and Virginia.[26] In the 1796 presidential contest between Jefferson and Adams, Beckley took on the job of personally managing Jefferson's campaign in Pennsylvania where he distributed packets of handbills to opinion leaders across the state. He also sent thousands of party tickets to voters listing the names of Republican candidates for public office.[27] Reflecting on Beckley's extraordinary efforts in Pennsylvania, which helped deliver Pennsylvania to Jefferson, Cunningham states, "There was system in his methods, purpose in his actions."[28]

In addition to John Beckley, Albert Gallatin, a prominent member of Congress from Pennsylvania, who would soon serve as Treasury Secretary in the administrations of both Jefferson and Madison, was instrumental in cultivating support for the Republican Party, particularly in the counties of western Pennsylvania.[29] Also assisting Madison was Aaron Burr, a high-profile lawyer and U.S. Senator from New York. Burr contested the presidency in 1796 and again in 1800. The controversial Burr, who had served as Jefferson's vice president, is most remembered for killing Alexander Hamilton in a duel in Weehawken, New Jersey on July 11, 1804. Burr's party building efforts helped to extend the reach of the Republican Party into New England, particularly in the states of Connecticut, Rhode Island, Massachusetts and Vermont.[30]

The name of John Taylor is also relevant with respect to building support for the Republican Party. "John Taylor of Caroline" as he was known was a U.S. Senator from Virginia and well known for his philosophical writings in defense of Jeffersonian ideals.[31] Clyde N. Wilson writes, "He systematically presented in his writings the principles of government and economy that Jefferson represented to the public and that John Randolph of Roanoke dramatized on the floor of Congress. Jefferson said that Taylor had seldom written a word with which he

---

[25] Cunningham, Jr. *The Jeffersonian Republicans,* p. 102.
[26] Ibid.
[27] Ibid., pp. 104-106.
[28] Ibid., p. 105.
[29] Ibid., p. 106.
[30] Ibid.
[31] Caroline was the county in Virginia where Taylor resided.

disagreed."[32] Although Madison was certainly the driving force behind the development of the Republican Party, which eventually became known as the Democratic-Republican Party, his party building efforts were clearly complemented by the efforts of several influential and politically connected individuals, all of whom were strong believers in the governing principles endorsed by Jefferson and Madison.

The Alien and Sedition Acts of 1798

Jefferson's strong second place showing in the presidential election of 1796 and the rise of the Republican Party in congressional and state politics, due principally to Madison's efforts as a party builder, were met not only with electoral resistance by the controlling Federalist Party, but also with an egregious attempt to legally suppress the viability of this growing party. What occurred was one of the most glaring assaults on civil liberties in the history of the United States. Knowing that the party of Jefferson and Madison was on the rise and which had the potential of becoming the country's dominant party, the Federalists in Congress passed in 1798 a package of laws titled the "Alien and Sedition Acts." The acts in no uncertain terms were intended to suppress the appeal of republicanism.

The suppressive acts are best understood as a reflection of the fears and animosity that many within the Federalist Party felt towards the Republican Party due to the party's close association with French emigres, compounded by the fact that France was perceived as an enemy of the United States during the undeclared Quasi War between the United States and the French Republic. There was a rising concern that both Jefferson, Madison and other members of the Republican Party had become too fond of French economic interests, and even French culture. The perceived association between Republicans and France persuaded Federalists in Congress to pass a body of laws which in their view would protect the sovereignty of the United States, while simultaneously curtailing the growing French presence on American soil. As David McCullough put it, "the infamous Alien and Sedition Acts of 1798 must be seen in the context of the time, and the context was tumult and fear."[33] Although McCullough suggests that President John Adams, a Federalist, was ambivalent about signing these acts into law, he nevertheless concedes that Adams should be held accountable for their passage.[34] The Alien

---

[32] Clyde N. Wilson, "The Writings of John Taylor of Caroline," Society of Independent Southern Historians; online at https:Southernhistorians.org. (Accessed August 30, 2023.)

[33] David McCullough, *John Adams* (New York: Simon and Schuster, 2001), p. 504.

[34] Ibid.

and Sedition Acts remain to this day a blot on John Adams' presidency and the Federalist Party.

French influence in the United States had been growing in various ways by the time of the Quasi War. A sizable number of French aristocrats who had fled France when the Revolution sank into the reign of terror had relocated to the United States, although a number of these aristocrats had actually arrived not from France but instead from the island of San Domingo in the Caribbean where slave revolts had forced their evacuation.[35] French newspapers were also appearing in the United States, along with French restaurants and schools run by French emigres. It was also suspected that French spies had been operating in the United States and providing intelligence helpful to the French military during the Quasi War.[36] French influence within the United States in multiple ways was becoming pervasive and it was the political party led by James Madison and Thomas Jefferson that was accused by Federalists of fostering this development. McCullough notes, the ruling Federalist Party was determined to crackdown on the "enemies at home."[37]

The Alien and Sedition Acts were passed by the Federalist controlled Congress and signed into law by President Adams in 1798. The view of Connecticut congressman John Allen reflected the almost paranoid view of many Federalist lawmakers towards Jefferson's party and supporters, "Let gentlemen look at certain papers printed in this city and elsewhere and ask themselves whether an unwarrantable and dangerous combination does not exist to overturn and run the government by publishing the most shameless falsehoods against the representatives of the people. . . . I say, sir, a combination, a conspiracy against the Constitution, the government, the peace and safety of this country is formed and is in full operation. . . . Are these approaches to revolution and Jacobinic domination to be observed with the eye of meek submission?"[38]

The law consisted of four separate acts. Three of the acts pertained to aliens in the United States, while one act targeted seditious activity.[39] The first alien-related act was the "Naturalization Act," which remarkably extended the residency requirement for American citizenship from five to fourteen years.[40] This act was specifically intended to restrict a wide range of immigrants of

[35] Ibid., p. 505.
[36] Ibid.
[37] Ibid., p. 504.
[38] Allen speech in *Debates and Proceedings in the Congress of the United States,* 5th Congress, 2093-98; quoted in Brands, *Founding Partisans,* pp. 346-347.
[39] Boles, *Jefferson,* p. 289.
[40] Ibid.

different ethnicities from joining and voting for candidates of the Republican Party. As Jefferson scholar, John B. Boles writes, "This act rested on the Federalist assumption that most immigrants tended to become Republican supporters."[41]

The second alien-related act was titled, quite simply, the "Alien Act." This act provided the President of the United States with unbridled authority to deport any foreign resident whose political views were deemed a threat to the country. The act of course allowed for discretionary interpretation on the part of the president. The act was directly aimed at supporters of Thomas Jefferson. Any vocal or printed support for the Republican Party could conceivably be interpreted by President Adams as a threat to the safety of America.[42] Under this law, political supporters of Jefferson could be deported. Expressing his thoughts on the Alien Act, Jefferson said it reminded him of what one would find during the Dark Ages.[43]

The third act related to aliens was titled the "Alien Enemies Act." This act, which attracted some support in Congress from across the aisle, allowed for the arrest and deportation of individuals who were from a country that was at war with the United States.[44] Although the United States and France were not in a declared war with one another, it was clear that the act would allow for the deportation of French emigres should Congress declare war against France. The three alien acts were specifically intended to suppress the increasing strength of the party associated with Jefferson and which Madison was successfully cultivating and expanding.

Although the acts concerning aliens were designed as suppressive political measures against the Republican Party, it was the fourth act which proved to be the most harmful to supporters of Jefferson. The fourth act titled "The Sedition Act" allowed for the prosecution of individuals engaged in political organization intended to challenge and undermine the policies of the federal government. It also allowed for the prosecution of individuals who published information and points of view critical of the federal government.[45] According to this particular act, those engaged in such "seditious" activity would be treated as traitors to the United States.[46] As Boles put it, "Under these broad terms, federal officials, including the president, could harshly suppress all political opposition. . . .

---

[41] Ibid.
[42] Ibid.
[43] Ibid.
[44] Ibid., pp. 289-290.
[45] Ibid., p. 290.
[46] Ibid.

Nothing like the law had ever existed on the American scene, and its expiration date – the last day of Adams' term of office – revealed its blatantly partisan nature."[47]

The Kentucky and Virginia Resolutions

Madison and Jefferson, angered over the blatant attempt by the Adams administration to suppress their political party, decided that resistance to the Alien and Sedition Acts was not only required, but also their personal responsibility. The two decided that the best response would be to anonymously author a dual set of resolutions condemning the acts. Their resolutions would initially be sent to the legislatures of Kentucky and Virginia, with the hope that once their resolutions were passed by both assemblies that other states would follow and pass their resolutions. Jefferson, who apparently conceived of this plan, authored the "Kentucky Resolutions," while Madison authored the "Virginia Resolutions." Despite residing at his hilltop home in Virginia, Jefferson's choice of Kentucky was understandable, as the land that became the state of Kentucky in 1792 was originally a part of Virginia. Jefferson thus had a close association with several political leaders in Kentucky who had roots in Virginia. One of these political figures was a political ally in the Kentucky state legislature by the name of John Breckinridge.[48]

Rutland described their plan: "Their strategy was disarmingly simple. They would draft a protest and plan of action, send the documents to friends in the state legislatures of neighboring states, as well as to Richmond, and urge all states to join in a general protest of the Alien and Sedition law on the grounds of their unconstitutionality."[49] Because the Supreme Court was firmly under the control of Federalist Justices, Jefferson and Madison wisely chose to target state legislatures to generate resistance to the acts, rather than depend on the high court for support.[50]

Although this was a joint effort on the part of Jefferson and Madison, this is not to suggest that the arguments articulated against the acts mirrored one another. Jefferson drafted nine separate resolutions attacking the acts. His resolutions, as expected, were introduced in the Kentucky legislature by Breckinridge.[51]

---

[47] Ibid.
[48] Burstein and Isenberg, *Madison and Jefferson*, p. 337.
[49] Rutland, *James Madison*, p. 157.
[50] Ibid.
[51] John Murray Allison, *Adams and Jefferson* (Norman: University of Oklahoma Press, 1966), p. 189.

Jefferson's resolutions as expected were quickly approved.[52] His nine resolutions not only condemned the Alien and Sedition laws as direct infringements on civil liberties, but, quite astonishingly, he argued that a state had the right to nullify a federal law within its own borders.[53] Challenging the constitutionality of the Alien and Sedition Acts was understandable and justified, while arguing in print that a state legislature possessed the authority to nullify a federal law was, to put it mildly, a radical proposition. According to Jefferson's line of thinking, the United States Constitution was first and foremost a "compact" among the states which therefore allowed each state to determine if a federal law was constitutional and worthy of compliance. A state legislature, in Jefferson's view, could thus be the final arbiter of a federal law's constitutionality.[54] Examining Jefferson's nullification theory, Feldman points out that Jefferson was basing his argument in favor of nullification on international law, and how a country after entering into a foreign policy treaty retained the authority to withdraw from the treaty if the treaty was no longer perceived to be in the country's interest. "Jefferson was depicting the Constitution as nothing more than the treaty of a federation."[55] In Jefferson's view, states therefore retained the authority to nullify acts passed by Congress because Congress was "a creature of the compact" and thus subject to the "final judgment" of state governments.[56] The compact theory of government articulated by Jefferson would reemerge several years later in the writings of South Carolina Senator John Calhoun who, as Mark Graber notes, relied on Jefferson's resolutions to argue that federal laws could in fact be nullified by a state legislature. Southern lawmakers would use the compact theory first articulated by Jefferson to justify secession from the Union.[57] Needless to suggest, it is quite stunning to learn that Thomas Jefferson, rated as one of our nation's great Founders, would advocate such a divisive and radical theory of government.

Madison's resolutions were submitted to the Virginia state legislature in Richmond by the writer and pro-Jeffersonian theorist, John Taylor of Caroline.[58] Like Jefferson's resolutions in Kentucky, the Virginia state legislature voted to

---

[52] Feldman, *The Three Lives of James Madison*, p. 417.
[53] Ibid., p. 418.
[54] Ibid.
[55] Ibid.
[56] Jefferson to Madison, November 17, 1798, *Papers of James Madison, 17:179;* quoted in Feldman, *the Three Lives of James Madison*, p. 418.
[57] Mark Graber, "Compact Theory of the U.S. Constitution," Center for the Study of Federalism; online at encyclopedia.federalism.org/index.php. (Accessed January 23, 2024.)
[58] Rutland, *James Madison*, p. 157.

approve them. Madison's resolutions challenged the constitutionality of the Alien and Sedition Acts by depicting them as direct infringements on constitutional rights. As the author of the Bill of Rights, Madison, as expected, would express strong opposition to the suppressive laws sponsored by the Federalist Party. However, rather than posit as Jefferson did that acts of Congress could be nullified within the borders of an individual state, Madison argued instead that states had the right to "interpose" acts they found objectionable.[59] In Madison's view, a state could prevent the enforcement of the Alien and Sedition Acts under this doctrine, although he did not believe nor did he articulate Jefferson's view that nullification of federal law was permissible under the Constitution.

Madison's reluctance to support Jefferson's position on nullification was understandable. After all, it was Madison, not Jefferson, who was responsible for the structure and ratification of the Constitution. Moreover, Article VI of the Constitution, which Madison was intimately familiar with, clearly established the supremacy of federal laws over the states, providing such laws were based on the Constitution. Madison therefore was not about to follow Jefferson's line of thinking that the Constitution was a compact among the states, rather than a compact among the American people. One cannot help but wonder what Madison must have thought when he first laid eyes on the resolutions drafted by his mentor and fellow Virginian. Writing to Jefferson, and trying to be diplomatic, Madison suggested that the best approach for challenging the Alien and Sedition Acts would be to use "general expressions" of opposition, rather than advocating such extreme resistance.[60]

In the end, the resolutions authored by Jefferson and Madison were approved by the Kentucky and Virginia legislatures, although no other state legislature chose to approve them. Jefferson's radical resolutions resulted in official rejections by seven states, while three states strongly condemned them.[61] Perhaps to Jefferson's surprise, support for the Union was much stronger among state lawmakers than he apparently realized.

Resolutions calling for the nullification of federal laws could be viewed by the Federalist controlled government of John Adams as an act of sedition, or perhaps treason. The result could have led to Jefferson's arrest, prosecution and imprisonment. Had Jefferson not called for nullification, but instead supported "interpose" as Madison did, which was a softer form of opposition,

---

[59] Feldman, *The Three Lives of James Madison*, p. 420.

[60] Madison to Jefferson, December 29, 1799, Hunt, VI, 327-9; quoted in Ketcham, *James Madison*, p. 396.

[61] Feldman, *The Three Lives of James Madison*, p. 420.

then it was likely that additional state legislatures would have joined their effort to oppose the Alien and Sedition Acts. Madison's support for interposition was acceptable, but not Jefferson's call for nullification. Washington, now in the final year of his life, was particularly troubled by Jefferson's radical response to the acts. On January 15, 1799, Washington drafted a letter to Patrick Henry in which he expressed concern that if Jefferson's Kentucky Resolutions were approved by other states that this would "dissolve the Union or produce coercion."[62] With so much resistance to the Kentucky Resolutions, it was evident, as Feldman put it, that "Jefferson had overplayed his hand."[63]

The identity of who penned the Kentucky and Virginia Resolutions remained a mystery for many years. Whether or not persons familiar with Jefferson's and Madison's choice of words and style of writing suspected them of authoring the resolutions is difficult to determine. Rutland comments that it took ten years after the Virginia Resolutions had been adopted for Madison to be identified as their author, and twenty-one years after the Kentucky Resolutions had been passed for Jefferson to be credited with drafting them.[64]

Precisely how effective the Alien and Sedition Acts were with respect to suppressing the development of the Republican Party is difficult to gauge with absolute certainty, although specific and documented acts of suppression did occur. From the time of their passage in 1798 to when they were repealed in 1801, the historical record indicates that twenty-six individuals were prosecuted in federal court for violating the Sedition Act. Most of these individuals were associated with pro-Jeffersonian newspapers critical of the Adams administration.[65] One such instance of political suppression was the arrest, prosecution and four- month prison sentence handed down to Vermont Congressman, Matthew Lyon. Lyon was the publisher of a pro-Jefferson newspaper titled *The Scourge of Aristocracy and Repository of Important Political Truth.*[66] To think that a member of Congress was sent to prison for printing a newspaper critical of the president of an opposing party is difficult to fathom in light of the freedoms enshrined within the

---

[62] Washington to Henry, January 15, 1799, *Writings of Washington, XXXVII, 87-90*; quoted in Ketcham, *James Madison*, p. 397.
[63] Feldman, *The Three Lives of James Madison*, p. 420.
[64] Rutland, *James Madison,* p. 158.
[65] Editors, "Alien and Sedition Acts," History.com., June 21, 2003; online at history.com/early-us-alien-and-sedition-acts. (Accessed September 9, 2023.)
[66] Feldman, *The Three Lives of James Madison*, p. 421.

First Amendment to the Constitution. Yet that is what happened when the Federalist Party was in control of the federal government.

The Election of 1800

As previously noted, the Republican Party won control of the federal government in the historic election 1800. Jefferson won the presidency, while both chambers of Congress flipped from Federalist to Republican control. The presidential election was ultimately decided in the House of Representatives due to the fact that Thomas Jefferson and Aaron Burr each received the same number of electoral votes. This was before the parties created presidential and vice-presidential tickets to run against one another and before presidential electors were required to cast separate votes for president and vice president. In 1800, and in previous presidential elections, presidential electors cast two votes for president, with the runner up in the electoral college becoming the vice president. Thus with each Democratic-Republican elector casting two votes for president, Burr, rather than coming in second, which had been anticipated, tied with Jefferson in the electoral college. It thus fell to the House of Representatives, with each state's congressional delegation casting one vote, to decide the next President of the United States. On the thirty-sixth ballot, Jefferson was finally elected president, thus ending the stalemate. Richard Hofstadter notes that the election of 1800 was significant in two respects. First, it represented a peaceful transfer of power from one party to the next, thus setting a precedent for future transfers of power; and second, because no candidate won a majority of the electoral votes, the election had to be decided in the House of Representatives, a less than democratic way to elect the first democratic president.[67] (The House of Representatives would again elect the president in 1824.)

The first orders of business for the new Congress, now under the control of Jefferson's party, was to repeal three of the four Alien and Sedition Acts. The only act that was not repealed was the Alien Enemies Act, which has remained an enforceable federal law to this day.[68] With Jefferson elected to the presidency and both chambers of Congress now in the hands of the Republican Party, it was evident that Madison's diligent efforts related to building a strong political party in opposition to the Federalist Party had resulted in much success.

---

[67] The election of 1800 is a long story that involved intrigue and much maneuvering behind the scenes. For an extended discussion, see Hofstadter, *The Idea of a Party System*, pp.128-140.

[68] Editors, "Alien and Sedition Acts," History.com. (Accessed September, 2023.)

The Republican Party had not only challenged the Federalist Party for control of the government, but had now eclipsed the Federalist Party as the ruling party.

When the Republican Party gained control of the federal government with the election of 1800, James Madison was not a member of the Congress. He was back home at Montpelier overseeing his plantation and the duties assigned to his slaves. Now with his mentor as President of the United States and the party he built controlling Congress, there was little doubt that he would be recalled to public service. Thus, in 1801 as soon as Jefferson took office, he nominated Madison to serve as secretary of state. With Republicans occupying a majority of seats in the Senate, Madison's nomination was easily confirmed. Madison would not only be returning to public service, but he would now be in charge of American foreign policy. Bruce Chadwick offers this view of Jefferson's predictable appointment of Madison:

> Jefferson had brought Madison to Washington with him as his secretary of state because the men were close personal friends and cofounders of the Republican Party, but there were other reasons. No one understood the workings and promises of American government more than Madison. Madison knew everybody in government from his years of service in the House. He was a smooth and clever politician who could help Jefferson write legislation and get bills passed (he had been nicknamed 'The Big Knife' for his ability to cut through problematic areas and move legislation through the halls of Congress).[69]

The challenges Madison faced during his eight years as secretary of state are discussed in the following chapter.

---

[69] Bruce Chadwick, *James and Dolley Madison: America's First Power Couple,* (New York: Prometheus Books, 2014), p. 85.

Chapter Six

Madison as Secretary of State

Madison served as President Jefferson's secretary of state from March 5, 1801 to March 3, 1809, the entire time that Jefferson occupied the presidency. As Brant states, "Nobody was surprised when President Jefferson nominated James Madison for Secretary of State on March 5, 1801. The offer had been tentatively accepted long before the election, and only extreme partisans questioned its fitness."[1] Commenting on Madison's relationship with Jefferson, Brookhiser put it this way, "No member of a cabinet had been so close to a president; none perhaps ever would be again."[2] It was also evident given the prestige of the office he now occupied that Madison would be Jefferson's successor to the presidency. In light of Jefferson's path to the presidency, it was becoming clear that the cabinet post of secretary of state would be the training ground for future presidents.

Madison's trip to the new federal city to assume his post was anything but pleasant. Rutland describes the difficult trip, "Heavy rains made the roads resemble quagmires ... and the trip was one mudhole after another."[3] Although the federal city, officially named Washington, D.C., had been meticulously designed by the acclaimed civil engineer Pierre Charles L'Enfant, the capital city when the Madisons arrived was nothing like the city that exists in contemporary times. Brookhiser describes the condition of the city, "The presidential mansion was a finished building, on the outside, at any rate, though the grounds were filled with the detritus of ongoing construction. The Capitol, a mile and a half away on a small hill was just begun. There were a few boardinghouses, a handful of shops

---

1. Irving Brant, *James Madison: Secretary of State 1800-1809* (New York: The Bobbs Merrill Co. Inc., 1953), p. 35.
2. Brookhiser, *James Madison,* p. 148.
3. Rutland, *James Madison*, p. 169.

and taverns, and a scattering of private homes (many of them built on spec). The roads were unpaved paths."[4]

Not long after their arrival, the Madison home under the direction of Dolley, his energetic, socially savvy, and politically astute wife, was thoroughly renovated and eventually became, as Ketcham writes, "one of the bright gathering places of the new Federal City during the eight years the Madisons lived in it."[5] Dolley proved to be quite the political spouse and hostess, often organizing social engagements with a wide range of important officials and their wives. The gatherings were intended to bolster opinions of not only herself, but also the political career of her husband, who she affectionately referred to as the "great little Madison." Cost describes Dolley as "one of the great female politicians of the nineteenth century, so capable was she at managing the social levers of political power."[6] Feldman notes that Dolley not only organized social engagements at her own house, but because Jefferson was a widower, "she presided when Jefferson held mixed-sex dinners."[7] Social interaction however never came natural to her husband, who was on the reserved and slightly shy side. For Dolley, however, managing and participating in social events was her "greatest skill."[8] Chadwick describes Dolley as "gorgeous, socially oriented, very friendly, and at ease with men and women of any background, and she was a great conversationalist. . . . She was completely in charge of meals, social events, receptions and an army of servants."[9]

Madison's house, only a few blocks from the White House, or what President John Adams referred to as "The President's House," was where the Madison family resided.[10] In 1801, the State Department consisted of several cramped buildings near the "President's House" and employed eight clerks, several of whom had worked for the State Department during the Adams administration. Madison decided to keep most of them in their present positions, rather than replace them with clerks drawn from his own party.[11]

When he first began his duties as secretary of state in 1801, there was nothing of pressing significance that required bold and difficult decisions. Most of Madison's initial duties were relatively mundane, labor intensive, and concerned

---

[4] Brookhiser, *James* Madison, p. 147.
[5] Ketcham, *James Madison*, p. 409.
[6] Cost, *James Madison*, p. 277.
[7] Feldman, *The Three Lives of James Madison*, p. 445.
[8] Ibid.
[9] Chadwick, *James and Dolley Madison*, p. 87.
[10] Cost, *James Madison*. pp. 276-277.
[11] Ketcham, pp. 409-410.

routine domestic and foreign policy matters; nothing that rose to the level of a major foreign policy decision.[12] Issuing reports to Congress, writing memoranda to governors and judges, filing official documents, and meetings with foreign ministers assigned to embassies in the nation's new capital were among Madison's duties.[13] Overseeing the appointment of ministers and consuls who had been appointed to posts in foreign countries was also one of Madison's most immediate concerns when he first took office.[14]

Even though much of Madison's initial work was mundane and bureaucratic, his excessive commitment to detail and the amount of time he devoted to every task weighed heavily on his health.[15] To further complicate Madison's health, the humidity in the federal city during the summer months was stifling. To escape the oppressive heat, Madison had to leave the city for the cooler mountains of central Virginia.[16] Despite Madison's penchant for thoroughness and precision, those who worked under him at the State Department found him to be an accommodating and fair-minded administrator. He was not condescending, nor was he an abusive department head. The U.S. State Department under Madison's leadership functioned within an atmosphere of trust and respect.[17] Although many of Madison's duties were primarily administrative when he first began his duties, it did not take long for myriad and complex issues to emerge. Most of these issues would test Madison's leadership skills, his political experience, and his foresight.

Judicial Commissions

As briefly discussed in the preceding chapter, the election of 1800 is regarded as a watershed election in the annals of American elections. Indeed, it was this election in which the Republican Party dislodged the Federalist Party as the ruling party of the federal government. It was also a unique historical event, as the power of one party passed to a competitive party in a peaceful, rather than a violent, fashion. This established a tradition which has remained a part of American politics to this day, with the one exception being the election of 2020 when supporters of the losing candidate stormed the nation's Capitol on January 6, 2021 to prevent the official counting and certification of electoral votes.

As part of the American political tradition, there is a transition period that occurs between the party that is coming to power and the party that is

---

[12] Ibid.
[13] Ibid.
[14] Burstein and Isenberg, *Madison and Jefferson*, p. 369.
[15] Cost, *James Madison*, p. 275.
[16] Burstein and Isenberg, *Madison and Jefferson*, p. 369.
[17] Ibid., p. 369-370.

relinquishing control of the government. In the aftermath of Jefferson's election in 1800, President John Adams, recognizing that his party would no longer occupy the presidency or control the Congress, decided that the federal judiciary would be the one branch of the federal government where the values and policies of the Federalist Party could still be preserved. Thus, to build a firewall against Jefferson's party, Adams decided to pack the federal courts with judges loyal to the Federalist Party. To achieve this blatantly partisan goal, the Federalist controlled Congress, which was now a lame duck Congress, passed The Judiciary Act of 1801 that authorized sixteen new federal circuit court judgeships.[18] Additionally forty-two justices of the peace positions for the District of Columbia were created with passage of the District of Columbia Organic Act. As Harold H. Burton, Associate Justice of the U.S. Supreme Court notes, "the Federalists had concentrated their hopes for the survival of the Republic upon the federal judiciary."[19] Because the judgeships for the justices of the peace were created and confirmed by the Senate only days and in some instances hours before Adams left office, several of these judges became knowns as the "midnight appointees."[20]

Whenever a federal judge is appointed, the constitutional procedure involves three distinct steps: First, the president nominates an individual for the judgeship. Second, the Senate reviews and confirms the nominee. Third, the confirmed individual is then delivered a commission, which finalizes the appointment. Those judges named to the federal circuit courts by Adams received their commissions on time, along with a majority of those individuals named as justices of the peace. However, because time had expired, four individuals who despite being nominated by Adams and despite being confirmed by the Senate for the justice of the peace positions never received their commissions. One such individual was William Marbury.[21] There simply had not been enough time for Adams' secretary of the state, John Marshall, to deliver all of the justice of the peace commissions before Jefferson took office.

When James Madison replaced John Marshall as secretary of state, he learned that Marbury and three other justice of the peace nominees had never received their judicial commissions. Because there was little love between the Federalists and the Republicans, despite the peaceful transfer of power, Madison, with

---

[18] Cheney, *The Virginia Dynasty*, p. 221.

[19] Harold H. Burton, "The Cornerstone of Constitutional Law: The Extraordinary Case of Marbury v. Madison," *American Bar Association Journal,* Vol. 36, No. 10 (October 1950), p. 805; online at https://www.jstor.org/stable/257399 (Accessed March 31, 2024.)

[20] Ibid. p. 806.

[21] Ibid.

Jefferson's blessing, chose not to deliver the remaining judicial commissions. This provided Jefferson with the opportunity to fill the vacant judgeships with members of his own party. Madison's decision not to deliver the judicial commissions resulted in a lawsuit waged by William Marbury against the Jefferson administration. Marbury was the plaintiff, while Madison, representing the Jefferson administration, was named the defendant.

Marbury was represented by Charles Lee. Lee had served as Attorney General under President Adams.[22] Lee based his lawsuit on Section 13 of the Judiciary Act of 1789 that authorized the Supreme Court to issue writs of mandamus to public officials instructing them to perform and carry out their official duties. It was Lee's contention that the Supreme Court should use this statutory authority to issue a writ of mandamus to Secretary of State James Madison instructing him to perform his public duty and deliver Marbury's judicial commission. The Supreme Court at the time consisted of six Federalist Justices. Four of the Justices had been appointed by President Washington and two by President Adams.[23] Jefferson and Madison anticipated a ruling that reflected partisan considerations.

The case *Marbury v. Madison* was heard and decided by the Supreme Court in 1803.[24] It is not who won or lost this case that makes the *Marbury* case historically significant. Instead, the significance of the case lies in the ruling issued by Chief Justice John Marshall who, upon reviewing how this case was brought to the Supreme Court, concluded that Congress by passing Section 13 of the Judiciary Act of 1789 authorizing the Supreme Court, to issue writs of mandamus to public officials had unconstitutionally expanded the Court's original jurisdiction. In Marshall's view, the Supreme Court's original jurisdiction was fixed in Article III of the Constitution and could not in any way be expanded by a simple act of Congress, which Section 13 had done. In Marshall's view, Section 13 was altering, in this instance expanding, the Court's constitutional authority. Marshall therefore deemed Section 13 of the Judiciary Act of 1789 to be in violation of the separation of powers doctrine as established in the Constitution.[25]

Commenting on the political dimensions of the ruling, Justice Burton notes, "The Court thus created no immediate conflict between the Executive and Judicial Branches of the Government. It thus decided the case in favor of Madison and

[22] Ibid.
[23] Ibid., p. 805.
[24] *Marbury* v. *Madison* 5 U.S. (1 Cranch) 137 2 L. Ed. 66 (1803)
[25] Ibid.

thus made it difficult for the Administration to object strenuously to the result."[26]The Supreme Court's ruling in *Marbury v. Madison* was the first time that a law passed by Congress was declared unconstitutional by the U.S. Supreme Court. The ruling stablished a lasting precedent known as *judicial review*. As a result of this ruling, courts in the United States have the authority to declare legislative acts unconstitutional; a unique feature of the American legal system.

Although there was nothing that Madison actually did to influence the Supreme Court's ruling, other than refusing to deliver Marbury's commission and being named as a party in the case, the fact of the matter is that such a ruling may never have been issued had Madison delivered Marbury's commission. Madison was therefore instrumental in what arguably is regarded as the most important Supreme Court ruling in the history of the United States. What Madison thought of this ruling, as Lynne Cheney comments, has never been recorded. It is unlikely, however, that Madison agreed with the precedent set by Marshall. Cheney reminds readers that Madison's Virginia Plan, which proposed a Council of Revision consisting of both the executive and judiciary with the authority to review and approve legislation, did not authorize the Council to declare laws unconstitutional. [27]

The Barbary Wars

Although most of Madison's public service prior to becoming secretary of state was related to domestic policy making, he was by no means a total novice in the field of foreign affairs. As Brant writes, "Madison had been initiated into diplomacy as a youth of twenty-nine in the Continental Congress. There, his activity in committees gave him the function of a foreign secretary before one existed."[28] Moreover, when Madison was as a member of the United States Congress from 1789-1797, he strongly supported the commercial activity of American merchant ships and was intimately familiar with complex issues pertaining to foreign trade.[29] Madison was thus prepared to lead the country in the area of foreign affairs and prepared to handle virtually any foreign crisis that threatened American interests.

Madison's first major crisis involved hostile action against American ships by countries located along the coastal regions of North Africa, a region known as the Barbary Coast. The countries, all of which were part of the sprawling Ottoman

---

[26] Burton, "The Cornerstone of Constitutional law," p. 881.
[27] Cheney, *James Madison,* pp. 312-313.
[28] Brant, *James Madison: Secretary of State 1800-1809*, p. 35.
[29] Ibid,

Empire, included Tripoli, Tunis, Algiers and Morocco. For several years, pirates from the Barbary countries with the support of their governments had been seizing American ships and American sailors. Seizures were followed with ransom demands for their return.[30] "Forced to do backbreaking slave labor, the prisoners were punished with the infamous bastinado, one hundred blows to the feet for even minor offenses."[31]

By 1801, the first year of the Jefferson presidency, the problem with the Barbary countries had become more serious than acts of piracy. The ruler of Tripoli, known as the "Bashaw" announced that his country was willing to wage war against the United States if the Jefferson administration refused to provide his country with payments for American use of the waters off the Barbary Coast. To further provoke the United States, the Bashaw, "on May 14, 1801, ordered the American flagpole chopped down as the symbol of a formal declaration."[32]

Rather than acquiesce to the Bashaw's demands, Jefferson, with the full support of his cabinet and Congress, ordered a squadron of naval ships to begin patrolling the Mediterranean with orders to destroy any hostile ship associated with the Barbary countries. "The captain of the American squadron carried clear instructions: to fight any or all of the Barbary States if they should declare war; and to safeguard commerce and 'chastise their insolence – by sinking, burning or destroying their ships' wherever they might be found."[33] That is exactly what the American navy did during Jefferson's first term of office. As Boles notes, the American navy, although small at the time, "plied the warm waters of the Mediterranean, sailing from victory to victory."[34]

From the very start of the crisis, Madison, as secretary of state, supported bold and decisive naval action against the Barbary countries. In Madison's view, a strong display of naval power against Tripoli and other Barbary powers would send a message of American strength, '"the object openly declared to every nation.'"[35] Although Levi Lincoln, Jefferson's attorney general, raised legitimate constitutional concerns about Jefferson's warlike decision in the absence of formal congressional approval, Madison, along with treasury secretary Albert Gallatin, strongly favored an unrestrained military response.[36] Madison's support

---

[30] Boles, *Jefferson*, p. 348.
[31] Burstein and Isenberg, *Madison and Jefferson*, p. 403.
[32] Rutland, *James Madison,* p. 174.
[33] Burstein and Isenberg, *Madison and Jefferson*, p. 403.
[34] Boles, *Jefferson,* p. 349.
[35] Cabinet notes, 15 May 1801, Ford, *Writings*, 1:294; *q*uoted in Rutland, *James Madison*, p. 174.
[36] Burstein and Isenberg, *Madison and Jefferson*, pp.403-404.

for American power to resolve the Barbary conflict set a precedent for future secretaries of state. The Tripolitan War, as Burstein and Isenberg note, "officially ended in 1805, when a combined sea and land offensive brought the prostrate ruler to terms."[37]

The successful use of American force in an international conflict, which involved both the American navy and marines, had long-term benefits with respect to perceptions of American power, "Putting Tripoli in its place gave America an upper hand in diplomacy, not just in the Mediterranean but also on the Continent, where it counted most."[38] Credit is attributed to President Jefferson for confronting the Barbary powers with military force and for securing the free passage of American ships off the coast of Africa. Yet there can be little doubt that Madison in his capacity as secretary of state was deeply involved in this historic conflict, thus elevating the international prestige of the United States.

Madison endorsed and understood the international benefits of a strong American navy. As a member of the Continental Congress and as a member of the Virginia House of Delegates, Madison had acquired knowledge about the Barbary pirates. He was cognizant of how detrimental their actions were to commercial intercourse.[39] John F. Schifalacqua writes, "The fact that Madison included issues concerning piracy, the institution of a navy, and commerce as justification for the Constitution in the *The Federalist Papers* suggests he was well aware of the connection between a robust free trade sustained by a national government and problems of piracy in the Atlantic world."[40]

The Louisiana Purchase

During his first term as secretary of state, Madison despite his admiration for the French Revolution, regarded the threat to the United States posed by Napoleon Bonaparte, who had gained control of France following the Revolution, as pressing and urgent. Madison's, concern involved the vast Louisiana territory, which included the port city of New Orleans. France, having lost Canada to Britain in the French and Indian War and fearing that it would also lose the Louisiana Territory to the British, transferred ownership of New Orleans and the territory to Spain, which at the time was an ally of France. It was the 1762 *Treaty*

---

[37] Ibid., p. 405.
[38] Ibid., p. 407.
[39] John F. Schifalacqua, "James Madison and America's First Encounter with Islam: James Madison's Engagement with Barbary Affairs Through the 1st Barbary War," *Penn History Review*, Vol. 21, Issue 1 (2014), p. 118; online at papers.ssrn.com. (Accessed March 2, 2024.)
[40] Ibid.

of Fontainebleau that officially transferred France's ownership to Spain. Elizabeth Clark Neidenbach states, "The secret treaty was made amid negotiations between Great Britain and the allied powers of France and Spain to end the Seven Years War (1756-1763). Together with the 1763 Treaty of Paris, which concluded the war, the Treaty of Fountainebleau reorganized colonial North America."[41]

However, under the potential military threat of Napoleon, Spain in 1800 signed another treaty with France that returned New Orleans and the Louisiana Territory to French control. As Charles Chamberlain and his coauthors note, "Even as Spanish Louisiana began to thrive, Spain itself was deeply troubled. Increasingly subject to the influence of France's new leader, Napoleon Bonaparte, Spain agreed in October 1800 to give Louisiana back to France in the secret Treaty of San Ildefonso."[42] In return, France gave Tuscany, a small European kingdom, which is now a city in central Italy, to Spain.[43]

Napoleon, who in 1804 would declare himself Emperor of France, viewed the Louisiana Territory as central to his imperialist ambitions. After having conquered much of Europe, Napoleon's hope, according to Gutzman "was to make New Orleans the center of a revivified French North American empire."[44] Cost observes that Napoleon considered the Louisiana Territory as the "breadbasket for his future West Indian conquests."[45]

Both Madison and Jefferson were deeply troubled by Napoleon's potential military presence on North American soil. They both feared that American national security and commerce would be threatened with the French military in control of New Orleans. Spain was never a major concern for Jefferson and Madison, but France under Napoleon's rule was. The port city of New Orleans in particular was extremely important for American commerce. Several thousand ships, approximately half of which were owned by American companies, passed in and out of this strategic port every year.[46] Madison, knew that dealing with Napoleon would be difficult, as evident from a letter he received from Robert Livingston, the American Minister to France. Livingston described the French Emperor as never open to constructive advice, egotistical and autocratic.[47]

---

[41] Elizabeth Clark Neidenbach, "Treaty of Fountainebleau," online at 64parishes.org. (Accessed November 7, 2023.)
[42] Charles Chamberlain, Lo Faber, and Lee Smith, "Spanish Colonial Louisiana," online at 64parishes.org (Accessed November 7, 2023.)
[43] Ibid.
[44] Gutzman, *James Madison*, p. 289.
[45] Cost, *James Madison*, p. 281.
[46] Ibid.
[47] Ibid.

Due to their concern with Napoleon's presence in New Orleans, Jefferson and Madison moved ahead with their plan to buy New Orleans from France. They persuaded James Monroe, who had just finished serving as Virginia's governor and who both Jefferson and Madison regarded as trustworthy, to travel to France as a special envoy for the purpose of persuading Napoleon to sell New Orleans to the United States. A challenging task indeed, although Jefferson and Madison knew that Monroe, more than any other public servant, possessed the diplomatic skills necessary to forge a deal with Napoleon.

Although Livingston was the Minister to France, it was Monroe's negotiating skills and his experience as a former Minister to France that would prove beneficial in his meetings with the French Emperor. According to McGrath, "Monroe spent several weeks meeting with Jefferson, Madison and French chargé Louis-Andre Pichon. He wanted every possible piece of information that would allow him to succeed in his mission . . . "[48] Monroe was also informed by Jefferson and Madison that if he succeeded in securing New Orleans from Napoleon, he would be named "minister extraordinary and plenipotentiary to Spain" with the goal of persuading Spain to sell the Florida territory to the United States. "Madison provided him with the appropriate letters for each country, the complete proposal to buy both New Orleans and Florida, and authorization to spend up to 30 million liras (roughly $5.6 million) for their acquisition."[49]

Much to Monroe's surprise, however, by the time he arrived in France, Napoleon had already decided that he wanted to sell not only New Orleans to the United States, but also the entire Louisiana Territory. The French Emperor's position was influenced by a massive slave rebellion on the French controlled island of Santo Domingo, an island in the Caribbean that today is known as Haiti. The rebellion was led by Toussaint L'Overture, who had been a slave on one of the island's plantations.[50] Despite a massive military attempt to crush the rebellion, the French were unsuccessful and suffered heavy losses. With French forces defeated, not only due to the effective guerilla tactics of the slaves in revolt, but also due to a deadly yellow fever that swept the island killing many French soldiers, including Napoleon's own brother-in-law General Charles LeClerc, Napoleon decided that his imperialist ambitions in North America, which depended on control over the West Indies, were no longer worth the effort.[51] As Cost notes, Napoleon decided to "cut his losses" and gave up on the idea of

[48] Tim McGrath, *James Monroe* (New York: Dutton, 2020), p. 226.
[49] Ibid., p. 227.
[50] Cost, *James Madison*, p. 283.
[51] Ibid.

creating a New France.[52] Moreover, and much to the astonishment of Monroe and Livingston, Napoleon offered to sell both New Orleans and the entire Louisiana Territory for $15 million. Monroe quickly agreed to the deal. Brookhiser captures the significance of this historic purchase, "With a few signatures, the United States nearly doubled in size. There had not been such a stupendous windfall since the treaty that ended the American Revolution, and this spurt of national growth had been accomplished without firing a shot."[53] Because the United States at the time did not have the revenue to pay for Napoleon's asking price, the Jefferson administration turned to Barings Bank of London and Hopes of Amsterdam for financial assistance. With the much needed assistance from Barings and Hopes, the American government was able to complete the deal.[54]

There can be little doubt that Madison, although not appointed as the point man for the negotiations, was involved in every facet of this historic purchase. He surely had persuaded Jefferson to select Monroe as the special envoy, and he must have recognized how important it was for the United States to acquire New Orleans for shipping and trade. He had also understood how important the Louisiana Territory was for the economic expansion of the United States. Jefferson and Monroe are the two who receive credit for this extraordinary land purchase, but Madison was surely behind the scenes from the very start of what became known as "The Louisiana Purchase." France officially transferred the Louisiana Territory including New Orleans to the United States on December 20, 1803. Cost notes that because Napoleon had viewed the Jefferson administration and the Republican Party as having favorable views towards France, that he would have been less likely to transact this sale had it been a pro-British Federalist administration negotiating the deal.[55]

There was however a surprise that awaited Jefferson and Madison once Monroe finalized the deal. Both had thought that the deal had included not only New Orleans and the Louisiana Territory but also a portion of Florida known as "West Florida." Brookhiser states, "New Orleans and Florida had been their maximum goal; even though they had won so much more, they still wanted all of what they had originally desired. And, for little more reason than their wanting it, they believed they had actually gotten it."[56] The situation with the Floridas was a complicated situation, which is why there was confusion when New Orleans and

---

[52] Ibid.
[53] Brookhiser, *James Madison*, p. 157.
[54] "The Louisiana Purchase," online at baringsarchive.org.uk/exhibition/the-louisian-purchase/ (Accessed June 27, 2024.)
[55] Cost, *James Madison,* p. 283.
[56] Brookhiser, *James Madison*, p. 158.

the Louisiana Territory was purchased. Spain, not France, owned West Florida. The Louisiana Purchase therefore did not include Spain's possession.

The Yazoo Scandal

At approximately the same time that Madison was setting his sights on acquiring New Orleans from Napoleon, a land scandal surfaced which involved the state of Georgia. So troubling were the revelations that Jefferson appointed a three member commission to investigate and resolve the problem. The commission consisted of Secretary of State Madison, Treasury Secretary Albert Gallatin and Attorney General Levi Lincoln. Madison, the most senior cabinet officer, was selected to head the commission.[57] As of 1802, Georgia was the only state that had retained its original land claims that extended into western territory, what today are the states of Alabama and Mississippi.[58] Why Georgia still retained its western land claims is related to a scandal that began several years earlier.

On January 7, 1795, with passage of the Yazoo Land Act, the state of Georgia sold thirty-five million acres to four companies involved in land speculation. The land was sold for the incredibly low price of $500,000.[59] But only one year after the sale, the Georgia legislature, which had now fallen under the control of reform- minded Republicans, voided the transactions by passing the 1796 Rescinding Act. The Act reclaimed the land for the state of Georgia.[60] The reason for reclaiming the land was due to a startling revelation: every Georgia state lawmaker, with only one exception, had been bribed by the land companies.[61] According to Jane Elsmere, "Members of both the Senate and House of Representatives in the legislature of Georgia were especially interested in the sale of the Yazoo lands. It seemed that every legislator, with the exception of Robert Watkins, was issued shares in one or more companies or else was offered some other inducements in return for his vote in passing the Act authorizing the sale of the land."[62] In fact the bribery scheme extended well beyond state lawmakers. George Lamplugh notes, "To bring off this coup, the leader of the Yazoo land

---

[57] Gutzman, *James Madison,* p. 291.

[58] Ibid.

[59] George R. Lamplugh, "Yazoo Land Fraud," *New Georgia Encyclopedia*, originally published September 12, 2002; last edited June 8, 2017; online at georgiaencyclopedia.org/articles/history-archeology/yazoo-land-fraud/ (Accessed, October 2, 2023.)

[60] Ibid.

[61] Brookhiser, *James Madison,* p. 151.

[62] Jane Elsmere, "The Notorious Yazoo Land Fraud Case," *The Georgia Historical Quarterly*, Vol. 51., No. 4. (December, 1967) p. 426; online at https://www.jstor.org/stable/40578730/ (Accessed October 3, 2023.)

speculators, the Federalist U.S. Senator James Gunn, distributed money to legislators, state officials, newspaper editors, and many other influential land-hungry Georgians."[63] Much to the chagrin of those who bought land from the land companies, the land which they thought they now owned was reclaimed by the state of Georgia. Due to the bribery revelations, the original land transactions were voided. A number of individuals who had purchased land from the land companies were from the New England states.[64]

With bribery confirmed and now made public, the scandal became known as the "Yazoo Scandal," as the land that had been bought by speculators and sold to investors was in "Yazoo country," named after the Yazoo River that flowed through the area and which joined the Mississippi River.[65] Following the land reclamation, legal complications emerged involving several different parties who had claims on the land: the Georgia legislature with the Rescinding Act claimed that the millions of acres that had been "sold" to land companies now belonged to the state; the land companies that bought land from the state, despite the fact that lawmakers and many others were bribed, objected to the state's reclamation of the land and claimed that the land was still theirs; those who bought land from the companies also claimed rightful ownership; the federal government also claimed that it owned the land, not the state of Georgia; and Native Americans with tribal settlements in "Yazoo country," which included, the "Creek, Cherokee, Choctaw and Chickasaw" nations, regarded the land as belonging to them, rather than the state of Georgia.[66]

Madison, heading the commission appointed by Jefferson and recognizing the extreme complexity of the land claims, decided that the appropriate solution would be to ask Georgia to cede the land to the federal government for the price of $1,250,000.[67] Because the price was appealing, Georgia agreed to the offer and ceded the land to the federal government. Of the thirty-five million acres acquired by the federal government, the commission agreed to use five million of the acres to resolve the numerous land claims.[68] With the federal government in possession of the land, Madison, Gallatin and Lincoln began to handle the claims of the aggrieved parties, although, as Burstein and Isenberg point out, "no party was entirely happy with the result."[69] Federal intervention to resolve the Yazoo

---

63 Lamplugh, "Yazoo Land Fraud"
64 Gutzman, *James Madison*, p. 291.
65 Brookhiser, *James Madison,* 151.
66 Ibid.
67 Gutzman, *James Madison*, p. 292.
68 Cheney, *James Madison*, p. 324.
69 Burstein and Isenberg, *Madison and Jefferson*, p. 415.

Scandal was certainly a bold plan, but one which Madison believed was not only the most practical solution, but also strategic for the purpose of expanding the country. New states, in his view, could be created from the land ceded by Georgia[70]

Gutzman notes that while Gallatin was the real architect of this plan, it was Madison who was viewed as the plan's originator. As a result, it was Madison who would bear the brunt of criticism from those who viewed the plan as an affront to states' rights. Chief among the critics of the federal government's intervention was John Randolph, the chairman of the Ways and Means Committee in the U.S. House of Representatives. Randolph, from Roanoke, Virginia, was Jefferson's cousin and a former House majority leader. A staunch Republican and firm believer in states' rights, Randolph was furious over Madison's blatant dependence on the federal government to resolve a scandal that should have been left to the state of Georgia to resolve. Gutzman states, "Not Jefferson. Nor Gallatin, but Madison was the target of Randolph's ire."[71] Randolph's attack on Madison was not only centered on Madison's federal solution, but he also tried in vain to link Madison to the land scandal itself, which was reckless and absurd. "Yazooism" became the term associated with the scandal, with Randolph fanning the flames to discredit the integrity and reputation of James Madison. Randolph not only alienated Jefferson and Madison with his claims, but also succeeded in driving a wedge between many Republican House members.[72] Spivak describes Randolph's polarizing behavior in this manner: "Randolph's extreme opposition to administration policies was destroying his political significance as it elevated his stature among his band of loyalists. His penetrating criticisms were always uncompromising, sarcastic, directed against what he perceived to be assignable villainy behind objectionable policy, and usually public."[73]

In his treatment of the Yazoo Scandal, Donald A. MacPhee identifies Randolph's fierce opposition to the government's handling of the Yazoo scandal as contributing to the emergence of the "Tertium Quids," a faction within the Republican Party firmly opposed to the policies of Jefferson and Madison.[74] MacPhee notes, "The 'Quids' have indeed often been called the first third-party

[70] Gutzman, *James Madison*, p. 292.

[71] Ibid.

[72] Rutland, *James Madison*, p. 177.

[73] Burton Spivak, *Jefferson's English Crisis: Commerce, Embargo, and the Republican Revolution* (Charlottesville: University Press of Virginia, 1979), p. 43.

[74] Donald A. MacPhee, "The Yazoo Controversy: The Beginning of the 'Quid' Revolt," *The Georgia Historical Quarterly*, Vol. 49, No. 1 (March, 1965) p. 23; online at https://www.jstor.org/stable/40578441. (Accessed November 1, 2023.)

movement in the United States."[75] Despite splitting the party and angering many, Randolph nevertheless succeeded in terminating the bold plan favored by Madison and his commission. According to Cost, "Randolph was aghast at this egregious expansion of federal authority, killed the deal in the House, and blamed Madison for the heresy."[76]

Randolph's decision to kill the deal did not however put an end to the Yazoo Scandal, as several years later the United State Supreme Court would hear a case involving a parcel of land that had been purchased in Yazoo country after the controversial sale had been rescinded by the state of Georgia. The case was *Fletcher v. Peck* decided by the Marshall Court in 1810.[77] In brief, John Peck had bought land in the "Yazoo" and after several years of ownership sold the land to Robert Fletcher. Fletcher, after purchasing the land, claimed that Peck did not have the legal right to sell this parcel of land because the original land sales had been voided by the Rescinding Act of 1796 when the bribes were discovered. Because Georgia had voided the original land sales, Fletcher claimed that Peck did not have legal ownership of the land and thus the sale was a "breach of contract." Fletcher's lawsuit eventually found its way to the U.S. Supreme Court where Fletcher's lawyer argued that the contract between himself and Peck should be ruled null and void because the land sale was illegitimate to begin with.[78] Yet despite the nefarious activity associated with the land sale, the Supreme Court issued a unanimous ruling in favor of Peck. Writing for the court's unanimous decision, Chief Justice John Marshall ruled that Georgia's 1796 law rescinding the land sales was in violation of the Contract Clause in Article I Section 10 of the U.S. Constitution. Private contracts, according to Marshall were binding regardless of circumstances. By declaring Georgia's 1796 Rescinding Act a violation of the Constitution, the Supreme Court in *Fletcher v. Peck* not only upheld the sanctity of private contracts, but extended the Court's power of judicial review over state laws.[79]

The "Floridas"

Madison and Jefferson, as previously noted, had their eyes on acquiring the region of Florida which was divided into West and East Florida. West Florida was the region which they thought had been included in the Louisiana Purchase. But

---

[75] Ibid.

[76] Cost, *James Madison*, p. 297.

[77] *Fletcher v. Peck* 10 U.S. 87 (1810)

[78] Fletcher v. Peck 10 U.S. 87 (1810) summarized online at oyez.www.oyez.org/cases/1789-1950/1ous87 (Accessed October 10, 2023.).

[79] Ibid.

despite still belonging to Spain, Madison continued to view the acquisition of both West and East Florida as a worthwhile goal.

The Florida peninsula was originally colonized by Spain in 1565. St. Augustine was the location where the Spanish military chose to begin their country's colonization of the region.[80] Despite conflicts with Native Americans and English colonists from the north, the colony located on the Florida peninsula remained valuable to Spain for the purpose of rescuing Spanish ships in distress and also to combat pirates interfering with Spain's commercial trade.[81] At the same time, Florida was also viewed by Spain as a strategic location to convert Native Americans to Catholicism. The Spanish monarchy and the Catholic Church heavily subsidized all facets of the colony's activities. To spread Catholicism, the Catholic Church had deployed a number of missionaries to the peninsula.[82] But Spain's allegiance with France during the French and Indian War proved to be an unwise alliance that resulted in the transfer of the Floridas when Britain ultimately defeated France. British control over Florida was formalized with the first Treaty of Paris in 1763.[83] British control over Florida however was short-lived, as only twenty-years later when the American colonies had achieved their independence from Britain, Florida was returned to Spain with the Second Treaty of Paris in 1783; the treaty which officially ended the American Revolution.[84]

Thus, it was Spain that had control over the Floridas when Washington was elected in 1789, when Adams was elected in 1796, and when Jefferson was elected in 1800. Because Jefferson and Madison were under the impression, albeit the wrong impression, that the western portion of Florida was included in the Louisiana Purchase, they both remained committed to acquiring West Florida, and possibly all of Florida, for the United States. The acquisition of Florida from Spain was among Madison's priorities during his years as secretary of state.

According to Ketcham, Madison's approach to acquiring Florida was to employ a "carrot and stick" strategy that in the end would strongly persuade Spain to sell the Floridas to the United States.[85] Writing to the American minister in

---

[80] Patrick J. Kiger, "How St. Augustine Became the First Permanent European Settlement in America," Updated August 29, 2023; history.com. (Accessed October 19, 2023.)
[81] Ibid.
[82] Ibid.
[83] "The U.S. acquires Spanish Florida," online@ history.com. (Accessed October 19, 2023.)
[84] Ibid.
[85] Ketcham, *James Madison*, p. 423.

Spain, Madison urged him to notify the Spanish monarch that not only was there a possibility that Britain would eventually seize the Floridas from Spain, which of course would not be in Spain's interest, but that relations with the United States could potentially become hostile should Spain refuse to cede the Floridas to the United States. "Protected by good relations with Britain and France, Madison adopted a firm, even arrogant attitude toward the weak and declining giant of the new world. He never doubted that all of Florida would some day be part of the United States, and he never doubted that despotic, corrupt Spain was unfit to possess it. This was manifest destiny. As long as he was in public office, Madison maintained a steady sometimes aggressive posture on Florida."[86] With two regions comprising the Floridas, Madison believed that West Florida could likely be acquired first followed by the acquisition of East Florida.[87]

Despite Madison's efforts to acquire the Floridas, the region remained under the control of Spain's government throughout his tenure as secretary of state. However, in 1810, when Madison was president, a rebellion among American settlers against Spanish control occurred in West Florida, which set in motion a series of events that eventually resulted in American control over the territory.[88] Although a meeting was arranged between Madison's secretary of state, James Monroe, and Spain's foreign minister, Don Luis de Onis, to negotiate the American acquisition of the Floridas, it still took several additional years before the United States would legally own all of Florida. Acquisition of the two Floridas, would finally be achieved under the presidency of James Monroe. Monroe's scretary of state, John Quincy Adams, closed the deal with the signing of the Adams-Onis Treaty in 1819.[89] "Minister Onis and Secretary Adams reached an agreement whereby Spain ceded East Florida to the United States and renounced all claims to West Florida."[90] Additional components of the treaty forged by Adams and Onis involved a further defining of the "western limits of the Louisiana Purchase and Spain surrendering its claims to the Pacific Northwest. In return the United States recognized Spanish sovereignty over Texas."[91] This historic treaty, also known as the Transcontinental Treaty, was ratified by the

---

[86] Ibid.

[87] Ibid., p. 424.

[88] Department of State, Office of the Historian, "Acquisition of Florida: Treaty of Adams-Onis (1819) and Transcontinental Treaty (1821)," online at https://history.state.gov. (Accessed October 19, 2023.)

[89] Ibid.

[90] Ibid.

[91] Ibid.

United States Senate in 1821.[92] Madison was in retirement by the time the treaty was signed.

Also related to the American acquisition of Florida, which would be remiss not to identify, were the military campaigns waged against the Seminole tribe and the Spanish by General Andrew Jackson. Jackson's campaigns were in no small part directly related to the American acquisition of Florida. Although Jackson's role related to the acquisition of Florida is a long story and one beyond the scope of this volume, one aspect of the American acquisition of Florida should be noted. In a letter to General Jackson from President Monroe dated December 28, 1817, the President had encouraged Jackson to not only neutralize the threat posed by the Seminoles, but also consider a broader campaign against the Spanish.[93] Monroe writing to Jackson, "This is not a time for you to think of repose. . . . Great interests are at issue, and until our course is carried through triumphantly . . . you might not to withdraw your active support from it."[94] Historian Jon Meacham questions whether Monroe was "hinting, and perhaps hoping" that Jackson would interpret the letter as giving him carte blanche authority to take all of Florida.[95] Regardless of what Monroe had in mind when drafting his letter, Jackson interpreted the President's letter as authorizing military action for the express purpose of acquiring Florida. Meacham writes, "Jackson moved against both the Seminoles and the Spanish and conquered Florida."[96] Once the transfer of ownership was formalized between Spain and the United States, President Monroe in 1821 appointed Jackson to serve as the governor of the Florida territory. As Monroe announced, "Smugglers & slave traders will hide their heads, pirates will disappear, and the Seminoles cease to give us trouble" when the people in Florida learn that Andrew Jackson will be serving as governor.[97]

Jefferson's Embargo

On December 22, 1807, per the insistence of President Jefferson and Secretary of State Madison, the Congress passed the Embargo Act intended to prevent American exports to Britain, while simultaneously prohibiting British

---

[92] Ibid.
[93] John Meacham, *American Lion: Andrew Jackson in the White House* (New York: Random House, 2008), p. 36.
[94] Monroe's letter to Jackson, December 28, 1817; quoted in Meacham, *American Lion*, p. 36.
[95] Meacham, *American Lion*, p. 36.
[96] Ibid.
[97] Monroe to Jackson, May 23, 1821, Monroe Writings, 6:180-85; quoted in Tim McGrath, *James Monroe: A Life* (New York: Dutton, 2020), p. 486.

merchants from exporting their goods to America. The embargo was Jefferson's response to a confrontation between a British and American ship off the coast of Norfolk, Virginia. The British warship, the *Leopard,* had demanded that its officers be allowed to board and search an American ship, the *Chesapeake*. The American captain refused the British order resulting in the British firing on the *Chesapeake,* killing or wounding twenty-one American sailors. To add insult to injury and to further humiliate the Americans, three of the *Chesapeake*'*s* crew were impressed into naval service by the British officers in command of the *Leopard.*[98] With Britain again at war with France, Jefferson decided to keep all American ships from engaging in foreign commerce with both countries. This would prevent American ships and sailors from being seized outside territorial waters in the event that war was to break out, particularly between the U.S. and Britain.[99] As Cost points out, the embargo "would also ensure that the United States could pick the time at which war might begin, rather than leaving it up to a random incident."[100]

Madison, like many in his party, was a strong advocate of the embargo and defended it as not only a security measure, but as an effective "instrument of commercial war."[101] So committed was Madison to Jefferson's embargo that he penned three anonymous editorials in the *National Intelligencer*, which at the time was the leading newspaper in the capital city. In his editorials, Madison vigorously defended the embargo and stated that the embargo would reflect the character and resolve of the American people. "Let the example teach the world that our firmness equals our moderation; that having resorted to a measure in itself, and adequate to its object, we will flinch from no sacrifices which the honor and good of the nation demand from virtuous and faithful citizens."[102] In addition to believing strongly in commercial warfare against Britain, Madison knew that the United States had the upper hand in imposing the embargo on British exports to America. This was due to Britain's greater dependence on the food grown by American farmers compared to America's dependence on the manufactured goods produced in Britain.[103] Madison emphasized this fact in one of his editorials. "It is not denied that an embargo imposes on us privations . . . but what are these compared with its effects on those who have driven us into the measure? We shall

[98] Gutzman, *James Madison,* p. 297.
[99] Cost, *James Madison*, p. 292.
[100] Ibid.
[101] Ibid.
[102] Madison editorial in *National Intelligencer,* quoted in Irving Brant, *James Madison: Secretary of State, 1800-1809,* p. 403.
[103] Cost, *James Madison,* p. 293.

be deprived of markets for our superfluities. They will feel the want of necessaries."[104] There was also little doubt that Madison's strident defense of the embargo was further motivated by partisan concerns. After all, it was the Republican Party, not the Federalist Party, that envisioned America as a magnificent "agrarian republic."[105]

Ketcham notes that Madison, even when he attended the College of New Jersey and studied under Witherspoon, supported the concept of an embargo to harm the British economy. His support for an embargo was further evident when he served in Congress between 1789 and 1794, during which time he called for retaliatory commercial measures against British trade.[106] "He felt commercial warfare would prove effective because British trade was fatally exposed at two points: hundreds of thousands of workmen and scores of wealthy merchants in England depended for their livelihood on goods sold to the United States, and the British West Indies depended on the adjacent mainland for food and lumber. Therefore, to shut off exports to the Indies and imports from Britain would bring the Empire to its knees."[107] In his role as secretary of state, Madison became the "faithful apostle of administration policy."[108]

Madison was apparently a driving force behind the embargo and often articulated in persuasive language why the embargo was a necessity. In Rutland's view, Madison was far more inclined to favor economic, rather than military warfare. "History taught Madison that wars not only created ruinous public debts, but also brought a concentration of power that inevitably spelled ruin to the people's liberties."[109] Despite Madison's position that commercial warfare was the best strategy for confronting British power, the embargo would nevertheless serve to heighten tension between Britain and the United States. This tension would eventually erupt in a declared war against Britain in 1812, a war that Madison in his capacity as the nation's commander-in-chief, would support and preside over.

Scholars who have studied the effects of the embargo have concluded that it did more harm than good to the American economy. Neither Jefferson nor Madison have received much praise for their support of the embargo. The embargo, as Peter Onuf writes, had by 1808, "devastated the American economy.

---

[104] Madison editorial in the National Intelligencer, December 28, 1807, *Papers of James Madison;* quoted in Cost, *James Madison.*, p. 293.
[105] Ibid.
[106] Ketcham, *James Madison,* p. 457.
[107] Ibid.
[108] Cost, *James Madison*, p. 293.
[109] Rutland, *James Madison*, p. 187.

American exports plummeted from $108 million to $22 million. Economic desperation settled upon the mercantile Northeast."[110] In one focused treatment of the embargo's effects on the town of Salem, Massachusetts, James Duncan Phillips captures the hardships caused by the embargo, "William Hunt, a Salem baker, gave notice that each destitute family could have a loaf of bread each Wednesday and Saturday at his bakery. A soup kitchen and other charitable projects were undertaken to relieve the growing distress. . . . By 1809, twelve hundred people were being fed at the soup kitchen, and about one-fifth of the town had been reduced to beggars."[111] A "fantastic failure, both in New England and the nation" was how Phillips summarized the impact of Jefferson's embargo.[112] Garry Wills observes that when Congress finally decided to repeal the embargo, it set the date for the embargo's expiration on the President's last day in office, "a kind of gratuitous insult to Jefferson."[113]

Madison's Performance as Secretary of State

Madison served a full eight years as President Jefferson's secretary of state. It is rare for a cabinet officer to serve the same president for eight years. Yet Madison has not been ranked by historians as among the best secretaries of state. In fact he is not ranked among the top ten.[114] This seems odd in light of Madison's influence related to shaping American foreign policy during the early years of the American republic. In Cost's view, Madison not being ranked as one of the best secretaries of state could possibly be due to the fact that his reputation as the "Father of the Constitution" was so profound that nothing he could do as a public office holder could ever match his role as a Founding Father.[115] Nevertheless, Cost still believes that Madison's less than impressive reputation as secretary of state is justified for two reasons. First, Madison's decisions as the head of American foreign policy were highly questionable in light of the fact that the United States while imposing an embargo on British trade still allowed "American vessels to ferry goods to and from" France's colonies located in the West Indies.

---

[110] Peter Onuf, "Thomas Jefferson: Foreign Affairs;" online at https://millercenter.org/prsident/jefferson/foreign-affairs. (Accessed February 26, 2024.)

[111] James Duncan Phillips, "Jefferson's 'Wicked Tyrannical Embargo,'" *The New England Quarterly,* Vol. 18, No. 4 (December 1945); online at https://www.jstor.org/stable/361063 (Accessed March 17, 2024.)

[112] Ibid. p. 478.

[113] Wills, *James Madison*, p. 55.

[114] "The Ten Best Secretaries of State," *American Heritage*, December 1981, Volume 3, Issue 1. Survey of 50 diplomatic historians conducted by Professor David Porter; online at americanheritage.com. (Accessed March 5, 2024.)

[115] Cost, *James Madison,* p. 299.

This, according to Cost, allowed Napoleon to continue his "wars of conquest." A second reason, according to Cost, pertains directly to the embargo itself, which "damaged the American economy, undermined the rule of law in the United States, divided the Republican Party, and worst of all had no effect on the British ministry."[116] Cost's perspective towards Madison's performance as secretary of state is harsh.

As President Jefferson's second term was winding down, there was little doubt that Madison was the heir apparent to the American presidency. This was an expectation from the time of his appointment as secretary of state. Heading the State Department was becoming the stepping-stone to the presidency. Madison followed that path to the White House where he would serve two terms as Jefferson's successor.

---

[116] Ibid. pp. 300-301.

Chapter Seven

President Madison

When Madison sought the presidency in 1808 after serving eight years as secretary of state, political parties during this time-period nominated their presidential candidates in congressional caucuses. This was before political parties began using national conventions to select their presidential candidates, and more than a century before presidential primaries made their appearance in presidential politics. The congressional caucus was a relatively simple mechanism for selecting a party's presidential candidate. Supporters of candidates would bring their names forward for nomination. Members of the party would then debate and vote for the candidates who they felt would best represent their party as president. The caucus was first used by state legislatures to nominate candidates for state offices. The success of the caucus at the state level persuaded the Federalists in Congress to begin using the same mechanism for nominating their party's presidential candidates.[1] Republicans followed the model of the Federalists and also adopted the caucus for nominating their party's presidential candidates.

Madison's Nomination

Although one might have thought that Madison's nomination for president was a foregone conclusion, this, surprisingly, was not the case. There was in fact some serious opposition to Madison's nomination. There was discussion that James Monroe, the former governor of Virginia, a key player involving the Louisiana Purchase, a former Ambassador to France, a former Ambassador to England, and whom Madison had defeated in his first bid for a congressional seat, also had his eyes on the presidency. In addition to Monroe, there was George Clinton, who had served for more than two-decades as New York's governor and who had served as vice president during Jefferson's second term of office. Monroe

---

[1] Norman A. Graebner, "Political Parties and the Presidency," *University of California Press*, Vol 25, No. 145 (September, 1953) p. 148; online at https:www.jstore.org/stable/45308516. (Accessed March 9, 2024.)

and Clinton, both members of the Republican Party and both with a base of support in Congress, were conducting stealth presidential campaigns. As a loyal Republican, Monroe had reservations about splitting the party. He had also been warned by Jefferson about this. Nevertheless, due to the insistence of the mercurial John Randolph, who was the former chair of the House Ways and Means Committee and who had a deep dislike for Madison, Monroe allowed his candidacy to go forward.[2] Feldman notes, Monroe "did nothing officially himself; but in a document he never published, he also made it clear that if elected, he would serve."[3]

To ensure her husband's nomination for president, Dolley, the skillful political spouse who knew how to cultivate positive opinions of her husband, held a series of dinner parties in which Republican congressmen were invited along with their wives. The dinner parties were engaging, lavish, and served to generate the political support her husband would need to win his party's nomination in the forthcoming caucus. Brookhiser captures the political value of Dolley's dinner parties, "Dolley's dinner guests were thus the electorate that would decide on Madison's nomination. All the dinner parties in the world could not have boosted a nobody, but Dolley did their bit to lift her already-prominent husband."[4] Jefferson of course was very supportive of Madison's nomination, as was Albert Gallatin, the popular and influential treasury secretary from Pennsylvania.[5] Their support, along with Dolley's dinner parties, would prove instrumental when the caucus votes were cast.

When the congressional caucus was held in January 1808, approximately 60 percent of the Republican members of congress who participated cast their votes for the presidential/vice-presidential ticket of James Madison and George Clinton. This was a solid endorsement of Madison by his own party, but by no means overwhelming.[6] Clinton, although still considered a presidential candidate, joined Madison as his vice presidential running mate. Yet a number of Republicans chose not to participate in the caucus, suggesting indifference and perhaps an unwillingness to go on record against Madison.[7]

Madison's political enemy, John Randolph, did all he could to prevent Madison's nomination. In harsh terms, Randolph spoke disparagingly of the ability and character of the man he vehemently opposed, "We ask for energy, and

---

[2] Feldman, *The Three Lives of James Madison*, p. 497.
[3] Ibid.
[4] Brookhiser, *James Madison,* p. 177.
[5] Ibid.
[6] Ibid.
[7] Ibid.

we are told of [Madison's] moderation. We ask for talents, and the reply is his unassuming merit. We ask what were his services in the cause of public liberty, and we are directed to the pages of the *Federalist.*"[8] Brookhiser notes that in Randolph's opinion, the *Federalist* essays were tantamount to "a devil's dictionary."[9] To further undermine Madison's candidacy, Randolph tried to persuade congressional Federalists, rather than Republicans, to nominate Monroe as their presidential candidate. Jefferson, aware of Randolph's divisive behavior, penned a note to Monroe, "Some of your new friends are attacking the old ones out of friendship to you, but in a way to render you great injury."[10]

Randolph's attempt to persuade Federalists in Congress to back Monroe was unsuccessful. It was unthinkable for Federalists, in light of their animosity towards Republicans, to nominate one of Jefferson's protégés as their party's presidential candidate. The Federalists decided instead to forego their congressional caucus and held a meeting in New York to candidate, quite remarkably, the same and unsuccessful ticket the party had nominated in 1804.[11] Once again, Charles Cotesworth Pinckney, a prominent South Carolina military man was nominated as the Federalist Party's candidate for president. Rufus King, a former U.S. Senator from New York, was again named the party's vice presidential candidate.

The Election of 1808

The election of 1808 was not very competitive. Madison won the popular vote in 12 of the 17 states and amassed an impressive 122 electoral votes to Pinckney's 47.[12] Clinton, Madison's running mate, won 3 electoral votes for president, while Monroe who had assembled an alternate slate of electors in Virginia, did not win a single electoral vote. Virginia was clearly Madison country. Madison won 14,665 popular votes in Virginia to Monroe's 3,408. Pinckney won a paltry 760 votes.[13] Reflecting on Madison's convincing win, Pinckney attributed his loss to the role Dolley played in helping her husband win

---

[8] John Randolph in Adams *(Jefferson)*, 1083; quoted in Brookhiser, *James Madison,* p. 177.

[9] Brookhiser, *James Madison*, p. 178.

[10] Jefferson in Norman K. Risjord, *Old Republicans: Southern Conservatism in the Age of Jefferson,* (New York: Columbia University Press, 1965), p. 64; quoted in Jules Witcover, *Party of the People: A History of the Democrats* (New York: Random House, 2003), p. 109.

[11] Witcover, *Party of the People*, p. 109.

[12] Ibid.

[13] Tim McGrath, *James Monroe: A Life* (New York: Dutton, 2020), p. 284.

the election. He suggested that he not only had to face Madison as a candidate, but in some respects also his wife.[14]

As evident from the election results, the spirit of republicanism was spreading across the land, although the Federalist Party was far from dead. According to Jules Witcover, Madison in 1808 won 40 fewer electoral votes compared to Jefferson's total in the election of 1804, while the same Federalist ticket had won 33 more electoral votes. Moreover, the Federalist ticket did better among the six New England states compared to its showing in 1804 by winning every state, with the exception of Vermont. Continued dissatisfaction among New Englanders with Jefferson's embargo reflected the voting results.[15] Nevertheless, despite signs of continued Federalist Party vitality, Madison's convincing win in 1808 suggested that the Republican Party had definitely surpassed the Federalist Party as the dominant party in American national politics.

The Embargo is Repealed

In February of 1809, only one month before Madison was inaugurated president, the Congress voted to end the embargo. The vote was bipartisan. Republicans, who no longer felt the embargo was effective, voted alongside Federalists who had opposed the embargo from the start. The bill repealing the embargo was signed by Jefferson. The designated expiration date was March 4, Jefferson's last day in office.[16]

The Non-Intercourse Act (1809)

Despite the fact that the embargo had been lifted, shortly before Madison was inaugurated, a weaker version of the embargo titled the Non-Intercourse Act was passed by Congress and signed into law by Jefferson. Madison, an enthusiastic supporter of Jefferson's embargo felt that the Non-Intercourse Act, although not having the same level of influence as the embargo, was still useful for the purpose of maintaining American neutrality and for preventing American merchant ships from traveling to "ports that remained under British and French control."[17] Spivak writes that Madison "hoped that nonintercourse would pinch Great Britain and conform, at least distantly, to his ingrained notions on the power of economic coercion as a tool of diplomacy and a weapon of war."[18] The new act however

---

[14] Ibid.
[15] Witcover, *Party of the People*, p. 109.
[16] Brookhiser, *James Madison*, p. 179.
[17] Burstein and Isenberg, *Madison and Jefferson,* p. 480.
[18] Spivak, *Jefferson's English Crisis,* p. 196.

was practically unenforceable. Burstein and Isenberg note that there were so many loopholes in the law "that U.S. vessels were able to trade with the British in neutral ports."[19] The Non-Intercourse Act lasted for approximately three years with very little effectiveness.[20]

Madison's Inauguration

James Madison was inaugurated the fourth President of the United States on March 4, 1809. Presidents, until passage of the Twentieth Amendment in 1933 which changed the date of the inauguration to January 20, were inaugurated in March. There was thus a long stretch of time from the fall election to inauguration day. The outgoing president was essentially a lame duck for a full four months.

The U.S. Capitol was still under construction in 1809. This required Madison's inauguration to be held in the House chamber of the Capitol.[21] A horse drawn carriage carried Madison to the Capitol for his inauguration. He invited Jefferson to join him on the carriage ride, but Jefferson, perhaps viewing such pomp and circumstance as slightly imperious, declined the offer. He decided to ride his own horse to the Capitol. Upon arriving, Jefferson tied his horse to a post and followed Madison into the House chamber.[22] Describing Jefferson's participation in Madison's inaugural ceremony, Feldman suggests that the former president's "show of republican self-effacement" consciously intended to minimize his presence at the ceremony, may have had the opposite effect and likely had called more attention to himself than to Madison.[23] John Marshall, the staunch Federalist Chief Justice of the Supreme Court, and certainly no friend of Madison or his party, administered the oath of office.

Madison's inaugural address has never been rated as one of the great or inspirational inaugural addresses. Yet Madison's address did provide a window to his view of America and his commitment to neutrality. His address, as expected, included admiration for Thomas Jefferson.

In his address, Madison expressed great pride in the progress that had occurred since the country's founding. He identified the "unrivaled growth" in American agriculture, commerce, manufacturing, the "useful arts," and how public revenue had allowed for a reduction in the public debt.[24] He made a firm

---

[19] Burstein and Isenberg, *Madison and Jefferson*, p. 480.
[20] Spivak, *Jefferson's English Crisis,* p. 197.
[21] Feldman, *The Three Lives of James Madison*, 502.
[22] Ibid.
[23] Ibid., p. 503.
[24] James Madison's Inaugural Address March 4, 1809; online at The American Presidency Project, https//www.presidency.ucsb.edu. (Accessed December 11, 2023.)

point to reiterate America's neutral stance towards the war between Britain and France, two countries he described as "belligerent powers" that historically and unfortunately had exhibited "rage against the other."[25] In his address, Madison also discussed how important it was to maintain unity among the states, a position he had strongly supported as a delegate to the Constitutional Convention. He also cited the importance of a standing army, essential in his view for the preservation of national security and personal liberty.[26] He expressed his admiration for previous presidents, with much gratitude, as expected, towards his mentor, Thomas Jefferson. "It is good fortune, moreover, to have the path which I am to tread lighted by examples of illustrious services successfully rendered in the most trying difficulties by those who have marched before me. Of those of my immediate predecessor . . . I may, however, be pardoned for not suppressing the sympathy with which my heart is full in the rich reward he enjoys in the benedictions of a beloved country, gratefully bestowed or exalted talents zealously devoted through a long career to the advancement of its highest interest and happiness."[27] Madison concluded his inaugural address by expressing confidence that America will be guided by "that Almighty Being whose power regulates the destiny of nations, whose blessings have been so conspicuously dispensed to this rising Republic, and to who we are bound to address our devout gratitude for the past as well as our fervent supplications and best hopes for the future."[28]

Madison's speech was concise and intellectual, and captured his views on foreign policy and other matters he deemed relevant. Yet despite his articulate and substantive speech, it may not have inspired those in attendance. Feldman writes, "Nothing in Madison's speech suggested that he felt any personal fulfilment or accomplished ambition in becoming president – or that he thought his election stood for some greater national transformation, as Jefferson's had in 1800."[29] Madison's inaugural address may not have been comparable to the eloquence of Jefferson's rhetoric, but it was nevertheless a clear and principled speech. In some respects, Madison's inaugural address reflected his low-keyed personality and selfless dedication to public service. Feldman further notes, "He knew that he lacked Jefferson's expressive flair or Washington's personal stature. He had not sought the presidency in fulfillment of the psychological drives that have powered so many into the office, for good or for ill. He had run because he believed he

---

[25] Ibid.
[26] Ibid.
[27] Ibid.
[28] Ibid.
[29] Feldman, *The Three Lives of James Madison*, p. 503.

could successfully navigate the dangerous shoals of global war . . . while maintaining neutrality."[30]

Cabinet Politics

One of the top priorities of a new president is to form a cabinet. Having served as secretary of state for eight years and intimately aware of the cabinet's important relationship to the president, Madison was determined to appoint a loyal and competent team of administrators. For the post of secretary of state, Madison wanted to appoint Albert Gallatin, one of his strongest political allies. Madison wanted to move Gallatin from his current post as treasury secretary to the state department where he would direct the nation's foreign affairs. Unfortunately, due to his loyalty to Madison and his position on many contentious issues, Gallatin had created too many political enemies in the U.S. Senate, thus precluding any chance of a confirmation. Opposition to Gallatin had even extended beyond Federalist senators. Among Republican senators there was a faction known as the "Invisibles" who were determined to prevent Gallatin from becoming secretary of state.[31] It was clear that Gallatin did not have the votes in the Senate to win confirmation. Maryland's U.S. Senator Samuel Smith, one of the "Invisibles" who strongly opposed Gallatin, notified Madison that the better choice for secretary of state would be his brother, Robert, who had served as secretary of the navy under Jefferson.[32] Madison, however, regarded Robert Smith as incompetent and inattentive to details. Knowing, however, that fighting for Gallatin's appointment would be an exercise in futility, he concluded that placating Senator Smith and the "Invisibles" would be less exhausting. Moreover, having served for eight years as secretary of state, Madison surmised that he could simultaneously perform his duties as president and the duties of secretary of state whenever the situation called for it.[33] Madison therefore nominated Smith for secretary of state who was confirmed by the Senate.

Other than the highly talented Gallatin, Madison's cabinet was less than impressive. According to Ketcham, "Political necessity and sectional balance seemed to force mediocrity on Madison for the rest of his cabinet."[34] Ketcham continues, "Thus at the outset, Madison found himself saddled with one of the weakest cabinets in American history."[35] Other than Gallatin who continued to

---

[30] Ibid.
[31] Ketcham, *James Madison*, p. 481.
[32] Ibid., p. 482.
[33] Ibid.
[34] Ibid.
[35] Ibid., p. 483.

serve as treasury secretary, Madison's cabinet picks were neither experienced for the position they held, nor were they the most reliable individuals.[36]

Less than two years into his presidency, Madison realized that Robert Smith had to be replaced as secretary of state. Smith, who was sharing sensitive information with the "Invisibles," seemed determined to undermine Madison's presidency. Smith was also issuing statements to Britain that were contradictory to Madison's position on foreign policy.[37] At the same time, Smith was not only performing his job poorly, which was evident in his incoherent policy memos, but because both Jefferson and Madison had served as secretaries of state, he too was starting to perceive himself as presidential. Smith, as Ketcham put it, was showing a "conciliatory posture" towards Britain that in his mind might rally pro-British Federalists to support his bid for president in 1812.[38] Madison was finally forced to fire Smith. However, before the official decision was announced, he had to first convince his fellow Virginian, James Monroe, to accept appointment as secretary of state. Although Madison and Monroe had become slightly estranged from one another, Madison was determined to put politics aside and to convince Monroe to accept the appointment. In Madison's view, there was nobody remotely close to Monroe with respect to experience and competence in the area of foreign affairs.

Monroe had recently retired from foreign service and was back home managing his plantation and devoting his time to Virginia politics. He had been serving as a member in the Virginia state legislature and had recently been elected for the second time as Virginia's governor. Nevertheless, Monroe was whom Madison wanted as his secretary of state and remained determined to recruit him. As Ketcham observes, "Madison valued Monroe's talents, his energy. His republican zeal, and the political support he could bring to the administration."[39] Once he convinced Monroe to accept the appointment, he could then rid himself of the incompetent and disloyal Robert Smith.[40]

In his effort to persuade Monroe to accept the appointment, Madison sent Monroe a letter, which McGrath describes "as close to an apology" that Madison could express to his former competitor and personal friend. "Differences of opinion must be looked for . . . within the compass of free consultation and mutual concession."[41] Monroe, who wanted to be secretary of state and who knew that

---

[36] Ibid.
[37] Ibid., pp. 484-485.
[38] Ibid., p. 485.
[39] Ibid.
[40] Ibid.
[41] Madison to Monroe, March 20 and March 26, 1811, *Papers of James* Madison, 5:801-3; quoted in McGrath, *James Monroe*, p. 294,

this post would be his path to the presidency, finally accepted Madison's offer. Madison had thus succeeded in getting the secretary of state he had always wanted.[42] He could now remove Smith.

Recognizing the political fallout that would come from firing Smith, Madison decided that the best approach was to give the disloyal secretary a soft landing. He called Smith to his office and softened the blow of dismissal as secretary of state by offering to appoint him Minister to Russia. Although Smith initially found the offer appealing, he concluded after further consideration that Madison's offer was intended to send him into political exile.[43] Smith therefore declined the offer. Following his dismissal, Smith launched a written attack on Madison's credibility and tried his best to elevate his own reputation in the eyes of the public. He authored a pamphlet approximately forty pages in length that included his virtues as a cabinet secretary. His self-promoting pamphlet printed in several newspapers, was titled, "Robert Smith's Address to the People of the United States." Smith's efforts to resurrect his reputation "demolished his career" and soon thereafter Robert Smith faded from public view.[44]

"Mr. Madison's War"

Tension between Britain and the United States had been building since the *Leopard* had shelled the *Chesapeake*, killing or wounding several American sailors. Although Congress repealed the embargo on the last day of Jefferson's presidency and repealed the short-lived Non-Intercourse Act that had been passed in 1809,[45] tension between the two countries continued to escalate. British impressment of American seamen under the pretense they were deserters from the British navy, despite the fact that many of those impressed were American citizens, continued to infuriate Madison and many members of Congress.[46] It seemed as if the British government with its powerful navy was determined to harass and show the Americans that despite the Treaty of Paris in 1783, which established American independence from Britain, America was still subservient to Britain. According to Gordon Wood, "The United States was trying to establish itself as an independent sovereign republic in the world, and Britain, much more than France, seemed to be denying that sovereign independence."[47]

---

[42] McGrath, *James Monroe*, p. 294.
[43] Brookhiser, *James Madison*, p. 190.
[44] Dewey and Peterson, *James Madison*, pp. 137-138.
[45] Broadwater, *James Madison,* p. 156.
[46] Cheney, *The Virginia Dynasty*, p. 250.
[47] Wood, *Empire of Liberty*, p. 667.

To further make life difficult for the Americans, the British were directly responsible for assisting Indian tribes in their effort to prevent American settlers from starting a new life in the Northwest Territory. In particular, it was the Wabash Confederation, led by the Shawnee Chief Tecumseh and his brother Tenswatawa, known among tribal members as "the Prophet," who posed the greatest threat to Americans moving westward.[48] Examining the conflict between settlers and Tecumseh, Wood notes, "From Prophet's Town at the junction of the Wabash and Tippecanoe rivers in Indian Territory, the Shawnee brothers spread their message throughout the region, resulting in an alarming increase in Indian raids on white settlers."[49]

Also contributing in a most important way to the rising tension between the United States and Britain was the war between Britain and France that had started in 1803. This war began during Madison's first term as secretary of state. During this war, Napoleon who had declared himself the Emperor of France, issued in 1806 the Berlin Decrees. The decrees were announced from Berlin where Napoleon was residing following the French army's defeat of the Prussian army. The decrees established French naval blockades of several ports on the European Continent with the intention of inflicting harm on the British economy. "No ship that stopped in Britain or its colonies would be permitted to land in France or a French controlled port."[50] The British government in 1807 responded to the Berlin Decrees with the Orders in Council, which "forbade neutrals to sail from port to port of Napoleonic Europe."[51] Napoleon in 1807 responded to the Orders in Council with his Milan Decree, which declared that any ship involved in trade with Britain would be considered a hostile vessel and subject to seizure.[52] Brookhiser writes, "Napoleon and George III's ministers issued escalating restrictions until each superpower forbade the United States to trade with the other in any way whatever."[53]

In his seminal article regarding the origins of the War of 1812, Madison scholar J.C.A. Stagg posits that although there have been multiple explanations offered by historians regarding what led to the War of 1812, the Orders in Council

---

[48] Feldman, *The Three Lives of James Madison*, p. 533.
[49] Wood, *Empire of Liberty*, p. 675.
[50] Brookhiser, *James Madison*, p.169.
[51] Ibid.
[52] Rutland, *James Madison*, p. 192.
[53] Brookhiser, *James Madison*, p. 169.

need to be understood as the prime contributor to this conflict.[54] According to Stagg, "The Madison administration decided to resort to war at that point when it concluded that Great Britain would never repeal its Orders in Council for as long as the Napoleonic Wars continued in Europe."[55] Although Stagg recognizes that other factors, such as British impressment of American seamen and British instigation of Indian attacks on American settlers in the western territories contributed to the hostility between the United States and Britain, he contends that those issues alone would not have led to the war.[56] The War of 1812, in Stagg's view, needs to be understood within the context of the war that was taking place between Britain and France, "Most of the maritime disputes between Great Britain and the U.S. were a result of the policies Great Britain adopted to defeat Napoleon and destroy his European empire."[57]

The Election of 1810

The turning point occurred with the congressional election of 1810, which resulted in a fierce breed of individuals elected to Congress who were determined to wage war against Britain.[58] "Full of energy and bravado, these young men would not stand by while the British insulted American rights at sea. They were also in a fury about Indian raids, in which they had lost grandmothers, aunts, uncles, cousins."[59] Among the new breed of congressmen was Henry Clay from Kentucky. Clay had relinquished his seat in the U.S. Senate in order to win a seat in the House of Representatives. Clay noted that "turbulence" was more fulfilling than "solemn stillness."[60] A gifted orator with a magnetic personality, Clay was elected Speaker of the House during his very first term in Congress. A strong supporter of President Jefferson's embargo and the core principles of the Republican Party, Clay led a contingent of newly elected congressmen known as the War Hawks. The War Hawks' chief objective was to convince President

---

[54] J. C. A. Stagg, "James Madison and the 'Malcontents': The Political Origins of the War of 1812." *The William and Mary Quarterly,* Vol. 33, No. 4 (October 1976), p. 557.

[55] Q&A with J.C.A. Stagg, "The War of 1812," Fifteen Eighty Four: Academic Perspectives from Cambridge University Press; online at https://www/cambridgeblog.org/2012/03/the-war-0f-1812-a-qa-with-j-c-a-stagg. (Accessed June 7, 2024.)

[56] Ibid.

[57] Ibid.

[58] Cheney, *The Virginia Dynasty*, pp. 274-275.

[59] Ibid.

[60] Clay, *Papers* 1:498, to Monroe, November 13, 1810; quoted in Cheney, *The Virginia Dynasty*, p. 275.

Madison that the time had arrived to declare war against Britain.[61] Brant describes Clay as, "Foremost of the militants . . . whose warlike spirit and capacity for leadership had been demonstrated in his one year in the Senate."[62] An ally of Clay, and also a supporter of war against Britain, was another new congressmen who would emerge as a prominent figure in American government. This was the strong willed and confident congressman from South Carolina by the name of John C. Calhoun.[63]

Madison's party enjoyed a major victory in the election of 1810. When the Twelfth Congress was convened in 1811, the party breakdown in the House of Representatives was 107 Republicans to 36 Federalists. In the Senate, 28 Republicans held seats compared to 6 Federalists, further evidence that the Federalist Party was in a state of decline.[64]

> Seventy new members were on the rolls of the Twelfth Congress and among them were a number of young men who were impatient with the way the elder statesmen had been running the country. The old Republicans were opposed to a large standing army, a large navy, imperialist ambitions and the levying of internal taxes, all of which they regarded as Federalist measures. They had let Great Britain bully and browbeat them[65]

Not one of the brash War Hawks was over 40 years old, and not one had any tolerance for the obsequious behavior of the older congressmen towards Britain. The young War Hawks knew exactly what they wanted and what had to be done, "empire and war" were their immediate goals.[66] The War Hawks also had their eyes on Canada to the north. They saw no reason why Britain should be allowed to have any land claims in North America.

The intense and warlike mood in Congress, despite reservations expressed by John Randolph and members of the Federalist Party, finally persuaded Madison to submit a message to Congress on June 1, 1812 requesting Congress to declare war against Britain. It was the first, but not the last time, a president would submit a message to Congress recommending a formal declaration of war against a

---

[61] Cheney, *The Virginia Dynasty*, p. 275.
[62] Irving Brant, *James Madison: The President 1809-1812* (New York: The Bobbs-Merrill Co., Inc. 1956), p. 380.
[63] Cheney, *The Virginia Dynasty,* p. 277.
[64] Francis F. Beirne, *The War of 1812* (New York: E.P. Dutton & Co., Inc. 1949), p. 64.
[65] Ibid.
[66] Ibid., p. 65.

foreign power. The transcript of Madison's historic war message identified four distinct grievances against Britain to justify the war. The subheadings are included by the author for instructional purposes.[67]

British Impressment of American Seamen

The practice, hence, is so far from affecting Britsh subjects alone that, under the pretext searching for these, thousands of American citizens, under the safeguard of public law and of their national flag, have been torn from their country and everything dear to them; have been dragged on board ships of war of a foreign nation and exposed, under the severities of their discipline, to be exiled to the most distant and deadly climes.[68]

British Blockades of American Shipping

Under pretended blockades, without the presence of an adequate force and sometimes without the practicality of applying one, our commerce has been plundered in every sea, the great staples of our country have been cut off from their legitimate markets, and a destructive blow aimed at our agricultural and maritime interests.[69]

Britain's Orders in Council

Not content with these occasional expedients for laying waste our neutral trade, the cabinet of Britain reported at length to the sweeping system of blockades, under the name of orders in council, which has been molded and managed as might best suit its political views, its commercial jealousies, or the avidity of British cruisers.[70]

Britain's Collusion with Hostile Indian Tribes

In reviewing the conduct of Great Britain toward the United States our attention is necessarily drawn to the warfare just renewed by the savages on one of our extensive frontiers, a warfare which is known to spare neither age nor sex and to be distinguished by features peculiarly

---

[67] All excerpts are from the transcript of Madison's message to Congress, June 1, 1812: Special Message to Congress on the Foreign Policy Crisis—War Message; online at httpls://millercenter.org. (Accessed December 2, 2023.)
[68] Ibid.
[69] Ibid.
[70] Ibid.

> shocking to humanity. It is difficult to account for the activity and combinations which have for some time been developing themselves among tribes in constant intercourse with British traders and garrisons.[71]

Madison concluded his war message with a strong statement indicating that for all intents and purposes, Britain had already declared war against the United States.

> We behold, in fine, on the side of Great Britain, a state of war against the United States, and on the side of the United States a state of peace toward Great Britain.[72]

Understanding how the Constitution defines the process for conducting war, Madison made it clear in his message that he must defer to the judgment of Congress on the matter of war, and that he was confident that Congress would do the right thing.

> In recommending it to their early deliberations I am happy in the assurances that the decision will worthy the enlightened and patriotic councils of a virtuous, a free, and a powerful nation.

Support for a war against Britain was intensely debated on the floor of the House of Representatives. The War Hawks led by Clay made a strong and convincing case for military action against Britain, while Federalist Party members, particularly those from the New England states which for years had benefited from trade relations with Britain and which were severely hurt by the embargo, strongly opposed going to war. As expected, speaking against the war in dramatic fashion was Madison's nemesis John Randolph.

> The question . . . is one of peace or war – a war not of defense, but of conquest, of aggrandizement of ambition. . . . a war foreign to the interests of this country, to the interests of humanity itself.[73]

Randolph continued:

> We have so increased the trade and wealth of Montreal and Quebec that at last we cast a wistful eye at Canada. Go! March to Canada! Leave the broad bosom of the Chesapeake and her hundred tributary rivers; the whole line of seacoast, from Machias to St. Mary's unprotected. You

---

[71] Ibid.
[72] Ibid.
[73] Randolph quoted in Beirne, *The War of 1812*, p. 68.

> have taken Quebec. Have you conquered England? Will you seek for the deep foundations of her power in the frozen deserts of Labrador?[74]

Despite debate, the decision to declare war was never in doubt. On June 3, only two days after Madison had submitted his war message to Congress, Calhoun, who was serving as chair of the House Committee on Foreign Relations, issued his Committee's report supporting war against Britain. On June 4, despite continued opposition from Federalists, the war bill was overwhelmingly supported on the House floor by a vote of 79 to 49.[75] Among the 79 House members who voted for the war, 48 had been elected from congressional districts in the South and the West, 14 represented districts in Pennsylvania, and only 17 were from districts located in the north. Among the 49 House members who voted against the war, 34 were from districts located in northern states, two congressmen were from Pennsylvania, while 13 were from districts in southern states.[76] The vote in the House reflected regional politics.

The war bill then advanced to the Senate. On June 18, after debate regarding the merits of the war, the Senate, following the lead of the War Hawks in the House, voted for war, 19 to 13; regional and party alignments were once again evident in the Senate votes.[77] It was obvious that going to war was not supported by both parties, nor was it supported by all of the states. It was instead "both a party war and a sectional war."[78] "About 81 percent of the Republicans in both chambers of Congress voted for the war (98 to 23), while every Federalist in both chambers voted against it (39 to 0)."[79]

Madison signed the war bill on the same day the Senate cast its vote for war. The day after, on June 19, he issued a proclamation to the American people stating that the United States was formally at war with Britain. Madison stated in his message that despite the feelings the American people might have about the war, it was essential for the people to support the war effort. Moreover, he stated that God was on America's side.

> I, James Madison, President of the United States of America … exhort all the good people of the United States, as they love their country, as they value the precious heritage derived from the virtue and valor of their

---

[74] Randolph quoted in Beirne, *The War of 1812* p 69.
[75] Beirne, *The War of 1812*, p. 93.
[76] Ibid., p. 94.
[77] Ibid. p. 94.
[78] Ibid.
[79] Donald R. Hickey, *The War of 1812* (Urbana: University of Illinois Press, 2012), p. 43.

> fathers, as they feel the wrongs which have forced on them the last resort of injured nations . . . under the blessing of Divine Providence of abridging its calamities, that they exert themselves in preserving order, in promoting concord, in maintaining the authority and efficacy of the laws, and in supporting and invigorating all the measures which may be adopted by the constituted authorities for obtaining a speedy, just and honorable peace.[80]

Some historians who have studied the War of 1812 have suggested that the War Hawks in Congress were most responsible for the war. Stagg refutes this point of view, "The belief that congressional actions played a vital part in pushing for the administration to war rests on a misconception about the relations between executive and legislature in the early Republic. Congress at that time was a loosely organized body, seldom capable of initiating or adopting major policy decisions independently of the executive."[81] Although there were vocal War Hawks in Congress, the decision to go to war in Stagg's view should be attributed to Madison, not Congress. "The role of Congress was thus far less decisive than most historians have believed, while the role of the president was far more important."[82] Moreover, a review of Madison's position on the subject of war discovered that throughout much of his public career he recognized that there were times when war was not only necessary but also desirable. Commenting on Madison's view towards war, Reginald C. Stuart writes, "Madison was reluctant to contemplate an Anglo-American war, but he accepted force as an integral part of international affairs. He was no pacifist. During the revolution he had argued for retaliation against the British for alleged atrocities . . . Subsequent considerations of the Constitution only confirmed that Madison recognized an intrinsic link between force and national policy that applied to republics as much as to other forms of government."[83] Because the war was so closely tied to Madison's presidency and his intense desire to wage war against Britain, a Massachusetts essayist by the name of John Lowell published a pamphlet pertaining to the war titled "Mr. Madison's War." Due to Lowell's pamphlet, the War of 1812 would forever be known by that name.[84]

---

[80] "June 19, 1812: Proclamation of a State of War with Great Britain," Millercenter.org. (Accessed December 11, 2023.)
[81] Stagg, "*James Madison and the 'Malcontents,'*" p. 599.
[82] Ibid., p. 560.
[83] Reginald C. Stuart, "James Madison and the Militants: Republican Disunity and Replacing the Embargo," *Diplomatic History*, Vol. 6, No. 2 (Spring 1982), p. 151; online at https://www.jstor.org/stable/24911290 (Accessed March 31, 2024.)
[84] Chadwick, *James and Dolley Madison*, p. 221.

As expected, public reaction to the declaration of war revealed a political divide among the American people. Those aligned with Madison's political party "found the news exhilarating," while members of the Federalist Party "greeted the news with alarm and foreboding."[85] However, despite the political division, the Madison administration with the support of Congress waged war against Britain.

The War of 1812 is perhaps one of the least understood wars in American history. It was by no means a bipartisan war, nor was it a war firmly supported among the different regions within the United States. In 1812, there were eighteen states, some of which were strongholds of the Republican Party, while others provided a reliable base for the Federalist Party. To complicate matters, the goals of the war were never made clear to the American public. Nevertheless, the War of 1812, which lasted for two and a half years, is the pivotal event which defined James Madison's presidency.

In his seminal volume titled *The War of 1812* first published in 1989 and then republished as a Bicentennial edition in 2012, Donald R. Hickey captures why the War of 1812 has never achieved the same fame and historical status as that of the other major wars fought by the United States.

> Why is this war so obscure? One reason is that no great president is associated with the conflict. Although his enemies called it "Mr. Madison's War," James Madison hardly measures up to such war leaders as Abraham Lincoln, Woodrow Wilson, or Franklin Roosevelt. Moreover, the best American generals in this war – Andrew Jackson, Jacob Brown and Winfield Scott – were unable to turn the tide because each was confined to a secondary theater of operations. No one like George Washington, Ulysses Grant, or Dwight Eisenhower emerged to put his stamp on the war and carry the nation to victory.[86]

Hickey notes that if the American people know anything about the War of 1812, their knowledge is likely confined to knowing that the White House and Capitol were torched by British soldiers, that it was under Andrew Jackson that the Americans defeated the British in the Battle of New Orleans, and that the "Star-Spangled Banner" was written by Francis Scott Key during the British bombardment of Fort McHenry in Baltimore Harbor.[87] Other than these events, most Americans likely know precious little about the origin of the war, nor for that matter where the battles occurred. Commenting on American perceptions of

---

[85] Hickey, *The War of 1812,* p 48.
[86] Ibid., p. 1.
[87] Ibid.

the war after it had ended, Hickey notes, "Although most Americans pretended they had won the war – even calling it a 'Second War for Independence' – they could point to few concrete gains to sustain this claim."[88]

When war against Britain was declared, the American military was unprepared to fight a superpower like Britain. The senior officers, which included the two major generals and the six brigadier generals, owed their stars not to meritorious service but instead to political patronage.[89] To further complicate matters, the appointments of new junior officers were delayed due to lethargic and bureaucratic nomination processes among the states.[90]

Soldiers in the enlisted ranks also had very little combat experience and desertion became a problem. To counter the high frequency of desertion, perhaps due to the ambiguity of the war's purpose, Madison issued a proclamation stating that army deserters would receive a presidential pardon should they return to active duty within four months of their desertion.[91] To boost enlistments, Madison authorized an increase in enlistment incentives from $31.00, along with 160 acres of land, to $124.00 and a doubling of land to 320 acres.[92] The dramatic increase in incentives proved effective, as the number of enlistments rose substantially. Many recruits however required extensive military training and were no match, at least initially, for the battle-tested British army.[93] As the war progressed, maintaining an adequate number of soldiers to accommodate the needs of units would remain an ongoing challenge, despite the incentives approved by Madison.[94]

The 1812 Election

In 1812, with war in its first year, another federal election occurred. Madison's vice presidential running mate in 1812 was now the former Massachusetts Congressman and Governor, Elbridge Gerry. Gerry replaced Vice President George Clinton who had died while in office. Although there was little doubt that Madison would be reelected president, there was nevertheless resistance to his reelection due to the war. Such resistance was not only evident among members of the Federalist Party, who truly despised the president, but resistance was also present within a faction of his own party. Close to one-third

---

[88] Ibid., p. 3.
[89] Ibid., p. 70.
[90] Ibid.
[91] Ibid., p. 71.
[92] Ibid.
[93] Ibid.
[94] Ibid., 109.

of Republican congressmen boycotted the caucus that nominated Madison for a second term.[95] As further evidence of their dislike for Madison, the Republican caucus boycotters from New York successfully persuaded DeWitt Clinton, the mayor of New York City and nephew of the deceased vice president, to challenge Madison in the election. Their resistance to Madison and the war was glaringly evident when the anti-Madison faction of Republicans met with Federalists to form a fusion campaign behind Clinton's candidacy.[96] The unusual alliance supported Clinton for president and added Philadelphia lawyer Jared Ingersoll to the ticket for vice president.[97] Nevertheless, despite what seemed like an effective strategy to dislodge Madison, Clinton's campaign was disorganized and incoherent. It was hardly the sort of campaign required to take down an incumbent president. According to Stagg, "The Clintonians, who had no official party name, tailored their message to the region and the audience. They said one thing to war Democratic-Republicans, another to peace Democratic-Republicans, and something else again to antiwar Federalists."[98]

It should be further noted that due to the unprincipled alliance between Federalists and a faction of anti-Madison Republicans, John Quincy Adams, the son of the former Federalist President John Adams, had become so disillusioned with the political antics of the Federalist Party that he switched his allegiance to the Republican Party.[99] At the same time, his father, also alarmed over the controversial fusion strategy involving his fellow Federalists, "not only endorsed Madison but also agreed to head Madison's electoral ticket in his home district of Quincy, Massachusetts."[100] Despite the political subterfuge and strange alliance against Madison, the president was easily reelected with 128 electoral votes to Clinton's 89. The election once again reflected regional politics. Madison won twelve states. These included Pennsylvania and eleven states located in the south. Louisiana had become a state in 1812 and cast its vote for Madison.[101] Clinton's fusion candidacy won seven states, all of which were clustered within the Northeast and New England, although, Madison was able to win Vermont.[102]

---

[95] J. C.A. Stagg, "James Madison: Campaigns and Elections," The Miller Center: online at https://millercenter.org/president/madison/camapigns-and-elections. (Accessed December 17, 2023.)
[96] Ibid.
[97] Ibid.
[98] Ibid.
[99] Ibid.
[100] Ibid.
[101] 270towin.com/1812_Elections/InterctiveMap.
[102] Ibid.

Despite Madison's landslide victory in 1812, the percentage of House seats occupied by Republicans declined from 75 percent in the Twelfth U.S. Congress to 63 percent in the Thirteenth U.S. Congress. In the Senate, the party's percentage of seats dropped from 82 to 78 percent.[103] Although the Federalist Party was still a competitive party, Stagg notes that the fusion strategy served to blemish the reputation of the Federalist Party as a credible alternative to the Republican Party.[104] The long-term consequences of this alliance would be further evident in the 1816 presidential election when Republican presidential candidate, James Monroe, won 16 states and 183 electoral votes. Rufus King, the candidate of the Federalist Party, won only Massachusetts, Connecticut and Delaware, resulting in 34 electoral votes. The election of 1816 would be the last presidential election contested by the Federalist Party.[105]

Madison's Second Inauguration

Madison's second inaugural address delivered on March 4, 1813 was focused almost exclusively on the war, which had now been in progress for slightly less than a year. His address served to inform the American people that due to the hostility of Britain, the United States had little choice but to declare war. "It was not declared on the part of the United States until it had been long made on them, in reality though not in name; until arguments and postulations had been exhausted . . . "[106] Madison stressed how the country's independence and reputation had been threatened by Britain, which necessitated a declaration of war. "On the issue of war are staked our national sovereignty on the high seas and the security of an important class of citizens whose occupations give the proper value to those of every other class."[107] He proceeded to describe Britain's transgressions against the United States, which included impressment, requiring Americans to fight against their own country, along with arming "savages . . . eager to glut their savage thirst with the blood of the vanquished and to finish the work of torture and death on maimed and defenseless captives."[108] He concluded his address by praising the efforts of the navy, and the heroic efforts of the American military.[109] It was evident in Madison's second inauguration speech that his second term

---

[103] Hickey, *The War of 1812*, pp. 239-240.
[104] Stagg, "James Madison"
[105] 270towin.com/1816_Election/InteractiveMap.
[106] Transcript of Madison's Second Inaugural Address, March 4, 1813; online at milliercenter.org. ((Accessed December 20, 2023.)
[107] Ibid.
[108] Ibid.
[109] Ibid.

would be consumed with the war against Britain. Indeed, Madison was so consumed with the war that during the second year of the conflict he became extremely sick and so immobilized that rumors began circulating that death was imminent and succession likely. Some suggested that Dolley, not the President, was directing the war effort.[110]

The War of 1812, as Hickey observes, was the most unpopular war in American history. There was never a national consensus regarding the necessity to go to war. Although there were no public opinion polls to measure support for the war, the war remained unpopular until the final peace treaty was signed. The Republican Party, with the exception of the anti-Madison faction, was closely associated with the war, while the Federalist Party was uniformly opposed to the conflict. The party divisions in Congress were profound. Of the 305 roll calls related to the prosecution of the war that were conducted in the House of Representatives from June 1, 1812 to February 14, 1815, 94.4 percent of Federalists on average routinely voted against the measures.[111] Of the 227 war related proposals introduced in the Senate, on average 92.5 percent of Federalists voted as a block in opposition to the war.[112] Never in the history of the United States had there ever been such intense partisan opposition on the floors of Congress to one of the nation's wars.[113]

The Hartford Convention

So opposed to the war were the New England Federalists that a convention was held in the city of Hartford, Connecticut to review the war's impact on the economies of New England states, and more broadly to discuss the effects of the war on the future of the Federalist Party. The convention was held from December 1814 to January 5, 1815. Federalists in Massachusetts initiated the idea of a convention and sent invitations to the other New England states to send delegates.[114] Connecticut and Rhode Island, both hotbeds of strong Federalist sentiment, quickly accepted the invitation, while the governors of Vermont and New Hampshire, although supporting Federalist concerns, declined the invitation. Nevertheless, despite the declinations, Federalist opposition was so strong in two townships in New Hampshire and in one township in Vermont that delegates from those local communities were selected to attend the convention.[115] Because

[110] Chadwick, *James and Dolley Madison,* p. 229.
[111] Hickey, *The War of 1812*, p. 261.
[112] Ibid.
[113] Ibid.
[114] Beirne, *the War of 1812*, p. 325.
[115] Ibid., p. 326.

attendance was somewhat sparce, the Hartford Convention, as Beirne notes, was "handicapped" from the start.[116]

The convention was conducted in total secrecy. The proceedings were released for publication to the *Hartford Courant*.[117] A list of grievances against presidents Jefferson and Madison, condemnation of the war against Britain, along with seven recommended constitutional amendments comprised the work of the Hartford Convention.[118] The seven amendments, in Beirne's view, reflected parochial interests intended to "suit the specific needs of New England with little consideration for the rest of the country."[119] Contained within the convention's report was also a hint at secession by the New England states, although this was tempered in the passage that read, "the severance of the Union by one or more States, against the will of the rest, and especially in times of war, can be justified, only by absolute necessity."[120]

The War of 1812 involved a number of maritime battles between the American and British navies. Naval battles were fought on the Atlantic Ocean, and on the Great Lakes. When the war started, the American navy had a total of only 16 warships compared to hundreds of British warships, although most of the British ships were deployed to fight Napoleon, not the United States. Fighting Napoleon was deemed by the British government a much higher priority.[121] Land battles between the Americans and British soldiers were also fought in a variety of locations in the United States and in parts of Canada.

The American military expeditions in Canada were unsuccessful.[122] In addition to encountering strong resistance from British troops in Canada, the Americans confronted loyalists who had fled to Canada during the American Revolution. Additionally, the Americans faced opposition from French Canadians and Indian tribes who, like the loyalists, preferred that Canada remain a part of the British Empire, rather than the United States.[123] Mancini comments, "Resistance to the American military became a nation-defining cause for Canada's people, who celebrate the war of 1812 to this day."[124]

---

[116] Ibid.
[117] Ibid., p. 330.
[118] Ibid., p. 331.
[119] Ibid.
[120] Hartford Convention report quoted in Beirne, *The War of 1812*, p. 330.
[121] Mark Mancini, "13 Facts About the War of 1812," Mental Floss; online at mentalfloss.com/article/559236/war-of-1812-facts. (Accessed February 10, 2024.)
[122] Cost, *James Madison*, p. 334.
[123] Mancini, "13 Facts About the War of 1812"
[124] Ibid.

Battles were also fought between the Americans and British-aligned Native American tribes in the Northwest Territory. In the year before the war was declared, American forces under the leadership of territorial governor William Henry Harrison had won a significant victory against Native American tribes led by the Shawnee chief Tecumseh. The "Battle, Tippecanoe" as Cost notes, "turned Harrison into a national hero and seemingly confirmed the fears that the Natives had become the cat's paw of the British."[125] Harrison's reputation would contribute to his election as president in 1840. With John Tyler as his running mate "Tippecanoe and Tyler Too" became the campaign slogan to mobilize voters for Harrison during the 1840 campaign.

Significant American victories during the War of 1812 included, among others, Captain Oliver Hazard Perry's dramatic naval victory against the British on Lake Erie.[126] Following the battle, Perry's message to his superiors became immortalized, "We have met the enemy and he is ours."[127] Moreover, an American victory, once again under the leadership of William Henry Harrison, occurred in the "Battle of the Thames." This fierce battle was fought in Canada (what became the province of Ontario) against British forces and Tecumseh's tribe. Tecumseh was killed during this battle resulting in the collapse of his mighty Confederation.[128] There was also the American victory in the "Battle of New Orleans," which elevated Andrew Jackson to an American legend. This battle was celebrated as the greatest American victory during the war, despite the fact that the historic battle occurred in 1815, shortly after the war had officially ended. Jackson's forces that repelled the British were a mix of American soldiers, Gulf Coast pirates, former slaves, and members of the Choctaw tribe.[129] Wood describes the significance of Jackson's victory in these terms, "The American victory at New Orleans was so overwhelming -- the British suffered two-thousand casualties, including the death of General Pakenham, to Jackson's seventy – that the Americans came to believe that the United States had really won the war and dictated the peace terms, even though the peace treaty had already been signed."[130]

---

[125] Cost, *James Madison*, p. 324.
[126] Feldman, *The Three Lives of James Madison*, p. 567.
[127] Perry quoted in Feldman, *The Three Lives of James Madison*, p. 567.
[128] Feldman, *The Three Lives of James Madison*, pp. 568-569.
[129] Mancini, "13 facts About the War of 1812"
[130] Wood, *Empire of Liberty*, p. 695.

The Treaty of Ghent

The Treaty of Ghent in 1814 brought an end to the War of 1812. The Americans claimed victory and frequently noted how the war was America's "Second War for Independence." In reality, however, neither country was the victor. The historic treaty was negotiated in the port city of Ghent, Belgium. Madison had appointed a distinguished commission of treaty negotiators, which included the treasury secretary, Albert Gallatin, John Quincy Adams who was serving as Minister to Russia, and James A. Baynard, a Delaware Federalist who Madison trusted. The War Hawk Henry Clay was eventually added to the negotiating team, along with Minister to England, Jonathan Russell. Madison appointed Adams to head the commission.[131] With Britain now gaining the upper hand against Napoleon on the European Continent, the Americans were concerned that the British might soon divert more of their resources and manpower to the war in America. Nevertheless, the American team of negotiators was "exceptionally strong" with four of the commissioners distinguished public servants.[132]

Russia, led by Czar Alexander I, with ulterior motivates, offered to send representatives to mediate the treaty. In the view of the Russian government, a peace treaty between the United States and Britain would allow the British to concentrate their efforts on defeating Napoleon, while allowing the United States to reestablish commercial trade relations with Russia. The Russian offer was accepted by the Americans, but rejected by the British.[133]

From August to December in 1814, the American and British negotiating teams advanced the interests of their countries by holding firm on key issues. British impressment of American sailors, Britain's control over Canada, the status of Britain's alliance with Indian tribes in the Northwest Territory, the naval and military activity of both countries in the Great Lakes region, American fishing rights along the Canadian coast, and Britain's right to navigate on the Mississippi River were among the main points of contention between the two negotiating teams.[134]

The Treaty of Ghent was finally agreed to by both countries and signed on Christmas Eve in 1814. However, despite five grueling months of intensive negotiations, nothing of importance had been resolved. The root cause of the war was never addressed, nor did the negotiators resolve how to create better relations

---

[131] Hickey, *The War of 1812*, p. 287.
[132] Ibid., p. 288.
[133] Ibid., p. 286.
[134] Ibid., pp. 290-297.

between the two countries. The war, in other words, never solved anything. As Beirne writes,

> From August through December the negotiators had struggled, yet after five months of labor not a single disputed point found settlement in the finished document. Some of these disputed points were left for future commissions to tackle. Impressment, that bitter bone of contention was was not mentioned. The treaty was, in substance, a mere agreement to let matters stand as they had stood before the war.[135]

Madison expressed relief when he learned that a peace treaty had finally been signed. The war, which his political opponents had routinely depicted as "Mr. Madison's War," had finally ended. Although little had been resolved, Madison still believed the war had value. "The President thus knew that though the Treaty of Ghent seemed to settle nothing . . . the United States by standing up to Britain, had won a second war of independence."[136]

The British government had already ratified the treaty by the time Madison on February 15, 1815 submitted the final text to the Senate for ratification. Weary of the war, the Senate on February 16 in a show of rare bipartisan support ratified the treaty by unanimous vote, 35 to 0. Madison received notice of the ratification on the same day and issued his final approval.[137] Although a stalemate with nothing of substance rectified, Brookhiser, Ketcham and Wood still identify value in this unpopular war. According to Brookhiser, the War of 1812 was "a war of national self-assertion --- a second war of independence. In such contests, the underdog has bragging rights. By not losing, America had won."[138] Ketcham states, "Despite the bungling and defeats early in the war, the grave weakness of the nation during it, and even the apparently armistice-like peace, the circumstances of its conclusion, mirrored in the exciting events in Washington in February 1815, produced a dramatic, gratifying effect."[139] Wood offers the strongest and most positive view of the war's value, "Although the treaty seemed to have settle none of the issues that had caused the War of 1812, it actually had settled everything. It was true that the treaty never mentioned the issues of impressment and neutral rights that were the ostensible causes of the war, but that did not matter. It was not merely the fact that the end of the European war rendered the issues of neutral rights moot; more important was the fact that the results of

[135] Beirne, *The War of 1812*, pp. 385-386.
[136] Ketcham, *James Madison*, p. 597.
[137] Hickey, *The War of 1812*, p. 300.
[138] Brookhiser, *James Madison*, p. 219.
[139] Ketcham, *James Madison*, p. 598.

the war vindicated what those issues had come to symbolize – the nation's independence and sovereignty."[140]

Madison as Commander-in Chief

Presidents, according to the Constitution, do not have the authority to declare war. That is a power delegated to Congress in Article I, Sec. 8 of the U.S. Constitution. Presidents, however, can request Congress to declare war against a foreign power, such as that which Madison did in his war message. Once war is declared by Congress, the constitutional responsibility for prosecuting the war then shifts to the president under Article II of the Constitution which designates the president as the nation's commander-in-chief. The American constitutional system, the brainchild of Madison, requires an elected civilian, not a military officer, to serve as the head of the U.S. military. Although some presidents have had extensive military experience, such as Presidents Jackson, Taylor, Grant and Eisenhower, others, such as Jefferson and Madison, were not military men.

The scholarly biographies of Madison do a fine job of covering the War of 1812, the politics associated with the war, the key battles, and the Treaty of Ghent. Sometimes missing in these works is a discussion of Madison's performance as the nation's commander-in-chief. It is well understood, as Hickey notes, that Madison was not a commander-in-chief in the same vein as that of Presidents Lincoln, Wilson and Franklin Roosevelt. Nevertheless, Madison was the commander-chief during the country's first declared war, which requires an appraisal of his performance.

Those who have examined Madison's role as commander-in-chief, have not showered praise on his leadership during the War of 1812. The scholarly assessments suggests that Madison was a rather poor commander-in-chief. Although Congress during the war was characterized by factionalism, negligence related to financing the war, and unnecessary delay in reestablishing the National Bank, which in 1814 could have prevented an economic crisis, the dysfunctionality of the legislative branch during the war years could still have been prevented had Madison demonstrated a more vigorous style of leadership.[141] As Hickey put it, "Cautious, shy and circumspect, Madison was unable to supply the bold and vigorous leadership that was needed."[142] The war may have been called "Mr. Madison's War," but by no means did Madison lead and prosecute

[140] Wood, *Empire of Liberty*, p. 697.
[141] Hickey, *The War of 1812*, p. 304.
[142] Ibid.

this war as one would expect from a commander-in-chief. The war "never bore his stamp."[143]

Madison's ineffective leadership during the war was further on display in his appointment of several less than competent cabinet secretaries along with his tolerance for generals with questionable experience and judgment.[144] Reflecting on Madison's leadership at the start of the war, John C. Calhoun, one of the leading War Hawks, commented, "Our President has not those commanding talents, which are necessary to control those about him."[145] Thus, the record does not suggest that Madison performed effectively in one of the most important constitutional roles assigned to the president.

Madison's Final Years in Office

With the war concluded, Madison had less than two years remaining as president. Even though there was no prohibition on presidents seeking a third term, the two-term tradition established by George Washington had set a precedent which Madison intended to honor. He would not seek a third term.

Most presidents in their final years of office become what are known as "lame ducks." Members of Congress feel under no obligation to support a president who is making his exit, and the focus shifts to whoever the next president might be and the policy goals of those planning to seek the presidency. Although presidents in the twilight of their presidency normally fade from relevance, this was hardly the case for President James Madison. Indeed, Madison's final two years in office were filled with creative legislative initiatives, some of which he had placed on the back burner due to the war, and some which reflected what he had learned from the war.

In his seventh State of the Union message delivered to Congress on December 15, 1815, a year after the Treaty of Ghent had been signed, Madison recommended a major reorganization and strengthening of state militia units. This would allow future presidents to rapidly mobilize militias for defensive purposes. Mobilizing state militias during the war was a serious problem that Madison had encountered. Madison also proposed a major reorganization and strengthening of the U.S. Navy with the goal of improving the navy's capabilities and efficiency during both war and peacetime.[146]

---

[143] Ibid.
[144] Ibid.
[145] Calhoun to James Macbride, April 18, 1812, in Meriwether et. al., *Papers of John C. Calhoun, 1:99-100;* quoted in Hickey, *The War of 1812*, pp. 304-305.
[146] Gutzman, *James Madison*, p. 329.

The biggest surprise was Madison's vigorous support for rechartering the National Bank. This must have come as a big surprise, particularly to members of his own party who most certainly remembered Madison's fierce opposition to the Bank when it was first proposed by Hamilton. Madison had apparently been persuaded by Gallatin, his former treasury secretary, that the Bank was in the national interest. The Bank was subsequently approved by Congress and rechartered with Madison's signature on April 10, 1816.[147] Discussing Madison's support for the Bank in 1816, Donald O. Dewey captures the President's view this way, "Madison explained that it was still his abstract opinion that the authority to charter a national bank could not be found in the pages of the Constitution. A lengthy series of precedents overruled his individual opinion. The bank had undergone a thorough discussion in Congress before it was established, it had been in operation for twenty years with annual recognition of it by Congress, it had even been extended into new states."[148] Madison thus recognized that the Bank had become a legitimate arm of the federal government and that resistance was no longer necessary. In a landmark ruling handed down by the U.S. Supreme Court after Madison had left office, the Court in 1819 upheld the constitutionality of the Bank based on the implied powers of Congress.[149]

Approaching the end of his presidency, Madison's legislative agenda included a proposal to establish a national university in the nation's capital. He also recommended tariffs on foreign imports to provide protection for American companies that manufactured items related to national defense.[150] At the same time, Madison focused on infrastructure with legislative proposals to build canals and roads.[151] Cost observes that towards the end of his presidency it was apparent that Madison had "abandoned the idyllic mythology of a virtuous republic populated with independent farmers" and had accepted Hamilton's economic vision for America.[152] "What emerged from the final two years of Madison's presidency, therefore was a hybrid ---Hamiltonian economics with Madisonian politics."[153]

---

[147] Ibid., p. 330.
[148] Donald O. Dewey, "James Madison Helps Clio Interpret the Constitution, *The American Journal of Legal History*, Vol. 15., No. 1 (January 1971); online at https://www.jstor.or/stable/844193/ (Accessed March 16, 2024.)
[149] *McCulloch v. Maryland.*,17 U.S. 316 (1819)
[150] Gutzman, *James Madison,* p. 330.
[151] Ibid.
[152] Cost, *James Madison*, p. 375.
[153] Ibid. 376.

Madison's eighth and final State of the Union message to Congress, once again delivered in writing, was presented on December 3, 1816. James Monroe, who Madison supported for president had recently been elected, thus maintaining the "Virginia Dynasty's" hold on the presidency.[154] In his final message to Congress, Madison reiterated his support for strengthening the hand of the president over state militias and continued support for infrastructure development. He again recommended the establishment of a national university located in Washington, D.C.[155] Although he was a slave owner and a firm supporter of the institution of slavery, Madison made it a point to note that the country during his presidency was the first to officially prohibit the importation of slaves from Africa. He also recommended in his message to Congress that legislation should be passed to prevent the illegal trafficking of slaves by slave smugglers.[156] Madison concluded his final message by identifying the virtues of the Constitution and how the Constitution was able "to contain in its combination of the federative and elective principles a reconcilement of public strength with individual liberty."[157] It was only fitting that the "Father of the Constitution" in his final message to Congress would highlight the beauty of the United States Constitution.

His Last Act as President

Madison's very last act as president was to veto what was known as the "Bonus Bill." The bill, which Calhoun had sponsored, "allowed for a $1,500,000 bonus paid by the Bank, along with future dividends on its stock, for a canal and road building scheme – 'internal improvements' in the language of the day."[158] Although Madison strongly supported infrastructure improvement, he opposed the Bonus Bill on the grounds that if passed it would extend a power to Congress beyond what was enumerated in the Constitution. In Madison's view, neither Congress' commerce power or the powers implied in the "necessary and proper clause," nor for that matter the "general welfare clause," permitted Congress to spend federal money in the manner that was being proposed in the Bonus Bill.[159] A firm believer in keeping the spending power of Congress limited to what the Constitution authorized, Madison, despite objections from members of his own

[154] Cheney, *The Virginia Dynasty*.
[155] Gutzman, *James Madison,* p. 330.
[156] Ibid.
[157] James Madison's Eighth Annual Message, *WJM,* 8: 375-85; quoted in Gutzman, *James Madison,* p. 331.
[158] Rutland, *James Madison*, p. 238.
[159] Ibid.

party, vetoed the bill.[160] "The president's strict constructionism took Congress by surprise and touched off a long debate over where, how and why Congress could dispense federal money."[161]

Monroe had won the 1816 election with an overwhelming 183 electoral vote count to Rufus King's 39. This election marked the end of the Federalist Party and the start of a period during which the Republican Party faced little to no opposition. With the war over and party politics calmed, Monroe would serve as president during a tranquil period which historians have dubbed "the Era of Good Feelings."[162] Madison attended Monroe's inauguration conducted on March 4, 1817. With his presidency officially over, the time had arrived for the Madisons to leave the capital. Gutzman writes, "Unburdened of public office, Madison joined Dolley in one last whirl of socializing. Then they headed home to Orange County."[163] Yet as the next chapter will reveal, although officially retired, Madison's commitment to public service was far from over.

---

160 Ibid.
161 Ibid.
162 McGrath, *James Monroe,* passim.
163 Gutzman, *James Madison*, p. 335.

Chapter Eight

Madison Retired – Still A Public Servant

Although Madison's many years of official public service were now over, this is not to suggest that when he returned to Montpelier that he devoted all of his waking hours to the management of his plantation and overseeing the duties of his slaves. Although the agricultural efficiency of his plantation was a priority due to his family's economic dependence on the sale of crops, which experienced a decline in prices when the "bottom fell out of the grain market,"[1] Madison in retirement was still able to devote considerable energy to an array of projects beyond the production of his plantation.

Madison's Notes From the Constitutional Convention

One project during Madison's retirement related to his legacy as the "Father of the Constitution." This involved a meticulous editing of his journal notes that he took in shorthand when serving as a delegate to the Constitutional Convention in 1787. Madison was aware that his notes would be the only detailed record of the debates, speeches, and key decisions that occurred at the Philadelphia Convention during that very hot summer. Madison was extremely protective of his notes and determined to make them, some of which were vague and incomplete, as informative as possible. In retirement he spent countless hours devoted to refining his notes "out of fear that his enemies would use it against him and that its incompleteness and errors would distort a strict constitutionalist approach to the Constitution."[2] So committed was Madison to avoiding future criticism of his notes, that he enlisted the help of Dolley's brother, John C. Payne, to make a fresh copy of his convention journal that would include "many of his emendations and corrections into the text."[3] A second reason related to Madison's

---

[1] Ketcham, *James Madison*, p. 623.
[2] Library of Congress, "James Madison and the Federal Constitutional Convention of 1787;" online at loc.gov/collection/James-Madison-papers/articles-and-essays/ (Accessed December 24, 2023.)
[3] Ibid.

careful editing of his notes, which were published four years after his death in 1840, reflected his desire to correct how he was portrayed in a partial body of notes taken by Robert Yates, one of New York's delegates to the Constitutional Convention.[4] Yates was one of the leading Antifederalists and identified as the author of the Brutus essays.[5] Yates' notes from the Convention were subsequently copied into a manuscript by John Lansing, another delegate from New York who opposed the Constitution. A complicated story followed resulting in Lansing's manuscript falling into the hands of Edmond Charles "Citizen Genet," a French diplomat to the United States and a critic of Madison.[6] Yates' notes, revised and heavily edited by Genet, were released in 1821. This body of notes troubled Madison, particularly because they contained inaccurate summaries of his positions on key constitutional questions, one of which was his perspective on federal and state relations.[7] Madison's careful revisions were thus intended to not only present an accurate version of the Convention's proceedings, which he wanted the public to read, but were also intended to counter misrepresentations of his positions at the Convention. Genet's goal, according to James Hutson, was to "discredit the Father of the Constitution."[8]

A three-volume set edited by Max Farrand is considered one of the most reliable treatments of Madison's final notes.[9] Additionally, a more recent and revealing treatment of Madison's notes, which examines in meticulous detail the changes and edits he made, is the acclaimed work of Mary Sarah Bilder.[10] One can picture Madison during his years in retirement poring over his original notes deciding with pen in hand what he wanted the public to read and not read. Much time during his retirement was devoted to his notes. His notes are now archived in the Manuscript Division of the Library of Congress. In an interview regarding her path breaking work, Bilder pointed out that Madison's notes were published as part of his public papers, not as a separate body of work. Yet "beginning in the mid-19th century, people began to understand the notes as if they were an official record of the Convention, something Madison himself was very adamant that they

---

[4] James H. Hutson, "Robert Yates's Notes on the Constitutional Convention of 1787: Citizen Genet's Edition," The Quarterly Journal of the Library of Congress, Vol. 35, No. 3 (July 1978), pp. 173-182. (Accessed April 27, 2024.)

[5] "The Founding Fathers New York;" online at archives.gov/founding-docs/founding-fathers-new York. (Accessed May 28, 2024.)

[6] Hutson, "Robert Yates' Notes"

[7] Ibid.

[8] Ibid., p. 179.

[9] Max Farrand, ed., *The Record of the Federal Convention of 1787, 3 volumes,* (New Haven: Yale University Press, 1911).

[10] Mary Sarah Bilder, *Madison's Hand* (Cambridge: Harvard University Press, 2015).

weren't. He insisted they were just notes taken by a member."[11] Bilder observed that many people today regard Madison's notes as having the same level of formality as congressional proceedings published in the Congressional Record.[12]

Mr. Jefferson's University

Thomas Jefferson, who strongly advocated a strict separation of Church and State, had been educated at the College of William and Mary, a college established during colonial times and rooted in the Anglican tradition. Yet despite his own education, Jefferson's dream was to establish a public university free of religious doctrine, with an emphasis on the classics, government, and law. A rigorous and secular public university was Jefferson's vision. He also insisted that his university once established would make no distinctions between freshmen, sophomores, juniors and seniors. Students would also select their preferred areas of study without having to take core requirements.[13] Jefferson further recommended that the mandatory teaching of theology, which was characteristic of most colleges at the time, including the college he had attended, should be strictly prohibited. "He was also extremely sensitive to the way boards of trustees at other major colleges, usually dominated by the clergy, imposed restrictions on what could be taught or what books could be read. He was insistent that his university not succumb to such forms of censorship."[14] With respect to the administrative functioning of the university he envisioned, Jefferson wanted his institution to be run by faculty and students, with oversight provided by a Board of Visitors. He was adamant that his university should be run without a central executive authority. "Self-government" was the core principal upon which Jefferson's university would function.[15]

In addition to his firm belief in academic freedom and secular education, Jefferson directly involved himself in the physical design of his university His goal was to create the appearance of an "academical village."[16] Jefferson was thus involved in virtually every aspect of the university he planned to create. This ranged from the institution's mission, the type of learning that would take place,

---

[11] Mary Sarah Bilder interview with Erik Owens, Boisi Center, p. 1.

[12] Ibid.

[13] Joseph J. Ellis, *American Sphinx: The Character of Thomas Jefferson* (New York: Vintage Books, 1998), p. 341.

[14] Ibid. p. 339.

[15] Ibid. p. 341.

[16] "Jefferson's Plan for an Academical Villiage," online at Monticello.org/research/ education/thoms-jefferson-encyclopedia/jeffersons-plan-academical-village/ (Accessed January 8, 2924.)

the architectural design of the university, the faculty who would be hired, and the manner in which the university would be governed. And who better to assist Jefferson in fulfilling his vision of an academical village than his friend and protégé' now living in retirement at Montpelier, James Madison.

Upon receiving Jefferson's invitation to help him create a university, Madison, ecstatic over such an opportunity, fully committed himself to Jefferson's project. Reflecting his strong commitment to religious freedom, Madison agreed with Jefferson that theology should not be a required subject of study. Yet Madison still insisted that students should at least be given the opportunity to read major theological works if they so desired. He therefore developed a catalogue of religious readings which he felt should be available on the shelves of the university's library. Works Madison recommended included those of "the Apostolic fathers and a good number of ante-Nicene fathers."[17] He also recommended to Jefferson that the religious writings of John Locke be made available to students, along with seminal works associated with Islam and the Quaker religion.[18]

Jefferson was grateful for having Madison join in his efforts to establish a first class state university. He also demanded a lot from Madison, perhaps more than Madison anticipated. When Madison missed the first meeting of the committee that Jefferson had assembled to review his plan, Jefferson sent him a sharp letter of rebuke in which he reminded him that in the future all members of the committee were expected to attend his meetings. Jefferson also sent a similar letter, quite remarkably, to Monroe who had recently been inaugurated president.[19] As Ellis writes, "The episode illustrates Jefferson's total immersion in his new educational and architectural venture; it never occurred to him that the outgoing and incoming presidents of the United States might have more important things to do."[20]

Madison not only helped Jefferson with the planning of his university, he also donated some of his own money to help with the building of the institution. Moreover, once the university was officially established, Madison was appointed by Jefferson to serve on the Board of Visitors. When Jefferson died in 1826, Madison succeeded Jefferson as the rector of the university, a position he held for several years.[21] The University of Virginia, which continues to be known as

---

[17] Gutzman, *James Madison*, p. 336.
[18] Ibid.
[19] Ellis, *American Sphinx*, p. 335.
[20] Ibid.
[21] Gutzman, *James Madison*, p. 337.

"Mr. Jefferson's University," was officially founded in 1819 in Charlottesville, Virginia. The university, Ellis observes, is "barely visible on a clear day" from Monticello.[22]

Although the building that houses the office of the president is named "Madison Hall," there is, oddly, no statue of Madison on the grounds of the University of Virginia. There is of course a statue of Jefferson on the campus, along with a statue of George Washington, even though Washington had nothing to do with the founding of UVA.[23] The absence of a Madison statue was noted by Jim Todd, a professor in the university's Woodrow Wilson School of Government. Todd expressed how unfortunate it was that no statue of Madison can be found on the grounds, particularly after all that Madison did to help found and lead the university.[24] Perhaps the time has arrived to recognize Madison's contributions to the University of Virginia in the form of a statue.

Slavery and Statehood

At the same time that Madison was helping his mentor establish a public university, he was drawn into an exchange with political figures regarding the complex issue of statehood and slavery. A supporter of slavery himself, along with the fact that the party he had formed had southern and pro-slavery roots, it was not too surprising that Madison would side with southern interests regarding this political controversy. The question arose when many Virginians after settling in the Missouri Territory decided to apply to Congress for statehood.[25] Their application for statehood however was met with stringent conditions proposed by a congressman from New York by the name of James Tallmadge.[26] Although Tallmadge was a member of the Republican Party, his legislative response stipulated that for Missouri to gain statehood it had to first comply with two specific conditions. First, transportation of slaves to Missouri after statehood could no longer be allowed. Second, those slaves in Missouri who had reached adulthood, defined as twenty-five years of age, were to be freed.[27]

The New York Congressman's conditions caused immediate division between lawmakers from slave states and those from states where slavery was

---

[22] Ellis, *American Sphinx*, p. 335.
[23] Jim Todd, "Madison's Role in the Founding of the University of Virginia," February 14, 2020; online at engagement.virginia.edu/learn/2020/02/14/ (Accessed January 29, 2024.)
[24] Ibid.
[25] Gutzman, *James Madison*, p. 337.
[26] Ibid.
[27] Ibid.

prohibited or less ingrained. With pen in hand, Madison responded to Tallmadge's conditions by supporting states' rights and the interests of slave owners. He took issue with Tallmadge's contention that the "1808 Clause" contained within the first paragraph of Article I, Section 9 of the U.S. Constitution, which prohibited the importation of slaves beginning in 1808, was intended to prohibit slavery in new states. Madison rejected Tallmadge's position by arguing that the intent of this Clause had absolutely nothing to do with prohibiting slavery among the states, but rather was intended to prohibit the importation of slaves to the United States from foreign countries.[28] Tallmadge's constitutional interpretation, in Madison's view, was incorrect with respect to the original intent of the "1808 Clause." To bolster his rebuttal, Madison drew from the notes he took at the Constitutional Convention as well as the *Federalist Papers*, several of which he personally authored.[29]

Following his treatment of the "1808 Clause," Madison then turned his attention to Talmadge's argument that Article IV, Section 3, known as the "Territories Clause," was yet another reason why Congress had the authority to prohibit slavery in new states.[30] As stated in this Clause "The Congress shall have Power to dispose of and make all needful Rules and regulations respecting the Territories or other Property belonging to the United States." Like his interpretation of the "1808 Clause" Madison dissected the "Territories Clause" and interpreted it as pertaining only to Congress' management of physical property, not slave property, in the territories. The Clause in his view did not give Congress the authority to prohibit slavery.[31] Madison made it clear that the "Territories Clause" was unrelated to slavery within a state. Thus, because states could decide for themselves whether or not to allow slavery, so too could Missouri once it achieved statehood. In Madison's opinion, if Congress prevented slavery in the new state of Missouri, this would have the effect of reducing the sovereignty of that state compared to other states.[32] Madison's constitutional interpretations, as Gutzman observes, "adopted the most 'southern' or pro-slavery arguments."[33]

Another Constitutional Convention

When Madison was in retirement, a constitutional reform effort arose within his home state which led to a state convention for the purpose of amending the

[28] Ibid.
[29] Ibid.
[30] Ibid., p. 338.
[31] Ibid.
[32] Ibid.
[33] Ibid., p. 340.

Virginia Constitution. Madison, who had helped draft the state's first constitution in 1776 was once again selected to attend the convention as a delegate from Orange County. The year was 1829. Thus, after fifty-three years, Madison was once again serving as a delegate to his state's constitutional convention. He was twenty-five in 1776, and seventy-eight in 1829. The convention was held at the state Capitol in Richmond.

Most of the convention's delegates selected for the convention were distinguished individuals with many years of public service.[34] James Monroe, who had served two successful terms as president, was chosen as a delegate. John Marshall, the current Chief Justice of the U.S. Supreme Court was also a delegate. Another delegate was the former Virginia governor, current U.S. Senator and future President, John Tyler.[35]

Madison nominated Monroe to serve as the convention's presiding officer. Monroe accepted the nomination and ably directed the convention's proceedings.[36] Not all of the delegates, which included Madison's political enemy, John Randolph, welcomed Madison's participation as a delegate, although the younger delegates who had only heard of Madison but had never met him were awed by his presence. They "saw Madison as a demigod whose thoughts and career had been guides for them for as long as they could remember."[37] As he did at the Constitutional Convention in Philadelphia, Madison positioned himself close to the front row and intensely followed the convention proceedings.[38] His dress and demeanor must have intrigued the younger delegates who likely marveled at his "old fashioned powdered hair, black clothes and shoe buckles."[39] At seventy-eight years old, Madison's dress was more in line with colonial times. It must also have been an extraordinary experience for the younger delegates to participate in the presence of two former presidents, one of whom was known as the "Father of the Constitution," along with the other highly distinguished delegates.

The two central issues before the convention pertained to voting rights for non-property owners, and the formula for allocating seats in the Virginia House of Representatives. The first contested issue involved the state requirement that only property owning males could vote.[40] Madison was instrumental in resolving the property issue by proposing that voting rights should be extended to

---

[34] Ketcham, *James Madison*, p. 637.
[35] Gutzman, *James Madison*, p. 353.
[36] Ketcham, *James Madison*, p. 637
[37] Ibid.
[38] Ibid.
[39] Ibid., pp. 638-639.
[40] Ibid., pp.637-638.

non-property owners, as long as such individuals were taxpayers.[41] His proposal was supported in committee and also supported on the floor. Voting rights were therefore extended in the state of Virginia. Madison had convinced his fellow delegates that with city populations increasing where property owning was less likely that it would be unfair for the rising populations in these areas to be denied the vote and controlled by the propertied class of Virginians. [42] Madison's argument was typical of his clear, intelligent, and low-keyed persuasive style.

With respect to the more complex issue of allocating representatives to the populations in eastern and western Virginia, Madison faced stiff resistance. Eastern delegates were adamant about keeping their advantage in the state legislature which was enhanced due to the number of slaves in that part of the state. Virginians in the western portion of the state however insisted that only whites should be counted for the allocation of representatives, not slaves who of course did not have voting rights. According to Ketcham, "Under the old constitution, counting slaves, white votes in the east had at least twice as much weight as white votes in the west."[43] Drawing from the compromise at the Constitutional Convention in 1787, Madison proposed that three-fifths of the state's slave population should be counted for representation purposes in the lower chamber. Yet despite Madison's efforts to create a more equitable system of representation for eastern and western Virginians, and despite the fact that he rose and spoke to the convention to defend his proposal, the one and only time he addressed the convention, he was unsuccessful in persuading a majority of delegates to support his compromise.[44] Ketcham writes, "eastern delegates defeated Madison's three-fifths compromise and then pushed through provisions maintaining eastern control of both houses of the legislature."[45] Madison thus resolved one issue pertaining to voting rights for non-property owners, but despite his efforts to forge an acceptable compromise, was unsuccessful in resolving how legislative seats should be apportioned in Virginia. Once the representation issue was decided, the constitutional convention was adjourned and Madison returned to Montpelier.

President of the American Colonization Society

Madison owned many slaves throughout the course of his adult life. Slaves were central to the functioning of the Montpelier plantation. A slave from the time

---

[41] Ibid., p. 637.
[42] Ibid. p. 638.
[43] Ibid.
[44] Ibid,. p. 639.
[45] Ibid., p. 639.

of Madison's childhood until the day he died routinely tended to his personal needs. As noted in a previous chapter, a slave tended to Madison's needs when he attended the College of New Jersey. While in retirement, Madison had come to the realization that when slavery was ended in the United States, which he believed would someday happen, freed slaves could never coexist alongside whites. He was in general agreement with Jefferson who articulated this very point in his *Notes on the State of Virginia*, the one book he authored and published.[46] "Blacks, Jefferson reasoned, hated whites, who gave them new reasons to do so every day; whites, he held, were prejudiced against blacks and were not likely to cease being prejudiced."[47] Madison, like Jefferson, could not envision thousands of former slaves living and intermingling with whites. Given the huge number of slaves in Virginia, another solution had to be found if southern slaves were ever emancipated.

The solution to this "problem" in the view of both Jefferson and Madison would be the creation of a colony where former slaves could be transported and where they could live in freedom with their families. The concept of colonization gained considerable traction in a number of southern states, as evident by the establishment of the American Colonization Society in 1816. Madison was selected to serve as the Society's president.[48] The Society, according to Cheney, "had many luminaries in its ranks – including Henry Clay, Daniel Webster, Francis Scott Key and John Marshall. It was nonetheless controversial, not so much because, as might think today, it advocated expatriating former slaves, but because it was regarded as an antislavery organization."[49]

The concept of colonization was very appealing to Madison, although he knew that implementation could be difficult. Under Madison's leadership and watchful eye, Society members considered a variety of locations in North America for the colony. Concluding that a colony in North America was less than desirable, the Society began reviewing the possibility of establishing a colony in Africa.[50]

To expedite colonization, Madison recommended that the federal government should not only buy slaves from slave owners, but also pay for their resettlement. With approximately 1.5 million slaves on American soil, Madison estimated that the total cost of the colonization project would be in the vicinity of

---

[46] Gutzman, *James Madison*, p. 355.
[47] Ibid.
[48] Ibid., p. 356.
[49] Cheney, *James Madison*, p. 433.
[50] Ibid.

$600 million.[51] To raise the necessary funds, Madison recommended that the federal government sell millions of western acres currently under its control to American settlers.[52] To those who had reservations about the federal government managing the colonization project and the cost involved, Madison replied, "It is the nation which is to reap the benefit. The nation therefore ought to bear the burden."[53]

In 1821, a land deal in Africa was finally agreed to between the American Colonization Society and African tribal leaders for the establishment of a former slave colony along a strip of land located on the west coast of Africa. This was a narrow strip of land that measured only thirty-six miles long and three miles wide.[54] Because the land was on the African Continent, Society members assumed that former slaves would appreciate being returned to their native homeland.

In 1822, the repatriation process formally began with a small number of former slaves transported from the United States to the designated strip of land which became known as "Liberia," i.e., "the free land."

Although never considered an official American colony, such as those established by European countries, Liberia was nevertheless governed for several years by the American Colonization Society. This situation lasted until Liberia in 1847 became an independent country.[55] From the very start of the colonization effort to the Civil War when slavery in the United States was officially abolished, "upwards of 12,000 freeborn and formerly enslaved Black Americans immigrated to Liberia."[56]

Like so many other important developments in American history, the name of James Madison is connected to the colonization effort. The development of a colony along the coast of Africa, and the eventual creation of an African country named Liberia reflected Madison's leadership while he was in retirement. In addition to Madison, the name of James Monroe is also associated with the colonization project. A strong supporter of colonization, it was during Monroe's presidency that the colonization project was officially set in motion. Monroe's

---

[51] Brookhiser, *James Madison*, p. 232.

[52] Ibid.

[53] Madison to Robert Evans, 6/15/19, M. 728-730; quoted in Brookhiser, *James Madison*, p. 232.

[54] Becky Little, "How a Movement to Send Formerly Enslaved people to Africa Created Liberia," April 1, 2019; online at https://www.history.com/news/slavery-american-colonization-society-liberia. (Accessed January 2, 2024.)

[55] Ibid.

[56] Ibid.

relationship to the colonization project is still evident in Liberia with the country's capital named "Monrovia."

An Extraordinary Retirement

Following his two term presidency, Madison in retirement lived for another twenty years. During his "retirement" he devoted his time and energy to not only the management of his plantation, which as noted experienced hard times and which had fallen into serious debt, but to a wide range of important projects with long term implications. Madison edited, revised, and apparently rewrote portions of his notes on the federal constitutional convention. His notes remain to this day the most authoritative account of what took place behind closed doors in Philadelphia during the summer of 1787.

In addition to his meticulous editing of his notes, Madison worked side-by-side with his longtime mentor and friend Thomas Jefferson to establish the University of Virginia. Following Jefferson's death, Madison served as the university's rector for several years. He is closely associated with the establishment of this first-class American university.

The slavery issue seriously challenged the United States Congress, particularly when it involved the admission of new states. The Missouri Compromise of 1820 was Congress' temporary solution to the problem. Although not a member of Congress in 1820, one might suggest that Madison's writings perpetuated slavery in the United States.

While in retirement and at the age of seventy-eight, Madison in 1829 participated in amending the Virginia Constitution. This is quite remarkable when one considers that in 1776 Madison, at the age of twenty-five, served as a delegate to the state convention where he helped write Virginia's Declaration of Rights and first constitution. Ketcham notes that Madison was the only delegate at the 1829 convention in Richmond who had participated as a delegate in the 1776 convention.[57] When one considers his key role at the Philadelphia Convention in 1787 and the moniker bestowed upon him as the "Father of the Constitution" one cannot help but wonder if there has ever been anyone in the history of the United States who has been more prepared to help guide the writing of a constitution than James Madison.

Finally, there is the project Madison immersed himself in during retirement that was related to the repatriation of freed slaves to Liberia. Madison not only endorsed the effort, but was selected to serve as the president of the American Colonization Society. The colonization effort can of course be viewed from two

---

[57] Ketcham, *James Madison*, p. 637.

very different perspectives. One perspective could argue that Madison and supporters of the colonization movement had concluded that an injustice had been perpetrated upon Blacks who had been captured in Africa and brought to the United States in chains. The establishment of a new homeland in Liberia for freed slaves was thus an attempt to provide them with a new life, free from white control and racial discrimination. A second interpretation, however, could posit that the colonization project reflected Madison's view, along with the views of those in the Colonization Society, that Blacks were inferior human beings incapable of co-existing in a society where laws and cultural norms were established by whites. The solution therefore was to find a location far from North America where former slaves could be "deposited," thus ridding white society of their presence. This brings us to the inevitable question regarding Madison's view of slavery. Although a difficult question to definitively address, the subject nevertheless deserves attention.

Madison as a Slave Owner

James Madison was born into a slave owning family. Along with his siblings, he grew up watching slaves assigned to many different tasks on the family plantation. There were slaves assigned to field work and slaves assigned to household duties. The children of slaves, of which there were many at Montpelier, served as playmates for Madison when he was a young boy. Madison grew up with an understanding that slavery was a way of life for plantation families in Virginia. A Virginia plantation, whether it raised wheat or tobacco, could not survive without slave labor.

As an adult, Madison, who had inherited more than a hundred of his father's slaves, had become very close to those who served as his personal servants. One such slave was named "Sawney" who had been willed to Madison by his maternal grandmother.[58] Sawney, who traveled with Madison when he went to college, was never freed and would continue to serve the needs of Madison and family members until the end of his own life. Another slave by the name of Paul Jennings also looms important among the slaves owned by Madison. It was Jennings, while working as one of the slaves assigned to the White House, who helped Dolley load valuable plates and articles including the Gilbert Stuart portrait of George Washington into a horse drawn wagon shortly before the British arrived to set fire to the White House and Capitol.[59] While at Montpelier during Madison's years in retirement, Paul would faithfully attend to Madison's personal needs. Madison

---

[58] Feldman, *The Three Lives of James Madison*, p. 4.
[59] Ibid., p. 586.

likely viewed both Sawney and Paul as members of his own family; slaves no doubt, but much unlike the field slaves that he also owned. Yet even if Madison did not have close relationships with all of his slaves, as he did with Sawney and Paul, there is no historical evidence to suggest that as a slave owner he treated his slaves in a cruel or inhumane manner.[60] Madison was not an abusive slave owner.

Scholars who address Madison's views on slavery suggest that despite owning more than a hundred slaves and never freeing any of them, he nevertheless had very conflicted views about the institution of slavery. For example, at the Philadelphia Convention in 1787, Madison expressed his opposition to the slave trade that he considered "dishonorable to the National character"[61] He also spoke against treating slaves as property and that it would be fundamentally at odds with the spirit of the Constitution "to admit in the Constitution the idea that there could be property in men."[62]

Madison's conflicted feelings about slavery apparently continued throughout his entire life. This was evident in a personal interview he had in 1835 with a writer of the Unitarian faith from England. The writer's name was Harriet Martineau.[63] In her interview with Madison, Martineau probed his thoughts on slavery. She captured Madison's thoughts in these words, "With regard to slavery he owned himself to be almost in despair." [64] She further observed that Madison recognized "all the evils that with which it has ever been charged."[65] Moreover, "He observed that the whole Bible is against negro slavery, but the clergy do not preach this."[66] Yet despite his recognition regarding the evils and immorality of slavery, Madison in his interview with Martineau continued to express optimism towards the efforts of the American Colonization Society and how Liberia was the solution for ending slavery in America. Martineau, who was familiar with the repatriation project, expressed bewilderment over Madison's unwavering commitment to the colonization project. She wondered how such an intelligent, thoughtful and accomplished man such as James Madison "could derive any

---

[60] Callie Hopkins, "The Enslaved Household of President James Madison," White House Historical Association; online at https://www.whitehousehistory.org/salvery-in-the-james-madison-white-house (Accessed January 10, 2024.)

[61] Michael Signer, *Becoming Madison,* (New York: N.Y., Public Affairs, 2015), p. 205; quoted in Paris Amanda Spies-Gans, "Princeton and Slavery: James Madison;" online at https://slavery.princetong-edu/stories/james-madison. (Accessed January 11, 2024.)

[62] Ibid.

[63] Brookhiser, *James Madison*, p. 236.

[64] Martineau I, 190-192; quoted in Brookhiser, *James Madison*, p. 236.

[65] Ibid.

[66] Ibid.

alleviation to its anxiety from that source is surprising."[67] Brookhiser understands why Martineau would express surprise over Madison's commitment to the Liberian project. He notes that the American slave population by the time of her interview with Madison had been increasing by 60,000 a year, and that only 3,000 former American slaves had actually been repatriated to Liberia.[68] Moreover, what Madison and those who favored colonization failed to realize was that Liberia, although on the African continent, was never the homeland of American slaves. The vast majority of American slaves were never born or lived on that thin strip of land along the west coast of Africa. In fact, the vast majority of American slaves had been born in the United States, not in Africa. Madison, who possessed such a sharp and analytical mind, must have known deep in his heart how unrealistic the colonization project was.

In addition to his support for the colonization project, Madison, although believing that slavery in the United States would someday come to an end, believed that slavery "as he practiced it was morally permissible, and even something to be admired."[69] As a slave owner, he was not like Jefferson who treated his slaves poorly, nor for that matter did Madison have sexual relations with his slaves, as Jefferson apparently did.[70] Madison could justify owning slaves because they were essential to the day-to-day operation of his plantation and their presence at Montpelier was an economic necessity. Because Madison treated his slaves in a humane way, he likely rationalized that his slaves, such as Sawney and Paul, were leading a better life than what they would have experienced had they lived in Africa. Madison could therefore rationalize owning slaves, as he was providing slaves and their children with a meaningful and better life. He knew slavery was immoral, but could still justify it. How Madison and other Founders involved slaves in their wills deserves some discussion.

Slavery and Wills

George Washington as Slave Owner

In his will, George Washington required that the slaves he personally owned were to be freed once his wife, Martha, who would inherit them, had died. Of the 317 slaves at Mount Vernon, Washington personally owned 123, while 194 were part of the Custis estate, which was Martha's side of the family. Washington did

[67] Ibid.
[68] Brookhiser, *James Madison*, p. 236.
[69] Feldman, *The Three Lives of James Madison*, p. 617.
[70] Ibid.

not have any legal control over the Custis slaves, only those he personally owned.[71]

Thomas Jefferson as Slave Owner

The record shows that among the hundreds of slaves he owned, Jefferson freed a total of only ten. Two he freed during his lifetime, three he let leave Monticello with his approval, and five as stated in his will were to be granted freedom after has death. Among the tiny number of slaves owned by Jefferson who gained their freedom, virtually all of them had the surname Hemings.[72]

James Monroe as Slave Owner

Throughout his many years in public service, Monroe owned approximately 200 slaves.[73] Of those he owned, there was only one slave who he set free. The freed slave was Peter Marks who served as Monroe's house servant for many years. As he was lying on his death bed, Monroe informed those who had gathered around him that following his death Peter Marks was to be set free. Monroe's "dying request," as it was described, was the only time Monroe had liberated one of his slaves.[74]

James Madison as Slave Owner

Madison died at Montpelier on June 28, 1836. He was 85 years old. He had become very feeble and labored greatly to breathe and speak. With death rapidly approaching, he was asked if he would prefer to kept alive a little longer so that he could die on July 4th, as Jefferson, Adams and Monroe did. Madison said that was unnecessary.[75] Thus, while having breakfast on the morning of June 28, he experienced great difficulty swallowing. When asked by his niece Nelly Willis, who had been making frequent visits to Montpelier to help her uncle, what the problem was, he replied, according to the recollection of his slave Paul Jennings, "nothing more than a change of mind my dear." With those final words, Madison passed away.[76]

In his will, Madison transferred ownership of his slaves, which numbered around 100, to his wife, Dolley. "I give and bequeath my ownership in the negroes

---

[71] https://www.mountvernon.org. (Accessed January 6, 2024.)
[72] https://www.monticello.org. (Accessed January 6, 2024.)
[73] McGrath, *James Monroe,* p.584.
[74] Ibid. p.576.
[75] Ketcham, *James Madison*, p. 669.
[76] Madison's final words in Paul Jennings, *A Colored Man's Reminiscences of James Madison* (Brooklyn, 1865), pp. 18-20; quoted in Ketcham, *James Madison*, p. 670.

and people of colour held by me to my dear wife, but it is my desire that none of them should be sold without his or her consent or in case of their misbehavior; except that infant children may not be sold with their parent who consents for them to be sold with him or her, and who consents to be sold."[77] According to his confusing and awkwardly worded will, there were some stipulations regarding how Dolley would handle ownership and the sale of her husband's slaves. It was clear that all of the slaves at Montpelier would now belong to her and that she was free to do as she pleased with them. Not long after her husband's death, Dolley, rather than freeing the slaves she had inherited, decided to sell a number of her elderly slaves at auctions, the money used to pay for debts that had accrued at Montpelier.[78] Dolley eventually relocated to Washington, D.C. where, as Cost notes, "in her own Dolley sort of way – she once more became the toast of the town."[79] Such a beloved former First Lady, Dolley was invited to numerous functions and was even awarded a seat within the House of Representatives.[80] To settle debts, she eventually sold Montpelier, along with several of the slaves she had brought to the capital city. Those that she did not sell were willed to her son, Payne Todd, who due to his own financial troubles sold them to pay for financial liabilities.[81] Dolley Madison died on July 12, 1849, thirteen years after her husband's death. She was buried in the city's Congressional Cemetery. After nine years, Dolley's body was exhumed and relocated to Montpelier where she was buried next to her husband's grave.[82]

[77] "Madison's Will," *WJM*, 9:548-52; quoted in Gutzman, *James Madison*, pp. 359-360.
[78] Gutzman, *James Madison* p. 361.
[79] Cost, *James Madison*, p. 398.
[80] Cheney, *James Madison*, p. 457
[81] Hopkins, "*The Enslaved Household of President James Madison*"
[82] Chadwick, *James and Dolley Madison*, p. 367.

Conclusion

Remembering Madison

James Madison's contributions to the American republic were profound. One is in awe when reviewing all that Madison accomplished during his adult life. A Constitution that has endured for more than two-hundred and thirty-five years along with a bill of rights that has protected the liberties of the American people are directly attributable to the vision and efforts of James Madison. Students to this day can also discover the depth and breadth of Madison's analytical mind by reading several of the *Federalist Papers* which Madison authored. So important are *Federalists* 10 and 51 that one will locate these classic essays in the Appendix of practically every textbook assigned to introductory courses in American government. The *Federalist Papers* along with Madison's skillful debating at the Virginia ratifying convention in 1788 were directly responsible for the ratification of the Constitution in the states of New York and Virginia, two states vitally important to forming a lasting Union. In addition to reading Madison's *Federalist Papers* which convincingly defend the value of a federal republic and the system of checks and balances, one should also read Madison's Helvidius essays to gain additional insight into the constitutional boundaries between the president and Congress in the area of foreign affairs.

Madison's notes on the Constitutional Convention, despite his extensive edits, still to this day provide scholars with the best account of this most historic meeting of delegates in 1787. His notes provide a window into the decisions and individuals responsible for what in the end was a magnificent governing document.

The establishment of a political party that represented the values of republican ideals and one that established the foundation for a party that has remained the oldest party on earth, is also attributable to the political vision and efforts of Madison. Moreover, despite the absence of a declared victory, the War of 1812, known as "Mr. Madison's War," elevated the morale and patriotism of the American people. America's "Second War for Independence" is directly related to the presidency of James Madison.

More can be said about Madison's contributions to the American system of government and his pivotal role as a Founding Father. Although Madison is not rated as one of America's great or near-great presidents, there is nevertheless greatness about Madison that is unrelated to his presidency. Madison scholars have suggested that his writings and ideals were so profound that they should still be consulted by those who occupy public office. Consider the eloquent words of historian A.E. Dick Howard.

> We are in reach of his conversations still, for Madison's words transcends the centuries. Much has changed in the United States since the times of the Founding Fathers, but Madison has much to tell us yet. And it may not be idle, from time-to-time, when faced with thorny issues of governance and equity, to wonder what Madison might have said and done.[1]

What Madison might have to say about several contemporary issues facing American government is precisely what this author contemplated while writing about this extraordinary public servant. A number of questions came to mind: What would James Madison have to say about the repeated pattern of wars waged by American presidents in the absence of thoughtful congressional debate and formal declarations? What would Madison have to say regarding the extensive use of executive agreements, which presidents now use to by-pass the Senate when making foreign policy? What would Madison say about the routine use of executive orders issued by presidents that are equivalent to law making? What might Madison have to say about bills signed into law by presidents which include signing statements comparable to line-item vetoes? It would also be instructive to hear Madison's thoughts regarding the development of a massive federal bureaucracy that has become home to more than a million unaccountable civil servants who structure public policy free from public constraint. At the same time, Madison's views towards the "deep state" would be welcomed. And what might Madison say about the intense polarization in contemporary American politics with elected lawmakers representing ideological *factions* and who have little comprehension or appreciation for the art of compromise? These and other questions came to mind when writing about the public service of Madison.

In closing, to preserve what is the most admirable form of government known to humankind, high school and college students, irrespective of race, religion or

---

[1] A.E. Dick Howard, "James Madison and the Constitution" *The Wilson Quarterly* (1976). Summer, 1985, Vol 9, No. 3 (Summer, 1985); online at https://www.jstor.org/stable/40256894 (Accessed January 7, 2024.)

class, should be required to come into contact with the contributions to American government associated with the work of James Madison. It is not an exaggeration to suggest that the future of the American republic depends on the preservation of the governing principles supported and brought forward by the man deservedly known as the "Father of the Constitution."

Bibliography

Books Consulted

Allen, W.B., Gordon Lloyd and Margaret Lloyd, eds. *The Essential Antifederalist.* Lanham: University Press of America, 1985.

Allison, John Murray. *Adams and Jefferson.* Norman: University of Oklahoma Press, 1966.

Amar, Akhil Reed. *The Words That Made Us: America's Constitutional Conversation.* New York: Basic Books, 2021.

Beeman, Richard. *Plain Honest Men: The Making of the American Constitution.* New York: Random House, 2009.

Bierne, Francis F. *The War of 1812.* New York: E.P. Dutton and Co., 1949.

Bilder, Mary Sarah. *Madison's Hand.* Cambridge: Harvard University Press, 2015.

Boles, John. *Jefferson: Architect of American Liberty.* New York: Basic Books, 2017.

Bowen, Catherine Drinker. *Miracle in Philadelphia: The Story of the Constitutional Convention May to September 1787.* Boston: Little and Brown, 1966.

Brands, H.W. *Founding Partisans: Hamilton, Madison, Jefferson, Adams and the Brawling Birth of American Politics.* New York: Doubleday, 2023.

Brant, Irving. *James Madison: The Virginia Revolutionist 1751-1780.* New York: Bobbs Merrill Co., 1941.

Brant, Irving. *James Madison: The Nationalist 1780-1787.* New York: Bobbs Merrill Co., 1948.

Brant, Irving. *James Madison: Father of the Constitution 1787-1800.* New York: Bobbs Merrill Co., 1950.

Brant, Irving. *James Madison: Secretary of State 1800-1809*. New York: Bobbs Merrill Co., 1953.

Brant, Irving. *James Madison: The President 1809-1812*. New York: Bobbs Merrill Co., 1956.

Broadwater, Jeff. *James Madison.* Chapel Hill: University of North Carolina Press, 2012.

Brookhiser, Richard. *James Madison*. New York: Basic Books, 2011.

Burstein, Andrew and Nancy Isenberg. *Madison and Jefferson.* New York: Random House, 2013.

Cheney, Lynne. *James Madison: A Life Considered.* New York: Viking Press, 2014.

Cheney, Lynne. *The Virginia Dynasty: Four Presidents and the Creation of the American Nation.* Viking Press, 2020.

Chernow, Ron. *Alexander Hamilton*. New York: The Penguin Press, 2004.

Cost, Jay. *James Madison: America's First Politician.* New York: Basic Books, 2021.

Cunningham, Noble E., Jr. *The Jeffersonian Republicans: The Formation of Party Organization 1789-1801*. Chapel Hill: University of North Carolina Press, 1957.

Dewey, Donald and Barbara Bennett Peterson. *James Madison: Defender of the American Republic.* New York: Nova Science Publishers, Inc., 2009.

Earle, Edward Mead. *The Federalist.* New York: Random House, 1941.

Ellis, Joseph J. *American Sphinx: The Character of Thomas Jefferson.* New York: Vintage Books, 1998.

Ellis, Joseph J. Founding Brothers. New York: Alfred Knopf, 2000.

Farrand, Max., ed., *The Records of the Federal Convention of 1787, 3 vols. New Haven:* Yale University Press, 1911.

Feldman, Noah. *The Three Lives of James Madison: Genius, Partisan, President.* New York: Random House, 2017.

Fried, Stephen. *Rush*. New York: Crown Publishers, 2018.

Grossman, Mark., ed., *Constitutional Amendments Volume I:* New York: Grey House Publishing, 2012.

Grossman, Mark., ed. Encyclopedia of the Continental Congress Volume II: New York: Grey House Publishing, 2012.

Gutzman, Kevin R. *James Madison and the Making of America.* New York: St. Martin's Press, 2012.

Hickey, Donald B. *The War of 1812*. Urbana: University of Illinois Press, 2012.

Hofstadter, Richard. *The Idea of a Party System.* Berkeley: University of California Press, 1969.

Ketcham, Ralph. *James Madison: A Biography*. Charlottesville: University of Virginia Press, 1990.

Maier, Pauline. *Ratification: The People Debate the Constitution, 1787-1788*. New York: Simon and Schuster, 2010.

McCullough, David. *John Adams*. New York: Simon and Schuster, 2001.

McGrath, Tim. *James Monroe: A Life*. New York: Dutton, 2020.

Meacham, Jon. *American Lion: Andrew Jackson in the White House*. New York: Random House, 2008.

Rakove, Jack N. *James Madison and the Creation of the American Republic.* New York: Harper Collins, 1990.

Rakove, Jack N. *The Beginnings of National Politics: An Interpretive History of the Continental Congress.* Baltimore: Johns Hopkins University Press, 1979.

Richard, Carl J. *The Founders and the Classics: Greece, Rome and the American Enlightenment.* Cambridge: Harvard University Press, 1995.

Rutland, Robert Allen. *James Madison.* Columbia: University of Missouri Press, 1987.

Schift, Stacy. *The Revolutionary: Sam Adams.* New York: Little and Brown, 2022.

Schlesinger, Arthur Jr. *The Cycles of American History.* Boston: Houghton Mifflin, Co. 1986.

Spivak, Burton. *Jefferson's English Crisis: Commerce, Embargo, and the Republican Revolution.* Charlottesville: University Press of Virginia, 1979.

Storing, Herbert J. *The Anti-Federalist Writings by the Opponents of the Constitution.* Chicago: University of Chicago Press, 1981.

Swanson, Mary-Elaine. *The Education of James Madison: A Model for Today.* Selma: The Hoffman Center, 1991.

Wills, Garry. *James Madison.* New York: Times Books, Henry Holt and Co., 2002.

Witcover, Jules. *Party of the People: A History of the Democrats.* New York: Random House, 2003.

Wood, Gordon, *Empire of Liberty: A History of the Early Republic, 1789-1815.* New York: Oxford University Press, Inc. 2009.

Wright, Benjamin Fletcher., ed., *The Federalist: The Famous Papers on the Principles of American Government*. New York: Barnes and Noble, 2004.

Journal Articles Consulted

Antieau, Chester James, "Natural Rights and the Founding Fathers – The Virginians," *Washington and Lee Law Review* Vol. 17, No. 1 (Spring 1960) pp. 43-79; online at https://scholarlycommons.law.wlu.edu/wlulr/vol17/Iss1/4.

Arkin, Marc M. "'The Intractable Principle:' David Hume, James Madison, Religion, and the Tenth Federalist," *The American Journal of Legal History* Vol. 39, No. 2 (April 1995) pp. 148-176; online at https://doj.org/10.2307/845899.

Burton, Harold H. "The Cornerstone of Constitutional Law: The Extraordinary Case of Marbury v. Madison," *American Bar Association Journal* Vol. 36, No. 10 (October 1950), pp. 805-808; 881-883; online at https://www.jstor.org/stable/257399.

Dewey, Donald O. "An American Liberia," *Pacific Historical Review* Vol. 31, No. 2 (May, 1962) pp. 179-182; online at https://www.jstor.org/stable/3636575.

Dewey, Donald O. "James Madison Helps Clio Interpret the Constitution," *The American Journal of Legal History* Vol. 15, No. 1 (January 1971), pp. 38-55; online at https://www.jstor.or/stable/844193.

Elsmere, Jane. "The Notorious Yazoo Land Fraud Case," *The Georgia Historical Quarterly* Vol. 51, No 4 (December 1967) pp. 425-442; online at https://www.jstor.org/stable/40578730.

Fairlie, John A. "The Separation of Powers," *Michigan Law Review* Vol. 21, No. 4 (February 1923), pp. 392-436; online at https://doi.org/10.2307/127683.

Garver, Frank. "Propositions Rejected by the Constitutional Convention of 1787," *The Historian* Vol. 6, No. 2 (Spring 1944) pp. 113-127; online at https:www.jstor.org/stable/24435972.

Graebner Norman A. "Political Parties and the Presidency," *Current History* Vol. 25, No. 145 (September 1953), pp.138- 143: online at https://www.jstor.org/stable/45308516.

Helderman, Leonard C. "The Virginia Bill of Rights," *Washington and Lee Law Review* Vol 3, No. 2 (1942), pp. 225-245; online at https://scholarlycommons.law.wlu.edu/wluir/vol3/Iss2/3.

Hughes, Charles Evans. "James Madison," *American Bar Association Journal* Vol 18., No. 1 (January 1932), pp. 854-859; online at https://www.jstor.org/ stable/25708450.

Hunter, Thomas Rogers. "The First Gerrymander? Patrick Henry, James Madison, James Monroe, and Virginia's 1788 Congressional Districting," *Early American Studies* Vol 9, No. 3 (Fall 2011) pp.781- 820; online at https://www.jstor.org/stable/23546676.

Hutson, James H. "Robert Yates's Notes on the Constitutional Convention of 1787: Citizen Genet's Edition," The Quarterly Journal of the Library of Congress Vol 35, No. 3 (July 1978), pp. 173-182; online at https://www.jstor.org/stable/2978/777

Ketcham, Ralph L. "James Madison and Religion – A New Hypothesis," *Journal of the Presbyterian Historical Society* Vol 38, No 2 (June 1960), pp. 65-90; online at https://www.jstor.org/stable/23325326.

Leibiger, Stuart. "James Madison and Amendments to the Constitution:1787-1789: Parchment Barriers," *The Journal of Southern History* Vol 59, No 33 (August 1993), pp. 441-468; online at https://doi.org/10.2307/2210003.

MacPhee, Donald A. "The Yazoo Controversy: The Beginning of the 'Quid' Revolt," *The Georgia Historical Quarterly*, Vol 49, No. 1 (March 1965) pp. 23-43; online at https://www.jstor.org/stable/40578441.

Munoz, Vincent Phillip. "James Madison's Principle of Religious Liberty," *The American Political Science Review* Vol 97, No. 1 (February 2003), pp. 17-32; online at https://www.jstor.org/3118218.

Ottenberg, Louis. "A Fortunate Fiasco: The Annapolis Convention of 1786," *American Bar Association Journal* Vol 45, No. 8 (August 1959), pp. 834-837; online at https://www.jstor.org/stable/25720900.

Phillips, James Duncan. "Jefferson's 'Wicked Tyrannical Embargo,'" *The New England Quarterly* Vol 18, No 4 (December 1945), pp. 466-478; online at https://www.jstor.org/stable/361063.

Scarberry, Mark S. "John Leland and James Madison: Religious Influence on the Ratification of the Constitution and on the Proposal of the Bill of Rights, *Dickenson Law Review*, Vol. 113, Issue 3 (2008-2009), pp. 733-800; online at https: //ideas.dickinsonlawpsu.edu/dira/vol113/iss3/3.

Schifalacqua, John F. "James Madison and America's First Encounter with Islam: James Madison's Engagement with Barbary Affairs Through the 1st Barbary War," *Penn History Review*. Vol 21, Issue 1 2014, pp.89-126; online at papers.ssrn.com.

Schultz, Harold S. "James Madison: Father of the Constitution?" *The Quarterly Journal of the Library of Congress* Vol 37, No 2 (Spring 1980) pp. 215-222; online at https://www.jstor.org/stable/29781852.

Smith, Robert W. "Foreign Affairs and the Ratification of the Constitution in Virginia," *Virginia Magazine of History & Biography* Vol. 122, Issue 1 (2014), pp. 40-67; online at https://www.jstor.org/stable/24392923.

Smylie, James H. "Madison and Witherspoon: Theological Roots of American Political Thought," *The Princeton University Library Chronicle* Vol 22, No 3 (Spring 1961), pp.118-132; online at http://www.jstor.com/stable/2640297.

Stagg, J. C. A. "James Madison and the 'Malcontents': The Political Origins of the War of 1812." *The William and Mary Quarterly* Vol. 33, No 4 (October 1976), pp. 557-585; online at https://www.jstor.org/stable/1921716.

Stuart, Reginald C. "James Madison and the Militants: Republican Disunity and Replacing the Embargo," *Diplomatic History* Vol 6, No 2 (Spring 1982), pp. 143-167; online at https://www.jstor.org/stable/24911290.

Tate, Adam. "James Madison and State Sovereignty, 1780-1781," *American Political Thought* Vol. 2, No. 2 (Fall 2013), pp 174-197; online at https://www.jstor.org/stable/10.1086/673130.

Wright, Benjamin F. Jr. "The Origins of the Separation of Powers in America," *Economica* No. 40 (May 1933), pp. 169-185; online at https://www.jstor.org/stable/2548765.

Websites Consulted

Chamberlain, Charles, Lo Faber, and Lee Smith, "Spanish Colonial Louisiana," online at 64parishes.org.

Congressional Research Service Reports; online at https://crsreports.congress.gov.

Department of State, Office of the Historian, "Acquisition of Florida: Treaty of Adams-Onis (1819) and Transcontinental Treaty (1821)"; online at https://history.state.gov.

Editors Note, "Madison's Election to the First Federal Congress October 1788-1789:" online at https://founders.archives.gov/documents/Madison/01-11-02-0219.

"Elbridge Gerry's Objections Letter to Massachusetts Legislature," online at; teaching americanhistory.org/document.

Founders Online, "Helvidius," No. 1, August 24, 1793; online at founders.archives.gov/documents/Madison/01-15-02-0056.

Founders Online, "The Virginia Plan," 29 (May 1787); online at https://founders.archives.gov/documents/Madison/01-10-.

History.com., editors, "Alien and Sedition Acts," June 21, 2003; online at history.com/early-us-alien-and-sedition-acts.

History in Charts, "The Significance of the 1794 Jay's Treaty," December 19, 2022; online at historyincharts.com.

Hopkins, Callie. "The Enslaved Household of President James Madison," White House Historical Association; online at https://www.whitehousehistory.org/salvery-in-the-james-madison-white-house.

James Madison's First Inaugural Address March 4, 1809; online at The American Presidency Project, https//www.presidency.ucsb.edu.

James Madison's Second Inaugural Address March 4, 1813; online at millercenter.org.

"John Witherspoon: Pastor, College President and Signer of the Declaration;" online at https://nassauchurch.org/about/princetoncemetary-bios/cemetary.

"John Witherspoon (1723-1794);" online at https://www.ed.ac.uk/alumni/services/notable-alumni/alumni-in-history/john-witherspoon.

Kiger, Patrick J. "How St. Augustine Became the First Permanent European Settlement in America," Updated August 29, 2023; online at history.com.

Library of Congress, "James Madison and the Federal Constitutional Convention of 1787;" online at loc.gov/collection/James-Madison-papers/articles-and-essays.

Little, Becky. "How a Movement to Send Formerly Enslaved people to Africa Created Liberia," originally published April 1, 2019, updated September 5, 2023; online at https://www.history.com/news/slavery-american-colonization-society-liberia.

National Archives, "The Bill of Rights," online at archives.gov.

National Park Service, "Congress Establishes the First Bank of the United States," online at nps.gov/articles/000/establishing-the-first-bank.html.

Stagg, J.C.A. "James Madison: Campaigns and Elections," The Miller Center: online at https://millercenter.org/president/madison/camapigns-and-elections.

Spies-Gans, Paris Amanda. "Princeton and Slavery: James Madison," online at https://slavery.princetong-edu/stories/james-madison.

The Founding Fathers New York; online at archives.gov/founding-docs/founding-fathers-new York. "Jefferson's Plan for an Academical Villiage," online at Monticello.org/research/education/thoms-jefferson-encyclopedia/jeffersons-plan-academical-village.

The House of Commons, "The Privy Council: history, functions and membership" November 15, 2023; online at commonslibrary.parliament.uk/research-briefings/chp-7160.

"The Ten Best Secretaries of State," *American Heritage*, December 1981, Volume 3, Issue 1. Survey of 50 diplomatic historians conducted by Professor David Porter; online at americanheritage.com.

"The Quasi-War with France (1798-1801)"; online at ussconstitutionmuseium.org/major-events/the-quasi-war-with-france.

Todd, Jim. "Madison's Role in the Founding of the University of Virginia," February 14, 2020; online at engagement.virginia.edu/learn/2020/02/14.

About the Author

Gary L. Rose, Ph.D. is Professor of Politics and Scholar in Residence at Sacred Heart University in Fairfield, Connecticut. A college instructor for close to five decades, Professor Rose has authored and edited fifteen books regarding presidential politics, constitutional law and Connecticut government. His constitutional law book, *Shaping a Nation* (2010) published in English and Chinese, is recommended reading by the National Association of Scholars for colleges and universities that have common reading programs. Professor Rose's book, *Haywire* (2017), an 800 page tome that meticulously tracks every dimension of the 2016 presidential contest, is one of the most thorough treatments of one presidential contest that has ever been published. His book *The American Presidency Under Siege* (1997) received a positive review by a leading presidential scholar in the American Political Science Review

In addition to his teaching and writing, Professor Rose provides routine political commentary for national, state and local media. His comments have been quoted in the *Wall Street Journal, New York Times, Washington Post,* and the *Hartford Courant.* He has appeared as a commentator on many television shows, including *NBC Nightly News* the FOX network and several news shows focused on politics in Connecticut. He is also the recipient of several teaching and scholarship awards and is frequently invited to speak before civic and business organizations. In 2011, Professor Rose was named the *Connecticut Professor of the Year* by the Carnegie Foundation for the Advancement of Teaching and the Council for Advancement and Support of Education (CASE).

Index

G

H

I

J

K

L

M

S

T

V

W

X

Y

www.ingramcontent.com/pod-product-compliance
Lightning Source LLC
Chambersburg PA
CBHW070543310726
48982CB00010B/1462/J

* 9 7 8 1 6 8 0 5 3 4 2 5 2 *